About the Author

VOLKER KUTSCHER was born in 1962. He studied German, philosophy, and history, and worked as a newspaper editor prior to writing his first detective novel. *Babylon Berlin*, the start of an award-winning series of novels to feature Gereon Rath and his exploits in late Weimar Republic Berlin, was an instant hit in Germany. The series was awarded the Berlin Krimi-Fuchs Crime Writers Prize in 2011 and has sold more than one million copies worldwide. He lives in Cologne.

About the Translator

NIALL SELLAR was born in Edinburgh in 1984. He studied German and translation studies in Dublin, Konstanz, and Edinburgh, and has worked variously as a translator, teacher, and reader. In addition to translation work, he currently teaches modern foreign languages in Harrow. He lives in London.

BABYLON
BERLIN

BABYLON BERLIN

BOOK 1

of the Gereon Rath Mystery Series

VOLKER KUTSCHER

Translated from German by Niall Sellar

PICADOR

NEW YORK

BABYLON BERLIN. Copyright © 2007, 2008 by Volker Kutscher. English translation copyright © 2016 by Niall Sellar. All rights reserved. Printed in the United States of America. For information, address Picador, 175 Fifth Avenue, New York, N.Y. 10010.

picadorusa.com • picadorbookroom.tumblr.com
twitter.com/picadorusa • facebook.com/picadorusa

Picador® is a U. S. registered trademark and is used by Macmillan Publishing Group, LLC, under license from Pan Books Limited.

For book club information, please visit facebook.com/picadorbookclub or email marketing@picadorusa.com.

The translation of this work was supported by a grant from the Goethe-Institut, which is funded by the German Ministry of Foreign Affairs.

Designed by Steven Seighman

The Library of Congress Cataloging-in-Publication Data is available upon request.

ISBN 978-1-250-18704-8 (trade paperback)
ISBN 978-1-250-18705-5 (ebook)

Our books may be purchased in bulk for promotional, educational, or business use. Please contact your local bookseller or the Macmillan Corporate and Premium Sales Department at 1-800-221-7945, extension 5442, or by email at MacmillanSpecialMarkets@macmillan.com.

Originally published in Germany as *Der nasse Fisch. Gereon Raths erster Fall* by Verlag Kiepenheuer & Witsch GmbH & Co.

First English translation published in Great Britain by Sandstone Press Ltd

First U. S. English translation published as an ebook original by Picador

First Picador Paperback Edition: January 2018

10 9 8 7 6 5 4

Spree-Athen is tot,
Und Spree-Chicago wächst heran.

—Walther Rathenau

PART I

THE DEAD MAN IN THE LANDWEHR CANAL

28th April—10th May 1929

1

When would they return? In the darkness even the smallest noise seemed infernal; the quietest of whispers grew to a roar. Silence itself became an interminable throb in the ears. He had to pull himself together but the pain was driving him mad. He had to pull himself together, to ignore the dripping sound of his own blood as it hit the hard, damp floor.

He had no idea where they had dragged him. Somewhere no-one could hear. A cellar perhaps? A warehouse? The room had no windows and there was only a faint glimmer of light, the same glimmer he had seen from the bridge as he gazed at the lights of a departing train, lost in thought. About the plan. About her. The blow had plunged him into darkness.

He shuddered against the ropes, the only things holding him up. His feet couldn't carry him, they hardly resembled feet anymore, and his hands no longer functioned. He put all his weight onto his arms to avoid touching the floor. The rope chafed. He was sweating all over his body.

The images kept reappearing: the heavy hammer, his hand, tied to the steel girder, the sound of his bones splintering and the unbearable pain, his cries that had grown into a single, loud cry. Unconsciousness. Then waking from the dark night, his extremities wrenched in pain. But the pain hadn't penetrated to his core.

They had enticed him with pain-removing drugs, trying to bend him to their will. He had to fight against his weakness. The sound of his own language had almost overwhelmed him, but their voices sounded colder and more sinister than the ones he remembered.

Svetlana had spoken the same language, but how different she had sounded! Her voice had sworn love, divulged secrets, been intimacy and promise itself, brought the great city to life once more. Even in foreign parts he could not forget the city. It was still his city: a city that had deserved a better future. Still his country: a country that had deserved a better future.

Hadn't she wanted the same thing? To oust the rogues who had seized power. He thought of the night they had spent lying awake in her bed, a warm summer's night that now seemed an eternity away. They had made love and confided their secrets, melded them into one big secret so that they might realise their dreams.

Everything had gone so well, but someone betrayed them. They had abducted him. And Svetlana? If only he knew what had become of her. Their enemies were everywhere.

He had known their questions in advance, answered without giving anything away. They hadn't even realised. They were stupid. Their greed made them blind. He couldn't let them know the train was already on its way. Not when the plan was almost complete.

The first blow was the worst. Everything that came afterwards merely served to disperse the pain.

Now, the certainty that he would die made him strong enough to endure never walking, never writing, never touching her again. He had made his peace with memories, but she was a memory he would never betray.

He had to get to his jacket and the capsule in its lining. If he had realised it was a trap, he would have bitten it long ago. In the darkness, he could just make out the outline of the chair it was resting on.

They hadn't tied him. After they had pulverised his hands and feet, they had simply hung him on the ropes so that they could work on him again when the pain roused him from unconsciousness. They hadn't left a guard behind, so certain were they that no-one would hear his cries. This was his last chance. The effect of the drugs was waning and, without the support of the ropes, the pain would be so unbearable that he would probably faint. Beads of sweat formed on his brow. Now!

He gritted his teeth and closed his eyes, stretched out both arms. First his elbows and then his whole body lost their hold and the lumps of mash that were once his feet touched the ground first. He cried out even before his upper body smacked against the concrete floor, where he writhed until the pain finally began to subside. Now he could move, could crawl forward on his elbows and knees, leaving a trail of blood behind him.

Soon he reached the chair and dragged down the jacket with his teeth, secured it with his right elbow and tore at the lining. The pain only made him angrier until he prised it open with a loud rip.

All at once he was sobbing uncontrollably and memory seized him, just as a predatory cat seizes and shakes its prey. He would never see her again. He had known it ever since they lured him into their trap, but now all of a sudden it was brutally clear, and he loved her so much. So very much!

Slowly he regained his composure. His tongue searched for the capsule, tasting dirt and lint, before it finally alighted on the smooth, cool surface. With his incisors, he carefully removed it from the lining. It was in his mouth now, the capsule that would end everything. A triumphant smile flickered across his pain-stricken face.

They wouldn't find anything. They would blame themselves. They were stupid.

He heard a door slam shut above him, resounding like a peal of thunder. Steps on the concrete. They were coming back. Had they heard him cry out? His teeth held the capsule, ready to bite down. He was ready now. He could end it anytime. He waited a little longer. Let them come in! He wanted to bask in his triumph until the final moment. He wanted them to see it. To stand by helplessly and watch as he escaped them.

He closed his eyes as they opened the door and bright light flooded the darkness. Then he bit down. With a quiet click, the glass shattered in his mouth.

2

The man was faintly reminiscent of Wilhelm II: the prominent moustache, the piercing gaze. Just like the portrait that hung in the parlour of every good German household during the Kaiser's reign—and still adorned the walls of many, even though he had abdicated over ten years ago and been growing tulips in Holland ever since. The same moustache, the same sparkling eyes, but there the similarities ended. This Kaiser wasn't wearing a spiked helmet; it hung alongside his sabre and uniform above the bedpost. In fact this Kaiser wasn't wearing anything, save a twirly moustache and an impressive erection. Before him kneeled a woman, no less naked, and blessed with voluptuous curves, paying her dues to the imperial sceptre.

Rath leafed limply through the photos that should, by rights, have aroused desire. There were further images of the real Kaiser's third-rate doppelganger and his playmate in action. No matter how their bodies were entwined, the prominent moustache was always in shot.

'Filth!'

Rath looked round. A cop was peering over his shoulder.

'Absolute filth,' the officer continued, 'An insult to his majesty. Time was you'd get hard labour for that.'

'The Kaiser doesn't seem too insulted,' said Rath. He snapped shut the file and pushed it back onto the rickety desk they had given him. The officer gave him an angry look from under his shako as he turned silently away and joined his colleagues. Eight uniformed officers chatted quietly amongst themselves, most of them warming their hands on cups of coffee.

Rath knew that the officers of the 220th precinct had more pressing concerns than providing support for a detective from Alexanderplatz. In three days though, the heat would be on. Wednesday was the first of May, and Commissioner Zörgiebel had forbidden all May demonstrations in Berlin. Despite the ban the communists were still intending to march and the police were nervous. Rumours of a planned putsch were doing the rounds:

the Bolsheviks would stage a revolution, would proclaim a Soviet Germany, even now, ten years on. In the 220th precinct, the police were at their most nervous. Neukölln was a workers' district. The reddest in all of Berlin, except perhaps for Wedding.

Every now and then, one of the officers stole a furtive glance at the detective inspector. Rath tapped out an Overstolz and lit it. He was about as welcome here as the Salvation Army in a nightclub.

Vice squad didn't have much of a reputation in police circles. Up until two years ago regulating prostitution in the city had been E Division's number one priority, and a kind of state-run pimping service, since only prostitutes registered with the police could ply their trade legally. Many officers exploited this dependence before a new law to fight VD transferred responsibilities from Vice squad to the local health authorities. Since then, E Division's remit encompassed nightclubs, pimps and pornography, though its reputation had scarcely improved. It seemed as though some of the smut its officers confronted in the line of duty had permanently attached itself to them.

Rath blew smoke across his desk. Rainwater was dripping from the shakos on the coat hooks onto the linoleum floor, green linoleum, reminiscent of the CID offices at Alexanderplatz. His grey hat looked out of place against the black leather and glittering officer's crests, likewise his coat, hanging in the midst of the blue police cloaks. Plain clothes, with nothing but uniform for company.

The coffee they had given him tasted like nasty black sludge in a misshapen enamel cup. So, the police couldn't make coffee in the 220th precinct either. Why should Neukölln be any different from Alex? All the same, he took another sip. It wasn't like he had anything else to do except wait for the phone to ring.

Reaching again for the file he noted that the various members of the Hohenzollern dynasty and other prominent Prussian figures depicted there were different from the usual schlock. The images weren't copies but premium high-resolution prints neatly arranged in a file. A buyer would have to fork out a pretty penny. No doubt they were intended for more rarefied circles. A roving magazine vendor had been selling them at the train station at Alexanderplatz, no more than a few steps away from police headquarters and the offices of E Division, when he caught the eye of a patrol unit and lost his nerve. The two officers had tried to draw the vendor's attention to a harmless magazine that had fallen from his sales tray but, as they approached, he hurled his entire consignment at them and took to his heels.

Fluttering in the air alongside the magazines were the glossy pornographic photos, just about level with the youthful officers' blushing cheeks. The young pair were so amazed at the artistry that they momentarily neglected to give chase but, when they finally did take up pursuit, the man had disappeared amongst the building works surrounding Alex. This caused the officers' cheeks to blush for a second time when they deposited their findings on Lanke's desk and submitted their report.

The head of E Division could be very loud. Superintendent Werner Lanke was of the opinion that congeniality undermined authority. Rath only had to think of how his new boss had greeted him four weeks before.

'I know you have connections, Rath,' Lanke had yelled, 'but if you think you can avoid getting your hands dirty you're very much mistaken! No-one gets an easy ride here! And certainly not someone whose presence I never requested!'

Rath's first month in E Division was almost behind him now. It had seemed like a punishment, and maybe that's what it was, even if he had only been reassigned and not demoted. He had had to leave Cologne, Homicide too, but he was still a DI and had no intention of hanging around Vice forever. He didn't understand how Wolter could put up with it, but the work was something his colleague almost seemed to enjoy.

Detective Chief Inspector Bruno Wolter, known by most of his colleagues as Uncle on account of his affable manner, was in charge of the investigation team as well as today's raid. Outside in the station yard, where the police van stood waiting, Wolter was discussing individual details of the planned raid with the two ladies from women's CID and the squad leader. They were just waiting for Jänicke's call.

Rath imagined the rookie sitting in the stuffy flat they had sequestered to observe the studio—a pair of binoculars in one hand, the other shaking nervously above the receiver. Like Rath, Assistant Detective Stephan Jänicke had joined Vice at the start of April, freshly assigned to Alex straight from police academy in Eiche. But the taciturn, blond East Prussian wouldn't let himself be put off by the teasing of older colleagues; he took his job seriously.

The telephone on the desk sounded. Rath stubbed his cigarette out and reached for the glossy black receiver.

The police van stopped in front of a large tenement house in Hermannstrasse. Police were not welcome in this part of the city. In the half-light of the archway which led to the rear courtyards, Jänicke was waiting, hands buried in the pockets of his coat, collar turned upwards and the brim of his hat pulled over his brow. Rath was forced to stifle a grin. Jänicke was doing his best to appear like a hard-nosed cop from the big city, but his eternally ruddy cheeks betrayed the country boy within.

'There must be a dozen people inside now,' he said, trying to keep pace with Rath and Wolter. 'I've seen a Hindenburg, a Bismarck, a Moltke, a Wilhelm I and a Wilhelm II, and even an Old Fritz.'

'Let's hope there are a few girls too,' said Uncle, heading towards the second courtyard. Two female officers smiled sourly. The plain-clothes men and ten uniformed colleagues followed the DCI through to the back of the tenement. Five boys were playing football with a tin can. When they saw the police contingent, they stood stock still, leaving the can to perform a final, clanking pirouette.

Wolter put a finger to his lips. The oldest, a boy of about eleven, nodded in silent assent. Above them, a window slammed shut. JOHANN KÖNIG, PHOTOGRAPHER 4TH FLOOR, proclaimed a brass plate by the entrance to the stairs.

Uncle had had to quiz one of his many informants in the Berlin underworld to track König down, as the photographer was unknown to the police. He made cheap passport photos for his insolvent Neukölln clientele, along with the occasional obligatory family portrait: infants on polar bear rugs, children with school satchels, newlyweds and the like. Until now there had been nothing to suggest he was rotten but for *one* entry in his record: political. You didn't have to break the law to attract the attention of the police.

It had been Rath's idea to go through the extensive files of Section 1A, the political police, where he stumbled upon a note that had lain dormant for ten years. In 1919, the politicals had registered Johann König as an anarchist, assigning him his own—albeit sparingly marked—index card. After the Revolution the photographer had ceased to be politically active. Now, though, his aversion to the pomp and circumstance of Prussian life had brought him into conflict with the law for a second time. No wonder, Rath thought. Being anti-monarchist with a name like *König* was never going to end well.

It seemed one of the younger officers was entertaining similar thoughts. 'The Kaiser is screwing at the King's,' he joked and gazed nervously around him.

No-one laughed. Wolter positioned the comic at the entrance to the rear building, and with the rest of the troops began to climb the dingy staircase as quietly as possible. Somewhere in the building a radio was blaring out a popular hit. On the second floor, a grey-haired old lady poked her nose into the stairwell, only to withdraw it again as soon as she saw the police, two women officers and twelve males barely making a sound. At the very top, they halted in front of a sign saying JOHANN KÖNIG, PHOTOGRAPHER, printed on yellowing cardboard that was already fraying at the edges.

Wolter turned to the squad leader and raised his right index finger to his lips. A good, strong kick would take the flimsy door clean off its hinges, but he brushed the squad leader to one side, taking a skeleton key from his coat pocket and busying himself with the lock. Before he pushed the door open, he drew his service weapon. The others did likewise, but Rath kept his Mauser in its holster. After Cologne he had sworn not to use his gun if he could at all avoid it. He allowed his armed colleagues to proceed and, from the door, observed the bizarre scene playing out in the studio.

On a green settee, a muscular Hindenburg was hard at it with a naked lady who was faintly reminiscent of Mata Hari. Next to them stood an ordinary private wearing a spiked helmet. Whether he would soon be disporting himself with Mata Hari or, indeed, be called to service by General Field Marshall Hindenburg wasn't clear. The rest of the actors, half of them naked, were engaged in animated conversation under the spotlights. A man with a goatee beard was crouching behind a camera and giving orders to the General Field Marshall.

'Turn Sophie's backside a little towards me . . . a little more. That's right. Hold still, aaand—yes, sir!'

No-one in the illustrious gathering noticed that a dozen police officers had entered the studio with their weapons drawn, the younger officers craning their necks to get a better view. There was a clatter as a spotlight fell to the floor and all faces turned towards the door, their expressions frozen. Only Hindenburg and Mata Hari refused to be thrown off their rhythm.

'Police! This is a raid,' Wolter cried. 'You're all coming down to the station! Leave everything where it is. Especially if it looks like a weapon.'

It didn't occur to anybody to resist. Some threw their hands in the air, others made instinctively to shield their genitals. All four women in the studio were wearing next to nothing or nothing at all. The female officers draped woollen blankets over them as uniform sprang into action. The first handcuffs clicked. König mumbled something about eroticism and artistic freedom, but fell silent when Wolter barked at him. And then the big names were handcuffed. Bismarck—click. Fridericus Rex—click. Old Fritz actually had tears in his eyes as he was clapped in irons. Hindenburg and Mata Hari had to be hoisted from the settee. The boys in blue were enjoying themselves.

Rath had seen enough and went back into the stairwell. There was no danger that anyone would escape. Gazing over the banister into the depths he removed his hat, his hands playing with the grey felt. When they were finished here, it would be back to the station for questioning. A lot of work just to nail a few rats who made their money taking pictures of people screwing with German national pride. They wouldn't get to the people behind it, the ones who made the real money. All that would happen was that a few poor bastards would end up behind bars. Lanke would have a result to take to the commissioner, and nothing would change.

Rath struggled to see the sense in it. Not that he approved of pornography, but he couldn't get too outraged about it either. It was how things were since the world had been thrown off its gimbals. The revolution in 1919 followed by hyperinflation in 1923 had turned first moral then material values on their head. Weren't there more important things to be concerned with, like maintaining law and order? In Homicide, he had known why he worked for the police. But in Vice? Who cared about a bit of pornography every now and then? Self-proclaimed moral apostles perhaps, for they too had found their place in the Republic, but Rath didn't count himself amongst them.

His thoughts were interrupted by a toilet flushing and a door opening halfway up the stairs. A slim man was about to pull his braces over his undershirt when he saw Rath. The DI knew that face: the pointed moustache, the gaze that now appeared more surprised than stern. The fake Wilhelm II barely needed a moment to take things in hand. With a single leap he cleared the banister and jumped down nearly half a floor. He continued with a crash, footsteps descending in jerky staccato.

Rath took up the chase instinctively, no time to tell his colleagues. It was so dark in the stairwell that he could scarcely make out the stairs. He stumbled more than he ran, but finally reached the ground floor. The daylight was blinding and he almost tripped over an officer who was picking himself up from the floor.

'Where is he?' Rath asked, and the young policeman, who only moments before had been cracking jokes about copulating Kaisers, gazed apologetically in the direction of Hermannstrasse.

'I'll deal with the fugitive. You call it in,' Rath yelled, bounding through the archway towards Hermannstrasse. It had stopped raining, and the pavement was glistening. Outside the tenement he saw the Black Maria, but where was Wilhelm II? There were building materials everywhere along the street, half on the pavement and half on the road: a mixture of beams, steel girders and pipes that pedestrians and cars were forced to make their way past, all set aside for the construction of the underground under Hermannstrasse. In the meantime the driver of the prison van emerged to give Rath a sign. Cursing, he clambered over a pile of wooden planks and spotted the porn Kaiser ducking and weaving down Hermannstrasse towards the square, his braces still hanging loose.

'Police, stay where you are!' Rath shouted, but his cry had the effect of a starting pistol on Wilhelm II. The Kaiser shot across the road and onto the pavement, effing and blinding as he careered past a handful of pedestrians.

'Stop that man,' cried Rath. 'This is a police operation!' Not one of them reacted.

'Save your breath,' he heard a familiar voice say from behind. 'People around here don't help cops.' Wolter tapped him on the shoulder. 'Now run,' said Uncle, and sprinted ahead. 'Together we can catch this rat.'

Rath was astonished at the speed with which the sturdy Wolter made his way down the slope at Hermannstrasse. Despite his colleague's extra bodyweight, Rath could scarcely keep pace. It wasn't until they had reached Hermannplatz that he finally caught up.

'Can you see him?' Rath panted. A stitch in his side forced him to lean against a streetlamp. Only then did he notice he was still holding his hat in his hand. He returned it to its rightful place on his head. Wolter signalled with a nod towards Hermannplatz.

The colossal shell of the Karstadt building towered above them. It was hoped the new department store would lend a touch of New York to provincial Hermannplatz. The official opening was planned for the summer, but for now all that could be seen was an enormous scaffolding, flanked by freight elevators and cranes. The two towers, on the north and south sides, reached sixty metres into the sky. Wilhelm II was racing towards the southern corner, moving diagonally across the intersection past a series of hooting cars, and only narrowly avoiding the number 29 tram as it made its way up Hermannstrasse, waiting until the last moment to execute a full-length dive across the path of the squealing brute before disappearing from the officers' view. They had no choice but to wait until the train rumbled past, and with that they lost sight of their man.

Across the intersection they surveyed the square.

'He couldn't have made it down to the underground,' Wolter said. 'There wouldn't have been time.'

'But there would've been time for *that,*' Rath said, pointing towards the construction fence, a hoarding plastered with posters and measuring several metres in height.

They approached together, searching for somewhere he might have clambered over. Someone had painted EXERCISE YOUR RIGHTS AND MARCH ON MAY 1ST in red across the hoarding, ruining several advertisements in the process.

Rath looked at Wolter but he must have seen it in the same instant. They made their way towards the *Sinalco* poster to take a closer look. The paper was torn under the C and the O. A dirty abrasion left by a shoe.

Wolter gave Rath a leg-up to haul himself up the slippery wet timber and peer over the top. Wilhelm II was running towards Urbanstrasse and had almost reached the opposite end of the building site. A decent effort, as the department store façade occupied the entire length of Hermannplatz, around 300 metres in all.

'He's headed for Urbanstrasse! Go and intercept him there!' he shouted to Uncle, before jumping over and taking up the chase once more. If Bruno could cut him off, he'd be theirs for the taking, but Wilhelm II had seen Rath, and was growing increasingly frantic. Now level with the north tower, he moved past the freight elevator that flanked it, directly towards the fence onto Urbanstrasse. Any moment now he'd be trapped, but then he stopped, turned on his heels and disappeared behind the steel framework of the elevator. The next minute he was climbing the struts, nimble as a rat. Rath barely gave the situation a second thought before following.

The porn Kaiser must have been a cat burglar or an acrobat. No match for a policeman lacking circus training. Rath swung himself onto the nearest ladder and ascended carefully, level by level, always mindful not to lose sight of the nimble, climbing rat. Today was Sunday and the vast building site was deserted. Only the two of them moved in the web of steel and timber until, suddenly, there were no more ladders. The scaffolding came to an end on the seventh floor, the main building didn't extend any higher, but the freight elevator by the north tower, which resembled an aborted skyscraper, had scaffolding for several more floors. Wilhelm had kept climbing. Was he headed for the spire? It looked as if he might be.

Rath groaned. Just don't look down, he told himself. Above, the Kaiser climbed onto the elevator struts sixty metres above ground. Rath fixed his gaze ahead, crossing a few metres of wobbly planks to reach the north tower. Then more scaffolding and another set of ladders. He could no longer see the Kaiser but it didn't matter, he just had to keep going. They'd get him in the end. When he reached the summit Rath was so out of breath he leaned his head against a cool iron girder, panting. Where was this guy, and why didn't the scumbag just give himself up?

There was no sign, but he must see that it was pointless. Rath felt his hands cramp around the iron girder as he fixed his gaze downwards. How was it the drop could be so alluring and yet so panic-inducing at the same time?

On Hermannplatz an endless stream of ants scuttled along heedlessly, while toy cars wheeled this way and that. His knees grew weak. Over the roofs, he could see as far as Kreuzberg, the great hall of Görlitzer station amidst a sea of houses and, in the distance, the chimneys of Klingenberg power station.

Was the fake Kaiser already on his way down? If so, Bruno would intercept him. If he was still scrambling around up here it would be *his* responsibility to nab him, Gereon Rath, vertigo or no. The whistling of the wind become unbearable as, carefully, he climbed down to a more sheltered level, and suddenly Wilhelm II was standing right in front of him, just as startled as the detective. He had lost half of his fake moustache during the pursuit.

'Fuck off, pig,' he said, his voice nervous and shrill and quite the opposite of majestic. Madness was in his eyes, an impression only intensified by the smear of greasepaint.

Cocaine, Rath thought, he's on cocaine, he's been snorting it in the toilet. Just what I need.

'C'mon pal,' he said, trying to sound as calm as possible, 'you must see this is pointless. Why don't you spare us any further trouble?'

'I ain't going to spare you nothing,' the man said in a thick Berlin accent, and suddenly a glistening piece of metal was in his hand. Great, Rath thought, a junkie with a shooter.

'Put that away,' he said, 'or give it to me, and I promise I won't have seen it. That I never saw you threaten an officer with it.'

'Story time over, arsehole?'

'I'll forget about you insulting a police official as well.'

'And when I blow a hole in your brain, will you forget that too?'

'I just want to have a rational conversation.'

The gun was trembling slightly. It was small calibre, but they weren't standing that far away from each other and it would be enough to kill a police officer.

'You're trying to sweet talk me until your mate comes. Fucking cop!'

The junkie didn't know how right he was. Wolter was clambering onto the planks behind him.

'My mate's waiting for you down below,' Rath said. 'Even if you shoot me, there's no way you'll get past him. He's got a gun too, and it's a damn sight bigger than that toy.'

'Shall I show you what it can do?'

In the same moment Wolter grabbed him from behind and, with both hands, held his right arm fast.

A shot rang out and Rath heard the bullet whistle past his ear. Wood splintered. He ducked instinctively.

The fake Kaiser looked horrified and momentarily forgot to resist. Wolter took his chance and slammed the man's right hand against a steel girder. A cry of pain, and the weapon crashed onto the wooden planks. Uncle swivelled the Kaiser round and rammed his right fist into his stomach. The man was already on his way down, but the brawny Wolter followed up with a left hook, sending the Kaiser sprawling onto the scaffolding boards. He aimed a final kick in the unconscious man's side and gasped for breath.

'Arsehole!' he said.

He cuffed the man to the scaffolding and picked up his pistol.

'That was close, Gereon,' he said. 'You should have used your gun.'

'I needed both hands to climb.'

Rath knew that Uncle was right and that he was deluding himself if he thought he could survive in Vice without a firearm. Police work was police work. 'Thanks, DCI Wolter,' he said finally.

'Thanks *partner*, we say around here,' Wolter replied, patting him on the shoulder. The DCI pulled out a pocket knife and pared the bullet from the wooded crossbeam. He took it over to the junkie, who had now come round and was struggling with the handcuffs, and gave him such a clout that his nose started to bleed.

'You should be grateful to me, you fucking arsehole,' said Wolter. The fucking arsehole spat blood. 'Do you know why?' Eyes flickering furiously. 'I just saved you from going to the scaffold as a cop killer.' More blood. 'But that still leaves you with *attempted* murder. Do you know what we do with people like you?' A shake of the head. 'You don't? Well, listen carefully. You get sent to Plötzensee, and there we tell the real hard cases that you're some godforsaken diaper sniper. Do you know what they do to kiddie-fuckers in Plötzensee? There won't be any guards stupid enough to interfere. I know people who *wish* they'd gone to the scaffold. People who wish their aim had been better.'

A horrified expression.

Wolter looked at Rath. 'What shall we do with this scumbag?' he asked.

Rath shrugged his shoulders.

Uncle Bruno turned to the junkie. 'Do you realise we're the only friends you have left?' He rolled the bullet between his fingers. 'This here is evidence. This is the bullet you shot at my partner. The one that almost killed him.' He stowed it in his jacket pocket. 'But maybe this bullet was never fired.'

Wolter waited until the man had processed what he was saying. Then he took the pistol by the barrel and dangled it at arm's length. The coked-up eyes tried to follow the weapon's arc.

'A Lignose. Nice model. Small but handy. Fires one-handed, right? 6.75 calibre, with your fingerprints on it. Bread and butter for any judge!' He replaced the pistol in his pocket. 'But I suppose it depends if a judge ever gets to see it.'

Suddenly the junkie rediscovered his voice. 'What do you want, cop?'

'Pay attention because I'm only going to explain this once. From now on you belong to me and my partner.' Wolter pointed towards Rath, who had edged closer. 'When we come to you with questions, you have the answers ready. Always. Doesn't matter if it's day or night.'

He removed the man's handcuffs and pulled him up. 'Why don't we see if you've understood? If you play ball, you might not even have to come back to the station.'

'I've never grassed on no-one. Find some other fink!'

'There's a first for everything. You of all people should know that.' Wolter produced a smile that was almost charming. 'You'll get used to it. Who knows, there might even be something in it for you. If we're satisfied with you.'

'And if I say you can shove it up your arse?'

'Just think about what I said about Plötzensee! It should make the decision easier.'

The glistening streets still reflected a white-grey sky, while clouds heavy with rain hovered over the city. A black Ford A shot across Kottbusser Damm with its soft top up, Wolter steering through the slow-moving Sunday traffic. Rath sat in the passenger seat, lost in thought. The real work would start when they reached Alex: questioning, questioning, and more questioning. By now König and his gang were stewing in the cells. Jänicke would have accompanied them to the station in the Black Maria. They would leave König and company in custody to simmer and then, with everything the porn Kaiser—real name Franz Krajewski—had told them, they could really begin to turn up the heat.

The fake Kaiser had talked like a blue streak on the scaffolding before they turned him loose. Rath had gained an insight into how Wolter recruited informants, and his brutality had surprised him. Now they were sitting silently alongside one another, Rath understood that Wolter's little number on the scaffolding had been meant as a lesson for the new recruit from the Rhine Province. Wolter seemed to read Rath's mind.

'If you lock up a rat like that, you'll get nothing out of him,' he said. 'Makes more sense for him to be running around Berlin knowing that we *could* lock him up, so scared he's afraid to fart without our permission. I'm telling you, that guy will save us a hell of a lot of work. As long as all that coke doesn't mess with his brain.' He laughed and rummaged in his jacket pocket. 'Whenever he thinks about this, he'll shit himself.'

Wolter fished out the bullet that was meant for Rath.

'Here!' he said.

'What am I supposed to do with that?'

'A souvenir. At the end of the day, *you're* the one he was trying to kill.'

Wolter stepped on the gas once they had gone under the elevated train at Kottbusser Tor. There was hardly any traffic on Dresdener Strasse.

'We're partners,' said Uncle. 'Now we even share an informant. That's just between us. It has nothing to do with anyone else.'

Turning Krajewski loose was against every rule in the book. Rath didn't feel too clever but their colleagues bought their story that the Kaiser had simply got away. No-one held it against them when they returned to Hermannstrasse empty-handed. Their colleagues laid the blame for the Kaiser's escape at the door of the young officer whom Krajewski had knocked over.

The boy's guilty conscience made him eager to please. In his desire to atone he had conducted a painstaking search of the studio. Rath and Wolter had overseen the work, Jänicke having departed with the suspects. They had found any number of plates and prints, more than enough for the public prosecutor. Enough to give König a good going-over too. Back on the scaffolding, Krajewski had revealed that the photographer had presented his gifted troupe with the chance to embark upon a career in film.

Pornography had been on the rise for a few years and dirty magazines were being sold on the streets and under the counter. It made sense for the dregs of the Berlin film industry to recognise the earning potential of these so-called 'educational films'. They were shown to initiates in back rooms and illegal night spots, generally in the better areas in the west of the city. Certain wealthy gentlemen had been known to take playmates into the performance with them so as not to waste any time putting what they had witnessed on screen into practice.

There was no way König was shouldering the costs alone. There would be other backers in the city's organised crime circles or amongst the upper classes in the west. Krajewski didn't name them, no matter how hard they pressed, but perhaps he really didn't know. Whatever the case, they still had a few pieces of information to rattle König. Perhaps enough to break up the pornography ring.

Rath examined the bullet. Small, shiny and unremarkable, yet it could have cost him his life. He looked across at Uncle, who was honking at a daydreaming cyclist on Oranienplatz. Had the man with the affable face really just saved his life? At the very least he had helped him out of a dicey situation. Nothing in the world gave Gereon Rath the right to criticise Bruno Wolter. He had broken the rules, but so what? Maybe that's just the way things were in this big, cold city and he'd better get used to it.

'If you want to make it here, you can't afford to be soft,' Wolter said. Rath was surprised at how well his colleague could read his silence.

'Make it in Vice?'

'We don't have it so bad. We get to gad about the night spots of the most exciting city in the world, which is also the most disreputable. There's something to be said for that. If the odd colleague turns up his nose, so be it. You get used to it.'

'Why don't you work in A Division?' Rath asked. 'With your skills and contacts?'

'In Homicide? If they want my skills and experience, not to mention my contacts, they can ask. Frankly, I'm not crazy about working for them.'

'But they have a good reputation!'

'Gennat's boys? The darlings of the press? Well, dealing with theft and murder will get you a lot further than raking up filth and smut.' Wolter looked at him as if assessing his worth. 'But it isn't easy to get in. Gennat's people are hand picked. You have to land something big. I mean really big. A Kaiser with his dick out won't cut it.' He laughed. 'But don't worry, even we lesser mortals are granted access to Olympus now and then. A Division is always borrowing officers from other units. You can run around playing at being in Homicide but, believe me, murder inquiries aren't half as exciting as they're cracked up to be.'

'That depends.'

'On what?'

'I used to be in Homicide. I was never bored.'

He hadn't told anyone in Berlin before. Commissioner Zörgiebel was the only one who knew Gereon Rath's personal file, and he had guaranteed his old friend Engelbert Rath that he wouldn't say a thing. Not even Superintendent Lanke knew all the details concerning his new recruit's service record. Wolter glanced at him.

'Do you miss the dead bodies?' he asked.

Rath had to take a deep breath, remembering a pale face and a pale body with a blood-encrusted bullet hole in the chest.

Wolter bypassed the big construction site on Jannowitz Bridge, which was always ripe for traffic chaos, and took the route past Märkisches Museum and over Waisen Bridge. Alexanderplatz was an absolute building site as well. Heavy steam hammers were driving the construction of the underground forward and had almost hollowed out the entire square. Traffic was diverted across thick timber planks, while site fences formed narrow passages for the pedestrian masses to push their way through. There were wooden beams supporting the steel railway bridge above Königstrasse.

They had just turned the corner at Aschinger's when they fell into the next trap. The Ford A got stuck behind a yellow Berlin city bus, which was blocking the already narrow temporary access route. *Berlin smokes Juno cigarettes* an advertisement revealed. Wolter cursed. A boy in his Sunday best stood on the steps leading to the upper deck, cocking a snook at them.

The vast brick expanse of police headquarters was already in view. The building wasn't called *Red Castle* for nothing; the great corner tower presided over Alexanderplatz like a medieval keep. It had taken some time for Rath to get used to the fact that even the officers referred to headquarters as *The Castle*.

'Let me out here, I'll get us something to eat,' he said. 'I'll be quicker on foot. See you back at the Castle.'

After scarcely ten minutes he entered the station from Dircksenstrasse.

This was where CID had their offices, on the same side as the city railway. His day-to-day work was interrupted by the peal and rumble of trains wheeling past his window. Rath greeted the cop at the entrance by raising the Aschinger paper bags in his right hand. Three *bratwurst* with mustard. In the left hand a tub of potato salad. The food from Aschinger's was better than the canteen. First they would take time to eat, and after that they would concentrate on the interviews.

It would be a while before they summoned the first of the gang from the cells. Let them stew a little longer. Rath's stomach rumbled as he climbed the steps. Apart from two cups of coffee—a good one at home and a bad one in the 220th precinct—he hadn't eaten anything today.

As he emerged from the stairwell into the grey corridor he paused, lost in thought, outside a glass double door with HOMICIDE written in white capital letters. He thought of Bruno's words in the car—*Gennat's boys—hand-picked.* In the long passageway behind the glass door, another door opened. Homicide was busy on Sundays too. A young woman was standing in the doorway. She shouted something back into the office before turning and moving down the passageway. Rath peered through the glass into a narrow face with a resolutely curved mouth, and dark eyes under black hair cut fashionably short. She wore a dark red suit and carried a file under her arm. Her shoes clicked across the stone floor of the long passageway at a brisk clip and, when she greeted a passing colleague, her smile conjured up a dimple on her left cheek.

'Don't get lost now,' a voice startled Rath from his daydream. He turned as if he'd been caught out. 'You still work for us,' said Wolter.

The glass door opened and the woman bestowed her smile on the officers from E Division.

'Good afternoon,' she said. Her voice was higher than he'd expected.

Wolter tipped his hat and Rath raised the paper bags. The woman looked at him in amusement almost, and he felt stupid and awkward. He lowered the paper bags and her smile returned. Rath wasn't sure if she was smiling or laughing as she continued on her way, her dark red suit becoming smaller and smaller, before disappearing behind the next glass door. Uncle patted him on the shoulder.

'Let's get something to eat before the real work begins. You look completely out of it. When was the last time you had a woman?'

'Ask me something easier.'

'No wonder you're not enjoying Vice,' Wolter said, 'if you're living like a monk. I'll make sure I introduce you to a few girls.'

'Forget it.' After Doris, Rath had had enough of women. She had dropped him as soon as the smear campaign had begun. Not even half a year had passed . . .

'Oh come on!' Wolter wouldn't let go. 'I know some great girls! In our line of work, you get around. Like I said: *I'm* not about to trade places.'

'Things don't look too bad in Homicide either.' He pointed to the glass door, the Aschinger bags still in his hand. 'Can you tell me who that was just now?'

'Charlotte Ritter, a stenographer in Homicide.'

3

'You take care of it, Rath, you know about this sort of thing,' Lanke shouted. They were sending him onto the roof again.

Behind Superintendent Lanke stood the silent figure of Police Director Engelbert Rath and, behind him, an army of uniformed officers. Above the white moustache, his father's eyes were icy and full of reproach. It was a familiar look, the same look he had assumed the first time little Gereon brought a bad report home from school. In contrast, Lanke's face was a fantastically grinning and sadistic caricature.

'How many more innocent people have to die before you get your arse up there? If you think you can avoid getting your hands dirty, you're very much mistaken!'

Rath gazed up at the roof, which seemed not only to be getting steeper but also to be growing in size. How the hell was he supposed to get up there? When he turned back the troops had all disappeared, replaced by rows of women with children. That was when the shooting started.

Row upon row went down, mown to the ground, dying mute as their children screamed. More and more children, and the more women who died, the louder the screaming became.

He hurried skywards, forgetting his vertigo, until suddenly the house was cloaked in scaffolding and he saw the sniper with a battery of rifles that he reloaded one after the other.

When he reached the upper platform the sniper lifted his shirt to reveal a pale, emaciated upper body with a gaping bullet hole. The blood had long since dried. It was the sort of wound you found on the corpses in the morgue. Clinical. Clean.

'How about that?' the sniper said in a reproachful whine. 'I'll tell my father.'

Rath pulled out his service revolver. 'Drop your weapon!' he cried, but the man trained his rifle on him.

'Drop your weapon! I'll shoot!'

The other man wouldn't be swayed. 'You can't shoot me. I'm already dead,' he said. 'Have you forgotten?'

A fuse blew inside Rath's head and his index finger pulled on the trigger again and again. The Mauser only clicked in response. Click, click, click, it went, as the other man quietly took aim and placed his finger on the trigger. He began to pull down, almost in slow motion . . .

'No!'

Rath was awoken by his own cry, suddenly wide awake and sitting bolt upright. His brow was cold and sweaty and his heart was racing. The clicking continued, but it was coming from the window. The clock on his bedside table showed half past one. He peeled himself out of bed, threw on his dressing gown and looked outside. Nürnberger Strasse was completely devoid of people. The only sound was that of the wind rustling through the trees, but there were three or four small stones on the window sill. Someone had been trying to wake him. He opened the window and leaned out.

The heavy front door opened and there was a short, sharp cry. 'What are you doing hanging around here like a bad smell?' a woman's voice asked.

A young girl, in her early twenties perhaps, entered Rath's field of vision, turning to look over her shoulder before hurrying towards the taxi rank. Weinert must have been entertaining again. Rath couldn't help but smile, but goodness knows what Elisabeth Behnke would make of it. The landlady was very strict about tenants receiving female visitors at night, and yet the intrepid Weinert had someone there most evenings. Who, he wondered, had Weinert's latest conquest bumped into down by the front door? Who had given her such a fright?

While he was still thinking he heard the heavy front door click shut and someone pull on the bell, followed by a hammering on the door to the flat. Rath stepped out of his room into the main hall. The door leading to Elisabeth Behnke's rooms was shut. No sign of Weinert either. He probably had a guilty conscience.

There was another crash against the door.

'*Kardakow,*' cried a deep, foreign voice, only slightly muffled by the closed door. '*Aleksej Iwanowitsch Kardakow! Atkroj dwer! Eta ja, Boris! Boris Sergejewitsch Karpenko!*'

He flung the door open and gazed into the baffled blue-green eyes of a scruffy, ragged figure. Tangled strands of dark blond hair fell over the man's gaunt, unshaven chin. Rath could smell the alcohol on his breath.

'What's all the racket?' he asked. The man stared at him with glassy eyes. 'You'd be better off going home to bed instead of banging on people's doors in the middle of the night.'

The man said something in a language that Rath didn't understand. Russian? Polish? He couldn't say for sure, but he was fairly certain the stranger had just asked him a question.

'Do you speak German?' he asked.

The stranger repeated his question. All Rath understood was that it was about a man named Alexej. 'I'm sorry, I can't help you,' he said. 'Go home! Good night!'

No sooner had he closed the door than the banging started again.

'That's enough,' he hissed as he threw the door open a second time, 'if you don't clear off this instant, there'll be real trouble!'

The man pushed him to one side and stormed inside. Only Rath's door was open in the hallway, and that was where the drunk staggered next. Rath rushed after him and grabbed him by the collar but, with a cry, the stranger pushed him up against the wall. A strong forearm pressed against Rath's neck; the man's face was so close that his alcoholic breath was almost unbearable.

'*Gdje Aleksej? Schto s nim?*' the man hissed before Rath kneed him in the guts. He doubled up momentarily but was soon back on his feet. '*Yob twaju mat!*' he cried, charging towards Rath, who dodged skilfully. The stranger crashed against the huge neo-Gothic wardrobe, taking a chunk out of its side.

Rath grabbed him by the collar, twisted his arm behind his back and dragged him into the hall. The drunk bellowed something incomprehensible, trying vainly to escape. Rath positioned him carefully before sending him on his way with a hefty kick. The drunk stumbled into the darkness of the stairwell, crashing against the door of the flat opposite. Rath slammed and bolted the door, and leaned against it panting. From the stairwell he heard a few muffled cries before the door banged shut and all was still.

'Has he gone?'

Rath looked up in surprise. The widow Behnke had thrown a crochet shawl over her nightdress and was standing in the doorway that led from the hall into the dining room and then to her private rooms. The landlady was in her late thirties and obviously lonely. If her gaze spoke volumes her hints could have replaced whole libraries. So far, he had resisted her advances. Start something with his landlady? With someone who wouldn't even allow female visitors? Out of the question! Right now though, she was allowing him a look at her ample décolletage. Elisabeth Behnke was obviously enjoying seeing her tenant short of breath.

'Come on, Herr Rath. I'll make us a tea. With rum. Just the thing to get over the fright. I thought all that nonsense with these Russians was finally over.'

He followed her into the kitchen. Once an opulent dining room, when she had been forced to sublet she had turned the old kitchen into a bathroom for her male tenants, and moved the kitchen units here.

'Drunken Russians on the rampage in strangers' flats in the middle of the night is a common occurrence here?' he asked at the dining table.

She looked at him and shrugged her shoulders.

'The previous tenant gave me more than my share of sleepless nights, I can tell you. Every so often your room would be teeming with Russians carousing until the small hours.' She lit the gas stove and placed a kettle on the hotplate. 'You'd think there were more Russians than Germans in this city.'

'Sometimes I think there are just too many people here in general.'

'They arrived just after the war, after the Bolsheviks drove them out. You'd hear more Russian than German on the streets of Charlottenburg.'

'That's still true in some of the bars on the Tauentzien.'

'I don't visit establishments like that. Cesspits. And there's you having to deal with them the whole time as part of your job, poor thing.' She fiddled noisily with the teapot as if to distract herself, before placing two cups on the table. 'To think Herr Kardakov seemed so refined when he first moved in three years ago.'

'Who?'

'The tenant before you. Herr Kardakov was an author, you know.' The kettle began to whistle. She poured hot water into the pot. 'A quiet tenant, I thought. What a mistake! They were always going on, these late night excesses.'

'. . . but you've banned me from receiving female visitors.'

'Do you mind? Herr Kardakov only ever had male guests. They talked and talked and drank and drank. You'd be forgiven for thinking by talking and drinking was how they earned their money.'

'So, how did they make their money?'

'Don't ask me. Quite honestly, I don't want to know either. Herr Kardakov always paid his rent on time, though I'm not sure he ever published a book. He certainly never showed one to me anyway.' She almost sounded hurt. Rath could imagine that Kardakov had also been obliged to resist his landlady's overtures.

'I suppose that visit just now must have had something to do with Herr Kardakov?'

'You can be sure of it.' Elisabeth Behnke poured tea for them both.

'I think the man's name was Boris. Does that mean anything to you?'

'No idea. There were so many of them coming and going.'

'Well, good old Boris demolished my wardrobe. Perhaps Herr Kardakov would be so kind as to pay for the damage.' *Or to buy me a completely new wardrobe,* Rath thought to himself.

She fetched a half-full bottle of rum from the wall cupboard and poured generously. 'He left in a hurry last month and there's been no trace since— though he still owes me a month's rent and the cellar's full of his junk. I've written to him at his new address several times. No reply. Do you think there's anything you could do? His name's Alexej. Alexej Ivanovitsch Kardakov.'

That was the name Boris had used.

'Maybe he'll show a little more respect if the police get involved,' she said, and passed him a cup. 'Drink up. It'll do you good after a shock like that. Although I'm sure you're used to it, as an officer.'

He didn't know quite what she meant. Was it the shock or the alcohol he was supposed to be used to? Probably both. Phew, she hadn't stinted on the rum! For a moment he suspected she was planning to get him drunk, but then he saw how she downed her own cup in one.

'Another?'

He finished his cup and nodded, feeling he could use a little self-medication. Not so much because of the stranger, but because of the dream he still hadn't managed to shake off. He'd sleep easier with a rum or two in his system.

'Forget the tea,' he said, and handed her his cup.

———

He awoke the next morning at quarter to nine, sat bolt upright and held his head in his hands. It was throbbing after the unexpected exertions of the previous evening. What on earth had he been drinking? More to the point, how much? He was in his own bed at any rate, albeit naked. A record was performing forlorn pirouettes on the gramophone. Rath groped for the telephone on his bedside table, almost getting tangled up in the cables. He could have reeled off Wolter's extension in his sleep. Uncle lifted the receiver and Rath mumbled an apology into the mouthpiece. He heard laughter on the other end of the line.

'You don't sound too good, old boy. A few too many last night was it?'

'First night for a week I haven't been in Hermannstrasse.' Rath had spent the previous six nights in the musty Neukölln flat, observing the comings and goings in König's studio, a shift that no-one else had wanted.

'True. In that case you've earned a day off.'

'You're more use to me rested,' Wolter said. 'Stay at home today.'

Rath didn't object. He hung up and was just about to turn round and get back to sleep when something warm under the bedclothes gave him a start.

Had he brought a woman back yesterday? For the life of him he couldn't remember. He remembered the dream and the strange Russian who had smashed his wardrobe, the tea with his landlady . . . the rum . . . the toast to friendship . . . He hadn't . . .

Rath pulled back the covers slowly, expecting the worst. The arm belonged to a set of blonde locks with a silvery tinge. Elisabeth Behnke was lying in his bed.

The last thing he could remember was the moment she had said to call her Elisabeth, after they had emptied the bottle of rum and started on the Danziger Goldwasser. They had kissed, he knew that. That was the custom when you toasted to friendship. But what had happened afterwards? Questions he couldn't answer. The only person who could was his landlady, who was currently stretching her ample and naked body beside him. She blinked into the light and pulled the covers over her breasts.

'Good morning,' he said, making every effort not to sound sarcastic.

'Good morning,' she said, almost shyly. At least she's embarrassed too, he thought.

'My God!' The alarm clock now showed nine o'clock. 'So late already. I should have made breakfast ages ago. Weinert's sure to complain.'

She used the bedclothes to cover herself until she realised that she was exposing Rath's manhood. She was still somewhere between getting up and sitting back down when there was a knock on the door. Quick as a flash, Elisabeth Behnke jumped back into her tenant's bed and disappeared under the covers.

'That's Weinert now,' she whispered.

The door opened slowly and Berthold Weinert poked his nosy head into the room.

'Good morning, sleepyhead,' he said and gave Rath a knowing wink. 'You couldn't lend me a few marks could you? There's been no sign of old Behnke this morning, otherwise I'd have asked her. Seems to be ill, hasn't even made breakfast, but I need to head into the office . . .'

'Help yourself.'

Rath pointed towards his jacket, which was folded neatly over the clothes stand, in sharp contrast to the dressing gown that, along with his pyjamas, formed a confused tangle on the floor somewhere between the door and the bed. Rath only hoped that Weinert wouldn't notice the blue chemise lying on the other side of the bed.

'Has your girl gone?' the journalist winked, as he searched the inside pocket for Rath's wallet. The conspiratorial glances were beginning to get on Rath's nerves. 'Behnke's like a hawk. I always send my girls home in the evening. Better safe than sorry. You were still going long into the night . . . and then the music! To think what old Behnke said about that Negro racket during the day!' He looked round, afraid that she might hear. 'You should tell your girl to be a little quieter. I've never heard a dirtier laugh! Not only that . . .' He fished a ten mark note from the wallet. 'Not that I minded, of course, just don't let her next door hear you!' He winked for a final time and left the room.

When he pulled the covers away, Rath saw that Elisabeth Behnke was blushing. 'I hope that blabbermouth didn't smell a rat,' she said.

'Didn't sound like it,' he said. 'Were you really laughing that much, Frau Behnke?'

'Call me Elisabeth.'

'Isn't that how all this started?'

'We're both adults, Herr Rath! I mean Gereon,' she said, more like her old self. 'I'm as keen to keep last night a secret as you are, but what's done is done. We don't have to go back to pretending we don't know each other.'

'Sorry,' he said. Her outburst had given him an erection. He pulled the covers tighter.

She stood up, having obviously decided she could live with his seeing her naked. Her voluptuous curves only intensified his erection, even once they had disappeared under her chemise. He turned over on his back.

'I'll make breakfast,' she said and left the room.

He lay in bed thinking. Elisabeth Behnke was almost ten years older than him. Her husband had fallen at the Second Battle of the Aisne in 1917. Rath remembered, back in the summer of 1918, after they had completed their basic training and awaited the call to the front, how they had felt that they were entering the final days of their lives. In the delirium of that time a zest for life was borne out of the fear of death. Sweating bodies writhed in bed with women who had all been older by ten years or more. Most had been married, their husbands either fighting on the front or already fallen.

Rath had just turned eighteen when he was called up by the Prussians and the draft had felt like a death sentence. He couldn't help thinking about Anno. He couldn't know that the war had entered its final year. His mother had cried, not wanting to lose another son. Her oldest had fallen during the first days of war. Anno the infallible, the eternal role model, but on this score Gereon had no desire to emulate him.

At the garrison they had felt like prisoners awaiting execution, and then all of a sudden the war was over. Before they fired a single shot in anger news of the mutiny at Kiel spread through the ranks and soldiers' councils were formed. As soon as it had become clear that no-one would arrest him as a deserter, Rath simply removed his uniform and went home to Cologne. Some of his comrades continued to play at war, joining the Freikorps as they crossed the country fighting communists. Private Gereon Rath listened to his father and joined the police. They too had given him a gun, as well as the desk that Anno Rath had occupied before the war.

He banished the memories and gazed out of the window where the sun was shining: the first day of spring to merit the name.

Rath's hangover finally dissipated in the fresh air. He took a deep breath and dug out the sheet of paper Elisabeth Behnke had given him. Luisenufer. Alexej Ivanovitsch Kardakov's new address was in Kreuzberg.

The street name had endured down the ages. Only a few years before, the Luisenstadt Canal had flowed between Urbanhafen and the Spree. Now there were children playing in the massive expanse of sand that the city had used to fill the harbour basin. Their shouts and laughter filled the clear skies. After the endless winter, spring had finally arrived. Rath had hated the Berlin winter, ever since he had stepped off the long-distance train at Potsdamer station to be greeted by a flurry of snow and traffic at Potsdamer Platz. The cold was entrenched in the streets until well into April.

His gaze wandered along the house façades to a pub, a hair salon, a dairy. He glanced at the sheet of paper again to check the number.

Breakfast with Elisabeth Behnke hadn't gone as badly as he'd feared. Neither of them breathed a word about what had happened, what could have happened, or what might have happened afterwards, but he had promised to take Kardakov to task over the outstanding final rent payment, over the junk in the cellar and the wardrobe.

The house he was looking for was beside the dairy. A train rattled across the elevated railway at Wassertorplatz as he entered the main house. He checked the mailboxes, including out back, but couldn't find the name Kardakov anywhere, or any name that sounded even vaguely Russian. He glanced again at the piece of paper. The address was correct, as was the house number.

He checked the mailboxes of the two neighbouring houses, but there were no Russians there either. Had he gone to ground to avoid paying his rent? Perhaps he simply hadn't changed the nameplate on the door. Rath went back to the first house. Before he could get there, the front door opened to reveal a face that was as surprised as it was mistrustful.

'Looking for someone?' The man was small and slight, his hat too big for his gaunt face, likewise his enormous moustache. There was a little steel helmet on his lapel.

'You could say that.' Rath dug out the piece of paper and read aloud. 'Alexej Ivanovitsch Kardakov.'

'Never heard of him. Is he supposed to live here?'

'He left this address.'

'That doesn't mean a thing with these Russians.'

'But *you* live in this house?'

'I don't need to tell you anything.'

'Perhaps you do.' Rath waved his badge, although he was not on duty. The man raised a conciliatory hand. 'What would you like to know?'

'Have you noticed anything suspicious in the last few weeks? Has anyone new moved in?'

'Not that I'm aware of.'

'Perhaps under a different name.'

'I'd like to help you, mate, but no. What's this guy supposed to have done?'

'Just routine questioning,' Rath said. He was regretting having shown his badge, strictly speaking it was illegal. He needed to get rid of this pesky witness before he became any more curious. It was obvious he couldn't assist any further. 'Thank you for your help.'

'Always at your service.'

Rath had already turned round when the stranger shouted after him. 'Hang on, officer! Are you here because of the row by any chance?'

'The row?'

'There was someone here in the middle of the night banging on the door so loudly that no-one could sleep. Crazy, he was. Afterwards, there were two of them fighting. The noise, well I'll tell you it was quite something. I thought they were going to kill each other.'

'And?'

'They were Russian. Hundred percent. Maybe it was the man you're looking for, but he doesn't live here. Definitely not. Only decent people live here.'

Rath tipped his hat.

'Many thanks.'

Strange, he thought, as he made his way via Skalitzer Strasse back in the direction of Kottbusser Tor. It seemed he wasn't the only one who'd had his sleep disturbed by a Russian.

4

The new month had got off to a good start. Rath was sitting at his desk, cup of coffee in one hand, cigarette in the other. In front of him were the photos. The print of Wilhelm II was the only one still with a question mark; a little secret he shared with Wolter. They had managed to identify all those who had been snapped, even the ones who had given them the slip during the raid. Yesterday, after he had softened up Old Fritz in the interview room, Rath had presented Uncle with a list of names.

For the first time since his arrival in Berlin, Rath felt halfway decent about himself and at one with the world. His gaze wandered out through the window, past the railway platform to the dark wall of the courthouse.

The day off had done him good, even if he had squandered it in fruitless inquiries. At least he had been able to avoid Elisabeth Behnke. She had cooked for him that evening, and he had told her about his futile search over a bottle of wine. This time he hadn't drunk too much, but had simply planted on her cheek a goodnight kiss that left everything open while promising nothing. The next morning, yesterday morning, he had arrived at work feeling fresh and well rested for the first time in weeks.

Wolter had pressed for results because time was short. 'We need to get a move on with our questioning. 1A will need plenty of space in the cells tomorrow. On the first of May our friends will be transferred to Moabit. We need to have something we can use by then.'

Well, now they did.

Section 1A, the political arm of the police, was in charge of the May actions, and obviously reckoned on making a lot of arrests. The communist press had been agitating for days. Commissioner Zörgiebel, meanwhile, had responded with an appeal that almost all the city's papers had carried: *If the communists have their way the streets of Berlin will be paved with blood. I am determined to assert the powers vested in me by the state and use all available means at my disposal*. It was clear what he meant.

In police barracks there was talk of civil war. Everyone knew the RFB—the alliance of Red Front fighters—had weapons, and many feared they would use them.

Accordingly, E Division's investigation was now less important. If the cells in Alex were to be filled with communists, then the pornographers would have to make way. Wolter had even been asked to postpone any further arrests until after the weekend, which had dulled Rath's sense of achievement a little. Despite the breakthrough they were forced to twiddle their thumbs.

He had managed to show his colleagues what he was about though; Detective Inspector Gereon Rath, the cop from the provinces. Bruno had been amazed. The rookie Jänicke likewise.

There was always a weakness, a wall of silence invariably contained a loose stone and, once you found it, the rest would crumble. In this case the loose stone was Old Fritz, who had squealed as soon as Rath threatened to subpoena his wife. Pure bluff, Rath hadn't known the old man was married. He didn't even know his name. The only person they'd been able to identify beyond any doubt in the last few days was Johann König and, like the rest of them, he hadn't said a word. They must have made a deal in the Black Maria while Jänicke had been half-asleep.

Rath had tried a few things before he had finally broken Frederick the Great, aka Old Fritz. The old man wasn't wearing a wedding ring, but he had the air of a respectable family man. Pressed in that sensitive spot, he had broken down and the names came gushing out. The stenographer had a job keeping up.

There was a knock at the door. Rath yanked his top drawer open and swept the prints from his desk. No-one else needed to see them, and he found them embarrassing. At the same time, some of his colleagues in E Division got a kick out of displaying their photo collections whenever a female CID officer entered. It didn't matter if the women blushed or came out with some saucy riposte, the men's laughter was always the same.

'Come in,' he cried. The door opened. It was Wolter. 'Why so formal?' Rath asked. 'Since when do you knock?'

Uncle grinned. 'Were you expecting visitors? I can see you've cleared your desk!'

'Not everyone has to see our evidence.'

'Especially not stenographers from A Division, am I right?' Wolter laughed. 'Come on, don't be such a sourpuss. You've got every reason to celebrate.'

'Why's that?'

'Because the calendar says Monday the first of May, and you're not in uniform. They're the ones out fighting the communists. While *we* get to stay warm inside.'

'Thanks, but I already know why I never wanted to join uniform.'

'Don't get your hopes up too soon. CID might still be needed on the streets.'

The entire Berlin police force had been on high alert since seven that morning, including both uniform and CID, sixteen thousand officers in total. They had called in those training at the police academy and mounted police had closed off all the parks. There was a strong police presence in the public transport depots, and uniformed officers had assembled in force in the city's working class areas.

'The Reds mean business,' said Wolter. 'Things are really kicking off at Alex. At least that's what Schultes said in the canteen just now. Both of his windows look out onto the square. Should we go and take a look?'

They weren't the only ones to find their way to Schultes's office. There was barely any space left by the two windows. Jänicke was there too.

'I wouldn't be going to Aschinger's today if I were you,' he greeted his colleagues.

A big crowd had gathered amidst the building-site chaos at Alexanderplatz, several thousand people tightly packed around the entrance to Tietz department store. A shawm band in marching order had turned the corner at Alexanderstrasse and was heading towards the square, followed by the grey uniforms of the RFB. Now and then a banner was raised and Rath recognised the faces that also adorned the front of Communist Party headquarters on nearby Bülowplatz: Lenin, Liebknecht, Luxemburg. A holy trinity of Ls.

Since arriving in Berlin, he had grown increasingly infuriated by the audacity of the communists, the way they decorated their party headquarters with the portraits and slogans of these enemies of the state. HAIL THE WORLD REVOLUTION! The sheer nerve of it, and now they were carrying these slogans in front of police headquarters. DOWN WITH THE DEMONSTRATION

BAN. KEEP THE STREETS FREE ON THE 1ST OF MAY! On an enormous piece of red fabric they had written: LONG LIVE THE SOVIET UNION, FIGHT FOR A SOVIET GERMANY! To the left was a resplendent Soviet star; to the right a hammer and sickle. More and more red flags were fluttering above the heads of those marching. An underground worker had planted a red flag on one of the steam hammers at Alex. High up in the offices of the Castle they could hear the crowd chanting: 'Down with the dem-on-stration ban!'

The grey and brown of the workers' caps was surrounded by the black of the shakos and the blue of the uniforms. Another police van emerged from Königstrasse and a troop of officers sprang from the platform, chin straps tightly fastened. The cops on the square formed a line of blue, drew their batons and stormed forth in unison. The chorus of voices quietened and ceased and a murmur went through the crowd. Batons began their whistling descent.

Those demonstrating on the front line ducked under the blows. Some fell and some were bundled into a Black Maria, amongst them a man with a red standard. Still the throng would not be deterred. A short step back and they were pressing forward once more. A wooden banner knocked the shako off an officer's head. The first stones were launched. The crowd had resumed their chant: 'Down with the dem-on-stration ban!'

'Have we taken on fire brigade duties as well?' Rath asked. At the tram stop in front of the UFA cinema down below, two officers were attaching a fire hose to a hydrant.

'New tactic,' Wolter replied. 'Water instead of batons. The demonstrators are about to get wet.'

Scarcely had the two officers connected the hose when the command sounded: charge the line! The officer with the hose waded into the middle of the crowd, which scattered in surprise. Some were knocked to the ground by the force of the jet, and sent rolling on the wet asphalt.

'Nice work. Watering the communists,' Wolter said.

'The commissioner's got the whole force on high alert for this?' asked Schultes. 'Socialist hysteria, that's what I call it. Later this afternoon these communists will be sitting back at home by the fire, drying their wet things. Enough revolution for one day. People will have had their fun and order will be restored.'

'I wouldn't be so sure,' said Wolter. 'The RFB are getting weapons and training from Moscow. They're not just playing.'

'We've always managed to bring the Reds into the line,' said Schultes. 'They tried to stage a revolution ten years ago and what became of it? The minute things get serious, they throw in the towel.'

'Let's hope so,' said Wolter and made a concerned face. 'At any rate, we can't allow this rabble to take over the streets.'

'No,' Schultes replied, 'but the Nazis with their brownshirts aren't much better. Better marchers perhaps.'

'They don't shoot police officers.'

Schultes fixed his gaze on Uncle. 'Law and order must be maintained at all times. You're right there, DCI Wolter.'

'That's the job of uniform, not CID,' said Rath. 'I for one am happy that we have nothing to do with politics, only criminals.'

'Politicians, criminals—who said they aren't one and the same?' Schultes replied and everyone laughed.

Rath gazed thoughtfully out of the window. Ten years ago the streets had also been turned upside down, but he hadn't seen anything like it since. His colleagues on the square were going about their business bravely, and not just with fire hoses. At this precise moment Rath wouldn't have liked to have been out there in his civvies.

5

The car hung from the hook of the salvage crane like an overgrown fish as dirty brown water poured back into the Landwehr canal. In the dark night, the crane's spotlight bathed the vehicle in bright, eerie light.

Detective Chief Inspector Wilhelm Böhm emerged from a large black Mercedes on Tempelhofer Ufer and put on his bowler hat. A few curious night owls turned from the salvage operation to admire the car, out of which there followed a slim, elegantly dressed woman carrying a shorthand pad, followed by a young man.

The black murder wagon was famous in Berlin. Equipped with numbered markers to secure evidence, camera, spotlights, an inch rule and tape measure, ordnance maps, gloves, tweezers, a transportable police laboratory, and all sorts of paraphernalia for the recording of evidence, it even housed a mobile office of folding table, chairs and a travel typewriter.

The car being lowered onto the wet asphalt of Möckern Bridge was a cream-coloured Horch 350. The soft top was down and there was a man at the wheel. DCI Böhm marched towards the police officer directing the operation.

'Have I just walked into Lunapark? What the hell are all these people doing? And why couldn't you have waited until Homicide arrived before starting the recovery? Did you at least manage to check the exact location with the divers?'

Without waiting for an answer, the DCI approached the vehicle. Pointless, he thought, trying to teach these idiots in uniform about modern-day police work. They still thought that restoring order to a crime scene was more important than securing evidence from it. Böhm glanced at the dead man behind the wheel.

'Gräf,' Böhm barked through the night. 'Make sure you get a photo before the doctor messes everything up.'

Assistant Detective Reinhold Gräf started lugging the heavy camera from the murder wagon. In the meantime the officer had recovered from being shouted at, and approached the DCI.

'Kemmerling, First Sergeant,' he said, pointing towards a gap in the canal fencing, right next to the bridge. 'That's where he went through. He must have hightailed it across Tempelhofer Ufer and come off the road.'

Böhm looked the corpse up and down and shook his head. 'How's he supposed to have driven with hands like that?'

Kemmerling winced as he caught sight of the dead man's hands. Individual fingers could barely be distinguished. Some of the joints were held together by skin alone; others were so contorted that simply looking at them was agony.

'How many people do you have here, Kemmerling?' Böhm asked.

'Five, sir. Most of my men have been withdrawn because of communist unrest.'

Böhm nodded sympathetically, he didn't have enough people either. The May disturbances had gone on for two days now. After slipping out of police control the confrontations had quickly escalated. There had been shootings and fatalities and communist strongholds around Bülowplatz, Wedding and Neukölln had been officially declared as trouble spots. All three were under siege and it seemed like civil war was about to break out.

'Four of you can get rid of the onlookers and seal off the crime scene; the fifth can help secure the evidence until ED get here. If they get here at all, that is.'

'Ahem . . .' it seemed Kemmerling didn't quite understand. 'Secure the evidence?'

'Don't touch anything or go inside anywhere. Just do whatever Homicide tells you,' Böhm said. 'Ritter,' he called into the darkness.

The stenographer stepped into the glare of the salvage crane.

'Put your pad away, Charly,' said the DCI. 'First, kindly show this gentleman how to secure evidence.'

In the meantime, Assistant Detective Gräf had assembled the camera and, for a split second, the crime scene was lit by the flash. It seemed almost as if the dead man was smiling for the camera.

Charly felt the officer staring at her dress, even though she was walking ahead of him. She had made the green dance dress only a few days before and knew that it accentuated her figure as well as revealing a not inconsiderable length of leg. She was wearing it today for the first time and, on the dance floor at *Moka Efti*, it had felt great. She had enjoyed attracting the attention of the men, which was never a bad thing on a first date. Jakob shouldn't go thinking she was a sure thing. That her heart started thumping whenever he so much as smiled at her was something she hoped he hadn't noticed.

The truth was everything had gone pretty well until a liveried valet held a sign up with her name. *Telephone for Fräulein Ritter.* She had guessed the call was from Homicide: Böhm was the only one who knew she was in *Moka Efti*—apart from Greta, of course, but she'd never have disturbed Charly tonight. Jakob was standing at the bar when she returned from the telephone booth. He had accepted that she would have to leave and, after accompanying her to the cloakroom, had even ventured out onto Friedrichstrasse.

When the murder wagon drew to a halt in Leipziger Strasse, with Böhm already ensconced inside and urging her to hurry, she couldn't have said if their taciturn exchange was a parting or a quarrel. Before the vehicle had gone far he had returned to the escalator. Yet another man incapable of dealing with her job?

She felt a little chilly. The short coat she was wearing over her dress wasn't particularly warm. Even at the start of May, the nights in Berlin could still be cold.

'Are you a gentleman?' she asked the officer as they reached the murder wagon.

'How do you mean?' he asked.

'Are you or are you not?'

'Of course . . .'

'In that case you can lend me your coat.'

He looked at her as though he had misheard.

'Don't worry, you're not going to have to lay it over a puddle. It's for me. It belongs to the Prussian police anyway. Or perhaps you'd rather not lend Homicide your support?'

She had to turn up the sleeves of the heavy blue coat twice, but immediately felt warmer. 'Thank you,' she said.

She passed the officer a pair of fabric gloves and slipped a couple of metal evidence markers into his hands. They trudged onwards. In his coat she no longer felt like she was being watched as she pressed on to the canal bank. The vehicle seemed to have burst through the wrought-iron canal fencing without braking. The posts had been bent downwards, and some had been ripped from their foundations.

The officer followed Charly's instructions and placed the first evidence marker at the point of impact. There was no trace of skid marks. In fact, it was hard to see what route the Horch had taken. One of the trees by the shore had a strip of bark missing. The car must have scraped past before colliding with the fencing. At most this had caused a change in direction. If the car had crashed head-on into the tree, they wouldn't have had to pull it out of the canal, although the man at the wheel would scarcely have fared any better. And his face wouldn't have looked nearly so good. Between the tree and the canal bank was only a few metres. If the gap in the fence was anything to go by, then the car must almost have hit it at right angles. But where had the vehicle come from before that? The case was beginning to interest her.

After she had given the officer further instructions she took a few steps down Möckernstrasse, which led from the canal to Yorckstrasse. Only the left side had been developed. The right side was dominated by a high brick wall that stretched along the pavement. Behind the wall was the site of the *Anhalter* goods station, with a few cars parked underneath the roadside trees. She had to strain her eyes in the dark, but found it eventually: on the wing of a jet-black BMW was a light-coloured paint stain, cream-coloured to be exact. Now she was sure. She called the officer over.

Out of the corner of his eye he had watched First Sergeant Kemmerling traipsing dutifully behind Charly, evidence markers in hand. He had given up his coat for her, another thing *he* hadn't thought of, even though it was his fault she was trailing through the cold in her skimpy dance dress. DCI Wilhelm Böhm was just an ill-mannered chump, and there was nothing to be done about it. Nonsense, he thought and looked over towards the Horch, which was illuminated again and again by the light of the flash. It's not my fault. It's his fault and his fault alone. The unidentified man we've just fished out of the canal is the one who's ruined our evening.

He watched the first sergeant move towards her, obviously finding it difficult to follow instructions from a woman. Had Kemmerling known that Charlotte Ritter didn't even hold the rank of detective he wouldn't have lifted a finger, which was why Böhm hadn't told him. He knew he could rely on Charly and that, on nights like this when he could barely muster enough troops, was particularly important. However, since she was out there securing evidence, he was now missing a stenographer and Böhm was no longer used to taking notes. The paper he held had been loaned by Gräf.

The DCI had made himself comfortable on the heavily padded bench seat of the murder wagon, the rear of which could be transformed into an office in next to no time, and was interviewing the only witnesses: a man and a young woman who had been sitting in a parked car on Tempelhofer Ufer when the Horch had crashed through the canal fencing.

The couple had been rather preoccupied and barely seen a thing. The vehicle must have come out of the darkness with no lights on. A loud noise had startled the pair. Fräulein Wegener had just had time to take in the roar of the motor and the spinning of the wheels before the vehicle hit the water. The man didn't appear to have seen anything. The pair of them climbed out of the car and ran towards the shore. There was nothing they could do except look on helplessly as the Horch overturned and sank. When they realised that their assistance would already be too late, they notified the police.

'Did you see or hear anything else?' Böhm asked. 'The noise of the brakes, or the driver calling for help? Were there other people in the car with him?'

Fräulein Wegener answered in the negative. 'If you ask me, he was completely out of it. Didn't react at all when the car went under. Maybe he was drunk.'

Or already dead, Böhm thought. He looked down at his notes. There wasn't a great deal there, and the few things he had written could scarcely be deciphered.

'Hmm,' he said and rose to his feet. 'I think that will be all for now. We have your details.' They climbed out of the murder wagon. Böhm left them standing where they were. He had caught sight of a familiar silhouette on the bridge.

'Mankind's progress is undeniable,' he heard the man on the bridge say. 'Floaters are driving cars now.'

Wilhelm Böhm had known Dr Magnus Schwartz for years. The doctor's cynicism was an occupational hazard which detective inspectors were not immune to. Maybe that was why Böhm had such a good relationship with the coroner, who was also a respected professor at the university.

'Good evening, Doctor! Did they tear you away from the opera?'

Schwartz turned from the dead man at the wheel. Under his coat, he was still in evening dress.

'Böhm! I should have known you were behind this!' the doctor shook his hand. 'No, I don't go to the opera. It's too loud for me. Reception at the dean's. Pretty dull conversation when you consider it was attended by the cream of the German intelligentsia.'

'You can be grateful that we dragged you away.'

'Just don't tell my wife!'

'So?' Böhm gestured towards the corpse.

'You'll scarcely believe it, my dear Böhm, but this man is dead.'

'Seriously?' Böhm feigned surprise. 'There's nothing quite like the word of an expert.'

The doctor undid the buttons on the dead man's double-breasted jacket and shirt. Then he inspected the inside of his mouth. 'Cause of death still unknown,' he said after a pause, 'but most likely he was already dead before he fell in the water. Would you like to hear any more guesses or can you wait until noon tomorrow? I'll know by then whether he had water in his lungs.'

Böhm didn't say anything.

'I thought as much,' said the doctor. 'Well now, these are all approximations and remain subject to change until we have the official result tomorrow. Male corpse, height over one seventy, weight around 65 kilograms, age mid-thirties, poor teeth, cause of death still . . .'

'Poor teeth?'

'That's a fact, not an approximation.'

'Then he must have been afraid of the dentist.'

'I don't think so. Judging by the ruined landscape of his mouth, he's been to a dentist. A bad one. Seems more likely he was unable to afford decent treatment.'

'And yet he drives a new car and wears an elegant dinner jacket. He's almost more stylish than you are, Doctor!'

'Maybe he preferred to spend his money on cars and clothes than on the dentist. You know how it is, fine feathers make fine birds. And wheels too! Nice car, that Horch. My colleague Karthaus drives one. Not that I'm jealous—what are you supposed to do with a crate like that when it goes off road and lands in the canal . . .'

'I think that's got less to do with the car than the roadworthiness of the driver.' Böhm gestured towards the dead man's deformed hands. 'Can you die of something like that, Doctor?'

'You can die of almost anything, my dear Böhm.' Schwartz adjusted his glasses with his index finger and took a closer look at the mash of skin flaps, flesh and bones. 'What a mess,' he said finally. 'That must have been very painful, but he most probably survived it.'

'Strange,' Böhm murmured to himself.

'My dear Böhm! You wouldn't believe the things people can survive.'

'No, I mean his face.' Böhm seemed as if he had awoken from a dream. 'Is that the face of a man who was in great pain shortly before dying?'

Schwartz didn't answer but focused instead on the deceased. The dead man seemed to be smiling peacefully.

6

They had been hauling people out of their beds since a quarter past six, searching everywhere, not just in the flats but in the attics and cellars as well. Officers were even rummaging for weapons in the bins. Rath never imagined he'd be back in Hermannstrasse so soon. Eight police squads had been deployed in the communist area of Neukölln alone.

The May disturbances had persisted into a third day. Communists and police had clashed repeatedly. Shots continued to be fired as war raged on the streets of Wedding and Neukölln. Building materials in Hermannstrasse had been used to erect barricades, and entire rows of street lights put out of commission by protesters throwing stones. Gangs of youths were taking advantage of the darkness and plundering shops.

The previous night, rioters had stoned the 220th precinct building in Selchower Strasse where, as recently as Sunday, they had launched the operation against König. Shots had even been fired and the affair was only defused by a police squad with an armoured car and two trucks.

Episodes like this exacerbated fears of a communist putsch while also stirring up the feelings of the police force. Every officer on the street—especially those in workers' districts—was nervous and ready to open fire.

In Rath's eyes, his colleagues' state of mind bordered on hysteria. When they had summoned him and Wolter to Neukölln, therefore, he determined to keep a cool head. On the morning of the third of May, Commissioner Zörgiebel ordered CID to assist uniform in their search of the city's trouble spots. Police squads had cordoned off the district on both sides of Hermannstrasse, from Boddinstrasse to Leykestrasse and a huge part of the city had become a no-go area. Uniform guarded the access points, and signs warned that heavy gunfire was expected.

When they began the house-to-house search, duty officers sealed off the entrances to courtyards, before uniformed troops, led in each case by two members of CID, combed the entire block. They had been met with the

same reaction everywhere: men cursing, women swearing, children crying—
but there had been no weapons. The more the morning wore on, the more
Rath felt that people knew something. Somehow, word had spread.

So far they had confiscated only a single revolver—and that after nearly
six hours of hard searching in at least four dozen flats, and the man they
had taken the weapon off wasn't even a communist. They had found an
embroidered text of the Internationale on the wall of his kitchen, but only
in the way that Christians might display Biblical quotations. The man was
a social democrat like the commissioner.

The operation was beginning to get on Rath's nerves, and judging by
his expression Bruno felt the same way. Pointless, it was a total waste of
resources, and yet the pair had struggled to suppress a grin when they saw
that Leykestrasse was on their list. That was where Franz Krajewski, the
junkie from the Karstadt department store scaffolding and their latest informant, had his digs. The porn Kaiser himself opened the door when they
called on him just after seven in the morning.

Krajewski's heart sunk into his boots as the crowd of uniformed officers marched past him into the flat. Rath and Wolter kept him in suspense
for a moment before Uncle trotted out the usual spiel, that police were engaged in a routine search for weapons throughout the district. Krajewski
seemed a little more relaxed after that. A trace of nervousness remained,
however, and Rath knew why. He had had the presence of mind to recover
a small bag of cocaine from the sugar bowl in the kitchen before uniform
got there.

'Lucky you met us a few days ago,' Rath whispered. 'Otherwise we'd
have found a shooter on you and you'd have had to come along with us.'

'What's all the fuss about?' Krajewski asked.

'You live in the wrong area. Too many communists. You should mind
what you hide in the kitchen.'

Krajewski turned pale, but uniform were already on the next floor up.
Rath lingered a moment before pressing the paper bag into Krajewski's
hands.

It was now just after twelve and they had worked through another three
blocks. House after house, flat after flat, but there was still a long way to go.

'I've had enough of this,' Wolter said, as the pair left another building
full of angry faces and furious protests—without finding a single weapon.

'Trench work,' said Uncle, and lit a cigarette while uniform got stuck into the waste containers in the courtyard.

Rath nodded. 'We're not about to find anything either.'

'Are you surprised? The fighters are all out on the streets. Thälmann's boys are stashing their weapons. 1A need to be more on the ball. It's these caches we should be cleaning out, instead we're searching workers' flats.'

Wolter made no secret of his aversion to the political police. He took a final drag and threw the half-smoked cigarette onto the courtyard. 'This is no work for CID. I'm sure uniform can manage for a while on their own.' At the rubbish containers a young officer was using a giant poker to root through ashes and waste. Uncle gave him a few instructions and pressed the list of addresses into his hand before making his way back to Rath.

'Let's go to Hermannstrasse, drop off the revolver and submit an interim report,' he said. 'They've got a good old-fashioned field kitchen and my stomach's starting to rumble.' Police had sequestered two private flats on the first floor of Hermannstrasse 207 to set up an operational base for the troops. 'Who knows, maybe we'll find someone looting or erecting a barricade on the way. At least then we'll have done something useful today.'

It wasn't until Hermannstrasse that they encountered anybody else, but still no-one they needed to arrest. All the streetlamps had been shattered and broken glass crunched beneath their feet. In several places stacks of wood for the construction of the new underground had been overturned across the carriageway. Not exactly barricades, they were more like minor traffic obstacles. Not that there were any cars on the road.

The tram wasn't stopping at Hermannstrasse today either as uniform had effectively sealed the trouble spot. No-one came in and no-one went out without police say-so. The Berlin public transport authority no longer sent any of its buses or trains into the communist districts anyway, as rioters had already wrecked several.

Shots rang out and Rath and Wolter sought cover in the entrance to a house. Uncle drew his weapon. Rath did likewise, having taken the episode on the Karstadt scaffolding to heart. He released the safety catch of his Mauser and poked his head out carefully from the entrance. An armoured car was rolling up Hermannstrasse, rattling its machine gun at irregular intervals. 'Idiots. Just like in the war. Under fire from our own side.'

They put their guns away. Standing in a house entrance in civilian clothing with a pistol in your hand was dangerous. It was all too easy for your own side to become confused.

'Your attention please, this is the police speaking,' a voice cried. 'Keep the streets clear! Move away from your windows! We're about to open fire!'

Really? Rath thought. We're about to open fire? They're announcing that a little prematurely. He peered round the corner and watched the armoured car roll onwards. The few people still on the streets took refuge in house entrances to the left and right. Behind the armoured car were two trucks carrying duty officers. The men had jumped down from the trucks and were cocking their rifles. Rath could feel how nervous they were. With anxious glances, they scoured the windows for snipers, weapons at the ready. For a short time it was quiet, then a rifle crackled and a glass pane shattered.

'Move away from your windows!' The voice was drowned by the crackle of rifle fire. The first shot had opened the floodgates.

A man was running across the pavement with his hands over his head as if they could shield him from bullets and falling glass. He came towards them in the entrance, pulled a key from his pocket and opened the heavy front door.

'Come on then,' he said, and held the door open. 'Inside before the pigs get you.' They burst into the house and the man ran upstairs. Rath banged the door shut and gazed after him.

'For fuck's sake, they're clearing the streets! Deploying a special vehicle. Why the hell didn't anyone tell us this was happening?'

'No idea,' Wolter replied. 'Probably because the whole thing's been planned by social democrats.'

There were more shots from the streets. Rath gestured with his head that they should move further back into the stairwell where they'd be safer.

Suddenly they heard a cry. 'No!'

Not a cry of pain or fear. A cry of horror.

They briefly exchanged glances and hastened upstairs. The door to the flat on the first floor stood open. They burst inside to be welcomed by petty bourgeois conservatism and comfort. Nothing here was remotely out of place, not a person to be seen or a voice to be heard. In the neighbouring flat, Richard Tauber was singing, his voice scratched out by a gramophone. The noise from the street penetrated through the open balcony door. From time to time there was a cry or an isolated shot as the commando receded into the distance. A gentle wind made the long curtain billow out and blow into the room.

There were two women lying on the balcony. Peacefully, as though they were sleeping, but they weren't sleeping. Blood was seeping from their heads and chests. The cry must have come from the man who was hunched over the older of the two, the man who had just opened the door for them. He was no longer crying out, but weeping silently. Having laid the head of the deceased on his lap, he was now stroking her bloody hair.

'Martha,' he said. 'Martha!'

The windows were boarded on the outside so there was barely any daylight in the shop. The man behind the counter didn't look much like a master butcher. Far too thin, pale face, hollow cheeks. Only the blood specks on his white coat gave him away, and his greeting.

'What will it be?'

'Police.' Rath showed his ID.

He had been on the move for quarter of an hour. No-one in Hermannstrasse seemed to own a telephone. The only public telephone he found hadn't worked but he struck lucky with Wilhelm Prokot the butcher. There was a sign on the door with a telephone symbol. *Telephone 20 pfennig per conversation*, it said below. Twice as expensive as a public telephone.

'There was me surprised that there were still people out shopping with all that racket,' grumbled the butcher. 'Do you and your colleagues want to occupy the shop?'

'I just need to use the telephone.'

'Out back,' the butcher nodded towards a door. 'It's not for free though.'

'The state will pay.'

Rath followed the man to a telephone hanging from the wall and asked to be put through to Hermannstrasse 207. The butcher remained in the doorway, looking on curiously. 'Do you have nothing else to do?' Rath barked.

'No,' said Prokot in his Berlin accent. 'Your people have scared off all my customers.' He disappeared back into the shop.

Rath asked to speak with one of the officers in charge of the operation. He gave a concise report of the fatal incident and received equally concise instructions in return: take down particulars, secure evidence, interview witnesses, have the corpses medically examined and removed, processes with which Rath was familiar from his time in Homicide. It annoyed him that they treated him like a novice here.

'Can you recommend a doctor?' he asked, as he pressed two 10 pfennig coins into the butcher's hands.

'What seems to be the matter?' the butcher asked.

The Berlin sense of humour did nothing for Rath. He ignored the stupid remark. 'Well,' he said simply, doing his best to conceal his displeasure.

'You're in luck. There's a doctor in the house above.'

The practice was directly above the butcher's shop. DR PETER VÖLCKER, GENERAL PRACTITIONER, read the sign next to the door. The waiting room was empty. The receptionist looked at Rath with surprise. 'An emergency,' he said simply, showing his badge. 'I need a doctor.' The woman led him into the consulting room where Dr Völcker was sitting at his desk.

The doctor was even more gaunt than the butcher and gave the impression of being strict and ascetic. He listened attentively as Rath briefly outlined the situation, took his hat and coat, and reached for the bag. Finally he sent the receptionist home.

'We're closing. There'll be no-one coming today anyway,' he said. 'No-one dares venture outside while the police are doing target practice.'

The sentence ought to have made Rath suspicious, but he didn't think anything of it. He didn't learn the truth about Dr Völcker until they had returned to the flat, Uncle having remained behind to comfort the grieving widower. Wolter was sitting beside the man, who appeared to have composed himself in the meantime, at the living room table.

'Where did you dredge him up?' Wolter asked.

The doctor greeted the widower briefly, offered his condolences and then disappeared onto the balcony.

'Do you two know each other?' Rath asked.

Wolter waited until the widower had joined the doctor on the balcony. 'You've really landed us in it there,' he began.

Soon Rath realised this was something of an understatement. Dr Peter Völcker was not only a doctor and head of the Neukölln public health department; he also had a seat and a vote on the local district council—as a member of the Communist Party.

In police circles, he was infamous, a troublemaker who enjoyed calling for inquiries and threatened legal action whenever police officers and communists clashed.

'Shit!' Rath commented.

'Succinctly put,' said Wolter. 'Nothing we can do now though.' He patted his colleague on the shoulder. 'Come on, we shouldn't leave the communist doctor alone for too long. Who knows what he'll try and foist on us?'

When they stepped onto the balcony, the two women were lying exactly where they had been found. The doctor had obviously examined them already. He was now standing by one of the wooden privacy screens that flanked the balcony, fiddling around with the wood. The widower hunched over the corpse of his wife.

'If you're finished, Doctor, you ought to fill out the death certificates,' Wolter said. 'The corpses shouldn't remain here any longer than is necessary. Have you recorded the death? In that case, don't waste any more time here and get back to your practice. There are bound to be some proles waiting to have their chicken eyes removed.'

'All in good time, my man,' Völcker replied. 'I'm still establishing the cause of death.' He turned round and presented both police officers with a large, sharp projectile. 'Here!'

'What the hell is that supposed to be?' Rath asked.

'You of all people should know. A police bullet. Not the first victim your colleagues have on their conscience.' There was something unbearably self-righteous about Völcker's tone.

'My dear doctor!' Wolter was like a steam boiler whose safety valves had opened to release high pressure in a sharp hiss. 'Perhaps you're unclear about the traditional division of labour. It's neither your job to secure evidence, nor to draw conclusions, and certainly not hasty ones!' He snatched the projectile from the doctor's hand. 'Whether it's a police bullet or not remains to be seen. We shall . . .'

'Murderers!' The widower had risen to his feet, his face no longer pale but red and distorted with rage. 'Murderers!' he cried again and hurled himself on Wolter. Rath pulled him back in an arm lock.

'Calm yourself down,' he said. At first the man tried to wriggle free, before growing quieter and finally beginning to sob. Rath gave him a consoling pat on the shoulder.

'Do you see what you've done?' Now Wolter was really yelling. Völcker winced inwardly.

'I'm not the one who made this man a widower,' replied the doctor.

'Are you trying to suggest that I . . .'

'Bruno!' Rath feared he would soon have to hold Wolter back too. Uncle paused mid-sentence and turned towards him, looking as if he might go for the doctor's throat at any moment. With a struggle he regained his composure.

'My dear doctor,' Wolter continued. 'As a scientist you should really be approaching a task like this from an impartial standpoint. I'm not sure if you're the right man for the job.' He turned to Rath. 'Call Dr Schwartz from the Charité hospital. He has more experience in this area.'

Rath left the two squabblers to their own devices. A short time later, he was standing in Wilhelm Prokot's shop for a second time. The butcher gave him a broad grin as he showed him to the telephone.

'Was the doctor able to help?'

Prokot had known exactly what he was doing when he pointed Rath in the direction of Dr Völcker. Rath would've liked to have slammed a fist into that grinning face but, instead, composed himself and asked to be put through to the Charité.

The black car could not have travelled faster if the two women in the zinc coffins at the back had still been alive. After they left the restricted area the driver put his foot down like a getaway car driver. Rath looked across at him.

'Slow down,' he said. 'Two corpses are more than enough.'

The driver muttered and laid off the gas a little. He had started grumbling when he heard they were going to the morgue in the Charité. Dr Schwartz was otherwise engaged but had requested that the two dead women be brought to him. Wolter had stayed behind in the flat, while Rath had been obliged to travel in the mortuary car with Dr Völcker between him and the driver. The Red doctor had insisted, and Wolter had given his consent. Thus Uncle was rid of the troublemaker, and Rath was lumbered with him.

The co-driver had groaned when he heard how many people were accompanying the two corpses. 'This isn't a police van, it's a mortuary car.'

Grumpily he had cleared his space, and was now sitting in the back between the coffins, cursing at each bend.

Although his eyes were open, Rath was scarcely aware of the world outside the car windows. He saw the traffic on Kottbusser Damm, saw the Friday hustle and bustle on Oranienstrasse, but it all seemed like a dream. Outside of Neukölln everything seemed normal again, but that normality was at the same time unreal. It hardly seemed credible that only a few kilometres away a state of emergency had been declared and shots were being fired, that people were dying. The image of the dead women had been burned into his brain. The younger of the two was only twenty-six years old, the older of the pair fifty. Their papers felt so heavy in the inside pocket of Rath's coat it was as if they were printed on lead.

Since the mortuary car had set off from Hermannstrasse, he hadn't exchanged a single word with Völcker. He observed the doctor's gaunt figure out of the corner of his eye, sitting in a creased grey coat that was slightly too big for him. There was a tinge of grey stubble on his pointed chin, and his eyes were focused on the road ahead.

Rath finally broke the silence. 'You're a doctor,' he asked, so suddenly that Dr Völcker gave a start, 'so why did you become a communist?'

For the first time since they had left Neukölln, Völcker looked at him. 'It doesn't tally with your world view, does it?'

Rath was annoyed by the doctor's self-righteous tone, and even more annoyed that Völcker was, in a way, correct. It always surprised him when academics called themselves communists. For Rath, communists grew out of the lumpenproletariat. People raised in an environment like that barely stood a chance. Either they became communists or they became criminals, or both. Criminals, communists—for many policemen they were one and the same. Didn't communists also want to steal? To dispossess the middle classes using violent means? The Penal Code called that robbery; the Commune called it revolution.

While Rath could half understand some poor devil pinning his last hopes on the communists, it made the intellectuals who preached revolution even less fathomable. They were the ones elevating robbery to an ideology. As long as it occurred on a mass scale, you could call it a revolution and justify it academically. It was these ideologues in particular that Rath couldn't stand, muddleheads who always knew best, who believed they had a monopoly on the truth. Völcker was someone he placed in this category, although the doctor didn't give the impression of being particularly muddled—just of being even more of a know-it-all.

'Have you ever been to some of the damp-infested hovels that certain people in this city still use to extract money from the working classes?' Völcker dug a little deeper when Rath didn't respond. 'Do you know the conditions some people are forced to live in?'

Rath was annoyed at having entered an unnecessary discussion with this intellectual Clever Dick. Of course he was aware of the tenement houses in the city's workers' districts, in the north, east and south: real slums, a disgrace, no question about it. But what did that prove? It was a reason to build bright, new estates for the workers—something that was happening too—but not to become a communist! He knew about the downsides of progress, the negative aspects of civilisation; he was a police officer. But he also knew about the communist agitators who preached the fight against the exploiters when they meant the fight against the police. How was the world supposed to become a better place with these loudmouths in charge? He had no wish to discuss this question with one of them.

'That doesn't give anyone the right to break the law,' he said simply. He was a policeman and it was his duty to maintain law and order. And the communists? Only today they had proved once again that they held neither sacred.

'Break the law?' Völcker's voice grew louder. The driver stared stubbornly ahead and stepped on the gas again. He obviously wanted to get this journey over as soon as possible.

'What kind of laws,' the doctor continued, 'prevent people from taking to the streets and expressing their opinion and . . .'

'Shooting police officers,' Rath finished the sentence.

Völcker gave him an angry look. 'The two women in the back of this car weren't killed by communists. That was the work of your esteemed colleagues!'

'If your people weren't constantly preaching violence the streets would be more peaceful.'

Now Rath was getting louder too. The thing that annoyed him most was that the doctor was probably right. The pointed bullet looked exactly like those used by the Prussian police force.

They were used in Cologne too. He thought back to the hearing and the evidence on the judge's bench. A bullet from a rifle had blasted a hole in the shoulder of the gunman, and would probably have been enough to put him out of action, though it hadn't actually killed him. It was another bullet that had dealt the fatal blow, one that had struck him right in the heart. 7.65 calibre. The ballistics report had revealed beyond any doubt that it had been fired from the service weapon of Detective Inspector Gereon Rath.

The hearing in Cologne wasn't even half a year past, and now the very same Gereon Rath was driving through Berlin in a mortuary car, accompanying two dead women to the morgue. Time and again, he was confronted by death in this job and he just had to deal with it. He had known that when he decided to become a police officer, but since the episode in Cologne it seemed as if every dead person he encountered was accusing him. The communist doctor saw things differently. Rath was a police officer, the police had shot the women, the police were guilty and therefore the detective inspector was guilty as well.

Rath looked out of the side window as they crossed the Spree, taking no notice of the people on Weidendammer Bridge. The silence between him and Völcker was icier than before, but there was no point talking to the man. They lived in different worlds. The driver sounded his horn as a pedestrian crossed Friedrichstrasse too slowly. The man looked round in horror, shaking his head as he gazed after the mortuary car.

At Oranienburger Tor the black car turned into Hannoversche Strasse. Shortly afterwards a yellow-brick building appeared on the right hand side of the road. The Charité morgue received them with Prussian indifference and sobriety, with a shrug that had turned to stone. The building had seen so many dead bodies come and go, more tragic cases than two women who had been shot on a balcony.

The driver negotiated the entrance with aplomb. In the back of the car, the zinc coffins made a clattering sound. The driver uttered yet another curse.

7

Only when they were on Dr Schwartz's marble table did the dead finally look dead. That morning, Wilhelm Böhm had thought the pictures Gräf had taken of the corpse from the Landwehr canal could be mistaken for passport photos—assuming you cropped the image to leave out the mangled hands. The deceased appeared almost friendly.

Here on the table the dead man looked different from yesterday, the head peering out from under the white cotton sheet Dr Schwartz had placed over it. Böhm cast an eye over the corpse and suddenly knew why: the dead man's body was now dry.

Despite Gräf's passport-like images, they still hadn't made any headway with the identification. The dead man hadn't been carrying papers and there was nothing in the pockets of his fashionable, double-breasted jacket, absolutely nothing. In all his years of service, Böhm had never seen anything like it. Even victims of robbery homicides had a handkerchief, a sweet wrapper or something that offered at least a tiny clue. Nor was the car any help. The Horch was registered to a Dr Bernward Römer, a lively character who had reported it stolen in the 113th precinct a week and a half before.

Charly had discovered that the vehicle had scraped past a car parked on Möckernstrasse and Böhm had found a metal rod in the footwell, which he had initially taken for a faulty car part, a piece of the steering rod perhaps, that might have caused the accident, but there was nothing missing. Apart from the dents from the canal fencing, the Horch was as good as new. Yet the solution was obvious: the rod had been wedged against the accelerator in order that a dead man might drive. Gräf and Charly were still trying to establish its origin.

This morning they had begun to scour the rectangle between Möckernstrasse, Tempelhofer Ufer and Grossbeerenstrasse for further witnesses. Böhm hadn't been assigned many men today, again, as most officers were in Neukölln or Wedding cleaning up the trouble spots. The accident at the

Landwehr canal probably had nothing to do with the May disturbances. Böhm was still calling it an accident, even though he was now certain it wasn't. The poor guy on the marble table had been murdered. At the very least, someone had wanted to dispose of his corpse instead of giving him a proper burial. That much Böhm could say already—without recourse to Dr Schwartz's wisdom.

He was thinking that he ought to have a couple of portraits made from Gräf's crime scene photos and send his men out again, when he heard the deep voice of Dr Schwartz as he entered the room at a brisk clip.

'Good morning Böhm. Sorry I'm late, but we're getting dead body after dead body at the moment. All hell is breaking loose in the city.' He shook Böhm's hand. 'Don't worry,' he said, when he saw the DCI's concerned face, 'none of them are yours. Most likely Reds, but a few women too. Seems like things are getting a little out of hand.'

'It was no different ten years ago. Almost always the wrong people die, and they're almost always killed by accident.'

Dr Schwartz pulled on a pair of gloves, approached the marble table and pulled back the cover. 'We can safely say that our friend from last night wasn't killed by accident. He was roughed up quite deliberately. There's almost no part of his wrists and ankles that hasn't been damaged: broken bones, torn ligaments, lacerations, a real mess. It looks as if someone fixed his hands and feet to a firm support and then struck with a heavy, blunt object. I'd guess with a hammer.'

'Dear God,' Böhm whistled through his teeth. 'These here?' The dead man's entire body was covered in bruises.

'Harmless in comparison. Haematomas that probably stem from physical blows. The mark on his chest could be from a cudgel. This one was probably from a kick. The man has been given a good beating by people who knew what they were doing.'

'You're saying there were several perpetrators?'

Schwartz nodded. 'Probably. It looks as though they spared his face. Professionals.'

'Career criminals?'

'They're not the only ones who know how to administer a beating. Could be boxers. Or policemen,' Dr Schwartz said. It was the kind of joke he always made.

'So what do you recommend?' Böhm asked. 'An internal investigation or a warrant for Max Schmeling?'

'All jokes aside, the people who did this were sadists. They have no . . .' Schwartz broke off as the big swing door suddenly opened and two covered corpses were rolled in.

'More May corpses?' Dr Schwartz asked.

One of the two men in white coats pushing the stretcher nodded. 'From Neukölln. Seems life expectancy is back on the rise in Wedding. They've had their big day already.'

'These are dead people you are talking about, gentlemen!' The reproachful voice came from one of two men who entered the room behind the white coats, a gaunt, strict-looking man in a creased grey suit. 'You ought to show more respect for the dead.'

'Especially when they're proles, isn't that right Dr Völcker?' said Schwartz. 'Long time no see. To what do we owe the pleasure?'

'Police bullets,' the gaunt man said tersely.

Völcker? The infamous communist doctor? Böhm rolled his eyes.

Völcker's tall companion intervened. 'These two women died as a result of gunshot wounds in Hermannstrasse,' he said. 'They were most likely caught by a stray bullet.'

Even before the tall man displayed his badge, Böhm knew that he was a colleague, even if he was rather too elegantly dressed for a police officer. Only cops talked like that, and tax officials.

'Rath, Detective Inspector Gereon Rath, E Division,' the policeman said. 'We spoke on the phone just now.'

Dr Schwartz gave him a nod and scratched his chin.

'Right,' he said. 'But now is not a good time. I'm in the middle of a meeting with DCI Böhm.'

Böhm thought he recognised the tall detective from the Castle, the newbie Lanke was talking about in the canteen. A careerist who was crawling up the arse of the commissioner.

'E Division?' Böhm grunted. 'What brings Vice to the morgue? Dead bodies aren't part of your remit, or are you responsible for the corpses yourselves?' The vice detective said nothing. 'I asked you a question, man,' Böhm roared, 'are you deaf?' Inspector Rath gave a brief start and stood to attention. Obviously a soldier with good old Prussian training.

'From the house-to-house searches in Neukölln,' he said. 'Happened to be on-site when the two women were hit.'

'Very good,' Böhm said, pleased. He would teach this conceited arsehole some manners. 'Now kindly take your load and be on your way. As you've just heard, this is not a good time.'

The tall detective seemed not to have heard. Instead he moved closer to the marble table and stared at the corpse, wide-eyed, as if he had never seen a dead body.

'What are you still doing here?' Böhm yelled. 'Did I ask you to identify the body?'

'Of course not, Detective Chief Inspector!' Rath stood erect once more.

'Then scram! You're holding things up.'

'That's right,' Dr Schwartz waded in, shifting his weight impatiently from one foot to the other. 'I must ask you to leave the autopsy table so that we can continue.' He pointed towards the clock on the front wall. 'I still have a lot to do today.' He gave the men in white coats a sign. 'Take these two women down to the cellar. I'll deal with them tomor—'

'Stop!' Völcker interrupted. The two men, who had already started to wheel the stretchers out, stood where they were. Schwartz looked at his colleague indignantly. 'Please excuse me, Dr Schwartz,' Völcker continued, calmer now, 'it wasn't my intention to interrupt you but, as it happens, I'm not here as anybody's gofer. I came to attend the examination of the two female corpses.'

Schwartz raised an eyebrow. 'As you can see, Dr Völcker, I still have a corpse to examine. The public prosecutor has ordered the autopsy. This takes priority.'

Völcker wouldn't let go. 'I have strong reason to suspect that these two women were purposefully killed by police. If you postpone the examination, it might look as if the police and the public prosecutor's office have something to hide.'

'I'll leave that to others to decide. I'm a doctor.' Schwartz could barely conceal the anger in his voice. 'As are you, Dr Völcker, need I remind you? It would be better if you refrained from expressing your suspicions.'

'The public prosecutor will order an autopsy anyway,' Völcker said.

'For the time being, the police have only requested that the body be examined. You know yourself that I do not have the authority to open up a corpse of my own accord.' He gazed at Völcker almost sympathetically over the rim of his glasses. 'An examination only, Dr Völcker, and if I do manage to get it done today, then it'll be for your sake. For old time's sake, let's say. If you would like to attend, then you're going to have to exercise a little more patience.'

Völcker didn't appear to notice the irony in Schwartz's voice. At any rate, he sat on the wooden bench that ran along the tiled wall. The two white coats disappeared without the bodies.

Böhm had had to be very careful not to give the communist doctor a piece of his mind. The man was disrupting things. Just like the cop from Vice who had dragged him here. When Dr Schwartz peeled back the sheet, the pain in the arse just stared at the dead man's mangled hands. The tall detective hadn't moved a millimetre from the marble table.

'Looks almost as if he was tortured.'

Böhm exploded. Enough was enough! Why did this man always have to have his two pennies' worth?

'You work in Vice,' he barked at the Clever Dick. 'Do you think that because this man is naked, that makes it your case? If you don't want to see someone actually being tortured, then I suggest you let us get on with our work. Do I make myself clear?'

'Yes, Detective Chief Inspector!' The tall detective stood to attention and performed an about turn.

Böhm's anger subsided as he turned back to Dr Schwartz. The vice detective took a seat on the bench next to the communist doctor, but the pair didn't speak.

'So, Doctor,' Böhm said, clearing his throat. 'Shall we continue? Where were we?'

'The injuries,' Schwartz said. 'They were most likely inflicted by professionals, and definitely before he died, as the haemorrhaging shows.'

'When did he die, and how?'

'The precise time of death is impossible to determine. I'd say the man has been dead for two or three days at the most. I'm afraid I can't say anything more for the time being.'

'So he was already dead when he entered the canal yesterday?'

'100%,' Schwartz nodded. 'He certainly didn't drown. We haven't found any trace of water in his lungs.'

'I didn't think it was a floater,' Böhm growled. 'If memory serves, you confirmed that last night. Don't keep me in suspense, Doctor. Enough of my time has been wasted today already.'

'The cause of death is astounding, however. You'll be surprised when you hear it. The man didn't die as a result of his injuries.'

'Surprise me, Doctor. I'm waiting.'

'Heroin,' Dr Schwartz said simply.

'Heroin?'

'Respiratory failure, caused by an overdose of diacetylmorphine; that is, heroin.'

'The cough medicine?'

Schwartz nodded. 'Cough tablets for morphine addicts. It used to be prescribed as an anti-asthmatic. Until people realised it was addictive. A particularly strong opiate, very hard to procure on the legal drugs market. On the illegal market, however . . . If you take too much of it, you stop breathing, but by that stage you won't notice a thing.'

8

Rath paused for a moment in front of the main gate to arrange his thoughts. The cool air did him good. He felt as if he had awoken from a morbid dream where a dead face had been staring at him. Something that could only be caused by a visit to the morgue. Before descending the steps, he lit a cigarette and inhaled deeply.

There was no doubt about it. It was definitely the Russian lying on the marble table. The man who had visited him a few nights before. The drunk who had wrecked his wardrobe. One moment alive, the next a case for Homicide. He took another long draw, turned up his collar and set off towards Oranienburger Tor.

Why hadn't he said anything? It was too late now. They would ask him why he had withheld the information and then—at the very least—institute disciplinary proceedings.

Rath felt his carefully suppressed rage returning. DCI arsehole! If everybody in A Division was as much of a bulldog as DCI Böhm, he wondered if it really was such a desirable place to work. He was yet to meet a bigger idiot in the whole of the Castle. In comparison even Lanke seemed like a charming, sympathetic paternalist. Naturally he hadn't told the bulldog anything, but it was more of a reflex than a rational decision.

What kind of information could he have passed on anyway? He knew almost nothing about the dead man. Boris had been in his flat that one time, a few days before this death, drunk, screaming and flailing his arms about. Rath wasn't even sure that Boris was his name; he only knew that he had been searching for a fellow countryman who had once lived in Nürnberger Strasse. And that he was now dead.

Heroin! A drug addict, driving into the Landwehr canal? How had the dead Russian sustained the injuries to his hands and feet? A very strange case, Rath thought. It was a strange case though none of his business.

At Oranienburger Tor he ignored the steps to the underground. Instead he lit a cigarette and continued to Friedrichstrasse station. The crowd of people on Weidendammer Bridge had grown since he'd driven over it in the mortuary car. Most of them had finished work for the evening and were on their way home or to the nearest pub, already thinking about dinner, families, their wives or a beer with friends. Here the city seemed frighteningly normal. How many of these people could imagine what was happening in Neukölln or Wedding? Whether shots were still being fired in Hermannstrasse? The events of the day had given Rath an upset stomach and only now did he realise that he hadn't eaten anything. There was an Aschinger here, directly behind the railway underpass on Friedrichstrasse. He decided to have a snack before heading home, and a beer or two. He flicked his cigarette into the Spree and fought his way through the crowd. In front of Friedrichstrasse station, the paperboys were crying out the evening's headlines. 'New street battles!'—'Further deaths in communist disturbances!'— 'RFB to be banned?'

'Strange!' Elisabeth Behnke lifted the broken padlock from the damp cellar floor. Someone had broken into Kardakov's storage area. 'That's my padlock,' she explained. 'I locked his cellar two or three weeks ago, so he couldn't sneak out his things without paying his final month's rent.' She held out the cheap, misshapen brass lock. 'I wonder who it was?'

Rath shrugged his shoulders and stepped into his predecessor's cellar. There was barely any light from the dim 40 watt cellar bulb and the air was musty.

'When was the last time you were down here?' he asked.

Elisabeth Behnke considered for a moment. 'Maybe last week.'

'The lock was still intact?'

'No idea. I wasn't paying any attention. My cellar is over there.' She pointed towards a few wobbly shelves, upon which a number of jars were gathering dust. Next to them was a big crate of potatoes.

'Does Kardakov still have a key to the main door?'

'Of course not.'

'Then it wasn't him picking something up.'

'It doesn't look as if anyone's ever picked anything up.'

Junk was piled to the ceiling. Along the back wall stood an old cupboard with a few framed pictures leaning against it, while the side wall housed a rusty bicycle. But for the most part it was boxes: box upon box, stacked one on top of the other.

'How long did he live here?' Rath asked.

She shrugged. 'Maybe three years.'

'Three years and all that junk!' He shook his head. 'You need an expert to go through that. Lucky I'm a police officer.'

'I'll go upstairs and make us a tea,' she said. He tried not to think what that might mean, and lifted the first box from the pile.

It had been his idea to look in the cellar. His interest in Kardakov had grown enormously since his unexpected encounter with Boris in the morgue. He couldn't get the image of his battered body out of his mind.

Only a few hours ago, his guilty conscience had been eating away at him, on account of his silence. Then he had sat at the counter of Aschinger's in Friedrichstrasse and dulled his conscience with a few beers. He tried to view things objectively, and realised that it was a sign. He knew a little more than Homicide. He knew that the dead man had been looking for some-one in Berlin. Maybe this was his chance. Why shouldn't he take advan-tage of it? It was what life was about, after all. He only had to think back to Bruno's words. *Gennat's boys are hand-picked. You have to land something really big.* No, he wouldn't do Böhm any favours, wouldn't confide the little he knew. He wouldn't break the rules either though, quite the opposite. He would present the commissioner with a solved case. And in order to do that, he would need to learn a little more about his mysterious predecessor. Handy, when you could begin the search in your own cellar.

After half an hour, all the boxes stood open in front of the wooden shed. Most of them had contained books. Book after book, almost exclusively in Russian. Rath couldn't even make out the titles. He didn't know a lot about the Cyrillic alphabet. The only thing that meant anything to him was a coffee-table book about St Petersburg, or Leningrad as people said these days. He was surprised that an author should have abandoned his books for so long and stored them in the cellar. There was only one box of per-sonal items, a few letters that Rath could make neither head nor tail of, all in Russian again. The only thing he could halfway make out was the date. He noticed that the letters weren't in chronological order but were bun-dled together higgledy-piggledy. In the middle of the pile was a number of programmes from the *Delphi Palace* in Kantstrasse. The artist Lana Nikoros, who was heavily billed, wore a mysterious smile in her photo. The Mona Lisa had nothing on her. Kardakov seemed to be a fan of the singer. He had collected programmes from several months, from October 1928 to March 1929.

In addition, Rath had also uncovered a few manuscripts. If Kardakov had use of a typewriter with Cyrillic keys he must have taken it with him. At least, it wasn't here. Amongst the manuscripts was a folder containing photos of a young man. Above a big nose, the dark eyes were deep in their sockets. Hollow cheeks and a mouth that twisted sadly. Elegantly curved lips. There was something almost feminine about that face and Rath suspected that Alexej Ivanovitsch Kardakov himself was staring back. If the man wanted to look like a poet he was succeeding. That melancholy Russian gaze.

Rath took the photos, pocketed one of the Delphi programmes, packed the rest of the junk back into the cellar and climbed the stairs. He hadn't found a great deal, nothing of much use anyway, but it was a start.

Elisabeth Behnke looked disappointed when after a cup of tea—without rum—Rath got to his feet and reached for his hat and coat.

'It's half past nine,' she said. 'Where are you going at this time of night?'

'It's Friday,' he said. 'I'm going dancing.'

'With whom?' She actually sounded a little jealous.

He showed her the photo of Kardakov.

The night was advancing towards dawn and the silhouette of the Memorial Church towered over the brightly lit mass of houses, the only building in the neighbourhood that wasn't drowning in neon light. It seemed to serve as a warning to revellers, with its dark, silent mountains of stone in the midst of the night-time racket. Rath walked past the church and went up the Kurfürstendamm, squeezing through a group of noisily laughing, drunk tourists he guessed were from somewhere near Stuttgart. He heard a strong southern German accent, at least, when one of the men made an indecent offer to a young woman walking by.

'Learn some German first if you want to pop your cherry,' the woman replied, suddenly no longer so coy.

The Swabian loudmouth blushed and fell into hurt silence while his companions grinned inanely. Rath was annoyed. For some reason, everyone from the provinces seemed to think they could let it all hang out in Berlin. In a way he was happy that, aside from his parents, nobody from Cologne knew he now lived here. It meant that no-one would be visiting. He could imagine some of his friends—his friends from before, mind—behaving in exactly the same way as the merry Swabian.

Rath glanced at the time. It was past midnight, and he hadn't made any headway. He felt the long day in his bones, having scoured the Russian bars in the neighbourhood as systematically as he had unsuccessfully.

He had thought his night-time operation would be easier when he questioned drinkers in the little Russian pub in Nürnberger Strasse, an establishment for those hankering after a taste of home. In the smoky bar with the low ceilings and Cyrillic menu he would have bet on finding someone who recognised Kardakov. A bet he would have lost, even though the place was barely five minutes from his flat, from the flat where Alexej Kardakov had lived until a few weeks ago. Either the Russians kept mum when someone ventured into their world or Kardakov really never had set foot in the bar. Rath suspected it was the former for, even in the cosmopolitan meeting points favoured by Russian intellectuals, he had only heard the word *njet* when he showed the Russian's picture.

Yet he felt sure that a man like Kardakov would come to this sort of place when he gave in to his longing for melancholy, alcohol and his fellow countrymen. Charlottenburg was the centre for Russians in Berlin. They had built their own world here with Russian bookshops, hairdressers and bars, a world in which you needn't speak a word of German to get by. Charlottengrad the locals called it.

He crossed Augsburger Strasse and counted his money. The *Kakadu-Bar's* neon sign was reflected on the wet pavement. Taxis kept arriving and spewing people out. He had come to know most of the bars in Berlin through work, but *Kakadu* was one of the few he also visited privately, stumbling in after prowling around town unable to sleep. It was situated where Joachimsthaler Strasse and Augsburger Strasse intersected with Kurfürstendamm, not far from his flat. Before he returned home he wanted another drink—and not tea mixed with rum. Besides, he liked the jazz band.

The red-gold room was jam-packed when he entered. The band drowned out the babble of voices and a number of couples were dancing. The stools by the long bar at the back were all occupied. Cockatoos and other exotic creatures romped around on glass panels that were illuminated from behind. In front of them quicksilver barmen positioned themselves against the glare to receive customers' orders with eager smiles.

Most of the drinkers in *Kakadu* had fat purses, the place wasn't exactly cheap. Rath placed himself between two men who looked as if they might keel over from their stools at any moment and waved a barman over. The man leaned closer to take his order, gazing at him as if he knew him although Rath knew this wasn't the case. It was how they had looked at him the first time too. It was just part of the service. Everyone should feel like a regular.

'An Americano please,' Rath said, leaning on the bar. Although the music went straight to his hips, he suddenly felt very tired. No wonder. He had been on the go since early morning.

The man placed a glass on the counter. Rath dropped a one-mark coin into his hands and pulled out the photo. The barman seemed bored. The smile had disappeared and he shrugged his shoulders. Discretion was part of the service here too.

Although he had hoped to avoid doing it in this bar, Rath placed his ID next to the photo. 'Have you really never seen this man?'

Another shrug of the shoulders. 'So many things happen here every day . . .'

'He's Russian,' Rath discreetly placed another mark on the counter.

The barman made the mark disappear even more discreetly under the palm of his hand and leaned in closer.

'The Russians usually keep to themselves,' he whispered. 'You should ask them.' He gestured in their direction with his eyes. 'Try your luck in the corner back there, but don't say you heard it from me.'

Rath looked round. At the other end of the room ten men were sitting at two adjacent tables. There wasn't a single woman amongst them. Rath moved slowly across the floor, one hand holding his glass, the other in his trouser pocket. The men took no notice of him whatsoever, as they were engaged in what was obviously a stimulating discussion. They were speaking Russian.

'A gathering of the displaced?' Rath asked. The conversation ceased immediately.

'Please excuse this interruption,' he said, displaying the metal badge on his jacket. 'CID. If you would be so kind as to provide some information about one of your countrymen.'

Rath removed the photo from his jacket and held it right under the nose of a blond youth. 'Do you know this man? Alexej Ivanovitsch Kardakov.'

The young man gazed at him through big blue eyes as if he hadn't understood a word.

Two men from the adjacent table stood up. One man's face was disfigured by a long scar across his cheek. It wasn't a duelling scar, more like a serious wound. He cast an eye over the large-size photo.

'No-one here knows this man,' said Scar Face.

Rath knew the man was lying before he had finished his sentence.

'Are you sure?' Rath gestured towards the blond. 'Your friend here didn't understand my question. Perhaps you'd be so kind as to translate?'

'Not necessary. He understood you.' The Russian puffed himself up. Rath could see his muscles flexing under the fabric of his dark suit. They wanted to do more than flex. 'Now might I ask you to leave us in peace? We Russians live amongst ourselves. We regulate our own affairs. We don't like it when Germans interfere in our business.'

'I'll weigh in wherever I please,' Rath replied provocatively.

The Russian's face turned red, his scar a shade of violet. 'You're lucky you're a police officer,' he said. 'We respect the agencies of law enforcement. Otherwise you'd be in trouble.' He paused theatrically. 'Big trouble. No-one talks to me like that. I have a good memory for faces. Just pray that you don't run into me off duty.'

'I'm never off duty.'

'A good cop doesn't drink on the job,' the Russian said and pointed towards the glass in Rath's hand.

'Then maybe I'm a bad cop,' Rath said. As laughable as this alpha male posturing was, he had no intention of showing this muscled ape the white feather.

The Russian became friendlier. He cast his eye over the photograph, took it from Rath's hand and feigned interest.

'We'd like to help you but, as I've already said, none of us have seen this man.'

'I'd like to ask your friends that myself.' Rath took an Overstolz from the packet.

'They'd all say the same thing.' The Russian produced a small matchbook and offered Rath a light.

A quick look around was enough to tell Rath that Scar Face was right. The others *would* all say the same thing.

'You can keep the photograph,' he said. 'Something might occur to you. You never know.' He finished his Americano and laid the glass on the table amongst vodka glasses. 'I'm here from time to time.' With that he turned and left the Russians.

For the first time that night, he was certain that he had run into people who knew Alexej Ivanovitsch Kardakov, but he had every reason to believe Scar Face. No-one in this company would say a word to the German police. At least not when either of the two Russian heavies was in the vicinity.

Rath was too tired to really care. Despite his fatigue, however, he made his way back to Nürnberger Strasse in the best of spirits. He had tasted blood and finally had the tiniest of clues. He also knew where he would continue his search. *Conditorei Café Berlin.* The advertising on the matchbook.

9

When Rath arrived at the office on Saturday morning, a little hungover, a little late and more than a little tired, Wolter was already hammering away on his typewriter. The type bars crackled against the paper like shots from a pistol.

'Morning,' Rath said, hanging his hat and coat on the stand next to the door.

Uncle looked up and raised an eyebrow. 'Morning,' he said. 'A bit late last night?'

'Just a bit,' Rath replied. 'Stephan not here yet?'

'Won't be coming today. The politicals just rang. 1A need him a little longer.'

'And *our* inquiries?'

'Not today. Vice has to wait. We're sticking with politics.' Wolter continued typing; it was obvious he didn't like it. Schmittchen wasn't there on Saturdays, Lieselotte Schmidt, their secretary who did most of the paper work. 'It's almost like a murder investigation, this. Ought to be right up your street.'

Rath ignored the jibe. 'Can I write down what happened to me yesterday first? It was quite an adventure.'

'Feel free. The Prussian police force is ideally equipped for precisely that task.' Wolter gestured towards Rath's desk, where there was another covered typewriter. 'Did you know that we have more typewriters than weapons recorded in our inventory?'

'Just CID or the entire police?'

Wolter shrugged. 'In Germany, it wouldn't surprise me if the *Reichswehr* had more typewriters than canons.'

Rath sat at his desk and removed the protective cover from his pre-war *Adler*. The black machine stared at him like a hostile insect.

'Were you able to satisfy our friendly communist doctor yesterday?' Uncle asked without looking up.

'Völcker? So comrades, come rally.'

'That's a good one.' Wolter laughed and, finally, stopped typing.

'It's from Dr Schwartz. He's known the Red doctor since university.'

'And what else did Dr Schwartz say? Did Völcker let him work in peace?'

'More or less. To begin with he played the outraged communist pain in the arse but, during the examination, he was astonishingly friendly. Even Schwartz teasing him didn't put him out.'

'People like him are never put out. That's why they turn out the way they do.'

'Maybe, but Völcker might also be happy with the result. It turns out a single bullet was enough to kill both women. It entered through the younger woman's chest and passed through her heart. The older one was hit in the shoulder but died of coronary failure. Probably the shock.'

Uncle pulled a disgusted face. 'The thing that annoys me most is that the communists make capital out of this. It's only because the social democrats are too stupid to plan an operation properly.' He tore a sheet of paper from the machine. 'Maybe this can get us out of it,' he said. 'I mean, who says it wasn't a communist bullet after all? It wasn't a police bullet anyway.'

'Your report?' Rath asked. 'Finished already?'

'Wündisch's people like to have everything early.' Deputy Wündisch was in charge of the political police. His department, 1A, was also investigating the deaths during the May actions. Rath skimmed the report. Brief, functional and precise, it was a shining example of police reporting, including a detailed account of Dr Völcker's appearance and the fact that it was the doctor who had removed the confiscated bullet from the wood. Wolter had formulated the report in such a way that one couldn't help suspecting the communist doctor of having exchanged the bullet himself. At least of having had the opportunity to do so and, with that, the pointed bullet was no longer worth a great deal as a piece of evidence.

'It was a police bullet,' Rath said. He didn't like the way Wolter's report skirted the truth, but sometimes there was no alternative. Dr Völcker would also manipulate the truth for his own ends—at least that had been Rath's impression in the morgue.

'A pointed bullet like the ones we use in our rifles,' Wolter agreed. 'I brought it to Ballistics myself. A pointed bullet given to me by a communist. Now what does that prove? Other than that there are communists out there who collect police bullets?'

Still reflecting on Wolter's relationship with the truth, Rath sat in a café in Tauentzienstrasse after work with a pile of newspapers on the table in front of him. He understood that there were different versions of the truth. Every police officer knew that, with each trial it was experienced afresh. Resourceful lawyers could call into question even the most unambiguous of facts, which made the work of the police all the more important. You had to provide the public prosecutor with evidence so watertight that no lawyer could pick it apart. Wolter had just done the exact opposite. He had made a piece of evidence inadmissible to protect police from communist attacks. Did the end really justify the means?

They would come before court with their differing versions of the truth, Wolter and Völcker, the cop and the communist, and what side would the witness Gereon Rath take? It was inconceivable that a police officer should testify against the police. If he did, he might as well pack it in. Most likely he would claim he hadn't seen anything, but he felt queasy about it already.

Was the cleverly fudged report another of Bruno's lessons? At various times, Rath had the feeling that he was trying to familiarise the provincial cop with the way things worked in Berlin. He knew that Bruno thought highly of him. Likewise, he had a high opinion of his experienced colleague, but what to make of these private lessons he wasn't sure. First the outburst on the Karstadt scaffolding and now the exercise in bending the truth, but perhaps that was what you did to survive in the big city. Perhaps Rath had been too naïve, even in a provincial city such as Cologne. Perhaps that was how LeClerk had been able to give him such a going-over in the press.

Rath remembered meeting Alexander LeClerk for the first time. The face of the man called to identify his dead son was like stone. On the marble table the deceased no longer looked like the madman firing at unsuspecting passers-by. He was a pale young man with dead eyes, who hadn't made it to thirty because Gereon Rath had pulled a trigger.

Passing one another in the corridors by Forensics, the policeman and the father, Rath hadn't known what to say or how to behave. He had offered his condolences, well aware of how inappropriate that was. LeClerk hadn't accorded him so much as a glance, showing no emotion in that stony face, neither grief nor anger.

Alexander LeClerk, one of the most important newspaper publishers in Cologne.

It started shortly afterwards, each day a new headline. The first: *Hail of bullets in St Agnes. Is our police force trigger-happy?* The name Gereon Rath appeared in the very first article.

LeClerk had obviously fed his reporters the background information and, in this first article alone, Rath's name was cited five times. Also mentioned was the fact that he was the son of the famous Engelbert Rath. *Triggerman Gereon Rath.* Each syllable a fresh bullet. His father had tried to bring his influence to bear, but that had only spurred LeClerk on and the media declared war on Rath senior too. About this time the decision was taken to remove Gereon Rath from the line of fire and he was granted leave of absence for the duration of the trial. When he resumed his duties post-acquittal, however, there was a fresh volley of headlines, each one more damning than the last.

The publisher seemed determined not to let his reporters rest until the career of Detective Inspector Gereon Rath lay in ruins. When it became clear that there wouldn't be a moment's peace for him if he stayed in Cologne, his father hatched a plan. Together with Otto Bauknecht, the Cologne Commissioner, he worked on Gereon until the latter finally agreed. Engelbert Rath made use of his connections with *dear old Karl*—he had been on first-name terms with Berlin Commissioner Karl Zörgiebel since their Cologne days—and arranged the transfer to Berlin. At the same time he laid a false trail in Cologne.

When the final headline appeared, Gereon Rath was sitting in a train bound for Berlin. This time his father's disinformation policy had worked. In Cologne only Engelbert Rath and Otto Bauknecht knew the truth and, in Berlin, only Commissioner Zörgiebel was aware of the Cologne past of Detective Inspector Gereon Rath, E Division, Alexanderplatz.

They had chosen Vice because there was a vacancy. Engelbert Rath somehow even managed to find something positive to say about his new role. 'At least you won't have to use your gun in a hurry.' This by way of farewell, as he passed his suitcase up to him on the train.

Rath watched silently as the platform and the waving people receded into the distance, and the steel truss of Hohenzollern Bridge hove into view. After a final look at the cathedral, he had unfolded the paper and read the headlines: *Triggerman resigns his post*. The truth was a pliable commodity, perhaps he should take a leaf out of Weinert's book. After all, he was in the same business as LeClerk. They twisted the truth in the whole of Koch-strasse, whatever it took to fit a particular paper. Omit something here, re-phrase it there.

Although his coffee was cold, Rath took another sip and gazed at the mountain of papers on the table. Though the majority had given the same importance to the May disturbances, every one painted a different picture. The only thing they could agree on was that these were the worst street riots in ten years. Even on the number of deaths, reports varied. Some papers went with the police statements, while others read more like adventure sto-ries or war reports. Rath wondered where the journalists got their informa-tion. The reporter from *Tageblatt* seemed at least to have been there as the liberal press wasn't completely reliant on the official reports. Although *Vos-sische Zeitung* had printed the commissioner's statement, clearly labelled as such, they placed it alongside their own reports, and the paper had coined a new word which was already doing the rounds. *Blutmai*—bloody May.

The large-scale police action had come in for criticism. The conservative and national press thought the police had basically acted correctly, though amateurishly, but didn't think the social democrats were capable of taking the drastic measures that were required. The criticism from the liberal papers, on the other hand, concentrated on the agitators from the far left and the far right, *who had grown intoxicated by the idea that the heavy rioting might, in time, result in merry civil war*, as *Vossische Zeitung* had put it. In the meantime they had also condemned the police as excessively brutal. There were too many innocent bystanders amongst the dead.

Zörgiebel would come in for flak. Engelbert Rath's old friend carried full responsibility and had as good as provoked the disturbances with his strict ban. The May Day demonstrations had gone off peacefully enough everywhere else, if one was prepared to overlook the odd fight between communists and social democrats.

Truth be told, however, it wasn't the criticism of Zörgiebel that Rath was interested in. He had wanted to learn more about a different police operation, one which the May disturbances had, without exception, banished to the back pages. For once the papers were all agreed on the subject of the dead man from the Landwehr canal.

Each one had described the case as a *mysterious death by the Landwehr canal;* each one could only offer the same basic information; and each one had published a picture of the deceased with the caption: *does anybody know this man?* In this case it seemed the Castle's public relations machine had been successful. All the major papers had gone with it. What choice did they have? Constructing one's own truth revolved around the art of omission, but the press had so little information they couldn't leave anything out.

Rath stirred his coffee, gazing out of the window at the Saturday afternoon crowds outside the KaDeWe department store. Almost without his noticing, his mouth curled into a faint smile. Böhm must be completely groping in the dark, A Division had a corpse that they couldn't even identify. Rath saw his chances of playing a role in the case improve dramatically.

'Another coffee, sir?'

The waiter wore a somewhat hurt expression. Rath surveyed him from top to bottom, as if his appearance might influence the desire for coffee.

'No, thank you. The bill, please.' He had read enough. It was time to act.

'The bill, sir? Certainly.' The waiter was unmoved. 'Then might we legitimately inform our patrons that the newspapers will be available today after all?'

The man in tails sped away to collect the bill. Rath didn't wait for him to return. He put his money on the table, tore a photo of the dead Boris from *Tageblatt* and took it with him. Now he had pictures of two Russians. Perhaps that would bring him a step closer to resolving things.

The tenement on Luisenufer seemed like an old friend by now. Only, the search for Alexej Kardakov interested Rath a great deal more than it had five days ago. In the courtyard he could hear someone beating a carpet. Rath stepped into the hallway and the smell of cleaning agent.

He started right at the bottom, in the caretaker's flat. SCHÄFFNER it said on the doorbell panel. He rang. Nothing happened. After a while he pressed the bell again. Finally he could hear noises: a bolt being pushed to one side, a key turning in the lock. The door opened a little and the head of a fat woman poked through the crack. 'Yes?'

'Sorry to trouble you on a Saturday but . . .'

Rath needed a moment to interpret her blank gaze, before correcting himself, 'I mean on *Sonnabend* . . .' He hadn't quite settled in the city linguistically either. *Sonnabend* was the word Berliners used for 'Saturday'. 'CID,' he continued, 'would you mind answering some questions?'

'You're not from around here!' came the suspicious reply through the crack in the door. 'Have you got any ID?'

He showed his badge through the crack.

'And what do you want?' She had a thick Berlin accent.

'Perhaps I could come in first?'

She stepped to the side and opened the door fully. 'Well, you'd better come in before the whole house sees it's the police. Make sure you don't get anything dirty!'

He wiped his feet and entered, squeezing past her.

'Why do you want to speak to me in particular?' she continued. 'Just be glad that my Hermann isn't here. He'd have told you where to go! Don't you have anything more important to do? This is a respectable house, we've never had any trouble from the police.'

A brown uniform cap was hanging on the cloak stand in the hall.

'Politically active, your husband?' Rath interrupted.

'You have to be, with the communists getting fresher by the day and the police losing control.'

She led him into a cosy living room. Although it smelt of cleaning agent here too, the air in the flat was somehow stale. The woman shifted her weight and followed Rath through the living room door. Hindenburg was hanging on the wall, next to the ex-Kaiser, both gazing sternly at the visitor. Rath couldn't help thinking of their doppelgangers in König's studio.

'Take a seat, Herr . . .'

'Rath, Detective Inspector Rath.'

'So, you've finally caught up with the Liebigs from the rear building?'

He almost sank into the yellow chair. 'Sorry?'

'If they aren't communists I'll eat my hat! Liebig senior was out on the streets on the first of May, even though it was forbidden. Didn't catch him though, your colleagues. Little snotbag came home talking big, with a red flag rolled under his arm. As for his wife . . .'

'Thank you. I will pass your information on.' He didn't think she noticed his sarcasm. He watched in astonishment as her weight almost pressed the sofa cushions down to the ground. 'But Frau Schäffner, I am here for a different reason.'

She squirmed on the sofa. 'I don't have much time. You've interrupted me in the middle of cleaning.'

'I'm looking for a man who's supposed to live here, but clearly doesn't.'

She stared at him blankly.

'Does the name Alexej Ivanovitsch Kardakov mean anything to you?'

'A Russian? There are no Russians living here.'

'No-one who's moved in in the past couple of months?'

'Not here. Brückner moved out of the first rear building. That is, my Hermann threw the red swine out because he couldn't pay his rent. There's someone new there now, but he's German, not Russian.'

'Kardakov has been in Germany a long time. Perhaps you didn't realise he was Russian.'

'Believe me, that's the sort of thing I notice. Besides, he has a German name.'

'Which is?'

She considered for a moment. 'Müller or Möller. Something run of the mill like that. Now that you ask, I realise I don't actually know. Probably because I've never seen him. I can only remember names once I've seen their faces.'

'You've never seen him?' Rath could scarcely believe that anything in this block escaped Frau Schäffner's notice. Herr Müller or Möller must have been invisible.

She shrugged her shoulders as if she herself were surprised by this gap in her knowledge. 'My husband must have seen him. He collects the rent.'

'How long has the man been living here?'

'Not very long. That's what I've been saying. Works as a night watchman as far as I know. At Osram's, Hermann said. During the day he sleeps. You can ask anyone here, he hardly ever shows his face.'

'One final question . . .' He took the scrap of newspaper from his pocket and pushed the photo of the dead Russian across the living room table. 'Perhaps you have seen this man?'

She glanced at the picture curiously and shook her head, then suddenly recognised him. 'That's the man from the paper. The guy they pulled out from the canal! Is that your Kardakov?'

'No, it relates to another case,' Rath said quickly and returned the scrap to his pocket. A dead loss. He showed her the glossy print. 'That's Kardakov.'

'Never seen him.'

He thought of something else. 'Did you hear anything about a fight a few nights ago? Here, outside?'

'We sleep at the back. The train makes such a racket out front. Means we don't always hear what's happening on the str . . .' She paused. 'But wait! There was a fight out in the courtyard. Someone was making such a noise we nearly fell out of bed. Hermann tried to get involved, but the trouble-makers had left by the time he got outside. Someone else must've sorted it out. Is that why you're looking for Kardakov? Did someone here complain? They should have come and spoken to us. Hermann would've dealt with it.'

'Two Russians fighting?' Rath probed.

'One of them was Russian, true. The other was German.'

'German? Are you sure?'

'Quite sure. The one who calmed things down, naturally, was the German!'

'And when was this?'

She considered briefly. 'No idea. Monday or Tuesday perhaps. Sometime at the beginning of the week.'

She looked at the clock on the wall. 'So.' She rose to her feet. 'Now I must ask you to leave. I'm not through with the cleaning yet and I still have to cook.' Rath was surprised by how quickly she emerged from the cushions. He had a lot more trouble with his own chair. It felt like he had almost drowned in it. 'You should take a look in the rear building,' she called after him, 'it's about time the police dealt with the Liebigs.'

When he was outside, Rath did, in fact, head towards the rear building. He wasn't so much curious about the Liebig family, as about the man who was apparently invisible. In the courtyard the first thing he did was to take a deep breath, happy to have escaped the sharp smell of the cleaning agent. The carpet rail was abandoned and the courtyard devoid of people, as if word had spread that police were there. In the second courtyard, Rath could hear a circular saw.

The letter boxes in the rear house revealed that a Herr Müller was indeed living there. Had Kardakov adopted the most banal of all German names? Or was there really a night watchman from the Osram plant living here? Rath climbed the steps to the first floor and rang.

In the flat all was quiet. He listened by the door. Not a sound. *He hardly ever shows his face,* the caretaker's wife had said. Rath glanced at the time. Almost half past four. Even a night-shift worker ought to be on his feet by now but after ringing and ringing the bell there was still nothing doing. Either Herr Müller was deaf or there was no-one at home.

Since he was already in the building, he climbed to the next floor and rang the bell marked LIEBIG. Everything was still.

Back on the street he lit a cigarette. He was just about to flick the match onto the street in front of the house, only to reconsider when he noticed a head peering from behind one of the ground floor windows. Frau Schäffner was just as nosy as he had imagined, which made it all the more bizarre that she had never seen Herr Müller. Rath tipped his hat to her.

Something about this address didn't add up. He decided to pay another visit to Luisenufer as he had to know who this invisible Herr Müller really was. Either he spoke with a Russian accent or else Kardakov had left Elisabeth Behnke a false address. Whatever the case, one thing was certain: Alexej Ivanovitsch Kardakov had gone to ground and didn't want anyone to find him. That it was rent arrears alone, however, he could no longer believe. Not after they had fished a dead Russian out of the canal. The disappearance of the one Russian was surely linked to the death of the other.

There was something else troubling him. Rath wondered whether he might have set eyes on Herr Müller after all. A small man with a hat that seemed too big for him. The man who had told him about the fight between the two Russians the first time he had visited. Frau Schäffner, on the other hand, was absolutely sure that it had been a Russian and a German. Who was telling the truth?

At any rate, there was something about the row that night. Boris had been looking for Kardakov here on Luisenufer too. The question was, had he found him? When he heard that there had been two Russians fighting, on his first visit here, Rath had assumed the answer was yes. If it was true that only *one* of the squabbling pair had been speaking Russian, then another solution presented itself. Namely, there had been a similar incident to the one at Rath's flat. Boris had awoken another complete stranger, thinking it was Kardakov. A fight followed, and Boris had pushed off, only to be murdered shortly afterwards. By the underground Kardakov, because someone had got too close for comfort? But what about the abuse Boris had suffered? What information had Kardakov been trying to extract, and why had Boris died of a heroin overdose?

Before Rath climbed the steps to the station at Kottbusser Tor, he trod out his cigarette sullenly. Spin it any way you liked, it just didn't make sense. Still, that was a feeling he recognised. It was how things usually were at the start of an investigation. They would change though, he had to be patient and he couldn't give up.

He boarded the train and travelled three stations westbound, alighting at Möckern Bridge. He wanted to see where it had happened.

10

He could see it as he crossed the canal. On Tempelhofer Ufer, close to the bridge, was a gaping hole in the canal fencing, secured by planks painted red and white. Passers-by scarcely paid attention to the temporary barrier. Rath sat on a bench in the shadow of the trees lining the promenade and lit his last Overstolz.

Though he seemed to be gazing aimlessly into the distance, he was registering every detail. To his left, where the car had crashed through the fencing, a tree was missing a large piece of bark. Otherwise the vehicle seemed to have pierced the gap between two trees almost exactly. With a dead man at the wheel! He tried to imagine how the whole thing might have happened. Boris had been sitting in the car, already dead, feet and hands broken. So who had been driving? Either someone was sitting in the car with him or someone must have wedged down the accelerator. Rath would have very much liked to know more details but, apart from what he had heard in the morgue and the little information carried in the papers, he knew nothing.

He crossed the street for a look at the houses on Tempelhofer Ufer. Presentable looking flats, they weren't the sort of place to have a high crime rate. On the bridge, on the other side of Möckernstrasse, was a kiosk. Otherwise there were no shops, just residential buildings, offices and the goods station. Rath walked slowly past the house entrances and checked the names on the mailboxes. No sign of a Kardakov, not that he had expected there to be.

Behind the kiosk marked the start of the goods station premises. The little stall probably supplied the railway workers with cigarettes, newspapers and beer. Kiosk owners were usually rewarding conversation partners for police. Rath made his way over.

'Overstolz, five six-packs,' he said, nodding at the figure in the darkness of the wooden stall. The man was so fat it seemed as if he was physically attached to his little cubbyhole. Rath wouldn't have been surprised if his huge upper body was screwed to a bogie. That was how it looked, at least, as he swung round and reached for the cigarettes.

'One fifty,' he said. 'Need a light too?'

'Please.'

The fat man passed him a box of matches. 'Did someone stand you up?' he asked unexpectedly. Rath gave him a questioning look. 'It looked as if you were waiting for someone just now.'

'Well,' Rath said, as he lit the first cigarette from the new packet, 'perhaps it wasn't such a good idea to meet here of all places.' He gestured towards the red-white planks. 'That's where he went through isn't it?'

The fat man nodded. 'Actually it was pretty nice to have my corner mentioned in the paper. Hasn't done anything for turnover yet, mind.'

'No legions of voyeurs and journalists?'

'Only a few cops so far, but they don't buy anything. They just ask questions.'

The kiosk owner didn't seem to think he was a cop. Fine. Rath wasn't here on official duty and the last thing he wanted was for Böhm's people to hear there was someone from Vice muscling in on their patch. He had put the badge he usually wore on his jacket in his coat pocket during the train ride. 'Did you see anything?' he asked, hoping the direct question wouldn't arouse suspicion.

The fat man was happy to talk. 'It happened in the middle of the night, and I close at six, but the next morning around five, when I was about to open up, there were two cops hanging around. CID didn't arrive from Alex until later and pestered me with all sorts of questions considering I didn't actually see anything.'

'Bet you see a lot here though?'

'There are always loads of people walking past.'

'Still, you must have good powers of observation.' Rath took a deep breath. 'I mean, you noticed me straightaway.'

'You have to keep an eye on people. There's always someone trying to steal something. A colleague of mine at *Schlesischer Bahnhof* had his stall burned down while he was inside. Petrol over the papers, light a match and see you later. A bunch of brats, couldn't have been more than fifteen or sixteen, and the cops haven't caught a single one. No wonder, the boys were sent by *Norden*, the kiosk was in their area and for some reason they didn't like the owner. I don't have any trouble with the *Ringvereine,* but you still need to be on your toes.'

Rath nodded. The *Norden Ringverein* had made the headlines only recently. After a bloody mass brawl on Breslauer Strasse, during which a Hamburg carpenter had been stabbed to death, the commissioner had banned two prostitution rings, one of which was *Norden.* In light of such violence, the police were forced to take drastic action. Normally, however, they tolerated the *Ringvereine,* associations that were supposed to help ex-cons reintegrate into society, but in reality deployed their singular abilities for profit. In short: the *Ringvereine* regulated organised crime in Berlin and had divided the city into different precincts. The police did nothing since the underworld was easier to control if it regulated itself, and excesses like those on Breslauer Strasse were rare. Murder was a crime that violated the *Ringvereine*'s code of honour. Some of the new associations, decried as rats by the more established organisations, no longer kept to the rules. Times were tougher these days.

'Is there a *Ringverein* here?' Rath asked the fat man. 'I thought they only had them in the east.'

'Don't go thinking there's no crime in Kreuzberg, my friend!' The man leaned forward ever so slightly—Rath suspected he'd have fallen off his chair otherwise—but enough to lend him a conspiratorial air. 'I wouldn't like to say,' he whispered, 'how many stolen goods are shifted day in day out back there. You should ask one of the workers here about the kind of people milling around the *Anhalter* goods station!'

'You don't think it could have something to do with the murder?' Rath gestured towards the shattered canal fencing.

'You'll laugh, but that's exactly what CID asked me too!'

Rath was just about to dig a little deeper when he saw them. Right on cue, two figures emerged onto the street from one of the houses Rath had visited a few minutes before. One of them was an assistant detective from A Division, whose name Rath didn't know. The other was a woman. Not a detective, a stenographer: Charlotte Ritter.

Rath disappeared behind the newspaper stands and leafed through the papers. Böhm had turned them loose, no question. Better if they didn't find him here. 'Is there anything about the dead man from the canal in here?' he asked, before treading out his cigarette.

'Try *Tageblatt*. It's more informative.'

The paper Rath was holding was the *Angriff*. A smearsheet favoured by the Nazis which regularly defamed the deputy chief of police. Dr Bernhard Weiß was Jewish and the *Angriff* didn't need any other justification for its attacks on the best criminal investigator in Berlin. The only reason Weiß hadn't been made commissioner was that he wasn't a social democrat. Or was it? Perhaps there were other reasons too. It wasn't just the Nazis who had a problem with Jews, but they were the only ones who hawked their anti-Semitism around.

The fat man held out a copy of the *Berliner Tageblatt* and Rath grabbed it, making sure he kept the pair in view as they moved towards Möckernstrasse. He would buy the paper so as not to arouse suspicion, despite having read it in the café just now. He searched for his wallet somewhat awkwardly, both liberal and Nazi newspapers wedged underneath his arm. When he looked up again, he saw the assistant detective crossing Möckern Bridge in the direction of the station, alone.

'Fifteen pfennigs,' the fat man said. Rath rattled around for change. He felt uneasy. How was he supposed to avoid Charlotte Ritter when he didn't know where she had gone?

The question was superfluous. First he saw her coat and slim ankles approaching from under the newspaper stands, the next moment she was standing before him. Her eyes were even darker than he remembered.

She seemed more surprised than he was. No wonder. He had had time to prepare himself for their meeting, admittedly only about four seconds, but that was enough to get a reasonable hold of himself.

'What a surprise,' he said, placing the papers and wallet on the counter and lifting his hat. 'Do you live around here?'

'I'm here on duty,' she replied.

'The lady works for the police,' the fat man prompted.

'The gentleman knows, he works for the police too.'

The fat man was visibly put out by the news.

'Could I have a packet of Juno?' she continued, and the heavy upper body turned once more to the shelf of cigarettes. 'Interesting mix,' she said to Rath.

He must have gazed at her dim-wittedly. She smiled and her dimple almost caused him to lose his composure.

'Your reading material,' she said.

There was something not quite right about seeing the *Angriff* and *Berliner Tageblatt* co-existing on the counter. 'I only need one of them,' he said.

'Let's hope it's the right one.'

He placed two coins on the counter and took *Tageblatt*. He wasn't political, but there was no harm in her thinking he was a liberal. Better than a nazi. Or a social democrat, as the rumour-mongers at the Castle had branded him when they learned that he had enjoyed protection from Zörgiebel. Meantime, the fat man turned to face them again.

'I'll have to fetch the Junos,' he said, detaching himself from his chair.

Rath was glad to be alone with Charlotte Ritter. 'Do even the stenographers from A Division do overtime?' he asked.

'When they're being used for murder inquiries, then yes they do.'

'The dead man in the canal?'

She nodded.

'You're being used as a CID officer?'

'Only sometimes, but I get paid as a stenographer. That doesn't change.'

'And what do the people you question say to that?'

'They don't even realise. I'm always on duty with an officer who shows his ID. Today I had the pleasure of traipsing round the houses with our very own Assistant Detective Gräf.'

The fat man returned and twisted himself back onto his chair with a groan.

'What brings you here?' she asked. 'Do you live here? In that case I'd have to question you as well.'

Rath gazed at the fat man, who was trying to open a carton of two hundred cigarettes, but floundering with the paper. 'I was meeting someone.'

'He was stood up,' the man from the kiosk said as he presented Ritter with a six pack of cigarettes. 'Not many people buy them,' he mumbled apologetically, turned his stool round and began loading the remaining cartons onto the shelf.

For a long time there was an awkward silence, but it came at the right time. No harm in Ritter thinking that the fat man had embarrassed him. At least she wouldn't realise that she had been the real cause.

'Twenty pfennigs,' the fat man said from the dark hollow.

She opened her handbag and searched for her purse. Rath made use of the opportunity to take his leave with a brief tip of his hat.

'See you on Monday at the Castle,' he said.

'Probably not. On Monday I have criminal law,' she replied, meeting his gaze.

Those dark eyes. He racked his brains for an answer. 'Well, have a good weekend anyway,' he said, and set off.

'Your change,' the fat man called after him as he crossed the street, but Rath pretended not to have heard. He crossed Möckern Bridge, but neglected to take the steps up to the elevated railway. She was bound to take the train, and after all that he didn't want to find himself sitting next to her. He continued to *Anhalter Bahnhof* on foot before splashing out on a taxi.

In *Café Berlin* no-one was sober. Those who hadn't indulged in sparkling wine had powdered their noses with cocaine in the elegant washrooms, and most had done both. The place was spread across three floors, likewise the abstract light sculpture housed on a giant pilaster. Below, the dance hall was attached to the wine bar, whose main attraction was the tropical jungle growing on the ground floor, where it seemed as if the neighbouring Zoological Garden had sprawled over its walls. Anyone hoping to escape the hustle and bustle made for the tea room or the cocktail bar on the first floor. Though dancing was restricted to the second floor, the music could be heard everywhere, elegant, fluid swing, not as quick or as hectic as in *Kakadu*, where the music positively assaulted your ears. A poster indicated that it was the *Excellos Seven* playing in such a civilised manner.

Rath stood by the railing on the first floor, eyeing the tables below, playing with a matchbook. He had bathed before throwing on his evening clothes. Goodness knows what Elisabeth Behnke must have thought as he left the house.

Although his eyes were on the faces below, Rath's mind was on an entirely different location and an entirely different face. A number of hours had passed, but his thoughts were still circling around the meeting at the kiosk. He couldn't stop thinking about her dark, inscrutable eyes. He felt as though he were in a bad love film where the women threw the men longing glances, although she hadn't done that. She had only looked at him, and he couldn't get that look out of his mind. Pull yourself together, he chided himself, not with someone from the Castle. Not with one of Wilhelm Böhm's colleagues!

The popping of a champagne cork returned him to the present. He didn't know exactly what or whom he was looking for, only that the Russian heavies frequented *Café Berlin*. And that they knew Kardakov. He was secretly hoping to see someone from the crew at *Kakadu*, the blond youth for example and, with a bit of luck, without his muscle-bound companions. Then he would be a little more talkative, despite the language barrier. Rath would see to that. The Russians needed to have their residency permits extended regularly, and a policeman could give them a lot of trouble.

Having scanned the whole room, he made for the cocktail bar where he found a free stool between an emaciated youth and a blonde who was dressed to the nines. After ordering an Americano, he took a photo out of his pocket and looked at it. Maybe he should try the direct route, he thought, as he watched the barman mix his Campari and Martini. While he was still waiting for his drink, he registered a movement out of the corner of his eye. The thin man next to him had risen from his stool a little too quickly.

No sooner did he have the man in his sights than the latter started to run. Agitated gaze, sunken cheeks. He jostled past an elegant woman, knocked the champagne glass out of her hand, and pushed her against her male companion. Both crashed to the ground. The woman cried out.

Rath put the photo away and chased after the man in the direction of the stairs, leaping over the downed couple. The barman gazed after him in astonishment, cocktail in hand.

The man was running towards the toilets! Rath knew the layout, he had thrown out a couple of pimps and their hookers only two weeks ago. Perhaps the thin man was one of them and had recognised him? Whoever he was, he was trapped, since he couldn't escape from the Gents. A couple of women began squealing and cursing, in amongst the odd suggestive remark. Obviously the thin man knew the lie of the land too, as there was a window in the Ladies that opened onto the courtyard. Rath left via the office, it was even quicker that way—you didn't have to squeeze through a narrow window. Just through the small anteroom and he'd reach the rear exit. Carefully he opened the door. Nobody there. He stepped back into the corridor, left the door ajar and waited. The man would have to go past if he wanted to reach the street. Rath saw him through the crack, and pushed the heavy iron door open just as he was running past.

A loud crash. Then a series of curses.

Rath stepped into the courtyard and pulled the man to his feet. Blood was running from his nose. Rath showed him his badge and got a startled expression like a deer in headlights. Big eyes flickered frantically. Cocaine.

'I knew straightaway you were a cop! What do you want?' His gums were still bleeding. The way he rolled his Rs suggested that he was Russian. Rath grabbed him by the collar and started yelling. As a police officer you couldn't show weakness, and in this city even being friendly was viewed as such. That much he had learned already.

'As far as I'm concerned you can snort cocaine until your nose falls off. I really couldn't give a shit. As long as you tell me what I want to know, you won't get any trouble from me.'

'What is it that you want to know?'

He shoved the photo of Kardakov under the Russian's nose. The other hand remained on his collar. 'Do you know this man?' The Russian hesitated. Rath got mad. 'Listen to me, my young brother! Until now I've tried to be friendly, but you'd better watch it, believe me. Stop trying to kid me. You know this man!'

'So what? Just because I know someone who lisps when he buys cigarettes doesn't mean I'm a snowman.'

Rath's ears pricked up. His predecessor had been dealing cocaine! Perhaps he should pop in to see Narcotics.

'Don't try and tell me you only snort the stuff!' he shouted at the Russian. 'But right now I don't really care. I'm looking for *him!*' He held the photo right in front of the thin man's face. 'So tell me what you know, and I'll leave you in peace.'

'You cops have no idea how hard it is to earn money in this city!' A discharge of blood and spittle landed on the pavement. 'Alexej wouldn't do it unless he had to. It's other people who earn the big money anyway, but you leave them be. The ones from high society who take the stuff too. Still, whenever it's a Russian there's trouble. You even expel them from the country. Doesn't matter if the Bolsheviks back home are after them.'

'If you want us to extend *your* identity card, then I suggest you show a little more cooperation.' Rath fished the yellow document from the Russian's jacket and pocketed it. 'You'll get it back when I'm satisfied with your answers. Who is Kardakov?'

'You haven't found him then.' The Russian smiled and his eyes grew smaller. 'You won't catch Alexej so easily. How did you come by the photo? Did his singer friend lose her nerve?'

Lana Nikoros. Delphi Palace.

'If anyone's about to lose their nerve, it's me,' Rath said, pulling the Russian up by the collar and slamming him against the wall. The guy was light as a feather. 'And believe me, you wouldn't like that. You definitely wouldn't like that.'

Rath heard his own voice, but it was as if another person was speaking. He couldn't help thinking back to Bruno's performance on the scaffolding. He was scaring himself a little. Had he already learned his colleague's lesson? At any rate, playing tough guy seemed to be working.

'OK, OK, don't get so worked up!' The Russian raised his hands in a conciliatory manner. 'Just don't tell anyone you've been speaking to me. You already know he's been earning a bit on the side.'

'Where do I find him?'

'No idea. Here and there. I haven't seen him for over a week. There were rumours your lot had nabbed him.'

'I don't believe a word you're saying.'

'Then why don't you ask the queens in *Eldorado*. They're feeling pretty nervous, because their source of cocaine's dried up.'

The place was for people who got a thrill from not knowing whether it was a man or a woman they were wheeling across the dance floor. At least half the women in *Eldorado* weren't women at all. They had looked in while they were on duty in Lutherstrasse, though without particularly disrupting business. Rath suspected that Bruno had informants here too.

'Does Kardakov sell anything apart from coke?' Perhaps they were investigating a murder on the gay scene, and the dead man from the canal had been Kardakov's lover. Although Boris hadn't seemed particularly amorous during his night-time visit to Nürnberger Strasse.

'I'm sure there are a few people who'd like a bit of Alexej, but he sends them all packing. They like him all the same. That's why they're missing him so much. The other guys dealing snow in Lutherstrasse aren't half as sweet.'

Rath glanced at the time. It was just after twelve. The party in *Eldorado* would just be starting. He left the Russian where he was and headed towards the taxi stand on Hardenbergstrasse.

'Hey, what's with my ID?' the Russian called after him.

'You'll get it back once I've found Kardakov.'

'And what if one of you cops asks for it in the meantime? Am I supposed to send them to you?'

'Just make sure you keep a low profile!'

'Hello, darling!'

The peroxide blonde behind the counter called herself Gloria but her real name was Gustav. She puckered her scarlet-red lips.

'You're looking chic,' she said. 'Flying solo tonight, where's Bruno got to? And that young blond colleague of yours?'

The dance floor in *Eldorado* was filling and the band was playing music you could tap your feet to. The smoke of countless cigarettes hung in the cosy room, which was dominated by the colour gold. Rath leaned against the bar and placed an Overstolz in the corner of his mouth.

'We're not married you know,' he muttered.

'You might be one day.'

Rath couldn't kick up too much of a fuss on Bruno's patch. He was the newbie, he had to watch out. The fact that he was investigating under his own steam went against every rule in the book. All the more so, given that he was withholding information.

'Gloria, darling?' He tried putting on a little more charm, and leaned against the counter with a smile.

'Yes?' She placed a glass in front of a man who uttered a very tipsy 'thank you, my dear,' and looked at her adoringly. A tourist who obviously had no idea he was talking to a man.

Gloria returned to Rath. The chains on her neck brushed the back of his hand as she leaned towards him. 'Nice of you to drop by again. There aren't too many good-looking cops out there.'

He held out a carton of cigarettes. 'Fancy a cigarette break?'

She grabbed one with her talons. 'If you have a drink with me.'

Shortly afterwards there were two glasses and a bottle of whisky on a table that was just far enough away from the band to talk. Gloria poured them each a generous measure.

'Out with it,' she said. 'Why is a cop offering me a cigarette and then standing me a drink? It can't just be because of my pretty blue eyes.'

She batted her false eyelashes.

'Got it in one, my dear!' He raised his glass to her and they drank. 'Although you do have very pretty eyes.' He showed her the photo. 'He must put in an appearance from time to time.'

She looked at Kardakov's soft features and drew on her cigarette, blew the smoke through her nose and nodded. 'He's Russian, isn't he? Cute guy. I hope you haven't locked him up? That would be a real pity.'

'Don't worry. At the moment I'm only looking for him because I'm trying to find out about one of his friends.'

'Has he done something wrong?'

'Not if you don't count dealing cocaine.'

'So, that's it.' Her voice grew colder. She looked first at him and then at the photo and he could see that she sensed a trap.

'No, don't misunderstand me. That doesn't interest me at all. Except insofar as it helps me find him.'

'I can't imagine that he deals snow here. The boss doesn't tolerate things like that.'

'It's possible he finds buyers here, isn't it?'

She shrugged her shoulders and refilled their glasses, leaning close in the process.

'I'm only saying what I'm about to say because every cop in Berlin knows it anyway. See it as a kind of remedial class for provincial cops.'

'Fine, so long as you don't tell Bruno I need the help.'

She laughed. 'Pay attention. If there's anyone dealing cocaine in this city, then you can assume that Dr Mabuse has a hand in it . . .'

'The guy from the cinema?'

'Just don't call him that. His real name is Johann Marlow. And don't ask me where he got his doctorate from. He probably bought it, just like he buys you cops. It doesn't matter what he's involved in, he always manages to keep his nose clean. He only knows Plötzensee from the outside. From waiting in front of the big gate to pick up his men.'

'What are you trying to say?'

'Your friend here . . .' she gestured towards the photo, 'it's not only you cops who are trying to find him. Dr M. is longing to see him too and has men out looking. There have been a few from *Berolina* here already. A couple of days ago. With a very similar photo.'

'*Berolina?*' Rath whistled quietly through his teeth. *Berolina* was one of the oldest *Ringvereine* in Berlin, a group for whom the code of honour still meant something. Murder was taboo. When they heard of gangs of thugs and pimps like *Norden* or *Immertreu*, the two *Ringvereine* the commissioner had forbidden following the bloodbath in Breslauer Strasse, the members of *Berolina* turned up their noses.

'So Marlow is in charge of a *Ringverein*,' Rath said.

'Don't say his name so loud!' She looked around. 'No, Dr M. doesn't belong to a *Ringverein*. He's far too clever for that. *Berolina* are still fronted by Red Hugo, but Red Hugo does exactly what Dr M. tells him. That way *Berolina* make more profit and Dr M. doesn't get his hands dirty.' Gloria took a final drag and stubbed out her cigarette. 'So,' she said as she stood up, 'duty calls.'

'Wait . . .'

She leaned over him once more. The chains on her neck jangled. He slipped her a five mark note. 'How do I find Dr M.?'

'You don't find him. He finds you.' She pinned the money to her garter. 'But if I could give you one tip? Go and see a variety show. The *Plaza* on Küstriner Platz only opened a few weeks ago. I hear they have a great line-up . . .' She planted a kiss on his cheek. As she fought her way through the crowd back to the counter, her hips swaying from side to side, most of the men in the room gazed in her direction, as did a few of the women who were dressed as men. Rath's eyes followed her until she reached the counter. She really did have a good figure. Especially when one considered that her name was Gustav.

11

'I just don't understand what's wrong with her! In all the years I've been living here, nothing like this has ever happened before. And now? The second time inside a week!'

Weinert fiddled awkwardly with the coffee pot and porcelain filter. It took a moment for him to set the filter on top. Neither of them had much experience with this sort of thing. Normally, it was the landlady who was responsible. Normally, the smell of fresh coffee was already drifting through the flat when they awoke. But today it had only been Weinert sitting in the kitchen when Rath had poked his tired, hungover head through the door. Now he was sitting at the kitchen table winding the coffee grinder, while Weinert placed the kettle on the stove top.

'She must be sick.' Rath defended the landlady. He hadn't seen the journalist for days. During the May disturbances he had been away almost the whole time, but today of all days he just had to be sitting at the breakfast table.

'Sick? She's been drinking, I bet you anything. It smells like a brewery in here. Yours truly has to live like a monk, while good old Frau Behnke's enjoying a boozy evening!'

The smell of sweet, strong liquor was still hanging in the air.

'It's only human. You shouldn't get so worked up about it,' Rath said. He tipped the coffee grounds into the filter bag. 'Just imagine if she was infallible. It doesn't bear thinking about!'

In truth he was happy she hadn't got out of bed. When he had got back to Nürnberger Strasse at around three that morning, she had been waiting for him. No sooner had he opened the front door than she had been standing in the hallway, propped up on the doorpost and gazing at him reproachfully. This time there was no shawl over her nightdress. In comparison, he felt almost sober. She fell into his arms and when he helped her into bed she tried to engage him in some sort of wrestling match. He freed himself and shortly afterwards she fell asleep. By the time he made it to his own bed, his alarm clock was showing half past four and he could sense how much the little hand was longing to click into place and trigger the alarm. He had let himself sleep until eight. Too little to be fully fit, but enough to get through the day.

The kettle emitted a shrill whistle that grew steadily louder.

'Of course, you're sympathetic,' Weinert grinned as he removed the kettle from the stove. 'Seems like you might have overdone it a little yourself.'

A pleasant aroma wafted through the kitchen as boiling water reached the coffee grounds in the filter. Rath inhaled appreciatively.

'An ancient rule 'tis and still true, who worry has, takes liquor too,' he pronounced.

'Old Behnke must have some serious worries in that case,' Weinert said, pouring the coffee.

Rath took the hot mug carefully in two hands and blew on it.

Weinert sat with him at the table and unfolded the Sunday papers. The disturbances were still dominating the front pages. 'The social democrats have really left you in the shit, haven't they?' he asked casually, without looking up.

'What?'

'The action against the May demonstrators, of course. Don't you think it was all a little heavy-handed? Over twenty dead. Any number wounded. A few whose lives are still in danger.' He began to read: *'We can't help thinking that the measures taken by social democrat Zörgiebel, above all the demonstration ban, were primarily motivated by party politics.'*

'Did you write that?'

'For three days it was like civil war in certain workers' districts, and all because your commissioner wanted to show the communists who calls the shots in Red Berlin. A minor dispute between Red friends and Red enemies of the state and he's misused the entire police apparatus to settle it. The deaths are just collateral!'

Rath feared that the journalist's interpretation wasn't so very wide of the mark. He shrugged. 'I don't know anything about politics, but it is the role of the police to restore order on the streets.'

'Don't give me that! I've been on the ground these last few days, and the police certainly haven't restored any order. Quite the opposite! The Reds would've gone home after an hour if you'd let them march in peace.'

'There were barricades, people looting, gun battles!'

'There are always people who exploit lawless situations. Smashing display windows, looting shops and generally letting it all hang out. I didn't see a single communist sniper. Only policemen opening fire . . .'

'. . . waiting to be attacked at any moment by the Red Front,' Rath finished the journalist's sentence. 'The RFB are armed.'

Now it was Weinert who shrugged. 'Of course, the communists with all their loudmouth posturing are at least partly responsible for the general hysteria as well. Even now they're still kicking up a fuss, milking every death for their own propaganda purposes, despite there being barely any communists amongst the deceased. On Wednesday three May victims will be buried in Friedrichsfelde, and Ernst Thälmann himself intends to speak at their graves. They're making martyrs of innocent victims, behaving as if revolution were imminent.

'The thing is, these idiots are actually playing right into the hands of good old Zörgiebel. If the communists were trying to stage a revolution, then sending the police in hard was the right thing to do. But the last person to die wasn't a communist. He was an unsuspecting journalist working for *The Daily Express*, who happened to be in the wrong place at the wrong time. Against that, the journalists who were driven out of trouble spots by police batons have actually been rather lucky. Likewise my colleague from *Vossische Zeitung* who escaped after being shot in the leg.'

Rath thought of the two dead women.

'You can see your commissioner's guilty conscience here.' Weinert showed him the story on page four. They had reprinted the photograph of the dead Boris.

'After all the police violence against journalists and the commissioner's smoke and mirror tactics during the May disturbances, the way the police have behaved towards the press on this case has been incredibly accommodating. No wonder, this corpse has come at just the right time for them.' Weinert struck the portrait with the flat of his hand. 'A death that has nothing to do with the disturbances. And the circumstances are so mysterious and gruesome. Hands and feet mashed to a pulp. That should keep the people of Berlin entertained for a few days. When the heroes from Homicide reveal the perpetrator, the police will be gleaming like a Persil sky. Brilliant and white! Feted by the press, feted by all of Berlin. Nobody will give a second thought to bloody May.'

Rath was lost in his own thoughts, but Weinert's theory seemed plausible. All that remained to be seen was who would play the hero. 'Don't tell me that's a story you wouldn't write,' he said. 'Don't tell me that if you had exclusive information about a murder inquiry that was on everybody's lips, you wouldn't write anything just because your story might be of use to the commissioner?'

Weinert smiled, looking like a shark with a cup of coffee. 'I'm always happy to receive exclusive information,' he said.

'Good to know.' Rath placed his empty cup on the table and stood up. 'Oh, and by the way, I lent you a tenner recently . . .'

'. . . which you'll get back tomorrow. I promise. I just haven't had enough time to go to the bank in the last few days.'

Weinert looked embarrassed. Rath made use of the opportunity. 'Maybe there's something else you can do for me today . . .' he said casually.

'Anytime.' Weinert sounded relieved.

'. . . I could use your car for a few hours.'

'One-nil!' he laughed. 'You can have it until four, and then I need it myself.' He waved the key. 'But be punctual. I'm meeting someone and without a car you'll leave me exposed.'

The journalist's sand-coloured sports car was parked in front of the door. Second-hand, but elegant. An American model, a Buick two-seater. A car you could use to impress women, but Rath just needed some wheels. If Weinert thought he was taking a girl out to the country, then so much the better.

The *Delphi Palace* was situated beside the *Theater des Westens,* looking like a jungle temple that had washed up in Charlottenburg with palm trees growing in the front garden. On the façade, where the programme attractions would normally be advertised, a large banner announced that the *Delphi* was temporarily closed. Rath had parked his car in Kantstrasse, directly in front of the gate, and was slowly climbing the steps to the front garden.

He was a little disappointed. He had been expecting to find the current programme displayed somewhere, so that he could see when Lana Nikoros was next performing, but the *Delphi* seemed completely deserted. The plants that flanked the path to the main door made a lamentable impression. A few exotic-looking wicker chairs, carelessly piled on top of one another and worn by the weather, stood in a corner of the garden. There were two flights of steps leading to the entrance. A sharp voice pierced the air.

'If you're one of Schneid's people, then I suggest you vacate the property this instant! Unless you want me to call the police?'

A man was rushing towards him from Fasanenstrasse.

'I *am* the police,' Rath said.

The man slowed his pace. He was so elegantly dressed it was as if he was preparing to go dancing. 'Really?' he asked as he drew nearer. 'Department of Building Regulations, Charlottenburg?'

'No.' Rath showed him his ID. 'CID, Berlin.'

'If Herr Schneid called you, then you can leave right now. He's not in charge here. We have every right to turn off the water and electricity.'

'I don't know any Herr Schneid. Perhaps you'd be so kind as to tell me *your* name.'

'Sorry.' He proffered a hand. 'Felten. I'm Herr Sehring's secretary.'

'Who?'

'You don't seem to know many people. Herr Sehring is an architect. The owner and builder of the *Delphi Palace*. May I ask what brings you here?'

Rath removed the programme from his pocket. 'A singer. Lana Nikoros.'

Felten took the programme and cast his eye over the photo.

'Oh yes, she has performed here. One of Schneid's artists.' He returned the programme to Rath. 'But there'll be new tenants here soon. Which means there'll be a new programme too.'

'I don't really care about the programme, but I do need to speak to this woman. I'm investigating a crime.'

'I'm sorry. I can't help you further.'

'Then where would I be able to find Herr Schneid?'

The man shrugged his shoulders. 'Not in his office at the *Delphi* at any rate. Bankruptcy proceedings have been launched against him.' He jangled a set of keys. 'I've got the keys here.'

'Perhaps you could take me to his office?'

Rath felt slightly uneasy as he followed Felten through the huge room, which did actually feel like a palace, opulent and bombastically decorated. A thin layer of dust had settled on the finery, scarcely perceptible but conveying a sense of decay.

Felten appeared to have read his mind. 'We'll get some life back in the old place soon,' he said, and gestured towards the scaffolding on the side wall. 'Work has already begun.'

They went past an inconspicuous-looking door that was standing slightly ajar. Felten closed it with a casual movement of the hand.

'Where does that lead?' Rath asked.

'The stairs into the cellar. Schneid has his office upstairs,' Felten said, before correcting himself. 'Had.'

He led him to the right and up a flight of stairs. They stopped in front of a dark, heavy door. Felten searched for the right key.

'You can come and go as you please?' Rath asked, surprised.

'No problem,' Felten grinned as the door opened. 'The liquidator is an old university friend of Herr Sehring.'

Inside the office it was dark.

'No electricity,' Felten said apologetically. He reached unerringly into a wall cupboard, took out a candle and lit it. Yellow light flickered over a dark, heavy desk and leather chair. Rath quickly located the artist directory. The details of any number of musicians were noted, along with male and female singers and dance artists. The directory also included addresses, artist names, special skills, and the size of the agreed fee. No Lana Nikoros. In one of the desk drawers Rath found Josef Schneid's business cards. He pocketed one. Felten made sure that everything was returned to its rightful place before locking up. Then he accompanied Rath outside.

'You should come by when we reopen,' he said then quickly added, 'when you're off duty, of course.'

Rath was happy to be rid of the man, off duty or not. He climbed back into the car and looked at the business card. Alongside the address in Kantstrasse was Josef Schneid's private address.

After the long, cold winter, May seemed to have brought more agreeable temperatures. Rath drove through Budapester Strasse with the top down. The first trees in Tiergarten were starting to come into leaf. A car like this was a wonderful thing, even if it wasn't cheap. He would have to ask Bruno how he could afford his Model A. As far as Rath knew, he was somehow able to claim any work-related trips in his private vehicle as tax exempt. There were certain colleagues who begrudged Bruno the luxury of owning a car. It was rumoured by some that Emmi Wolter had brought money into the marriage. CID officers were not particularly well remunerated. Even the DCIs, to say nothing of a simple detective inspector.

Well, Rath might not have a rich wife, but he did have a neighbour with a car.

Tiergartenstrasse was a good address. To the left the green of the park; to the right houses with extravagant façades. The old West's heyday was over. Today those who could afford it were building their villas a long way out, in Grunewald, but Rath paid more attention to the house numbers than the mouldings. He parked the Buick under a tree just before Kemperplatz.

There were so many mouldings on the façade of Schneid's house that it looked as though the plaster cast angels would have to fight it out to retain their place. The owner was at home. A valet led him into a drawing room that was every bit as impressive as the façade; few signs of bankruptcy here. Rath didn't have to wait long before Josef Schneid appeared leaning on a cane, a commanding figure in a robe, sporting an old-fashioned beard.

'Lana Nikoros? Of course I know her. I stole her from Fritz. A shame that we had to close temporarily, I fear she may have gone back to him. This feud with Sehring is taking up so much of my time, don't ask me where my artists are. He kicked them all out, the staff too. These bankruptcy proceedings he's started, they're just a way of getting rid of me. I'm standing in the way of his new tenants.'

'Fritz?'

'Buschmann. He runs several variety theatres in the city, as well as a few dance cafés. You just have to study the Berlin night scene carefully, then you'll find Lana for sure.' Schneid played with the silver knob on his cane.

'Perhaps you have an address for me?'

'An address? No. I got her together with the band, and that's how I paid her too, through the band.'

'Which band?'

'Russians. They could play jazz, I tell you. Just like the Negroes in the

Cotton Club! Ilja Tretschkov is the band leader's name. If you can find him, you'll find Lana.'

'She's a Russian too?'

'Yes, what were you expecting?'

Rath glanced at the time as he emerged back onto the street. He still had time. Given that he was already out in the car he might as well make the most of it.

An hour later he finally parked the Buick in the atrium at the station, having driven for any number of kilometres in what ultimately amounted to little more than a jaunt around Berlin. First he had returned to Möckern Bridge and driven slowly along Tempelhofer Ufer, without really knowing what he was looking for, probably for a glimpse of Kardakov. He didn't recognise a single face amongst the Sunday afternoon strollers, now examining the scene of the accident, not even one from the Castle. Soon it would cease to be a crime scene altogether, but simply a ruined section of canal fencing, whose repair the city council would put off for as long as possible.

Next he drove into the eastern part of the city, over the Schilling Bridge into the Stralau quarter and the centre of Friedrichshain. He hadn't dared to get out at Küstriner Platz, which wasn't the sort of place you could park a sand-coloured American sports car and expect to find it intact upon your return. The area around *Schlesischer Bahnhof* was amongst the most notorious in Berlin. Uniform only dared to venture onto the streets in small groups, and CID kept as low a profile as possible. The area was firmly in the hands of criminals and, as there wasn't a lot that police could do, they left it to the *Ringvereine* to maintain order.

Plaza had once been a station. However, no trains had stopped there for over forty years. Since then the buildings of the former *Ostbahnhof* had been used as warehouses. Jules Marx had converted the giant station concourse into a variety theatre that housed almost three thousand spectators. It had only opened at the start of the year. Rath first explored the long side of the great building, where the street was still called *Am Ostbahnhof*. Only the front part of the station had been converted into a theatre. At the back there were still a number of warehouses, many of which had gone to rack and ruin. Next he drove slowly along the newly renovated station façade.

The big neon letters which formed the name *Plaza* were still switched on. At the main entrance, multi-coloured placards promised an evening themed around the Wild West. Not without a certain irony, Rath thought. In Berlin, the east was wilder than the west.

No sign of Johann Marlow. *You don't find him, he finds you.* Rath couldn't help thinking of Gloria's words. He didn't even know what Dr M. looked like, which was the reason he had driven to the Castle and was now trudging up the stairs. I Division was located on the top floor and was home to the *Erkennungsdienst*, the identification service.

There was no mention of a Johann Marlow anywhere in the files. The man didn't have a single conviction or file note. He hadn't even so much as driven through a red light at Potsdamer Platz. The same was true for Alexej Ivanovitsch Kardakov. Until now he had successfully concealed his coke dealing from the Berlin police. A trip to see his colleagues in Narcotics was thus rendered superfluous. Rath returned to the ground floor.

The offices in the western wing were all locked up. Sunday. Closed for public business. As far as Rath knew, the passports office was usually open on Sundays, or at least part-staffed. He trawled through the various doors before striking lucky. Just as he turned the corner and opened the connecting door to the north wing, he saw a grey-haired official who was already in his coat. The old man was just about to lock the door to his office.

'Home time!' he said, as Rath addressed him. 'One o'clock.'

'Come on! CID are working today too. Criminals don't keep office hours.'

'I still need to go to the form storage room.'

'And you can. I just need a little help with an address.'

The grey-haired man sighed. The key turned back in the opposite direction.

'Well, I just hope that CID will do me a favour when I need one.' The man led him into a neat and tidy office and rummaged around in his jacket pocket for his glasses case. Behind a low wooden barricade, which normally kept the public at arm's length, stood meticulously arranged rows of desks, shelves and filing cabinets. 'Which Division do you work for?' he asked.

'E Division.'

The old man put on his reading glasses and surveyed him briefly.

'What letter?'

Rath almost said 'E' again before he realised what the man meant.

'K,' he said simply.

The man noisily opened a roll-front cabinet.

'And the whole word?'

'Kardakov.'

The man had already pulled out a drawer and started to search.

'Alexej Ivanovitsch Kardakov,' Rath added, hoping to do the official a favour.

The latter abandoned his search immediately. 'That doesn't sound like a German name to me,' he said.

'It isn't. Kardakov is Russian.'

The official rolled his eyes, slammed the drawer shut, closed the roll-front cabinet and jangled a bunch of keys. 'Couldn't you have said right away?' he asked. 'Come with me.'

He led Rath through three further offices that all looked the same as the first.

'Room 152. Alien passports office,' said the man when they had reached the fourth office. The rest Rath knew already. Roll-front cabinet, drawer, search. It didn't take too long. The official pulled an index card from the drawer.

'There he is . . . Kardakov, Alexej Ivanovitsch. Born 25th July 1896 in St Petersburg, Russia, registered in Berlin since 15th December 1920 . . .'

'I need the address!'

'All in good time, young man.' Another reproachful glance from over his spectacles. 'Registered in Berlin since 15th December 1920 . . .' the man repeated with a composure that nearly drove Rath spare. He was exactly the kind of Prussian official the police could do without. '. . . resident in Nürnberger Stra—'

'That's his old address.'

'My dear inspector! Might I ask why you are bothering *me*, when you seem to know all the answers?'

'Sorry, but the man moved out of that address a month ago.'

The official glanced over the card. 'There's no mention of it here. Kardakov has been living at this address for three years.' He took another look. 'In a week's time he has to extend his yellow identity card, foreigners need to do that every six months. That's most likely when he intends to give notice of his move. Perhaps you could come back then. On the 16th May I'll be able to tell you more.'

'Many thanks. You've been a great help,' Rath said, as pleasantly as he could manage. Inside he was seething. He'd have liked nothing better than to throttle the old man. 'Wait,' he said. The official was already standing by the door. 'Please wait! There's one more thing you can do for me. A woman's address. Lana Nikoros.'

The official grumbled, but did as he was told.

'Doesn't sound much like a German name either.'

His visit to the Castle was not very productive. Neither at the records office nor at the passports office did he get any information that might advance his inquiries. There wasn't even a Lana Nikoros registered in Berlin, but at least he knew that Kardakov would soon be obliged to renew his ID. If he didn't appear for that, it would be clear that he really had gone to ground. If he was only interested in not paying his final month's rent, he would not run the risk of wandering around Germany as a foreigner without valid papers.

Big white letters interrupted Rath's thoughts. HOMICIDE. He stared at the glass double door. Somehow he had ended up on the first floor. Force of habit? He had stood in front of the very same door a week ago, which was when he saw her for the first time. Today the passageway was devoid of people. He made a quick about turn and headed towards Vice. All he needed now was to run into Wilhelm Böhm, but their corridor was quiet too. There was no noise coming from the offices, no sound of voices, no rattling away on the typewriters. A floor higher, where the politicals were based, was still a hive of activity. The May actions had filled the police holding cells. In contrast there wasn't a single person working in E Division. Just the right place to do some thinking.

The door wasn't locked. He had expected to find a deserted office, so was all the more surprised to discover one of his colleagues.

'Stephan!'

The rookie Jänicke was sitting at Uncle's desk, buried in a mound of papers.

'Hello, Gereon!' Jänicke was just as surprised as Rath. 'This crew not giving you any peace either? I wanted to have another look at the files on König. I can't get the man out of my head. An upstanding photographer, and then this filth.'

'The König file from 1A? It's in my desk. I'm the one who dug it out, not Bruno.'

'Right!' Jänicke stuffed the papers on the desk back into Wolter's drawer and closed it. 'I'd have been looking for a long time.'

Rath's desk drawer was still relatively empty. He found the file with König's political inclinations and threw it over to Jänicke. 'Here.'

His colleague was a good catcher. Word was that he played handball.

'Thank you!' Jänicke took the file to his desk. 'And what brings you here on a Sunday?'

Rath had no desire to feign an interest in the porn investigation, only to spend the rest of the day poring over the König file with the rookie. That he was looking for a Russian named Kardakov had nothing to do with the young man.

'Boredom,' he said. 'I don't have a car I can wash.'

Jänicke laughed. 'Now I know why Bruno isn't here.' He cleared his throat. 'Well, I had no intention of spending my whole Sunday here. Hertha are playing against Südstern today. Are you coming?'

'I thought you played handball?'

'In my youth I was a football goalkeeper for Viktoria Allenstein. I didn't start playing handball until police academy at Potsdam. I was in goal there too.'

'Hertha will win anyway,' Rath said. 'They always take the Berlin Championship.' He made as if he was looking for something in his desk. 'I'll be on my way soon too. I just wanted to see . . . Ah, there it is!'

He removed the wallet that he had placed in the drawer three seconds before and pretended to be relieved. 'There was I thinking one of the pickpockets at Alex had nicked it. I was ready for a weekend without any money.' He put the wallet back in his pocket and moved towards the door. 'See you tomorrow then.'

For forty-eight hours they hadn't set eyes on their colleague and now, on today of all days, Jänicke turns up again! Rath felt that their unexpected meeting had been more embarrassing for the rookie than for him as it wasn't exactly kosher, rummaging around in other people's drawers. Did Bruno know about it? Probably not. Rath decided not to say anything either. That way Jänicke would be worried he *might* say something. Couldn't hurt if the rookie felt obliged to do him the odd favour.

In the stairwell, Rath realised how hungry he was. Only half past one. He still had enough time to eat something here, although not in the canteen. Instead of the atrium, he made for the exit at Dircksenstrasse. The railway arches were lit by a few thin rays of sunshine.

There was a gusty wind blowing over Alex and he had to hold his hat as he turned into the square. Even on a Sunday there was a large crowd milling around between the construction hoardings. A magazine vendor was pedalling his dubious wares, at 20 pfennig each: Ehe magazine, fascinating and piquant. Rath wondered whether the porn merchant, to whom police owed their successful search, would appear again. He pushed through the crowd, squeezed past a bread trolley in front of Aschinger's and went inside where it was dark but pleasantly warm and smelt of beer and cigarette smoke.

He took a Sunday paper from the hook and looked for a free table. When the waiter came, he ordered *Sauerbraten* with dumplings and a beer and unfolded the paper. The photo of the deceased Boris had been printed again today and had advanced several pages towards the front. The article was bigger, but it contained no significant new details. Böhm wasn't making any progress.

'Ah-ha! I see you don't just advertise Aschinger products. You eat here too!'

He gave a start, his thoughts rudely interrupted by a smiling Charlotte Ritter in a dark coat. He folded the paper hastily and mumbled a greeting.

'Is there still space on this table?' she asked.

'Of course.' He stood up and straightened her chair, gazing at her slim neck and realising how good she smelt.

She sat down and, before he could say anything stupid, the waiter arrived with his food.

'A coffee for me,' she said and wished him *bon appétit*.

'Thank you.' He would have liked to bag the *Sauerbraten* and go. 'We meet again,' he said instead. 'Been at the station today too.'

'What do you mean 'been'? I'm just about to go back. Böhm has only let me off the leash for a moment. We've got a lot to do, another busy weekend.' She shrugged as if to say: what the hell? That's just the way it is.

'Any progress?'

'Progress would be an exaggeration. It's a strange case with barely any clues. I fear that *Aquarius* will keep us occupied for some time yet.'

'*Aquarius*?'

'Even if it's not a classic floater. What else are we supposed to call the case when the victim doesn't have a name?'

'You don't know his identity?'

'If we knew his name, we'd be a lot further forward, but I'm afraid we're not making any headway. Although Zörgiebel wants results by the day before yesterday.'

Weinert had been right. The fat man was putting his foot down, he wanted a quick result. The homicide team were the most popular police officers in Berlin, as popular as UFA film actors, and A Division had a fantastic detection rate. No question: Dörrzwiebel, as the commissioner was known amongst officers, on account of his desiccated onion-like complexion, was under pressure. They had given him the nickname when Karl Zörgiebel was still commissioner in Cologne.

'I thought A Division was concentrating on the May fatalities.'

She shook her head. '1A are taking care of that on their own. The politicals haven't had so many deaths to deal with for a long time. It's mass processing like you wouldn't believe. It would be easier for us to investigate a May corpse, as the details are usually easy to establish. Even if it wouldn't make us many friends on the force.'

'What do you mean? '

'Let me put it this way. Obviously there were too many police bullets fired during the skirmishes. And too few communist bullets.'

She seemed to be well informed.

'In that case 1A is the best department for the job,' he said. 'Their officers are used to being a little unpopular.'

The waiter placed a pot of coffee on the table and poured.

'Is the coffee in E Division as bad as it is in Homicide?' she asked.

'You know that I work in Vice?'

She laughed and her dimple almost knocked him off his feet. A good thing he was already seated.

'When someone frequents the same corridors as Parabellum Wolter,' she said, 'then he probably works with him too. Powers of deduction are a pre-requisite for a job in Homicide, even for stenographers.' She sipped cautiously from her coffee.

'Parabellum?' It was the first time he'd heard the nickname.

'The guy used to be an instructor on the range. One of the best marksmen the Berlin police have ever had.'

'Seriously?' He wouldn't have thought that Bruno had it in him. Rath realised he'd never seen him fire a gun. Working in Vice, you seldom had recourse to use your weapon.

'You should spend more time in the canteen. You hear interesting things about your colleagues there. About you too.'

'About me?' He was surprised. 'Do you know my name then?'

'Oops,' she said, placing her hand over her mouth so conspicuously that he knew it wasn't meant seriously. He couldn't help but smile. 'Don't sit here playing the innocent,' she said. 'You already knew that I was a stenographer yesterday. Which means you've collected more information about me than you're letting on, and I sincerely hope that includes my name.' She sighed theatrically. 'What can you do? It's a small world, and an even smaller Castle.'

'One of the best marksmen the Berlin police have ever had. Old Bruno!' Rath shook his head. 'How does someone like that end up in Vice?'

She stirred her coffee and smiled at him. 'How did *you*.'

'That's a long story. Much longer than a cup of coffee, I'm afraid. You'd be better off asking in the canteen.'

'There might be a lot of people talking about you, but they don't *say* very much.' She pointed to the table in front of her. 'Besides I've got a whole pot of coffee here.'

'My story'd take longer than a whole coffee morning.'

'Does that mean I have to invite you for coffee and cake if I want to hear your story, Herr Rath?'

'At the very least.' Then after a moment's thought, he came out with it. 'And what do I have to invite *you* to, if I want to hear *your* story?'

'I think dinner should suffice.'

———

He was still thinking of her as he drove aimlessly through the city, relishing the empty early Sunday afternoon roads. What had she been looking for at Aschinger's? She could just as easily have had coffee in A Division. There was even an ample supply of cakes there, the cake-addicted Chief of Homicide Ernst Gennat would see to that. Was she sounding him out on Böhm's behalf, because of their meeting at Möckern Bridge? Was her flirting part of the plan?

It was time to go home. The stretch of road he had just driven would have been something for his father, if he ever came to visit, that is. It was ideal for provincial tourists such as Engelbert Rath, from Alex to Königstrasse, past the town hall and the City Palace, over the Palace Bridge towards Unter den Linden, past the armoury and the guardhouse, left onto Charlottenstrasse, a lap of the Gendarmenmarkt, then via Leipziger Strasse and Wilhelmstrasse past the government departments, back onto Unter den Linden and through the Brandenburg Gate.

A slice of Prussia for that model Prussian officer Engelbert Rath, pride of the Cologne police force, and a much more enjoyable drive in Weinert's Buick than in one of *Käse*'s tour buses. Still, Rath wasn't expecting a visit anytime soon. His father had only called him twice in Berlin, both times at the station, and had only ever asked how his son was getting on in E Division. That was how it had been with his old man for as long as he could remember. He was never off duty. His mother had dialled his private line in Nürnberger Strasse on several occasions, but Rath could do without her worried calls. His father's indifference was preferable.

At Potsdamer Platz he was obliged to wait at the crossroads. Quarter past three. The lights had just changed to green when he saw the poster on the advertising pillar. Behind him a taxi driver beeped his horn. Rath let him pass and turned into Potsdamer Strasse. Behind *Josty* he turned right, parked the car and ran the few metres back to the corner.

The advertising pillar stood in front of a house-high billboard that shielded a building site from the pavement below. Its letters may have been considerably smaller and more unassuming than the monstrous script on the billboard behind it, but he had read it correctly. *Ilja Tretschkov live*, proclaimed a poster for the *Europa-Pavillon*. He noted the time and returned to the car cheerfully. Could be just the thing for Charlotte Ritter. Besides, there was a cinema in *Europahaus* too. All in all, the day had been a real success. Time would tell what the evening might bring.

Weinert was waiting when Rath returned to Nürnberger Strasse. It was five to four. He coasted to a halt in front of the journalist, applied the handbrake and climbed out.

'Bang on time,' Weinert said appreciatively, and took his place in the driver's seat. 'How did you like the car?'

'Better than Berlin public transport, at any rate.'

'You can say that again.' Weinert took off the brake and engaged first gear. 'Have fun at your officers' meet.' He sped away.

Rath couldn't make sense of what he had just said, but when he opened the door to the flat, he heard voices from the kitchen. Elisabeth Behnke had a male visitor.

He went to his room and hung up his coat. His gaze fell on the Pharus-map he had hung next to the broken wardrobe, a box of pins in his hand. The first he had placed by the Landwehr canal, right next to Möckern Bridge, where they had fished Boris's body out of the canal; the second by Nürnberger Strasse 28, where Boris had come looking for Alexej Kardakov shortly before his death. He had placed further pins by Luisenufer, by the zoo level with *Café Berlin*, and by *Eldorado* in Lutherstrasse. Kardakov's trail. It led to Küstriner Platz. The *Plaza*. And the man from whom Kardakov obtained his cocaine.

Rath came a step closer to the map and removed the pin that marked the abandoned *Delphi Palace* on Kantstrasse, pricking a spot next to *Anhalter Bahnhof* instead. *Europahaus* on Königgrätzer Strasse, the place where Ilja Tretschkov had found a new engagement. Hopefully, Lana Nikoros too.

Rath removed the photos of the two Russians from his pocket, the noble print of Kardakov and the newspaper cutting of the dead Boris, and pinned them next to the map. He added the *Delphi* programme with the portrait of the singer.

What did these three have in common? The singer was Kardakov's girlfriend, and she was Russian. Was she perhaps married to Boris? Had the lovers killed the husband and fled? Rath shook his head. Next he took Josef Schneid's business card from his wallet and clipped it onto the programme.

He took a step back and contemplated the Pharus-map, like an artist contemplating his work. Sometimes he seemed to spy a pattern, a connection, a proximity between places or a correlation of some other kind, but the pins were spread indiscriminately across the city. The trails of Boris and Kardakov converged at a single point: Nürnberger Strasse 28. For years Rath had been in the habit of indicating important places in an investigation on a map, but in all that time he had never had cause to mark the location of his own flat.

There was a knock on the door. Weinert surely wasn't back yet. Perhaps it was Elisabeth Behnke requesting that he joined them in the kitchen? He opened a door of the wardrobe whose gothic carvings concealed the photos on the wall as well as a small part of the map. 'Yes?' he said. The door opened.

'Surprise,' said a male voice.

Rath was indeed surprised. 'You?' he said.

Bruno Wolter stood laughing in the doorway.

'You can close that mouth of yours,' he said. 'I thought, if I'm paying Elisabeth a visit, I should check if my colleague's at home too. Just wanted to see how you're settling in.'

Bruno had arranged the flat for him because he knew the widow Elisabeth Behnke, having served with her late husband during the war. In fact, he had notified the young widow of her husband's death. Rath had repressed the details—just as he had everything connected to the war.

'I didn't see your car,' he said. 'You've been visiting E . . . you've been visiting Frau Behnke?'

Wolter took a step inside the room. He was already in his coat, carrying his hat in his hands. 'I bring her flowers every year on the anniversary of her husband's death. Helmut Behnke was the best comrade a man could have wished for.'

Rath swallowed. So that was why she was drunk last night, her husband had fallen twelve years ago. She had been drunk, looking for a little human warmth when he strolled through the door.

Uncle looked around the room. 'Very cosy,' he said. Then his gaze fixed on the map. 'Only, this corner looks almost like a superintendent's office.'

'Or a confessional,' Rath said. He thought the wardrobe was far more conspicuous than the map. It had nothing to do with Bruno anyway.

'Did the Russian kick that in?' Wolter gestured towards the side of the wardrobe.

Elisabeth must have been talking. 'Just some drunk.'

'Has he turned up again?'

Yeah, as a corpse, Rath thought, but shook his head.

'I told Elisabeth that she shouldn't take on a Russian as a tenant. They only cause trouble. Doesn't matter if it's a Bolshevik, a Tsarist, or whatever.' Suddenly he was looking Rath straight in the eye. 'That's why I recommended a colleague to her. Hopefully *he* won't cause her any trouble.' It sounded like Elisabeth had kept on talking. The question was what had she said.

'Would you like something to drink?' Rath asked, and took a step towards the door. He wanted to get Bruno out of his room before he saw the map. 'Perhaps we should go into the kitchen . . .'

Wolter waved his hands dismissively. 'Don't put yourself out on my account. I've been very well looked after. I'm about to go anyway, I just wanted to pop in.' He considered for a moment. 'Perhaps we could have a beer together tonight? At my house in Friedenau? Emmi can make us something to eat.'

'That's very nice, thank you. I'm afraid I can't tonight though . . .' Rath shrugged apologetically. 'I'm going to the theatre.'

'I understand,' Wolter said and a little grin spread across his features. 'It's about time you emerged from your cell. I hope she's cute!'

A car beeped outside.

'I have to go,' said Uncle. He put on his hat. 'See you tomorrow then.'

Rath went to the window and peeked out carefully from behind the curtain. In front of the main door there was a black Ford by the roadside, Bruno's Ford Model A. At the wheel was a young man whom Rath didn't recognise. Did Bruno have a son? He realised he still didn't know a great deal about his colleague. Bruno climbed in and the vehicle drove away, essaying a rapid U-turn before disappearing off towards Tauentzien. Friedenau was in the other direction. Obviously Bruno didn't want to head home yet.

He instinctively turned up the collar of his jacket as he alighted from the city railway at *Schlesischer Bahnhof.* Hopefully it wasn't immediately obvious he was a cop. Wearing a police badge here was not a good idea. Today his Mauser was sitting loaded in a shoulder holster under his jacket. Its presence reassured him. In this part of town, you never knew what might happen.

Indeed, that was precisely the attraction for many revellers: a night in Stralau alongside rakish criminals and beautiful women, stealing furtive glances at them from the neighbouring table. This was more exciting than being out and about in mundane West Berlin. On Kurfürstendamm you ran the risk, at most, of being beaten up by a horde of SA stormtroopers for not looking Aryan enough, while with a bit of luck here in the east you could actually watch a shoot-out between real-life hoodlums.

It was already dark when Rath reached Küstriner Platz, where even the street-lighting was dimmer than in the city or in Charlottenburg. It almost seemed as if the streetlights were ashamed of what they were obliged to il-luminate. The neon letters outside *Plaza* cast further light into the dark-ness, while the three floors up to the roof balustrade and the old station clock were bathed in spotlights. *Plaza* glowed like a small, bright island in this murky district.

Taxi after taxi paused in front of the entrance to spew out well-dressed patrons, adventurous tourists from the west. People from the neighbour-hood who had saved to attend a performance arrived on foot or by bike. Rath mingled with the motley assortment of guests, drifting along with the crowd past the box office, through the foyer and cloakroom and into the vast auditorium.

What Jules Marx had done with the former station concourse was im-pressive. An enormous auditorium opened out above Rath. With no corners, only a series of soft curves, *Plaza* had almost three thousand seats, and tonight it looked as if almost all of them would be filled. There were already more than a thousand people inside and the orchestra was playing, though the music was scarcely audible amongst the clamour of the audience.

Rath looked around. How Marlow was supposed to recognise him in a crowd of three thousand people was a mystery. He took his seat and leafed through the programme, at the same time fiddling conspicuously with a photo of Kardakov.

'Is he appearing too?' his neighbour enquired, a thin woman with glasses who looked like a recorder teacher.

Rath mumbled something about an acquaintance and the lady blushed and turned away. He could tell what she was thinking. His other neighbour showed no interest whatsoever. Perhaps he had overheard the short conversation with the recorder teacher. Rath put the photo away angrily. In the meantime, the lights had gone out. The first act on stage was a magician who looked like a witch doctor, followed by lasso acrobats in cowboy costumes, and a knife thrower dressed as an American Indian. When yet another cowboy began singing a lament about loneliness on the prairie, Rath wanted to throw tomatoes at him. He gritted his teeth, but stuck it out until the interval.

As the rest of the audience made its way to the foyer, he stayed put and gazed around. People pushed past but, in amongst the melee, there was no-one that stood out. He didn't know what he was looking for, didn't even know what Marlow looked like. What was he expecting? A gangster boss like Al Capone? A fat man in a white suit, flanked by two heavyweight wrestlers? He didn't see anyone who set his alarm bells ringing. In the meantime, the auditorium had almost emptied. He followed the others into the foyer.

Once again he held the photo casually alongside the programme as he strolled through the groups of smoking, drinking and chattering people. Obviously the portrait of Alexej Kardakov left the people here cold. Why had Gloria sent him to *Plaza*? What did Dr M. have to do with the variety theatre? Perhaps it belonged to him and Jules Marx was just a front man? Then Dr M. would hardly visit every performance. More likely he'd be in an office somewhere. He should have pumped Gloria for more information in *Eldorado*.

Maybe he should go upstairs and take a look at the office.

'Stop, you can't go up there!'

He had scarcely taken three steps before one of the tail-coated ushers whistled him back.

Rath tried his best to come across like a businessman. 'Excuse me,' he said, 'but I would like to speak to someone from management . . .'

'Are you unhappy with the line-up?'

'It's not that,' he lied. 'I need to speak to Herr Marlow urgently. I was told I might find him here.'

'I'm afraid you've been misinformed. There's no Herr Marlow working here.'

'Dr Marlow, then?'

The usher raised his right eyebrow. 'As I said just now, you must have been misinformed. Now might I ask you to get down from the steps?'

'The name means nothing to you?'

'Not that I'm aware of.'

He had reached the end of his tether. The audience was already streaming back into the auditorium. He let the rest of the show wash over him, without seeing a Great Marloni pull a rabbit out of his hat or a Dr M. turn in a sparkling display of knife throwing.

He hadn't seriously expected to find Marlow amongst the performers, but there had to be some connection between Dr M. and *Plaza*, he thought, as he trudged back to the city railway with a herd of audience members. Or else Gloria had fooled him. Would she have dared? Unlikely. At *Eldorado*, they relied on Vice cops being friendly. Perhaps he was just here on the wrong day. That, or Marlow had found him a long time ago and had no intention of speaking to him.

With several hundred people streaming towards *Schlesischer Bahnhof* from *Plaza* Rath didn't notice the one on his tail.

12

There was a general air of depression at the Castle on Monday morning. The grey corridors appeared even greyer than normal. The large-scale action around May Day had lasted three days and turned into a disaster for police command. Press reaction was devastating and Berthold Weinert wasn't the only journalist to condemn their actions. The word *Blutmai* was doing the rounds, just as *Vossische Zeitung* had conceived it.

There had been twenty-two recorded fatalities, and many of the wounded were still critical. The police had used huge amounts of ammunition: 7,885 shots had been fired from police pistols, and a further 3,096 from rifles and machine guns. The Berlin police accounts were a model of Prussian exactitude.

As far as confiscated weapons were concerned, however, officers had less counting to do. They could have spared themselves the house-to-house searches in Wedding and Neukölln. Though it had been a large-scale action, with hundreds of flats thoroughly searched, the yield had been negligible, perhaps a dozen revolvers and pistols, two or three rifles. There were more weapons in the shooting gallery at the funfair.

On the command floor they were already hard at work constructing the story of a communist coup that had been prevented by the brave efforts of police officers. Since early morning, they had been searching communist offices not only in Bülowplatz but across the whole city using the register of names. The Prussian Interior Ministry had used the May disturbances as a pretext for banning the RFB.

Shortly after work began, a meeting was called for officers from all departments and Commissioner Zörgiebel greeted them personally in the large conference room above the main entrance. Dörrzwiebel had hardly changed since his Cologne days, an obesity-prone former union secretary who had been entrusted with running the police force because the social democrats were in power and had offices to fill. He was a politician rather than a criminal investigator, even after all his years as police chief, and rarely seen by officers. Normally, he sent his deputy to meetings such as this. Dr Bernhard Weiß was the leading specialist at the helm of the Berlin police, and an outstanding criminal investigator, too perfect to be popular with colleagues but universally respected. That gave him a distinct advantage over Zörgiebel. Weiß had expressed reservations about upholding the demonstration ban on the first of May, but Zörgiebel had wanted to push it through with consequences that, by now, were well established.

After the police chief had thanked the officers for their commitment during the 'communist riots', he changed topic. Zörgiebel knew that CID didn't enjoy being roped in to political work and felt that such work should be carried out by Section 1A alone. The majority of officers gave a satisfied nod when he revealed that he had gathered them for a different reason. The latest unsolved fatality required everyone to pull together, its swift resolution was of the utmost importance to demonstrate that the police still called the shots. Zörgiebel appealed to CID to display a united front and requested that all divisions from Section IV aid Homicide wherever possible, so long as they didn't neglect their day-to-day duties. 'You all get about in this city, gentlemen,' he concluded, 'so make the most of your contacts!'

DCI Böhm approached the lectern. Rath would have liked to bombard him with paper balls, like when he was at school. With *wet* paper balls, that is. He looked for Charlotte Ritter but there wasn't a single woman there. Well, someone in A Division had to be working, he thought, if the men were all present in the conference room looking important. Buddha Ernst Gennat wasn't up on the podium either, but he knew the chief of homicide preferred investigative work to noisy gatherings such as this.

And it really was noisy.

'Gentlemen!' Böhm barked so loudly that his colleagues in the first row visibly winced. 'Thank you first of all for appearing in such numbers. We are still pursuing all lines of inquiry. Our biggest problem is that we are yet to identify the deceased. Our number one priority, therefore, is to establish who we dredged from the Landwehr canal.'

The DCI held the newspaper photo in the air. 'This picture was published in all major newspapers at the weekend. We have had a few responses from the public, but unfortunately nothing we can use. No-one seems to have known this man. At least, no-one who will admit it. We believe it is possible that he doesn't come from Berlin at all. That he was the victim of a violent crime is beyond doubt and his injuries cannot have stemmed from the car accident. The autopsy . . .'

Rath had already heard most of what the DCI was reeling off. There hadn't been any major developments over the weekend. Two assistant detectives went round distributing photos, the same ones that were in the papers but a good deal sharper. Rath could now see that a wet lock of the Russian's hair was hanging down over his forehead. His skin was glistening in the flashlight.

König's women were putting them to a lot of trouble. They had remained resolutely silent to this point, but now it all came gushing out. For this they had a new member of the group to thank, part of the yield they had harvested from Old Fritz's breakdown. Unlike the men in König's photo stories, who were cast in their roles because of their similarity to prominent Prussian figures, the women were all professionals, prostitutes from Unter den Linden or Friedrichstrasse. They had been identified beyond doubt, and subsequently given a good grilling. The breakthrough came when Rath managed to make Sylvia Walkowski, or Squealing Sylvie, believe that her arrest had come about solely as a result of Red Sophie's loquacity. Red Sophie, or Sophie Ziethen, had dazzled as Mata Hari on the day of the raid.

Then the floodgates really opened. When Sophie heard that Sylvie had blabbed, she started talking too, angering the women in the neighbouring cells. Little by little, they learned that the majority of the women didn't just earn their money through prostitution and pornography but also in illegal nightclubs—most of them by dancing nude. Two of them worked in *Pegasus*, whose speciality was women parading in the uniforms of the various Prussian wars—bottomless—while gentlemen from the audience pinned medals on their most voluminous body parts. Currently the ladies were all in police custody, wishing death upon one another. No-one envied the female wardens in the women's wing, where Squealing Sylvie was living up to her name.

There were eight illegal nightclubs on their list, their locations spread across the city. A huge amount of work lay ahead. They had to discreetly assemble information, as well as prepare and plan the raids. They wanted to raid all the clubs in a single evening, before word of the operation got round.

'Just like in the old days.' Uncle had telephoned Lanke and requested that twenty police vans be placed at their disposal next Saturday evening. 'Back then, these sorts of operations happened regularly. We'd cart people back to Alex by the vanload, and in the main conference room, where Dörrzwiebel just preached his sermon, we would separate the wheat from the chaff.' He rubbed his hands.

'Picking up in pick-ups,' Jänicke joked.

'No time to enquire about some dead man,' said Wolter. 'A Division can get their shit done on their own.' He took the photo from the conference room, ripped it in two and threw it in the wastepaper bin. Jänicke had carelessly flung his photo on the desk. Rath, meanwhile, had stowed his copy in his jacket pocket. He had no intention of throwing it away.

Bruno fixed him with a sidelong glance, but didn't say anything, just got back on the phone. Uncle wasn't stupid, but Rath didn't think he had become suspicious during his surprise visit the day before. Rath was still new to the city. Why shouldn't he have a map on his wall? There was no way Bruno had been able to see the pins from the door. Nevertheless, he did know that Rath had once worked in Homicide.

Shortly afterwards, once Jänicke had left, Wolter took him to one side.

'Have you tasted blood, Gereon? Want to show those glamour boys in Homicide that you're a glamour boy too?'

Rath wasn't about to let himself be intimidated. Böhm distributing the photos gave him an excuse to continue investigating Boris's death. 'The commissioner has officially requested that we support A Division in their efforts to solve a particular case,' he said, alarmed by how bureaucratic he sounded. 'And that is precisely what I intend to do. No more, no less.'

'You don't have to prove anything to me, Gereon. You've already shown that you're a good cop, and it's my assessment that goes into your personal file.' Wolter gave a brief pause before uttering his next sentence. 'Or is it that sweet little stenographer you're trying to impress? In which case I'm afraid I can't help you.'

That hit him like a blow to the solar plexus. Inside, Rath had to gasp for air. Why did Bruno want to hurt him? Because he felt hurt himself? Because he sensed that a colleague whom he had to come to appreciate in a short space of time, felt drawn towards the other side of the glass doors? He had probably experienced that all too many times before.

'Look at the facts, Bruno,' he said. 'If I can help solve a murder inquiry, then I will. You can't ask me to defy the instructions of the commissioner.'

'I only ask that you place yourself fully at the disposal of E Division. What do you think is going to happen if you help Böhm with that stupid corpse of his? You'll do well to get a thank you! He'll take your information and use it to solve the case and it'll be him Dörrzwiebel pats on the shoulder.'

Bruno was probably right, but Rath had no intention of helping Böhm. He just had to be careful that he didn't put Bruno's nose out of joint. 'The commissioner's orders apply to everyone.' He was already behaving like his father, hiding behind official regulations when he didn't want to give anything away.

'Not so formal, my boy. As long as you are committed to our work you can do as you please. Just don't forget who you're working for. If I think you're confusing the letters E and A too often, I might not be so willing to stick my broad shoulders between you and Lanke.'

'Do you have any complaints? We're about to raid a heap of illegal nightclubs. That's something, isn't it? Lanke I can deal with on my own.'

Wolter laughed. 'Lanke? No-one should pick a fight with him without back-up. He's more dangerous than a pimp who's had his car scratched!' Uncle proffered his hand. 'Come on, let's forget about it. I'm just a little overworked at the moment. We shouldn't be arguing.'

Rath hesitated for a moment, but the furrows on Wolter's brow had vanished almost as soon as they had appeared.

'Actually, I wanted to ask you round,' Uncle continued. 'I'm entertaining a few friends at my place tomorrow, and it would be great if you could make it.'

It was the evening he had reserved for Charlotte, but he couldn't tell Bruno that yet. The invitation was an attempt at reconciliation, he had to accept and he wanted to accept. Bruno had called him a friend and he needed friends. He'd have to put Charlotte off.

'Wednesday evening? That should be fine, as long as I don't have to do any overtime. I have a strict boss.'

'No overtime on Wednesday. We'll do it tonight. What we don't get done on Wednesday, we'll work off on Friday!'

13

It was already dark when he stepped onto the small forecourt at Friedenau station, but the streets in this neighbourhood were well lit and already it felt different from *Schlesischer Bahnhof.* He couldn't help thinking of his visit to *Plaza*. He would try one more time. He had spoken to Gloria again yesterday evening before heading home and falling exhausted into bed. 'If he wants to talk to you, then he'll talk to you,' she had said, almost a little insulted. 'If not, then there's nothing you can do.'

Bruno had made them work overtime yesterday as well as on Monday, but he had been true to his word and sent them home at five today. They had got a lot done, but would have to work on the public holiday tomorrow. Still, there was no reason why Rath shouldn't leave the office promptly and go out. First to the cinema, then to eat, and after that perhaps to dance. With Charlotte.

He had spent Monday searching all over the Castle for her. Discreetly, of course, as he couldn't just march into A Division, but he had taken every opportunity to get out of the office. He had looked in Aschinger and the canteen, and on several occasions lingered in the corridor outside the glass doors of Homicide. When he returned home late that evening, he hadn't even seen her, let alone spoken to her, but an idea had come to him as he gazed at the telephone next to his bed. CID officers like him had to be available, and they all had a telephone line. She was only a stenographer, but she was ambitious. There must be a tiny chance, even if he didn't really believe it. He leafed through the telephone directory and came across an entry. *Ritter, C., Spenerstrasse 32, NW HANSA 3919.* Perhaps he'd be in luck. He waited to be put through, praying that it wouldn't be a Carl or a Christian on the other end of the line.

'Overbeck,' a woman's voice answered.

Wrong number? He almost hung up instinctively, but recovered himself.

'Good evening, Inspector Rath here. Please excuse me for disturbing you so late, but is Fräulein Charlotte Ritter . . .'

'As long as the station calls before midnight, it isn't late—that much I've learned by now. Wait a moment.'

The receiver was placed next to the cradle.

'Charly,' he heard the woman shout. 'Telephone for you. The station!'

He heard the slamming of doors, steps, and a loud clatter as she picked up the receiver.

'Böhm?' It was her voice. 'Böhm, is that you?'

'No, Rath here.'

A pause. 'Oh!?'

He had managed to surprise her at any rate.

'Good evening, Inspector,' she said, 'I do hope you're not trying to rope me into one of E Division's operations.'

'No, it's a private matter.'

'About arrangements for Wednesday evening?'

So, she hadn't forgotten their vague plans to meet.

'No,' he said, 'it's about arrangements for Thursday evening.'

Another pause. Exactly as he had feared. 'I could only get tickets for Thursday.'

'Tickets?'

She was curious.

'*Phoebus Palace.*'

'A cinema? There were only tickets for the public holiday?'

'The cinema in *Europahaus*. Not so easy to get tickets there. Besides, there's a little extra into the bargain. I've reserved a table in the *Europa-Pavillon.*'

He didn't know if she had really swallowed his lie, or if she was even free on Thursday. 'So, what's on at the cinema?' she replied.

It wasn't far to the Wolters's house from the station. Fregestrasse, a quiet street, was lined with trees, the houses solidly middle-class. Rath was reminded of Klettenberg in Cologne. Rath recognised Bruno's Ford, as well as a large Horch and even a Maybach. Walking through a small front garden he straightened his jacket, rang the bell and looked upwards. A nice two-storey house, not a villa but hardly a shack, and the only detached house here as far as he could see. A woman opened the door. Rath recognised her face from the photograph on Bruno's desk.

'Good evening, Frau Wolter.' He presented her with a bouquet of flowers.

'Thank you! You must be Herr Rath? Bruno has told me a lot about you.'

He entered and looked around. The flat was generously proportioned. A flight of stairs led to the top floor. There were lots of coats hanging on the coat stand, amongst them two *Reichswehr* jackets, and he could hear a babble of voices and the clinking of glasses from further inside.

'Let me take your hat and coat,' Emmi Wolter said.

'Thank you.'

'Just follow the noise. Your colleague, young Herr Jänicke, is here as well.'

The rookie too? Jänicke's relationship with Bruno wasn't exactly friendly, but Uncle wouldn't want to exclude the third member of their team.

Emmi Wolter rushed ahead of him and opened the door. 'Please. Let me just put these flowers in water. What can I get you?'

'A cognac, please.'

Thick cigarette smoke hung in the air in the large drawing room. A dozen men were present. *A few friends.* He couldn't see Stephan, but Bruno was standing next to two *Reichswehr* officers and a serious looking civilian. When he caught sight of Rath, his face brightened.

'Gereon! Good of you to come.'

'You don't often get the opportunity to polish off a colleague's supplies.'

'Stephan is here too, but I've no idea where he's lurking.' He led him towards the three men with whom he had been speaking. 'Gentlemen, may I introduce my most trusted colleague, Detective Inspector Gereon Rath?'

Rath gave a brief nod. Wolter continued with the introductions.

'Major General Alfred Seegers . . .' A grey-haired man with thin lips and a gaunt face made a bow. '. . . Senior Lieutenant Werner Fröhlich . . .' A blond man in his mid-forties saluted with his cognac glass. 'And this is Paul Geitner,' Wolter introduced the civilian last. Pinned to Geitner's lapel was a sparkling red-white button with a black swastika. 'All former comrades-in-arms. War welds people together. Unfortunately, Helmut Behnke is missing. He was one of us too.'

'Did you serve, Inspector?' Seegers asked. A Prussian from the old school, he reminded Rath of his father.

'Yes, but not on the Front. The war was over before I received my marching orders.'

'So many young men ready to fight. We could have won if those November criminals hadn't stabbed us in the back!'

Rath was familiar with these pronouncements. In Nationalist circles, they were seen as good form. For his part, he was happy not to have been used as cannon fodder, but he couldn't say that here.

'Things are going to look up soon,' said Wolter. 'Ah! Thank you, Emmi.'

Emmi Wolter had appeared with a cognac glass, which she presented to Rath, who had no desire to talk about the lost war.

'To our host,' he said.

'To the best marksman the German army ever had,' seconded the gaunt Major General. The men clinked glasses.

Seegers took him to one side. 'Were you part of the operation against the communists?'

Rath nodded.

'The one time the social democrats try to take decisive action, it goes sour.' Seegers shook his head. 'Bruno told me everything.' The officer clapped him on the shoulder. 'No offence meant, young man, I'm not attacking you. Orders are orders, it's your superiors that failed. The social democrats just aren't capable.'

'At least they've banned the RFB now.'

'Good joke, isn't it! The Reds are laughing up their sleeves! Those social democrats aren't even capable of raiding a single arms cache, but they think they can maintain control with a ban. It's laughable! The Red Front had illegal arms caches before the ban. They'll have them still.'

'I don't think the commies are ready for a revolution. They'd like to be, but really they're a bunch of undisciplined layabouts.'

Seegers laughed. 'I like you, young man. A bunch of layabouts, indeed! But for how long? The red army has capable officers, and Moscow is supporting the German Red Front to the best of its ability! If the gold that everyone's after at the moment falls into the wrong hands, then good night. The Reds will be able to afford weapons that your police can't possibly hope to compete with and, with our miserable force of one hundred thousand men, we'll be powerless too.'

'What gold?'

'Does the name Sorokin mean anything to you?'

'Should it?'

'Ancient Russian nobility. Provided generations of officers for the Tsar's army.' Seegers produced a small, silver case from his uniform jacket and opened the cover. 'Would you like one?'

Rath took a cigarette. Seegers gave him a light and lit one for himself.

'The last generation deserted the Tsar and switched allegiance to Kerenski.' Seegers breathed smoke in greedily, like a vampire sucking blood. 'Not that the Bolsheviks cared. They bumped off the liberals just as they did the monarchists and only a handful of Sorokins managed to escape, forced to leave their legendary hoard behind. The Reds searched every inch of the Sorokin castles before turning them into barracks and factories, but found nothing.' He paused, his silence pregnant with meaning. 'They say it's turned up again!'

'Stalin will be pleased.'

'Wrong, young man!' Seegers waved his hand dismissively. 'Stalin is beside himself. Gold worth around eighty million *Reichsmark* is alleged to have been smuggled out of the country. Do you know to where?'

Rath had no idea and shrugged his shoulders.

'The rumour is that the Sorokin gold is in Berlin!'

'Eighty million? That's an incredible sum!'

Seegers nodded. 'That's why Stalin is so afraid. Especially now, after sending Trotsky into the wilderness. He's worried the money could be invested in counter revolution. I wouldn't put it past the Sorokins. Stalin is counting on the worst. Why do you think there are so many Chekists in Berlin at the minute? Thälmann's people are helping them with the search—in the hope that they get a piece of the action too.'

'How do you know all this?'

'In the *Reichswehr* one hears things.' Seegers cracked a grin and winked, looking grotesque, as if his gaunt face couldn't deal with so much expression at once.

'And the communists are after this gold?'

'Everyone who knows about it is after it. The word is the courier buckled and kept everything for himself. At any rate, it didn't arrive where it was supposed to arrive.'

'With the Sorokins?'

'Or their political allies. People say the liberal Sorokins have joined forces with *Krasnaja Krepost*, to snatch power from Stalin.'

'With who?'

'*Krasnaja Krepost*. It means something like 'red fortress'. Communist dissenters. Like Trotsky. Perhaps he's involved in it too, and that man can assemble an army.'

'Why are you telling me all this?'

'Because it's about Germany's future, young man. You were a soldier. We are comrades-in-arms! This gold cannot be allowed to fall into the wrong hands.'

'Why hasn't the *Reichswehr* reported this to the political police?'

'In this matter, there are no reports. Nothing official. People in the police whom we trust can be informed, but the political police, as an apparatus, must never learn of this affair. Do you understand? I've told you in confidence as well. A friend of Bruno is a friend of mine.'

'I'm honoured by your trust.'

'It's not just a question of trust, young man, it's a question of comradeship. The German *Reich* is only permitted one hundred thousand soldiers. Laughable! But there are many men who are good soldiers, even if they don't wear the field grey uniform. Germany needs good soldiers, and a good police officer is always a good soldier too. The police and the *Reichswehr* should stick together in matters that concern Germany.'

'I think you've come to the wrong man. For me police officer and soldier are two very different things. I should know, I've been both.' It was about time he gave this officer a piece of his mind. Rath had bitten his tongue because he wanted to hear Seegers's conspiracy theory to the end. 'I became a police officer to help maintain law and order and ensure the streets are safe, not to play soldiers or war, and certainly not civil war.'

Seegers raised his hands in appeasement. 'I didn't mean to offend you, young man. No-one wants war, but Germany has many enemies and if they want war then we should be forearmed. I am certain that when the Fatherland calls to arms, you will answer that call too. Once a soldier, always a soldier. You're a soldier, my friend, there's no point denying it, and we need people like you!'

Rath spotted Stephan Jänicke in the room next door. 'You'll excuse me,' he said to Seegers, 'but I need to go and say hello to a colleague.'

'Just have a think about what I said,' Seegers called after him.

Rath went over to the rookie, who was standing in the room with his glass, looking a little lost.

'Hello, Gereon!' Jänicke was relieved to see him.

Rath toasted his health. 'Dear old Bruno still seems to be very attached to his army days.'

'Yes, a whole lot of soldiers. Or at least former soldiers,' Jänicke said. 'Must be to do with his age.'

'Just old comrades. I'm afraid we don't quite fit.'

'*You* were a soldier, Gereon.' It sounded as if Jänicke regretted not having been part of the war.

'I did the basic training, and then it was over. I was lucky.'

Emmi Wolter came round with a tray. Rath reached for a devilled egg. 'Where were you the whole time?' he asked. 'We were worried about you. Almost got Missing Persons involved. You didn't get lost, did you?'

Jänicke seemed embarrassed. 'Isn't so easy to find the toilet in this house. It was engaged below, so I came upstairs.'

Emmi Wolter laughed and the eggs on the tray wobbled. 'Just imagine, I found Herr Jänicke up here groping helplessly in the dark, searching for a light! And to think the bathroom was just behind the next door!'

Jänicke blushed red. 'Well, it is rather a big flat.'

'Yes, we even have two bathrooms,' Emmi Wolter said, not without pride.

'Then the chances of finding one should be even greater,' Rath said.

The lady of the house giggled. 'Bruno said you had a sense of humour. I hope you're having a good time.' She lowered her voice. 'Sometimes Bruno's friends talk a little too much about the war.'

'That's OK,' Rath said. 'We're happy here.'

'If you want to speak to a colleague of yours, Bruno always invites Rudi Scheer along too. The only policeman who comes here regularly, for years at that. Bruno's other colleagues come and go, but he's always had a good relationship with Rudi.'

Scheer? There was no-one by that name in E Division.

'He's responsible for the armoury,' she continued. 'The pair of them used to work together. Should I introduce you?'

The armoury. Parabellum Wolter. Of course. He still hadn't asked Bruno how he, the marksman, had ended up in Vice.

'That's very kind of you, but I'm a little short on time. I just wanted to look in quickly. We're back on duty tomorrow, and need to be well rested.' Jänicke nodded in agreement. 'We have a strict boss!'

She laughed. 'What a shame, but I understand. Work is work. That's what Bruno always says when he makes himself scarce. You must come and see us again, both you and your colleague.'

'I promise,' Rath said.

Wolter didn't seem disappointed when his two colleagues took their leave a few minutes later. The slight redness in his cheeks betrayed the alcohol level in his blood. He clapped them jovially on the shoulders as his wife led them out.

'Phew,' Rath said, as he and Jänicke made their way towards Friedenau station. 'Bruno's old friends! You'd never believe there were so many soldiers. Especially when the *Reichswehr* is only allowed one hundred thousand men.'

'It's more than that. Police are soldiers too.'

Rath stopped short. 'Sorry?'

'It was suggested to me this evening that the police and the *Reichswehr* should work more closely together. Unofficially, of course.'

'Major General Seegers?'

Jänicke nodded.

'He was probably on a recruitment drive. He put the moves on me too.'

'Do you think Bruno's working for the *Reichswehr* in an unofficial capacity?'

Rath shrugged. 'I can't imagine that. He just has too many friends in the army, indulging their reminiscences of the old days. Seegers was drunk, that's all. They told me something about a Russian hoard of gold that's gone missing in Berlin and that the commies are supposedly trying to pinch. Worth eighty million, he said. What a load of rubbish. You can't smuggle that much gold from Russia to Berlin unnoticed.'

Jänicke raised his eyebrows but said nothing as the men proceeded towards the red-brick building of the little station.

14

He had hardly slept and yet he was in the best of spirits when he entered the office on Thursday morning. With a tune on his lips that he barely recognised himself, he flung his hat in the direction of the hat stand, and landed it. Jänicke whistled appreciatively through his teeth.

'Where did you learn to do that?'

'You either can or you can't.' Rath took off his coat. 'Bruno not here yet?'

Jänicke gave a shake of the head. 'I think the party yesterday was too much for him.'

Schmittchen, their secretary, had already brewed coffee. From the outer office they could hear the incessant clattering of her typewriter. Ratatata—quick as a machine gun. Any number of official requests and judicial rulings were still necessary before the raids on Saturday. She had to work through the public holiday too.

'Before I forget, someone just rang. He only wanted to speak to you or Bruno though,' Jänicke said.

'And?'

'I tried to take down his number, but he said it was nothing to do with me. He said he'd ring later.'

Right on cue, the telephone on Rath's desk sounded.

'That'll be him,' Jänicke said.

Rath picked up. It was Wolter. He mumbled something about coming in later and gave a few terse instructions. Rath had only just hung up when the phone rang again.

Rath recognised the voice straightaway. Franz Krajewski.

'Bit early for you to be up and about, isn't it?' he asked the porn Kaiser. 'On Father's Day too.'

'I can't talk for long, but I need to speak to you. If you could do me a favour, then I have some information that might interest you.'

'I've already done you a favour, haven't I?' Rath tried to sound as innocent as possible, as if he were speaking to a girlfriend. Jänicke couldn't find out who he had on the other end of the line.

'I could really use another.'

'Why should I?'

'Just listen to what I have to say.' Krajewski's voice grew softer. 'You're still looking for these films, right? If you want to attend a screening . . .'

Rath pricked up his ears. 'I still haven't had breakfast,' he said. 'Perhaps we could get a bite to eat.'

'Just don't come to Neukölln!' His voice sounded alarmed, even though it came very softly through the receiver.

'I wasn't intending to pay you a visit. We're going out.'

'But not to Alex. Too many people know me there.' Krajewski was still whispering. It was hard to understand him. 'The *Grinzing* in *Haus Vaterland*. It's only tourists who go there.'

Rath could be there in quarter of an hour on the underground.

'Half eight?'

'Half eight, and you're paying!'

'I'll decide that after the meal.'

He hung up and reached for his hat and coat.

Jänicke looked up in surprise. 'That was a fleeting appearance.'

'Already forgotten today's a holiday? If Uncle comes, tell him I'm out and about. Just need to check something.' He gave a conspiratorial wink, exactly the kind he couldn't bear seeing from Weinert. Let the rookie think he was meeting a woman. 'Be back in an hour or two.'

Haus Vaterland was an enormous pleasure dome near Potsdamer Platz. Everything under one roof: a large cinema, several pubs and restaurants, everything from a Turkish café to a Wild West themed bar. Berliners tended to avoid *Vaterland* but there was still an unbelievable whoopla there every night. Rath remembered how he had spent his first evening in Berlin at *Rheinterrasse* in *Vaterland*—they didn't even have Kölsch, just wine that was far too sweet and vinous older women on the hunt for single men. A sobering evening; he hadn't been back to *Haus Vaterland* since.

There wasn't a lot going on here in the mornings, but at least at this hour Rath wasn't obliged to fork out to enter the complex. In the evenings that was standard here. The tourists were always flabbergasted when they had to pay again at the cinema box office. The *Grinzing* was trying to look like a Viennese Heuriger, and less like a coffee house. Artificial greenery crept up the walls, while Chinese lanterns hung from the ceiling. When Rath entered, Franz Krajewski was already sitting at a white covered table, before him a cup of coffee and a glass of white wine. The man was drawing nervously on his cigarette. Rath sat down and placed his hat on the table, not intending to stay long.

'Starting at breakfast time?' he asked.

Krajewski gave a forced smile. 'Always a joke at the ready, your local bobby!' He fell silent for a moment before continuing. 'I need a favour,' he said. Rath's silence made Krajewski nervous. He continued talking. 'People are saying there's something up. You're planning something big, am I right?'

It was astonishing how fast the bush telegraph worked in this city. Word of the planned raid must have trickled through from a leak at the Castle.

'Who's the informant here? That's not how this works, you should know that by now. You tell me something and then maybe I'll be in such a good mood that I pay for your breakfast.'

'I know how it works, and I am going to tell you something. I just don't fancy getting picked up by one of your colleagues. I ain't much use to you in the can.'

Rath said nothing. His hands played with the small calibre projectile he had fetched from his pocket.

Krajewski raised his hands in appeasement. 'OK, you're the boss. But you should have a think about what I've said.' He fell silent as a waiter approached their table to take Rath's order. He didn't continue until they were alone again. 'If you want to see an interesting cinema performance: *Sonnabend*, at twelve.' He leaned in and spoke even more softly. '*Pille,* a secret cellar bar in Motzstrasse, just by Nollendorfplatz. There's a back room there, that's where the fun'll be.'

Rath put the bullet back in his pocket. 'Sounds good. If you're talking shit, there'll be trouble. If I don't find anything I'll assume you've stitched us up, do you understand?'

Krajewski nodded. The waiter came and placed a cup of coffee and a glass of water on the table. Rath pushed the photos that he always carried across the table.

'Do me another favour?' he said. 'Do you recognise either of these men?'

Krajewski grabbed the picture of the dead man. 'He was in the paper, right?'

Rath nodded.

'No idea, only place I've seen him.'

'And him?' Rath gestured towards the photo of Kardakov.

'Hmm . . .' Krajewski furrowed his brow. 'Looks familiar. What's he supposed to have done?'

'He deals coke.'

Krajewski shook his head. 'Then I don't know him. Must've been thinking of someone else.' He passed the photos back to Rath and downed his glass. 'Who's paying, then? I need to know if I can order something else.'

'You can choose. Either I do you a favour or I pay your bill.'

Krajewski considered for a moment only. 'Favour it is then.'

'Good.' Rath stood up and put on his hat. 'Then a little tip. Stay home at the weekend.'

He'd been hit by something. Without knowing how it had happened, he found himself back on the ground; every bone in his body was aching. He felt as if he had been run over by an express train, only they didn't operate on the first floor of the police station. Clearly it was a person.

'Can't you look where you're going?'

He recognised the voice. It was worse than an express train. Rath looked up. Correct! DCI Böhm.

The homicide detective stood firm as a German oak on the grey stone floor; Rath on the other hand was lying supine. Having almost fallen back down the stairs he was holding his aching shoulder. Admittedly, he had hurried up the stairs rather quickly, a little giddily even. Krajewski's tip-off had given wing to his steps. It had come at just the right time and dovetailed perfectly with their plans for Saturday. He sensed today was going to be a good day, and now this. He had just made it to the half landing when the door that led from the stairwell to the corridor had hit him like a ton of bricks, landing him face up on the floor.

'Use your eyes, man! You almost knocked me over!'

Rath didn't say anything. His hat had rolled off his head and the photos had fallen out of his pocket. He gathered everything back up.

'Aren't you going to say anything to me?' Böhm asked. He narrowed his eyes.

Rath struggled to his feet and placed his hat back on his head. 'Me? If you'll pardon my saying so DCI Böhm, it's *you* who should be apologising,' he said, going on the counter-attack.

Böhm hadn't been listening. 'If you know something about that dead man you've just returned to your pocket, then you should tell me,' he said simply.

Rath smoothed down his suit and fell silent.

'You could start by telling me who that was staring up at me?'

The son of a bitch had seen Kardakov too. Did he also know that Charlotte had met him at the Landwehr canal? Rath had to take care that Böhm didn't become too suspicious, which wasn't so easy. Being suspicious was part and parcel of the job, and Böhm was suspicion personified.

'An E Division investigation,' he said. 'A cocaine dealer, with a possible connection to a porn ring.' That was the link he'd come up with in case he needed to explain why he was investigating a case that was outside his remit. The solution to the Landwehr canal murder as a by-product of the pornography investigation, so to speak. It was the coke which allowed the link to be constructed. 'We've got things to do too,' he continued. 'You mustn't think we're all scrambling to help Homicide.' He took the picture of Boris from his pocket, staying on the offensive. 'I know colleagues who have thrown this photo away. You should be happy I'm supporting A Division.'

Böhm looked even grumpier.

'Fine,' he said at length. 'But my joy will be somewhat confined if you're only carrying this photo around, and I don't hear from you. Let me make one thing clear, if you have something to say to me, then say it. I don't like it when people move in on my territory.'

Rath took an Overstolz from the packet, unmoved. Just stay cool. The obnoxious fool couldn't know anything. Böhm took every opportunity to rant at subordinates.

'Have I made myself clear, Inspector?'

'Yes, Detective Chief Inspector, sir!' Rath lit his cigarette and inhaled. He didn't exhale until Böhm passed him and was crashing down the stairs.

———

She was happy to leave a little earlier today. The atmosphere in Homicide wasn't the best. Böhm wasn't making any headway, his mood was deteriorating and it was nothing to do with working the holiday shift. The way he had stormed out of the office just now! Like a steamroller. She knew that her boss had a choleric streak, but usually they got on fine together. He accepted her, and she gave him credit for that. Still, for the moment it was best not to tangle with him. With him outside, the atmosphere was more relaxed. Gräf, who had been crouched behind his desk as if ducking to evade a series of blows, sat up straight and inhaled deeply.

She thought about the evening. She didn't want to wear the green dress. It brought bad luck. Thursday again. Exactly a week ago her last date had ended in sublime failure. Yesterday was the first time she had gone out since her abortive evening in *Moka Efti*. With Greta. They had talked about men all evening and agreed on one thing. You shouldn't get involved with guys who couldn't accept you as a working woman. That she had already arranged to meet someone else was something she hadn't told Greta. In fact, she hadn't told her anything about the newbie at the station. Probably because she felt guilty about meeting another man so soon after the disaster in *Efti*. And one from the Castle at that. But Greta didn't have to know everything, did she?

It was good that he'd already been here for half an hour and bought tickets early. It was getting full inside *Phoebus Palace*, almost as if the crowd was bearing out his telephone lie about the difficulty in acquiring tickets. While people pressed inside, Rath stood at the showcases examining the publicity photos. Gustav Fröhlich as a cop and a woman who reminded him vaguely of Charlotte, only that she was far more done-up. But that's just the way it was in film; even the men wore lipstick. Even if they were playing a cop. He couldn't help but grin as he imagined all the hard-boiled cops from Alex with their lips painted red.

The film was called *Asphalt*, a police drama. He hadn't known what was on when he invited Charlotte to the cinema. *Phoebus Palace* had presented itself solely because of its proximity to the *Europa-Pavillon*. Both were housed in the new complex inside *Europahaus*. So much the better that it was a film about police officers, although it looked more like a slushy romance than a crime thriller. The film was due to start in five minutes, but there was still no sign of her.

The noise around him grew ever more lively. Besides the cinema, *Europahaus* was home to several restaurants, cafés and dance halls. Almost like in *Haus Vaterland*, only that it was less of a racket here, since the various restaurateurs were competing against one another, as opposed to in *Vaterland* where everything had a single operator. A skyscraper was set to crown the whole complex at *Anhalter Bahnhof*, but for the time being it only existed on paper. The Department of Building Regulations had only recently granted planning permission, after the architect had reduced the number of floors to ten.

Below, in the parts of the building that had already been completed, business was booming. *Europahaus* had the reputation of being sophisticated and metropolitan and was correspondingly popular with Berliners, who heralded anything that cemented the capital's reputation as a world city.

Then he saw her climbing out of a taxi on the other side of Königgrätzer Strasse, wearing a short coat and a red skirt. He waved and could almost have embraced the nearest passer-by out of joy when she smiled as she spotted him.

The evening wouldn't be cheap for him, of that she was certain. She was enormously hungry as she entered *Europa-Pavillon* on his arm, and the waiter led them to their table. The film had lasted an hour and a half and by the end she had been hoping that her stomach wouldn't rumble during the performance. Fortunately, the band had been playing pretty loud. He hadn't tried to exploit the darkness to take her in his arms or kiss her a single time. He wasn't one of those types. If he was, she would have passed on dinner, no matter how hungry she was. But this way, there was nothing to prevent them from spending a pleasant evening.

She liked the *Europa-Pavillon* too. The restaurant and dance hall were spread across two floors with orange-gold the dominant colour, interspersed with silver ornaments, the furniture mahogany. The waiter led them upstairs to the gallery. She was wearing the red skirt that, until now, she had only worn to work. He shouldn't go thinking she had dressed up for him. Nevertheless, Greta had caught her carefully applying her make-up and checking in the mirror to see how it showed off her legs. Her friend hadn't said anything, but a pair of raised eyebrows had given her to understand that she owed Greta an explanation.

The waiter showed them to a table next to the balustrade. From there they could look down on the dance floor, upon which several couples were already swaying. She liked the music, a brisk swing, and it was only the singer that struck her as overly schmaltzy. The waiter returned to their table with two menus and two glasses of *Heidsieck Monopole*.

'I took the liberty of ordering us something to drink,' Rath said and raised his glass. So that was why he had been whispering to the waiter before.

She smiled nervously as she toasted his health. She had liked his twinkling grey-blue eyes from the start, right from the very first time he had happened upon her at the Castle. She surveyed his appearance. Elegant—even if he was wearing a brown suit he could have worn to work, indeed probably had worn to work. Just like her and her red skirt. They could have set off right away and started investigating. Instead they were perusing the menu.

The waiter came with the wine and took their order. They decided on the fish.

'I lied to you,' she said, once the man in tails had departed again. 'My story isn't half as long as I said. I just wanted to have dinner.'

'In that case you'd better hope I don't call in Fraud Squad.'

'Please, no!' She raised her hands in mock horror. 'I'll tell you everything, Inspector. Only I'm afraid that *everything* isn't very much at all.' She took a sip of wine. 'Born and bred in Berlin. Moabit to be precise, right next to the criminal court. Something like that leaves its mark: I've been working for CID for four years now as a stenographer, but I wouldn't like to do it for the rest of my life.'

'What would you do instead?'

'I'm studying Law.'

He whistled appreciatively through his teeth. 'Do you want to be a senior civil servant?'

'We'll see. I do think there aren't enough female CID officers.'

'How do you combine the two?' he asked. 'The work and the studying, I mean.'

'I only work for Homicide from Thursday until Sunday, that's what we've agreed. So I don't complain when I have to work late or go out into the field.'

'Most murders happen at the weekend.'

'Tell me something I don't know.'

'And you have to clock in every weekend?'

'Most of the time. The others are happy if they can get out of a weekend shift.'

'Then you can't have much free time.'

'Not at the moment. I save my free time activities for the evening.'

'So long as A Division doesn't call.'

'Right.'

He raised his glass. 'Let's drink to Böhm having mislaid your phone number, at least for tonight.'

They clinked glasses for a second time. The waiter came with the food and they were silent for a time.

'You still haven't told me how you ended up in Vice? Did you fall in love with a jewel thief you were supposed to be bringing in?'

That was what had happened to the cop in the film just now. He had then killed her gangster boyfriend. In the end the jewel thief had saved her beloved cop by confessing, and had gone to jail for him. Pretty far-fetched, but good fun nevertheless. It just didn't have much to do with normal police work.

He didn't seem to think so either. 'Chance would be a fine thing,' he said. 'But the reality is less romantic. I wanted to come to Berlin and there was nothing else available at Alex.'

'Where have you come from then?'

He looked at her in astonishment. 'Don't tell me you can't hear it.'

'The Rhineland?'

'And there was me hoping I'd got rid of my accent. I've even caught myself imitating the Berliners.'

'Actually I wanted to know what unit you used to work in.'

'Everything from grievous bodily harm to Homicide.'

She was astonished. A detective who had already worked in Homicide had willingly transferred to Vice because he wanted to come to Berlin? It wasn't something everyone would have done. She resumed her eating in silence, deep in thought.

'Why did you want to join the police?' he asked.

'Because there are too few women in this job, and because I've got something against people who think they can do whatever they want and get away scot free.' She hadn't needed long to consider. 'But actually it's not yet guaranteed that I'll become a police officer. I need to study first,' she added quickly.

He nodded seriously. 'You're right. There's nothing worse than having to close the file on an unsolved case.'

'Yes. Luckily we don't have too many wet fish under Gennat.' That was what they called unsolved cases at the Castle. He seemed to know the expression. 'A Division has an extremely high detection rate,' she added, and could have bitten her tongue in the same instant.

'In that case, our colleague DCI Böhm is currently skewing the statistics,' he said. 'When I saw him in the conference room on Monday, I had the impression that this wet corpse was threatening to become a wet fish.'

She nodded. 'True. It's not looking good. I came back today after a three day break, and the investigation hadn't progressed since Sunday. That doesn't happen often.'

'Do you have any idea who the dead man might be?'

She shook her head. 'We've been through every missing person's file since 1927, we've asked all residents several times, almost all the papers have printed his picture, and yet, apart from the usual idiots, no-one has been in touch. It is pretty strange that no-one knew the deceased.'

He nodded. 'Scarcely credible. A dead man's found in a city of four million, and not one of those four million has seen him before in their lives.'

'Someone must have seen him.'

'You mean the killer?'

'Exactly. But he's not going to get in touch, is he?'

'And you've got nothing at all to go on?'

'If you've worked in Homicide before, then you'll know what it means to have an unidentified corpse. Normally you look for the perpetrator in the victim's immediate circle: friends, enemies, family, business partners. Only, how are we supposed to do that if we don't even know who it is that's died?'

'And you don't have any other leads?'

'We barely have anything. The man was wearing an expensive suit, no-one knows him and he has lousy teeth. He was driving an expensive car, but it was stolen. He was tortured and died of a heroin overdose. He had already been dead for eight to ten hours when the car went into the canal. Someone wedged the accelerator with a metal rod. Curiously enough with the steering rod of an Opel. None of it hangs together.'

'Do you like your boss?'

'Böhm?' she shrugged her shoulders. 'What do you mean, like? He isn't as grumpy as he makes out.'

'Every division's supposed to be helping Homicide solve this case. Was that his idea?'

'Of course not. That comes from Zörgiebel himself. He wants to see results soon, and sometimes mass actions like this can help, although the press appeal has been a disaster up until now. There's a 500 mark reward set aside from the public purse for information.'

'So that's how the social democrats go about spending our taxes?'

'I take it you're not a party member?'

He shook his head. 'Don't talk to me about politics. Working for 1A is the only thing worse than Vice. They even spy on their own colleagues.'

The waiter cleared away their food.

'I never even thanked you for the invitation,' she said, and took a Juno from the packet.

He gave her a light and gazed briefly into her eyes. She felt a slight tingling sensation.

'Thanks for your company,' he said, and lit a cigarette for himself. 'You're the nicest person I've met so far at the Castle.'

'Hardly a difficult competition to win right now. You're not exactly flavour of the month. People say you've been crawling up Zörgiebel's backside and that's the reason the commissioner is protecting you.'

'Protecting me? Is that a joke? Is that why I'm working in Vice?'

She waved her hand dismissively. 'I'm just telling you what people are saying in the canteen. It was probably Lanke who started the rumour. He wanted to reinstall his nephew in the position that you are currently occupying. It's your fault he's still stewing in Köpenick.'

'Köpenick? Has he fallen out of favour?'

'I don't think young Lanke has ever been in favour. He came to Alex fresh from police academy five years ago and started messing things up right away. By now the dust has settled and Lanke wants him back. He had even agreed it with Dörrzwiebel, but then you came along.'

'Not even Bruno's told me anything about that.'

'Wolter? Of course not. At the Castle you hear everything. Unless it's about you. But believe me, Wolter is happy that Lanke Junior's passed him by. He must have welcomed you with open arms, am I right?'

'And why are you telling *me* all this?'

During dinner he watched the band playing one floor below with no female singer. If anybody sang, then it was Ilja Tretschkov himself. He was better at playing the trumpet. The band leader seemed to have split from Lana Nikoros, or she had split from the band. That much, at least, he still wanted to ask Tretschkov.

Straight after dinner he had led Charlotte onto the dance floor. She was a good dancer, but the look in her eyes was confusing him. He had to make sure he didn't forget why he was here. The *other reason* he was here. They had been in the *Europa-Pavillon* for over two hours and the band had been playing uninterrupted the whole time. Only now were they taking a break. The dancers applauded as the musicians took their bows. A café violinist filled the break in the music with a few schmaltzy numbers, but no-one paid him any attention. The audience were more interested in Tretschkov's musicians, who had made a beeline for the bar.

He led Charlotte back to their table. The bottle of champagne in the cooler was almost empty. He waved the waiter over and ordered another, excused himself and disappeared in the direction of the toilets. Just before the toilet door, he swerved towards the bar. She couldn't see him anymore, despite her excellent position in the gallery.

Ilja Tretschkov was sitting at a table with his musicians, in front of him a large beer that was already half finished. Rath showed his badge discreetly, so that only Tretschkov could see.

'I need to speak to you for a moment,' he said. 'Preferably in private.'

Tretschkov stood up. They found a seat in a quiet corner by the bar.

'My papers are in order,' the musician said before he sat down. His German was almost accentless.

'It's not about you. It's about a singer. Lana Nikoros.'

'Have you found her?'

'How do you mean?'

'So you haven't. Probably wouldn't be good if the police found her.' His face alternated between hope and disappointment. 'I'm worried about her. After we had to leave the *Delphi*, she just didn't show up anymore. Even though she knew we had a new engagement'.

'What do you mean she didn't show up?'

'We've been playing in *Europa-Pavillon* for two weeks. Before that we practised here a few times. She knew the dates but didn't turn up. She's never done that before, and we've been working together nearly two years.'

'Have you tried to contact her?'

'Of course, but it was hopeless. You've probably already been in her flat too. Almost everything's still there, it's only her that's missing. And a few things besides. As if she's gone away somewhere.'

'You've been in her flat.'

'In Kreuzberg. Luisenufer. I have a key.'

Rath nodded. He could have bet that he knew the number.

'It's not what you think,' Tretschkov was quick to explain. 'We're colleagues and friends.'

'Luisenufer,' Rath repeated. 'But she doesn't live there under the name Lana Nikoros . . .'

'No, that's her stage name. Her real name is Sorokin. Countess Svetlana Sorokina. A famous name in Russia . . .'

The Sorokin gold! Rath could scarcely believe it. *Lana Nikoros was one of the Sorokin clan. The girlfriend of Alexej Kardakov!*

The musician continued: '. . . and that's why she's living incognito in Berlin, that's why there's a common name on the door of her flat. Otherwise the Soviets would have discovered her long ago.' It sounded as if that was what he feared had happened.

'What does Stalin want from her?'

'What does he want? She belongs to the one of the most distinguished noble families in the country. Do I need to remind you what the Bolsheviks did to the Romanovs!'

He had stayed away too long. A woman like Charlotte shouldn't be left alone. When he returned there was someone with her at the table. A greasy, smarmy type with a nutcracker's laugh. Some unsavoury show-off who thought he was the bee's knees and didn't realise that she found him repulsive. Rath hated guys like him and felt anger rising within him. Or was it jealousy? He brushed the thought aside.

'Excuse me, but this table is reserved. Would you please leave us alone?' The man laughed. 'Is the lady reserved too?'

Rath could see in his eyes that his big talk wasn't genuine, he'd snorted it up in powder form in the toilet just now.

He leaned over towards the man. Then he seized him by the crotch so quickly that he didn't have time to react. It was all he could do to sit with teeth pressed together, not daring to move. All this played out in the shadow of the table cloth, so that Charlotte couldn't see what was happening.

'Listen to me, my little snowman,' Rath whispered with his mouth pressed against the man's ear, sounding as if he were kindness personified. 'You were stupid enough to sit down with your coke at a table of cops. If you don't leave this place within the next ten seconds, then you won't just have trouble pissing for the next few weeks; I'll also make sure you end up behind bars. Do I make myself clear?'

He underlined the final question by tightening his vice-like grip. The popinjay nodded eagerly. He had turned blue-red. Even the strip of his scalp, which could be seen through his perfectly straight parting, had turned red.

'So,' Rath whispered. 'If you don't want to spend the next year inside, then you'll apologise as soon as I let go, but not before you bow politely in front of the lady!'

The man nodded, stood up and managed to perform something approximating a bow to Charlotte. Then he went down to the foyer in an oddly nimble manner that made him look as if he had soiled himself. Charlotte gazed after him in confusion.

'The alcohol's probably gone to his head,' Rath said, as he re-joined Charlotte. She seemed impressed.

'Do you do that to everyone who gets in your way?' she asked.

15

The clock was set for an hour earlier than usual. He hadn't slept long. *They* hadn't. Rath was already awake as the hand was just about to click into place and trigger the alarm. With a single blow he silenced the tinny monster before it could make any noise. Black hair lay on the pillow beside him. It wasn't a dream. He stroked her and kissed her on the nape of her neck, felt her waking up. She lay still so that he could continue kissing her. When she turned round she smiled at him.

When had it happened? Shortly after he had given the gigolo a piece of his mind, Tretschkov's musicians had returned to the stage and he had led Charlotte to the dance floor. Charly! They had danced, and she had looked at him in such a way that he simply couldn't help it. At first it was only their noses that had touched, then he had kissed her, just softly, but she had reciprocated in kind.

They danced a little while longer but didn't dare kiss one another again. Not in public, on the dance floor. Then he led her from the floor back to the table with their hands entwined. They had ordered another drink and gazed in each other's eyes and suddenly things became serious between them. She was the first to rediscover her smile.

'Now?' she asked.

'Maybe we should call each other by our first names?' he suggested.

She laughed. 'I'm Charlotte, but everyone apart from my mother calls me Charly.'

'At the Castle too?'

'There, I'm Fräulein Ritter.'

'I'm Gereon.'

'A strange name. Never heard it before.'

'A Cologne saint. My parents are very Catholic and very Rhinish.'

'I want more from you, Gereon.'

They had already begun in the taxi.

Now she was lying next to him, stroking his cheek and smiling. The bed cover slid away, and the sun shone on her slim body. He felt his desire returning, but they didn't have time for that now. They had to make haste.

He hadn't wanted to emulate Weinert, who always sent his ladies home in the middle of the night. Not with Charly! He wanted to fall asleep next to her and wake up next to her, but now he didn't have the faintest idea how he was going to sneak her past Elisabeth Behnke unnoticed. That he wasn't actually allowed to receive any female visitors was something he had already confessed to Charly. 'I always wanted to do something illegal,' she had said simply, and so he had guided her quietly to his room. Even though he hadn't seriously reckoned with the possibility, he had nevertheless taken the precaution of removing the map from his wall and concealing the photos before he had set off towards *Europahaus*.

They gave themselves a lick and a promise by the wash basin that stood on the old-fashioned dressing table in his room. In front of the mirror they got themselves halfway fit for the working day at the Castle. It seemed to work. Rath was the more rumpled, but Charlotte looked fantastic anyway, even if she needed a little time to do her hair. She was missing a stocking, but soon standing in front of him ready to leave.

He opened the bedroom door and looked across the corridor. No-one there. The smell of coffee reached his nostrils. Charly remained in his room until he waved her over. She shot quickly across the corridor into the stairwell and descended on tiptoes. Rath closed the door as quietly as possible and returned to his room. They had negotiated the worst; Charly was outside.

He threw on his coat, took his hat and was about to follow her when the kitchen door opened. Elisabeth Behnke stood in her dressing gown. This time though, it was high-necked.

'Good morning!' She refrained from saying Gereon.

'Good morning, Elisabeth!'

'No breakfast?'

'Thank you, but I have lots to be getting on with today. Didn't I say that to you yesterday?'

'Have you already been downstairs? I thought I heard the door.'

'I had forgotten some important papers.' He glanced at the time. 'But now I really do have to go!'

He put on his hat and ran downstairs where Charly was waiting. She had hidden in an entrance. You could tell the woman worked at the Castle.

Barely an hour later they entered the station as inconspicuously as they had crept out of the flat. After a quick breakfast they had got on the underground at Wittenbergplatz, and had sat, love-struck, next to one another for a time. Nevertheless, as soon as the train was nearing Alex, they had begun to distance themselves from one another. The probability that a colleague would get on grew with each station. Rath gave Charly a final kiss and rose to his feet at Spittelmarkt. At Alex they proceeded to disembark from different doors and, shortly afterwards, strolled through the station like two strangers. Even six metres below the ground, Alexanderplatz resembled a building site. Charly had been first to arrive at the Castle; Rath had examined a few train timetables, before likewise setting off towards Dircksenstrasse.

The office was still empty, but the post had been delivered. On his desk Rath found a package. When he recognised the foreign stickers, he knew straightaway. There was only one person who sent him post from abroad, and who knew his new work address. For a moment, he even forgot about Charly as he cut the cord and opened the package. Newspaper cuttings in English poured out. The package was well padded with a letter on top, but his curiosity was initially reserved for something else. A new record! He examined the flat cardboard square and, with a practised movement, allowed the record to slide out. *Fletcher Henderson Orchestra,* he read, *Easy Money Blues.* Fresh from New York! He wanted to listen to it right away.

Only one man sent him packages like this, a man who, in his father's world, no longer existed: Severin Rath had taken the mail boat to America in the spring of 1914 and never returned. Not when the war broke out in August and the Fatherland called him up for military service. Nor, some four and half years later, when the war was over.

Gereon understood back then and even more so today. Engelbert Rath hadn't, and the shame of housing a traitor to the Fatherland had affected him deeply. Not even the hero's death suffered by his eldest son could

offset it. Quite the opposite: it was almost as if he held Severin responsible for Anton's death. Engelbert Rath had allowed his second son to die
through his silence alone. Severin was no longer discussed, and his letters
went unanswered. They weren't even read until, at some point, they stopped
coming.

No-one, not even Ursula, knew that Gereon had tried to find his brother
after the war. Not so very easy, since the old New York address was no longer valid, and many people in the city had anglicised their German names
to avoid being interned on Ellis Island. After a laborious exchange of letters with the US authorities, who didn't always react in a friendly manner,
he had finally located a Sevron Rath in Hoboken, New Jersey. And he had
actually written back. *Poste restante.* As agreed. That was when the first jazz
record had been enclosed. The start of a little collection.

Rath took the black disk from its sleeve and held it like expensive porcelain. Midnight-blue, silver font. *Come on, Baby,* the title said on the other
side. Which straightaway reminded him of *her* again. Charly was sitting
only a few rooms away. The thought of that alone made him crazy.

Stephan Jänicke interrupted his daydreaming. The rookie stormed
through the door, full of energy, surprised to find another colleague in the
office so early.

'Didn't you say you were going out yesterday evening?' he asked.

'I'll sleep at the end of the month,' Rath said and wrapped the package
back up. That was what he had said to Charly last night as well. When they
had fallen into his bed. But not to sleep.

He realised he was aroused just by the thought of it. It was high time
he got this woman out of his head, at least for a few hours! He had to work.

It was to remain no more than an honourable intention. He hadn't been
able to banish her from his thoughts all day, no matter how hard he tried.
Time and time again Bruno had caught him daydreaming. Even as they
were planning the raid! Even Jänicke seemed to realise something wasn't
right with Rath. It had come to a head when he encountered her in the
corridor. He addressed her formally, said hello, remaining polite and dis-
tant as they had discussed. And Charly? She pulled him by the tie into an
office and kissed him. Thank God it was empty.

'If anybody comes,' Rath said and looked around.

'Don't worry, the owner's on holiday.'

Before he closed the door, he looked into the corridor. No-one had seen anything.

Then they fell into each other's arms.

'I want to see you tonight,' she said.

'Sadly that's not going to happen. The meeting.'

'I know. Work is work. You don't have to tell that to an old Prussian.'

'Exactly. And I'm afraid there's no time for play today.'

'Then I want to play a little now,' she said and kissed him again.

Ultimately he had had to hobble back to his desk with an erection, glad not to encounter anyone. By the time he arrived he could, admittedly, walk normally again, but he was still in a state of confusion. He couldn't get anything more done. Finally, Bruno allowed him to go home.

He'd have liked to have her beside him in *Plaza* too. Even if he knew, of course, that it wasn't possible. No-one from the Castle knew he was here, and they certainly didn't know why. Nor was anyone allowed to find out. And so he sat at the bar in the foyer of the variety theatre, sipping on his Americano.

The line-up had seemed even more boring than on Sunday, five days before. This time Rath stood up when the lonely cowboy appeared. His neighbours in the auditorium had been able to enjoy the strangled voice of the tenor as before, and had whispered to each other and laughed. This time it hadn't been a recorder teacher sitting next to him, but a man with a monocle and a grey beard, who was accompanied by an elegant, young woman. Unmistakeably from the West. They'd soon be laughing on the other side of their faces, he thought, as he pushed past them towards the exit.

Barely five minutes later, they joined him at the bar. The monocle man sat on the barstool next to him, the woman one place further on. Rath ordered another Americano. After the disaster on Sunday he considered a new tactic, and the bar was the perfect starting point. Most of the people getting drunk in the foyer were from the West. Even though *Plaza* was an innocuous island in the middle of an area full of disreputable establishments, they couldn't help gazing around every so often, as if they were expecting a knife fight, or at the very least fisticuffs or a police raid. However, there was nothing disreputable in the slightest about this particular people's variety theatre. A disappointment. The young woman seemed to be entertaining similar thoughts.

'It's not very exciting here, sweetpea,' she said to the monocle man.

Sweetpea sipped at his drink and stroked his grey beard.

'You're right, Angel. I'm used to something different. This here is a rather tame nightspot. Halbach should have warned us. Not even champagne, just cheap sparkling wine. We should drink up and go. I know a place where you won't know what's hit you!'

'First of all I need to go and powder my nose,' Angel said.

'Then we should drink up quickly.'

Rath's ears pricked up. *To powder one's nose* was one of the cues he had been waiting for.

'Excuse me,' he addressed the grey-bearded man. 'I just happened to overhear your conversation. You said you knew a place nearby?' The man examined him suspiciously. 'You know,' Rath continued. 'There's no *cocoa* on the menu here. I know my way around Tauentzien, but in this area . . .'

The man seemed to have understood. He looked more friendly now.

'You must be from Charlottenburg?'

Rath nodded.

The man clapped him jovially on the shoulder.

'My good man, nothing beats a wild night in Charlottenburg, but there's a place here that we in the West can only dream about. If it was on our side, the peelers would have raided it long ago, but here the cops don't dare. Our good fortune! In *Venuskeller* they have everything you need to be happy.'

They didn't have to go far. Sweetpea led them into Posener Strasse. Once there, he steered them determinedly towards a dilapidated tenement house. The mouldings were already crumbling from the façade. No neon signs, no placards, nothing that in any way pointed to the presence of nightlife. Nothing apart from a few dark figures. Though scarcely visible, there were men loitering around the street corners and in the shadows of houses, as well as a lone figure standing in the entrance gate. He was very elegantly attired, dressed in a dinner jacket and bow tie under a light coat. As far as his stature was concerned, however, he was more reminiscent of a boxer than a gentleman; his eyes were indistinguishable under the shadow of the brim of his hat, unlike his enormous chin. Rath was ready for anything, from a clean blow to the pit of his stomach to a gun barrel pointed at his head. The only thing he wasn't ready for was what came next: the man was exceptionally friendly.

'Gracing us with your presence again Herr Director General?'

Sweetpea was clearly proud that they knew him here. He grew at least two centimetres.

'Needs must, my good man, needs must. Want to show my friends here where the real party is.'

Angel looked bored. Rath was now certain that she wasn't a luxury whore but some spoilt, high-born daughter out for an adventure, whom the old man had picked up somewhere. She wasn't his wife at any rate.

'Of course, Herr Director General. Have fun.'

The man cleared the way, and they went into the inner courtyard. A red light was burning in the entrance to one of the cellars above an iron door. Herr Director General knocked. Twice long, three times short, a pause, three times short, once long and twice short.

The door opened without a sound, and all of a sudden the muffled clamour of voices and muted sound of wild jazz music penetrated through to the outside. They were examined by a man who made the gorilla out on the street look like a capuchin. Once he had looked them over thoroughly he stepped to one side. The music drew ever closer as they proceeded through a dark corridor. Red Chinese lanterns on the wall gave off a dim light. A cloakroom attendant took their coats, and a liveried valet pulled back a heavy leather curtain that reached to the floor.

From one moment to the next the background noise became louder. They had to raise their voices to talk to one another. The large room they entered didn't seem like a cellar at all, but rather a throne room bathed in red light. Everywhere on the walls Cupids made of plaster were firing their shafts. A waiter led them to their table by the stage, which was the shape of a large mussel. On it a fake American Indian was currently disporting himself with a real Caucasian woman, who despite having her hands tied to a stake, was otherwise very amenable. *Venuskeller* seemed to have leaned heavily on *Plaza* in its choice of themes.

'Well, did I promise too much?' the Director General said, when they had sat down and he had sent the waiter off with a one hundred mark note. The performances on the stage didn't appear to surprise him. Rath, on the other hand, was rendered speechless, even though he was used to seeing a thing or two working for Vice. Even Angel seemed to have gone a little red in the cheeks, but then perhaps it was just the light. Her eyes still looked bored.

The waiter returned with a bottle of champagne, three glasses and a small, silver sugar bowl. The Director General was obviously feeling generous. After they had toasted their health with champagne, he passed the sugar bowl first to Angel and then to Rath.

'There's cocoa on the menu here,' he said, 'and it's very good too! Try a little, my good friend.'

Rath hesitated. He had never taken cocaine before, but he couldn't back out now. He might as well show his badge or go home.

'No false modesty!' said the grey-bearded man. 'Take it! We Charlottenburgers have to stick together in places like this.'

Rath took a small pinch from the bowl. He'd just have to see it through. Angel was already in the process of preparing herself a little line on her pocket mirror, beside which she had laid a small, silver tube.

He had reckoned with all sorts of possibilities: with seeing stars, a variety of colours, bright lights, but all he felt as he snorted the white powder was numbness. His whole nose was numb. He wouldn't have noticed if someone cut it off, but then he felt the cocaine taking hold of his brain and all of a sudden he was wide awake. It was as if someone had turned the music up, and yet he could understand the numerous voices talking over one another considerably better than before. He felt himself positively oozing energy and lust for life.

The young woman was also transformed. Suddenly she could smile, which lent her a charm that he had never thought her capable of possessing. Only now did he realise just how young she was. Twenty at most. The Director General was fifty at the very least, if not sixty.

'I want to dance, sweetpea,' she said.

The Director General waved her away. 'Not with me!' How about you, my young friend?'

Angel was already pulling him from the table. The dance floor was at the other end of the room, directly in front of the gallery with the band. There were people dancing ecstatically, thrashing around alongside couples with their arms tightly around one another. She pulled him towards her straightaway and placed her arms around his neck.

'You're a real sweetie, do you know that?'

'You're not the first to have noticed.'

He tried to free himself from her arms.

'Oh, what have you got there!' The shoulder holster. She looked at him as if the weapon aroused her. 'You can count yourself lucky the gorillas at the entrance didn't frisk us! Are you a crook or a cop?'

'In this neighbourhood you can't be too careful . . .'

She shoved her tongue down his throat. It took a moment to free himself. She smiled.

'You can shoot if I'm too dangerous for you!'

Already she had a hand on his crotch.

'I see you have another weapon here,' she breathed heavily into his ear, 'we really ought to try it out!'

He obviously wasn't cut out for the wild life. He tore himself away and left her standing. She didn't seem to mind. He heard her laugh as he fought his way through the room. A good thing it was dark. By the time he reached the table his erection had disappeared again. In the meantime, on the stage a cowboy had caught the American Indian in his lasso. The woman, now freed from the stake, was thanking him accordingly. The Director General looked on with interest.

'That was quick,' he said, as he noticed Rath. 'You must excuse me. Vivian can sometimes be a little demanding. I prefer to leave her to others but she's amusing, isn't she? Once she's tired herself out, I'll pick her up again. Then she's just right for someone my age. I have to think of my heart, my doctor says.'

Rath sat down. 'You know your way round.'

'You have to study life, my good friend, and it works best in places such as these. Is it your first time in this neighbourhood?'

'At this time of day at least.' He removed the photo from his jacket pocket and placed it beside the sugar bowl. 'Actually, I'm looking for this man. A Russian. Alexej Kardakov. He's supposed to come here from time to time.'

The Director General sounded very understanding. 'A good-looking guy!' he laughed. 'If Vivian only knew who she was trying to seduce!' The grey-bearded man clapped him on the shoulder, shaking with laughter. 'No hard feelings, young man, no hard feelings.'

Another person he had shown the picture who thought he was gay. No matter. Better than being taken for a cop in a place like this. The waiter came and brought a second bottle of champagne. He cleared away the used silver tubes and the sugar bowl. He shot the photo a glance that was conspicuously discreet and disappeared once more.

Meanwhile, the Director General had regained his composure.

'Excuse me,' he said and wiped away the tears from his eyes. 'But that is simply too funny. I don't think that's ever happened to Vivian before. She's taken up with women before, but with a homosexual man . . .' He fetched a monocle from his waistcoat and examined the photo in detail. 'I'm sorry,' he said finally, 'but I'm afraid I don't know your friend. Does he come here regularly?'

Rath was about to reply, but he could see from the face of the grey-bearded man that someone must have been standing behind him. He turned and saw a man in an elegant, white dinner jacket. Above his sparkling eyes, a receding hairline gleamed in the red light. He smiled and the corners of his eyes crinkled.

'I can see that you're having a good time, Herr Oppenberg! I'm delighted!' The man in the white dinner jacket gave a bow. 'Sebald. I'm the manager of this establishment.'

'Pleased to meet you.'

'I'm afraid I must borrow your companion for a moment.'

'I hope you're not going to throw him out!' Oppenberg laughed and lit a cigar. 'We were having an amusing discussion, which I'd very much like to continue.'

'This won't take long, Herr Oppenberg.' The manager turned to Rath. 'Could I please ask you to follow me. There's someone who'd like to speak with you.'

Rath put the picture away and followed Sebald to a door beside the dance floor. In the meantime, Angel Vivian was attracting even more attention than the three actors on the stage. She had pushed her dress down and was dancing bare-breasted on the gallery with the band. She had a well-rounded bosom, like fresh apples. The men's eyes were beaming, the ladies' less so. The manager smiled and shrugged as if to say: that's just how it is in *Venuskeller*, you won't experience this sort of thing anywhere else.

Instead he said, 'This way, please.'

They entered an office that was furnished in a modern style. Rath had expected to see Marlow, but the leather chair behind the enormous desk was empty. They moved across the room, at the end of which Sebald opened a second door. A staircase led upwards. In the courtyard the gorilla from the main entrance was waiting with Rath's hat and coat. He pressed the items into his arms and began to frisk him.

'Where are we going?' Rath asked.

The gorilla pulled Rath's Mauser from his jacket, then his wallet, before passing both to Sebald with an apologetic shrug.

'You're slacking, Benno!' the manager said coldly and removed the Prussian police ID badge from the wallet. 'Rath, Gereon, Detective Inspector,' he read. 'First you let in someone with a shooter, then it turns out he's a cop.'

Benno tried to appear contrite, as far as that was possible for a man of his stature. Rath didn't think he was doing a particularly good job.

'Well, well,' Sebald's mood improved quickly and the smile returned to his face. 'That a film producer who is not averse to forbidden pleasures and a cocaine-addict actress should come to us with a cop, of all things, is not something we would expect. If the cop himself is a user, then perhaps it's no bad thing. He becomes a guest like anyone else.' He pocketed the wallet and the Mauser. 'Might I assume your visit is of a private nature?'

'Purely private.'

The two men led him back to Posener Strasse. He was familiar with the remainder of the journey too. They were going back to the *Ostbahnhof*. Only not, this time, to *Plaza*, whose neon sign was still bathing Küstriner Platz in a garish light, but to the back end of the former station, where it was as dark as the far side of the moon. Benno knocked on an iron door.

'It's us, Liang!'

A slim man opened, his suit cut as elegantly as Benno's, but fitting considerably better. His lustrous black hair was tied back in a long ponytail. Impenetrable, narrow eyes examined them. Rath had heard that China was the land of smiles, but this Chinese man wasn't smiling. Sebald handed him Rath's badge and the Mauser. He accepted both and let them in, leading them through a large, dark warehouse. Beyond it he opened a door, which led to a room that appeared to be completely out of place, as if it had been transplanted from an English country house. It was almost as big as the warehouse, but fully furnished, a mixture of drawing room, library and study. An open fire flickered on the opposite wall. Behind a desk, which was even bigger than Sebald's, sat an elegant but stockily built man in a black suit. He was speaking on the telephone and making notes. Only as they were approaching the desk did he look up and motion for them to sit down. Rath sank into a black leather chair. The Chinese man dealt with their hats and coats and remained on his feet. After he had taken the coats away, he placed Rath's papers and the Mauser on the desk. Then he took up position behind it, hands clasped together. The man at the desk hung up and took a quick look at Rath's ID.

'Good evening, Herr Rath. Did you enjoy *Venuskeller*? We don't often have police officers as guests.'

'Johann Marlow I presume?' Rath said, taking an Overstolz from his jacket. 'May I?'

He was amazed. It was clear he was sitting in a criminals' lair and that the criminals knew he was a cop, yet he wasn't afraid in the slightest. The coke was still at work. Marlow raised an eyebrow briefly, and the Chinese man placed a heavy brass ashtray by Rath's chair. He took up position behind the desk once more.

'You know your way round,' Marlow said. 'There aren't too many police officers in this city who would recognise me. The few who do are well paid.' He took a cigar from a metal container himself, and cut off the tip. The Chinese man provided him with a light and he puffed with relish. 'But I don't think we're paying *you*!'

Rath lit a cigarette. 'No,' he said casually.

'Perhaps we could make a deal?'

'What makes you think I'll help you? I'm a police officer and you deal cocaine.'

'I only see to it that people get what they want, and these days that means cocaine. Amongst other things.' Marlow leaned back like a Pomeranian squire. 'The law of supply and demand is the only law that a businessman should adhere to.' He smiled politely. 'Not least, it was my supply that satisfied a demand on your part, as Sebald informs me. Perhaps I can help you in other ways too. In business, giving goes hand-in-hand with taking.'

Rath cursed his own foolishness. Why on earth had he taken Oppenberg's cocaine? Marlow was putting him under pressure. The drug made him susceptible to blackmail—and it made him brave. Both he could do without. Brave was just another word for rash. He had to pull himself together and be careful as hell.

'I'm not here to make a deal,' he said.

'Let's have a little chat. You can decide after that.' Marlow's voice, soft as velvet just now, became ever so slightly sharper when he turned to the manager. 'Sebald, you shouldn't leave your club unattended for so long, and Benno is better at the door than in a soft chair.'

The manager and the gorilla stood up. The Chinese man escorted the pair of them outside.

'It should be easier to talk now,' Marlow said when they were alone. He drew thoughtfully on his cigar, before continuing. 'Sebald tells me you're in possession of an interesting photo. I'd be curious to hear where you have it from.'

'You just spoke about giving and taking. Actually, I'm here to ask you a few questions.'

Marlow laughed. The Chinese man had returned without a sound and placed a glass first in front of his boss and then in front of the inspector. He poured them both whiskies.

'To giving and taking,' Marlow said and raised his glass. 'Tell me where you got the photo and ask your first question.'

The stuff *tasted* good too. What did this man want from him? 'From a cellar,' he said.

'I see.' Marlow drew on his cigar and gazed after the smoke rings. 'I'd like to place my cards on the table, Inspector. My people were also in that cellar. I am in possession of a similar photo.'

'Why are your people looking for Kardakov? Has he been misappropriating cocaine?'

'Why don't you tell me why the police are looking for him.'

'Allow me to place my cards on the table. The police aren't looking for him. *I'm* looking for him.'

'Why?'

He had a moment of sudden inspiration. 'The Sorokin gold.'

Marlow appeared unruffled but Rath sensed that he had scored a bull's eye. It took a little too long for the man to formulate his next sentence. A wave of a finger and the Chinese man refilled Rath's glass.

'Don't you think you're overstretching yourself a little there? Is it not a few tons too heavy for someone acting on their own?'

'Who said I was acting on my own?'

'You don't have the police force behind you at any rate.' Marlow laughed. 'Perhaps you're dreaming of an early retirement! You wouldn't be the first cop to switch sides. Are a few corrupt colleagues involved too? The one who pulled the courier out of the canal? Perhaps he wasn't even dead and you managed to squeeze a little more out of him? And now you're going after the big money? Be careful. Even with a whole heap of cops, you're still out of your depth.'

The courier! Rath's ears had pricked up, yet he was trying to appear as bored as possible. Marlow was obviously talking about Boris.

'Do you know why Kardakov went underground?'

'Probably because he's playing his own game.'

'And the courier? Why did he have to die?'

'Inspector Rath! Don't play dumber than you are, what do you know about the gold?'

'That it's in Berlin.'

Marlow gave a forced smile. 'Nor should you make the mistake of playing *me* for a fool. Let's get down to brass tacks! You want the gold and I want the gold. We both know something. If we combine our information and our capabilities, then perhaps we have a chance of getting it. What else do you know?'

Rath shrugged. 'That it's supposed to be worth around eighty million.'

Marlow laughed loudly, but he sounded anything but amused. 'You need to tell me something more than I already know!'

'I'd love to, but clearly you know so much that I can't.'

Marlow stubbed out his cigar. It looked as if he was squashing a bug.

'Perhaps I should give you a little more time to think about it. Kuen-Yao will see you out.'

'How can I reach you?'

'If you want to speak to me, come to *Venuskeller*. But for that reason only! If you want to have a good time, go somewhere else. Sebald doesn't like cops taking coke in his club.'

The Chinese man stood behind him holding his coat and hat. Rath stood up.

'Goodbye, Inspector,' Marlow said. 'Kuen-Yao will return your weapon when you are back on the street.'

'Thanks for the whisky,' Rath said.

'The pleasure was all mine. It was nice to meet you, Inspector,' Marlow said in a friendly tone that sent a shiver down Rath's spine. 'I hope for a little more cooperation the next time we meet.'

It sounded like a threat, and no doubt it was supposed to be one.

Sometimes he regretted not having a car. The neon signs outside *Plaza* were out and the taxi rank at Küstriner Platz looked as abandoned as a bank vault after a visit from the Brothers Sass. There were no more trains running at this hour either. A good thing he didn't have to go into the office tomorrow. He wasn't on duty again until the evening—when Operation Nighthawk was set to go off. He would take *Venuskeller* off the list. No-one needed to know where he had been tonight. They wouldn't get to Marlow with a raid anyway, only to his front man, Sebald. Worse still, Marlow would know who to thank for this blue-uniformed company away day.

The nearest taxi rank was at *Schlesischer Bahnhof.* He had no option but to set off, turning up the collar of his coat and burying his hands in his pockets. A penetrating wind was blowing across the square. It seemed a storm was brewing.

He tried to assemble the pieces of the puzzle. Lana Nikoros, alias Countess Svetlana Sorokina, tells her lover, Alexej Kardakov, about her family's gold and they decide to smuggle it into Berlin. To this end, they engage the services of a courier, a Russian named Boris. Why a courier? Is he taking the gold to Berlin, or just a message? Whatever the case, the courier dies after looking for Alexej Kardakov in a foreign city. He seems to be furious with Kardakov. Why? Did he pull a fast one on him? Play his own game, as Marlow put it? At any rate, Kardakov and the Countess go to ground. Perhaps they deprived Boris of his rightful reward, or eliminated an accessory? Before making off with the gold.

Rubbish, he thought. In order to get that amount of gold from the Soviet Union across to Germany, you needed more than one helper in Russia and in Germany. How did Marlow know about the gold? Coincidence? Had Kardakov blabbed, or had he deliberately got the underworld king involved? Somehow they had to convert a lot of gold into cash, and that was only possible with connections such as Marlow had. And in Russia? The Sorokins still had friends there. What had the *Reichswehr* officer at Bruno's said about communist separatists who called themselves *the Red Fortress*? Was Kardakov one of them? Why not? A hack writer . . .

A sound interrupted his thoughts. He stood still and listened. Nothing there. He looked around. The streetlamps were casting such a wretched light that the exterior walls of the houses lay in darkness. There was no-one to be seen. It had been raining. The wet pavement reflected the weak light. As he walked on, he thought he heard something again—an echo of his own steps. He was now certain that he was being followed. Someone was walking behind him who didn't want Rath to see him. This neighbourhood wasn't safe, especially not at this hour. He felt his left side, at the Mauser still in its holster.

At the next turning he veered to the right, even though the station was now in sight. He wanted to be certain. The echo continued. Rath increased his tempo, then stopped abruptly and turned around. There was still no-one there. Nevertheless, the house façades were in such darkness that he would be protected from view simply by moving along the walls. Rath waited until the next street and darted sideways again. He moved to the nearest courtyard entrance and leapt inside. His pursuer had also fallen into a cautious trot, but stood still for a fraction of a second too long.

Again Rath heard the artificial echo of his steps. He listened into the night, heard raindrops dripping onto the asphalt from gutters and window ledges. In between times, he thought he could hear the sound of soles on cobblestone. Only very softly, but it was there. His pursuer still hadn't given up. Rath retreated inside the courtyard, still keeping the entrance gate in sight. He had to conceal himself, had to surprise his pursuer.

He looked around. It wasn't a normal courtyard he had stumbled across. In the dim glow of the courtyard lighting, he could make out a construction fence, behind which a new building was being raised. In front of it was a trailer. Another look in the direction of the entrance, and within a few strides he was in the shadow of the trailer. From here he had a good view of the gate. It had started raining again.

He didn't have to wait long. The shadow of a man in a hat and coat. Not a flat cap, just a normal wide-brimmed hat, the latest in fashion. One of Marlow's people? Had Dr M. sent Benno or a similarly friendly customer after him?

The man stopped, obviously considering whether he should enter the courtyard. And then he approached, still slowly and cautiously, moving along the exterior wall, gazing around time and again. Rath unbuttoned his coat and jacket and loosened the push-button on his holster. He waited until the man reached the courtyard and released the safety catch of his Mauser. With weapon drawn he emerged out of the shadow of the trailer.

'Looking for me?'

The unknown figure stood still, the surprise had worked. He turned his head, seemed to consider if he could still escape, and then drew closer. Silently.

'Stop! Stay where you are!'

Rath trained his pistol on the stranger.

The man was still a few paces away from him. Not particularly big, it wasn't Benno, at any rate.

'Why are you following me . . .'

The man took another step closer.

'Stay where you are, I said!'

Rath's voice grew louder. The man was still silent, but was now standing still.

'We can just as easily talk at the station, if it's too uncomfortable for you here,' Rath said. 'Then you won't need to worry about where you're spending the night.'

He couldn't make out the eyes under the shadow of the hat, but the narrow mouth had twitched at the word *station*. It was only a threat, Rath wasn't seriously intending to take the man to Alex. And then he thought for a moment that he was the one who had been lured into a trap.

Behind him he heard a resounding clang, a small, wet explosion.

Instinctively he turned his head. There was no-one there, just a hissing, white puddle on the pavement and shiny, red-brown shards. Above him a window slammed shut and, in the same instant, he was attacked.

A firm grip clasped his right forearm and pulled it to one side, turning the muzzle of the pistol painfully downwards. Rath lost his balance and fell to the ground. It happened so slowly it was as if time had been frozen. It seemed to take minutes for him to crash onto the wet stones.

While he was still falling the shot went off. A reflex. He squeezed the trigger without taking aim. Without the first idea of what had happened. The shot was earsplittingly loud.

Along with the crack he heard a loud metal noise, almost like a gong, and then the zing of a ricochet. Still he fell endlessly but with the grip of the other man loosening. His pursuer crashed to the ground too, thudding against the pavement barely a metre away.

Rath climbed to his feet, ready for the next attack. He had the Mauser in his hand and could aim again, keep the aggressive terrier in check. But the man stayed down. The hat had rolled from his head to reveal a face that Rath still didn't recognise. Thinnish lips, a crooked nose that hinted at numerous punch-ups, an eye that was wide open. Only one. There, where the other eye ought to have been, was a gaping dark hole. In the dim light, the blood running in a thin rivulet over his pale face appeared almost black.

Rath stood holding his right ear; it ached and there was a buzzing noise. Only now did he understand what had happened. Or try to understand. Was it the mixture of alcohol, cocaine and adrenaline that somehow made the whole scene seem so unreal? But it was real, terrifyingly real. He could kick the corpse with his foot.

He saw a shiny metal object next to his foot and could almost have laughed. A mundane, everyday manhole cover, through which the rainwater drained from the paved courtyard, had sealed his attacker's fate. As in billiards, the angle of incidence is equal to the angle of refraction.

As if someone had kicked in a glass pane and the reality behind it was only just revealing itself now, Rath became aware that he was standing next to a corpse. Next to a person who had been killed by a bullet from his Mauser.

Who would believe his story? There was a corpse, and here's Detective Inspector Gereon Rath, pumped full of cocaine and alcohol, claiming it was all just a mistake? He realised he wasn't going to be able to sell that to anyone. He could hear the public prosecutor posing his questions: could you explain to us again why you took cocaine, Inspector? I see, to get closer to Herr Marlow, very interesting. And what did you want from him? What on earth were you doing in a notoriously shady part of town in the middle of the night?

This time he wouldn't escape the courts in one piece. Let alone the press. A cop who shoots a person dead during a cocaine high—the boys in Kochstrasse had been waiting for a headline like that since the Kaiser abdicated.

He looked around. All the windows remained dark, but at least one person must have seen them fighting. Rath examined the brown shards. From the white of the puddle, nothing had remained, only a few little bubbles that were frothing. A familiar smell reached his nostrils. Next to the wet shards lay a metal holder with a porcelain stopper. A beer bottle. Some sleepless voyeur up there had dropped a beer in fright.

A witness!

So what? Don't panic! A shot here was nothing unusual. No-one would expose themselves to the questions of the accursed cops, just because they had been witness to a shoot-out. He was telling himself all this, like a kid who claims not to believe in ghosts but is still afraid of the dark. He instinctively pulled his hat further down over his eyes, but then his thoughts were clear; he knew exactly what he had to do.

He replaced his weapon and began to search the pockets of the deceased. He recoiled as something pricked him in the finger. A lapel pin, no weapon, not even a wallet. Just a small, stylised steel helmet. Rath threw it into the drain. Then he buttoned the dead man's coat to the top, put his hat back on his head and began to pull him by the collar of his coat.

The rain became heavier, as he hauled the heavy body to the construction fence and looked for a gap. He found the loose plank and gave one of the neighbouring planks a little nudge until the gap was big enough to drag the corpse through. He looked around. The contractor hadn't got very far, only the foundations and the floor panels had been laid. Rath climbed into the excavation and tested the concrete with a timber beam. Still not set, they must have only poured it today. He dragged the dead man down and located a shovel from the trailer. He wiped down the lock with a handkerchief after he had broken it open. His dry mouth was making him crazy. He almost took a beer from a crate that was lying next to a rusty bike, but he managed to control himself. Instead he poked his tongue out into the rain.

As if in a frenzy, he dug a hole in the fresh concrete, placed the man inside and shovelled the concrete back over the top. There was a little left over, which he spread out. Then he returned the shovel to the trailer and wiped down the handle with his handkerchief. He wiped down everything he had touched, including the loose planks in the fence, once he had straightened them again. The rain would hopefully have washed away the blood from the courtyard by the morning.

Rath looked down at himself. His dark coat was glistening with rainwater, mud and concrete. He tried to rub away the dirt but it was pointless, he was only spreading it further. The way he was looking, he couldn't show himself to a taxi driver. He went back to the trailer, retrieved the bike and gave it the once over. There wasn't enough air in the rear wheel, but for his purposes it would do.

His gaze wandered once more over the dark apertures that looked out onto the courtyard. He wasn't sure whether anyone had seen him, but he was sure that in this darkness no-one could have made out his face under the shadow of his hat. Even if there was someone here who enjoyed speaking to the police.

He wheeled the bike through the entrance to the courtyard. Still no-one on the street. He pushed off and jumped into the saddle. The bike bumped across the cobblestones. As long as he wasn't stopped by a colleague for riding without a light he would be home within half an hour.

PART II

A DIVISION

11th May—21st May 1929

16

The rain was still beating on the roof of the car. The beat rose to a hiss as the car door opened and a huge body sank, with surprising force, onto the black leather of the rear seat. Liang must've lent a helping hand. The door closed with a resounding clunk and wouldn't be opened again until Johann Marlow gave the signal. Through the ever-changing pattern of the raindrops on the windscreen, Marlow could see the dark coat of Liang Kuen-Yao, who had remained outside to ensure that any thought of escape died a premature death.

Marlow looked at his guest without saying a word. The man had thrown on a trench coat, upon which the rain had left dark traces, but underneath he was wearing only pyjamas. His grey face could have done with a shave, while his eyes told of too little sleep. The smell of alcohol, sweat and rain permeated the vehicle. Despite their tiredness, his eyes danced anxiously to and fro. In trying to mask his anxiety he ended up sounding a little brash.

'What's the big idea? Why is your Chinaman dragging me out of bed in the middle of the night? I have to be at Alex at six tomorrow. I need my sleep!'

Marlow turned his attentions to a cigar that was as thick as his thumb, calmly cutting off the tip. He allowed the snapping noise of the cigar cutter to take effect before answering. His guest had already seen once what else the device could be used for.

'I had a visit from one of your colleagues today, and I ask myself why I didn't know anything about it,' he said.

'Come again? Can't be anything official. The raid isn't until tomorrow . . .' He corrected himself upon looking at his watch. '. . . until *this evening.*'

'Not a raid, a lone cop. Rath, Gereon Rath. Does the name mean anything to you?'

The man considered, but all that followed was a shrug.

'He doesn't work in Narcotics anyway.'

'I don't pay you just to keep Narcotics off my back. I'd hope that you picked up on a little bit more than that at Alex.'

'Who told you Vice were planning a raid? I can't know everyone at the station. It's probably someone new.'

'There can't be that many new people arriving at Alex from the Rhineland. Keep your ears to the ground!'

'From the Rhineland?' The man hesitated. 'Maybe I have heard something about the guy. What was his name again?'

'Gereon Rath.'

'I'm not quite sure, could be from Vice. They've had someone new foisted on them. From Düsseldorf or Cologne. He's supposed to be a friend of the commissioner.'

Marlow nodded thoughtfully.

'You have a name now. See what you can do with it. I want to hear more tomorrow.'

A small hand movement sufficed for Kuen-Yao to open the door. It had stopped raining. The man stayed in his seat and looked around uncertainly.

'Go and have your well-earned sleep,' Marlow said, almost friendly now. 'We'll speak again tomorrow evening.'

No sooner was the man outside than Liang closed the door again. He didn't bother to accompany him back into the house. He went straight to the driver's door, threw the umbrella onto the floor space in front of the passenger seat and reclaimed his place behind the wheel. There was barely a drop of rain on his coat, as if he had never been outside.

'To Peters?' he asked simply.

Marlow shook his head. 'That'll do, Kuen-Yao. We're going home.'

The Chinese man started the engine, and the brand new, gleaming, jet-black *Standard 8* rolled onto the carriageway.

The streets were filling with cyclists as the first workers pedalled towards the factories. Liang steered the big *Adler* Limousine calmly and safely through the dawning city. The night-time storm clouds had dispersed as suddenly as they had arrived. Only on the eastern horizon did they continue to paint the morning sky in strips of red. It promised to be a beautiful day. In the rear-view mirror Marlow gazed into the eyes of the Chinese man. They were inscrutable.

Bruno Wolter was a morning person. Getting up at six didn't bother him, but today he gazed pensively out of the window, and not just because he knew it was going to be a long day. A beautiful morning. It must have rained in the night, as there were puddles glistening on the asphalt. In Fregestrasse the birds chirruped in the trees, doing all they could to mark the start of a sunny spring day, but he wasn't listening. He scraped shaving cream from his face as if blindfolded, and mulled things over. The calls yesterday evening had pursued him into his dreams and were still whirring around his head. He didn't think there was any reason to worry. They had planned everything carefully, but you never knew.

One thing, at any rate, was clear: he would soon be rid of the new detective inspector. And yet he had grown accustomed to the lanky figure. He was a little too ambitious for someone who had no idea what was going on in this city but, still, he would most likely get his wish and be transferred to Homicide. Well, enjoy, my friend! The half-shaved face grinned in the mirror.

'Bruno,' he heard Emmi call from below. 'Coffee's ready.'

After breakfast, he felt better. Emmi carried his brown briefcase to the door and passed it to him as he stepped out of the house. He gave her a quick, dry kiss and went to the black Ford that was parked in front of the house and drove away. He watched her disappearing in the rear-view mirror.

Emmi was the kind of woman he had always wished for. She admired him, she was attentive—and she didn't ask any questions. He could do no wrong by her. She trusted him completely. Until now he hadn't disappointed her, and they had been married for over fourteen years. When war broke out and he was called to arms, he had made his proposal. Emilie von Bülow was much sought-after but he won the race for her hand and they used his first leave to get married. It was good to have someone to write to in the field, and that's what he had done, regularly and in detail. She had sent him at least one letter a week. As the war tightened its grip, and the soldiers were no longer granted leave of their trenches, things continued to take shape in Berlin. Little by little, Emmi furnished the house her parents had bought for them, while he defended the Fatherland for a paltry sum, with which they could never have afforded such a place. But they weren't fighting for the pay, none of his companions were. They were fighting for the future of Germany, a position that his father-in-law fully supported.

The longer the war continued, the more sordid it became and, for many of his companions, it became a question of returning home in one piece. Not for him, he had hope until the end. They had been in the heart of enemy territory for four years, but Germany's future was up the spout when the Reds sent the Kaiser packing and signed the surrender—and this despite the fact that his unit hadn't retreated a millimetre for three years. They held their position in the middle of France without yielding, in the heart of enemy territory, but suddenly everything disintegrated and the country they had fought for no longer existed. It was still called Germany but it was no longer their country.

Nevertheless, he had remained with the police, whom he had already served under the Kaiser. Even with the social democrats in power, someone was required to maintain law and order, and he had never given up hope of the Germany he had fought for and wanted to serve further. He retained contact with his old comrades who had survived.

He parked the Ford in front of the *Josty* branch on Kaiserallee and looked for a sunny spot on the terrace. Shortly afterwards a waiter brought his coffee, and Wolter leafed through the papers. They were all reporting on the Young Plan. Idiotic prattle, these negotiations in Geneva. He rustled the paper impatiently, gazing up from his reading to take in the entrance to the café terrace and the wide pavement on Kaiserallee. His mood was deteriorating rapidly. He didn't have forever.

After waiting three quarters of an hour and ordering a second coffee, he had had enough. The man was usually reliable, but today of all days he was blowing him off. As if Wolter didn't have enough on his plate. He placed the exact change angrily on the table. As he stepped back down from the sunlit terrace onto Kaiserallee, he tried to calm himself. Don't get nervous, he thought. He had been in this game long enough. The best thing he could do was to wait for the evening, when he would learn more. Until then he had more than enough to do.

The silhouette of a man emerged from the shadow of the newspaper kiosk on the other side of the road. As Wolter slumped onto the driver's seat of his car, the man hailed a taxi.

17

Rath couldn't have been asleep for long when the sound of the telephone interrupted his dreams. He blinked out of gummy eyes and groped for the receiver.

'Hello,' he mumbled.

'Gereon?'

All at once the voice made him feel wide awake.

Charly!

He sat up.

'Good . . .' he looked at the alarm clock. Half past ten. 'Good morning.'

'Good morning, late sleeper!' She sounded cheerful. 'I thought if we're not going to see each other at the Castle today, then we should at least speak on the telephone.'

'Yes,' he said simply. His thoughts were caught in the tangled dreams of the all-too-short night, and a few scraps were hanging there still. Her call had wrenched him from a deep sleep into which he had only just fallen. When he tried to clear his thoughts, he suddenly became aware that the one-eyed man from his dreams was real. The events of the previous night were catching up with him like a scraggy dog pursuing its master: unloved but faithful nevertheless. In his head a film projector began to whir, showing the pictures that had hounded him in his sleep: the stranger's attack, the shot, the blood in the empty eye socket, a dead man disappearing in concrete. Silent. Pictures without sound, but still needle sharp.

'You sound as if I've woken you up?'

Her voice stopped the silent film, and Rath felt as if he had been found out. Felt as if the projector had also been running for Charly, and that she had caught a glimpse into the furthest reaches of his soul. He hadn't even told her anything about Cologne yet. How the hell was he supposed to tell her about what had happened last night? He waved his hand in the air as if he could banish these thoughts like a pesky fly. One day he would tell her everything, all this nonsense too. Just not now.

'I'm actually still in bed,' he said. Good God, he felt lousy! Why did she have to call?

'Alone, I hope.'

'You know I always smuggle ladies out of the house at the crack of dawn.'

At least she laughed. He heard a noise that sounded like the beep of a horn. She would never call him from the office, not with so many keen-eared cops around. Probably a public telephone somewhere at Alex. Her voice grew quieter. 'A shame you didn't have to smuggle *me* out this morning,' she whispered.

Her voice! He yearned for Charly more than he cared to admit, and above all more than he could allow. He had other things on his mind. 'Maybe a good thing too,' he said, more sharply than he had intended. 'I had a lot of sleep to catch up on.'

'You didn't *arouse* the impression of needing much sleep yesterday morning.'

Her innuendos were making him crazy. Why couldn't she just leave it? 'Well, I can be a real show-off sometimes.'

'Not today. You sound more like someone who doesn't want to be disturbed.'

'Nonsense,' he said, although he knew she was right. 'I'm just a little tired. I've got a lot on my plate.'

'I know,' she said, 'the meeting yesterday, your raid today. I've got a lot to do as well. I'd still like to be with you though.'

'And I with you,' he echoed her answer, knowing it wasn't true. As much as he longed to be near her, he could scarcely be with her now. How he would have liked to take her in his arms, smell her, feel her body, but in another universe, another world in which the events of the previous night had never taken place. He had lied to her about some meeting or other the day before. Instead, he had met with a criminal and buried a dead man: a harmless white lie that had suddenly taken on a meaning all of its own. How was he supposed to show himself to Charly now?

'With me?' she laughed. 'That's not such a good idea at the moment. I'm in a telephone box. It would be a little tight. And I need to get back to the Castle, but perhaps Böhm will let me out early enough for us to see each other before it kicks off tonight. When do you start?'

'This afternoon. We still need to prepare a few things.'

'I think I get out around two. Time for a coffee in the *Letzte Instanz?*'

Not such a bad idea actually. The *Letzte Instanz*—Last Resort—was situated in Klosterstrasse near the police station, and, despite the name, was hardly frequented by police officers. Still, Rath fobbed her off. He hoped he didn't sound as cold as he felt at this moment.

'I'm afraid I can't,' he said, 'I've still got loads to do.' *Like covering my tracks, by burning bloody, concrete-smeared items, for example. And buying a new suit; and preferably a new pair of shoes while I'm at it.* 'And I need a little more sleep.'

'Sleep? I'll sleep at the end of the month!'

He noticed that his laughter sounded forced. She had caught him off guard.

'What's wrong with you? Is something the matter?'

'Should there be?'

'I'm feeling pretty stupid at the moment. Shouldn't I have called?'

'Of course not!' He knew it didn't sound the way he had intended it to. 'I'm just a little tired, that's all.'

'Well, you'll have plenty of opportunity to sleep it off in the next few days. I won't be bothering you at any rate, not if you don't want me to. You have my number. At work and at home.'

The receiver in his right hand fell like a sandbag used to test the gallows before an execution. He kept hold of it, lost in thought. Outside the window, the sun was shining, banishing all traces of the night-time thunderstorm. He felt wretched. The sound of her receiver slamming into the cradle had cut him to the quick. At the same time, he was relieved. He couldn't have endured speaking to her for another second.

Far too many tangled thoughts were racing through his mind. He had to bring order to this chaos, recall what had happened. What he had done, and what he still needed to do.

No-one had seen him as he had pedalled back through the thunderstorm to Charlottenburg. He had thrown the bicycle into the Landwehr canal at Lützowufer and completed the journey by foot. The birds had been chirruping as he finally stood in front of the door at Nürnberger Strasse. Nevertheless, he had acted as if by clockwork, mechanically, without thinking about what he was doing. Because he knew what had to be done. First get out of the clothes as quickly as possible. Jacket and suit were ruined, the concrete, dirt and blood stains a giveaway, and he had left the print of his brown box calves umpteen times in the construction site sludge. A shame about the shoes, but they had to go. Everything had to be disposed of. That was what he had wanted to take care of this morning. Before he had sunk into a brief sleep, he had packed everything away into the smaller of the two cases that had accompanied him to Berlin, and shoved it back under the bed.

He stood up and looked himself in the mirror on the small dressing table. Quite presentable really, if you ignored the stubble and dark circles under his eyes. A bath would do him good. He threw on his dressing gown and went across into the dining room. The breakfast table had been cleared, there was only a single place still laid for him. The coffee in the pot was cold. He poured himself a cup and drank it in one gulp. It didn't have to taste good, it just needed to work. He didn't have any appetite and left the bread-basket untouched. He knocked on the door that led to his landlady's rooms. No reaction. Was she out or just offended?

'Elisabeth, I'm taking a bath,' he called through the door as a precaution. The last thing he wanted was for old Behnke to hit on the idea of cleaning her tenants' bathroom at this precise moment.

In truth he didn't think she would get any ideas, but upon withdrawing to the bathroom with a towel and fresh items of clothing, he locked the door nevertheless. He opened the fire flap in the boiler, lit a little newspaper and made up the fire with a briquette. While the boiler slowly heated, he got undressed. Next he unrolled the towel and allowed his dirty things to fall on the floor tiles. He removed a pair of scissors from his wash bag and cut the damp, rain-scented material into strips. First the jacket then the suit. Rag after rag went into the boiler, until finally everything had disappeared in the flames.

A little later he was sitting in the warm water, deep in thought. He still didn't know how he was going to get rid of his shoes, but the best thing was probably to throw them into the canal like the bicycle, at a different location of course, a few kilometres away. He had to go to Kreuzberg today anyway, and the house on Luisenufer was located close to Urbanhafen. Before E Division took up their duties once more, he wanted to have another look at Countess Svetlana Sorokina's flat.

He had to solve this damned case now more than ever. All this snooping had put someone's nose out of joint. The terrier they had put on him had only confirmed that he was on the right track. Marlow had a hand in it, he had probably sent the little man after him, the one who was now lying dead in the concrete. Dr M. had something to do with Boris's death and Gereon Rath would figure out what. At any rate Marlow knew about the Sorokin gold. Alexej Kardakov had worked for him, and was a friend of Countess Sorokina. The pretty couple had disappeared, while a third Russian was dead.

When he emerged from the cooling bathwater, he felt a good deal better. The old thirst for action was returning. Before he left he took another look inside the boiler. He could no longer make out any textile remains, only ash. His favourite suit didn't exist anymore. Now all he had to do was get rid of the shoes and hope that the construction work in the Stralau quarter was making good progress.

'Do you come by every *Sonnabend* now? Because you know my Hermann's out of the house, is that it?'

She had recognised him straightaway. The stairwell smelt of cleaning agent, just as it had the week before, and he was interrupting her housework again. The pail was still standing in the stairwell.

'I need to ask you a few more questions, Frau Schäffner.' Rath neglected to show his ID this time. She let him in all the same. He avoided sitting and remained where he was. She waved a duster pointedly over the shelf.

'This time I'm looking for a woman . . .'

'I'm already spoken for!'

'. . . a single woman who lives in this house.' He wouldn't be put off by her lewd sense of humour. 'A woman who has been away quite a while.'

'Well, why didn't you say so last week? Bombarding me with questions about some Russian! You must mean that Steinrück. Thinks she's quite the elegant lady that one, yet she can barely afford that little room in the attic. But *she's* no Russian, I'd know if she was.'

He decided not to rely on Frau Schäffner's judgement of character. He hadn't told her he was looking for a Russian woman, and it was none of her business anyway. He had her open up the flat. She fetched the key from a wooden shed in the courtyard and panted theatrically as she struggled up the stairs in front of him. Ingeborg Steinrück lived at the top of the first rear building. The caretaker's wife stood behind Rath curiously as he switched on the light in the windowless hall.

'I'm sorry I interrupted your cleaning,' he said. 'Please feel free to continue.'

She gazed at him uncomprehendingly.

'I'll bring the key back when I'm finished,' Rath said. 'Or should I just hang it in the shed?'

For a brief moment her eyes flared with suspicion. He thought there might be a hint of frustrated curiosity too, but she turned without a word and went down the stairs, leaving the keys in the lock. At least she had sufficient respect for authority not to ask for a search warrant. Rath went in.

It looked tidier than he had expected. Probably the work of Ilja Tretschkov. Even the flowers under the little skylights, the only natural source of light, seemed to have been watered. The flat consisted of an attic room, in which there was just room for a bed, a wardrobe and a small table, as well as a small kitchen and an even smaller bathroom. At all events, it didn't look like the residence of a Countess, whose family owned a legendary fortune. The only hint of luxury was the electric hairdryer, which lay under the mirror in the spotlessly clean bathroom.

Rath's gaze wandered through the room, looking for some sort of clue, something that might tell him which way to steer the investigation. Above the bed there was a bookshelf. Everything in German. Not a single Russian title, not even Russian authors. Rath leafed through the books. Nothing unusual, no notes, nothing. This woman had made every effort to conceal her Russian and aristocratic roots. The paper basket under the table was empty. If she had really fled, then she must have been careful not to leave any clues. If there was anything she had overlooked, Tretschkov would have found it long ago. It looked as if the man had swept the place thoroughly.

He didn't find a single photo, not on the walls, not on the bedside table, not in the drawers. No posters, nothing that hinted at her career as a singer. He removed the *Delphi* programme from his pocket and threw the face on it a glance. A pretty woman, why had she disappeared?

There were only three possibilities: either she had fled in a mad rush, she had been kidnapped—or someone had murdered her. Had she eloped with Kardakov? Had Stalin's people carried her off to Moscow? Or did Kardakov have her on his conscience as well as Boris—because he wanted to appropriate the gold and they were standing in his way, the courier and the owner of the gold? Rath didn't know enough about Kardakov to say whether he would be capable of something like that. Nevertheless, in this job he had been obliged to learn that people had the ability to do far worse things than you could guess by looking at them.

The wardrobe was still full of simple but tasteful clothes. He took an autumn-coloured dress from the hanger and examined it. The Countess must be a dainty little thing. He rummaged through the whole wardrobe. There was a winter coat hanging there too—had she scarpered after the heatwave, or had she been forced to leave it behind? The coat must have been older than it looked, a part of the lining was torn. No, not torn, but cleanly unstitched. He took a closer look. It looked as if someone had tried to retrieve something from the lining, and that someone had obviously been successful. He searched the whole coat and found nothing. Now he examined the room more carefully. Nothing, clinically clean. He would have to pay Tretschkov another visit.

A short time later, he stood opposite Frau Schäffner again. She had worked her way up the stairs of the rear building with her pail, and was gazing at him with a face as red as beetroot, dripping with sweat.

'You're here?' Rath was astonished. 'Weren't you cleaning the stairs of the front building just now?'

She gasped for breath. Her fat upper arms wobbling as she noisily wrung out the cloth.

'Did you think my work was done with the front building? You've got some nerve!'

He ignored the reproach in her voice. It sounded as if the whole world was to blame for the fact that Margarete Schäffner had to clean the stairs, but especially the Berlin police and Detective Inspector Gereon Rath.

'Good nerves are a pre-requisite for employment with the Prussian police,' he said and jangled the bunch of keys.

'Where am I supposed to take those now?'

'Give yourself a break and take them back. I'd like to ask you a few questions anyhow.'

'More questions?' She let the cloth fall into the metal pail and wiped her hands on her apron. 'Do you want to take out a subscription, it might make things cheaper!'

Dim but with a ready tongue. He ignored her tone. At least she had stood up and was accompanying him downstairs.

'Do you know how long Frau Steinrück has been away?' he asked, still in the stairwell.

'What do I know? Two weeks maybe. Maybe longer. She was always away somewhere.'

'Is there someone in the house who knows her better?'

'Steinrück? You're joking! She doesn't mix with the likes of us! We hardly saw her, she was always in bed, and usually out in the evenings.'

'Like the gentleman here.'

'Pardon?'

Rath gestured towards the door of the flat they had just passed. 'Herr Müller,' he said. 'He works nights too.'

He held the door to the courtyard open for her, and she heaved her body through.

'At least Herr Müller has a reason. He goes to work.'

'And Frau Steinrück doesn't? She's a singer, isn't she?'

'That's what she said, but we hardly ever heard her sing. There are other ways for a woman to make money at night.'

'Did she have visitors from time to time?'

'From time to time? Again and again, and they were exclusively male!'

'The Russian whose picture I showed you last week, was he one of them?'

'How should I know? It was dark when they arrived.'

They had arrived at the front building. She opened the flat, went in and hesitated as Rath remained outside.

'Well, what's the matter?'

'You tell me.'

'Aren't you coming in?'

'Thanks for the invite but I've already asked everything I needed to. Goodbye.' With these words, he raised his hat, turned round and walked away. He could picture her face, even though he had turned his back on her. It took about a second for her to rediscover her voice.

'To think, I walked across the courtyard for that? You could have asked me that in the stairwell! That's just . . .'

When the heavy front door clicked shut he could no longer make out what she was saying. He didn't even bother to suppress a grin as he made his way past the big windows of the dairy towards the elevated railway.

It was shortly after four o'clock when Rath arrived at the Castle. He hoped he wouldn't run into Charly, but she must have left the station a long time ago. He could have spared himself the visit to Ilja Tretschkov as he returned from Schöneberg with nothing more than the new suit he bought at Tietz near Alex. A brown cheviot suit for sixty-eight marks was a typical cop's suit. Not too expensive, in case you made a mess of it on duty. *Or while burying corpses in your spare time.* He had forked out almost twenty marks for a new pair of shoes. Yesterday's expedition was costing him dear, and he still had to get himself a new coat. In his old trench coat, he looked like a sleuth from the political police.

He placed the paper bags with his shopping on the desk. Bruno and the rookie still weren't there, and he decided to put on his new things. He was in the middle of stuffing his shirt into his new trousers when the telephone on his desk rang.

'Rath, CID.'

'Likewise.'

There was only one person who answered like that. Police Director Engelbert Rath. Great! The last thing he needed right now was his father's well-meaning advice.

'What a surprise,' Gereon groaned into the receiver. 'How did you know I was in the office?' He wedged the receiver fast with his shoulder and carried on getting dressed.

'I'm a criminal investigator, my boy,' said Engelbert Rath, laughing his short, loud laugh. Even through the telephone his father sounded like someone who'd lay a hand on your shoulder and slip a cigar into your mouth while he chewed your ear off. 'All joking aside, your landlady told me you were working this afternoon. It's good to show a little commitment.'

Elisabeth Behnke had answered his telephone. What business did she have in his room? Nosy cow! A good thing he had taken the little suitcase with him this morning and disposed of the contents.

'And yourself? You're still in Krebsgasse, are you?'

'Impressive powers of deduction, my boy!'

'Call it investigative instinct,' he said, fastening his belt, 'you ought to send your secretary away earlier. There are no typewriters clattering next door at home. How is mother doing?'

'Oh, you know, her knee. But otherwise she's fine. She sends her love.' Engelbert Rath's voice took on a familiar, paternal tone. 'You should get in touch with her,' he said. 'She'd like to know very much how you're faring in Berlin.'

'Would she like to know how her son in New York is faring as well?'

'I don't know what you're getting at.'

'If she wants to know how I am, then she should ring me and ask.'

'You know how she is. She doesn't want to impose. It's just she's always so pleased when you get in touch.'

'I've hardly been away two months.'

'Please, I'm asking you, boy.'

'Fine, I'll ring her one of these days.'

'There, you see! And what's the latest with you?'

I buried a person yesterday, Gereon thought, *but otherwise it's business as usual.*

'I've had a lot on my plate. We've got a big operation on tonight . . .'

'The raid? Karl told me about it.'

So the old man had been speaking to Dörrzwiebel on the phone. At least that meant top brass were aware of E Division's work.

'You're doing a good job, my boy,' his father continued. 'The commissioner thinks very highly of you.'

'Not just because of my surname I hope.'

'Now, don't be so sensitive!'

'It takes a little getting used to when your own father calls your superiors by their first name.'

'But you know all about that.'

Gereon knew all too well. At police headquarters in Cologne, Police Director Engelbert Rath was not only a high-ranking police official, but a legend. Someone with whom nearly all high-ranking officers in Krebsgasse were on first-name terms—and for the most part proud of it. Gereon had seen his transfer to Berlin as a chance to escape his father's shadow. But that shadow was far-reaching.

'So what did old Dörrzwiebel say?'

'You know I don't like that nickname!'

Of course he knew. That was the reason he had used it.

'Sorry. It just slipped out somehow.'

'You've settled in well with Vice squad in the meantime, I hear.'

'It's not exactly my favourite department, even if there'll be lots going on tonight for a change.'

'Thanks to your work, my boy! Believe me, those at the top are aware it was you who made the decisive breakthrough. Maybe you'll get to work in a more interesting department soon. Karl said that you'll soon be assigned to a homicide team.'

'That's normal here. Nothing unusual, everyone gets a turn. And then after four weeks, you have to step back in the ranks.'

'Could be. But Karl knows you from Cologne, and he knows you've no business being in Vice. There'll soon be a post free in A Division that needs to be filled by an inspector.'

'Aha!' He already sensed what was coming.

'Karl would like you to fill it. Naturally he can't argue your case in front of Gennat using your testimonials from Cologne. That remains classified, we don't want the old stories to resurface. But he wants to give you the chance to show your talent.'

'What's that supposed to mean?' He felt his tone become more aggressive. Couldn't the old man just stay out of his life for once?

'Don't get angry. You know the commissioner sets great store by having every employee deployed according to their skills. Karl has already spoken with the chief of homicide about the possibility of giving you some responsibility as part of one of their teams. If you deal with that successfully, my boy, and we have no doubt whatsoever that you will, then you'll have an excellent chance of taking up that free post. Good news, isn't it?'

As if in a trance, he stared at the map on the end wall of the office, on which they had marked the most depraved places in Berlin with little multi-coloured flags. The old man had set it all up beautifully. There it was,

Detective Inspector Gereon Rath's big chance! Zörgiebel himself wanted him ushered into A Division. With a little nudge from Engelbert Rath.

'No-one's said anything to me about working in Homicide yet,' he said. 'Let alone what great things I'm supposed to do there.' It was a half-hearted protest. He was angry with himself, and not just about his response. Whenever he spoke with his father, he ended up feeling like a little boy.

What had he managed to achieve in a week? He had startled an underworld boss, set the Russian camp in Berlin against him, and secretly disposed of a corpse at night. Quite a balance sheet! If his father had phoned the day before, then none of that would have happened. No gunshot, no dead man. He would have continued performing his duties in E and calmly awaited his transfer to A. So many ifs and buts.

His thoughts were interrupted by Engelbert Rath's impatient voice.

'Don't you think?' the telephone groaned once again. He had no idea what this *don't you think* referred to.

'Sorry?'

'Are you listening to me at all?'

'The connection was very bad just now.'

'I said that officially you don't know anything about it either. But I suppose it's better you're informed, don't you think? You know my motto: knowledge . . .'

'. . . is power.'

That old slogan. Rath had always thought his father would've been better off in the political police.

18

Although the sun had disappeared behind the houses many hours before, there was still a pleasant summer warmth on the streets. The audience from *Theater am Nollendorfplatz* was spilling out of the evening's final screening, as two trucks turned the corner and hurtled into Motzstrasse. The cinema-goers gazed after the vehicles, whose tyres came to a squealing halt a few metres behind the American church. The tailboards opened almost simultaneously and men in blue uniforms sprang one after the other onto the asphalt. It seemed like something was about to happen!

A few curious cinema-goers were obviously anticipating the continuation of the film in real life and strolled over. Others moved off discreetly in the opposite direction. Some revellers had reason to avoid contact with the police, even as onlookers.

Rath stood next to Wolter by a green Opel on the opposite side of the road, observing the spectacle. Stephan Jänicke was sitting in the back with a pale man, whose hands were cuffed to the canopy hinge. They had overpowered the lookout, who had been hanging around discreetly outside *Pille*, only a few minutes before. Following a brief tête-à-tête inside the vehicle, Uncle had had no trouble in extracting the secret knock which, as if by magic, would open the steel door of the cellar bar. He climbed out of the vehicle and gave the plain-clothes officers at Nollendorfplatz the agreed signal. It took less than two minutes for both trucks to roll into position.

Rath and Wolter crossed the street, and the officers looked at them expectantly, ready for action. Having received a brief wave from Wolter, they followed the two CID officers through a courtyard entrance. Uncle descended the steps and knocked on the basement door. Three times short, twice long, and a hatch opened in the steel door. The muffled sound of music could be heard.

'You're a little late, sweetheart,' said a surprisingly high-pitched voice. A pair of eyes could just be made out in the hatch, pupils dancing nervously from right to left. Someone was missing the guard who normally escorted the guests to the door.

'Where's Johnny got to?' All of a sudden the voice sounded suspicious, and no longer so inviting.

'He's gone for a piss,' said Wolter, at the same moment sticking the barrel of his P.08 through the hatch. 'But my friends and I can come in anyway, right?'

The door opened to reveal a gaunt transvestite in a velvet green dress, whose slightly too muscular arms were raised in the air.

'Did Red Hugo send you? You must be suicidal if you think you can make trouble here. You're not coming through with that!'

'We're not suicidal, but we do have plenty of back-up.' Wolter gestured towards the top of the stairs with a brief toss of the head. 'And besides, we have uniforms, my dear. Get ready to spend a night in Alex.'

He passed the man in woman's clothing towards the back, where he was received by two cops and placed in handcuffs. One troop went inside with Wolter and Rath, the other remained outside to take care of the clients and note the number plates of the cars that were parked in front of the courtyard gate.

There was a frenzy of activity as the officers descended the steps into the long, dark passageways that led to the pleasure rooms. Half a dozen men were hanging around, and some of them had only just realised what was going on. Wolter revealed the badge on his jacket and moved through the basement vault with his weapon drawn. Rath followed with his Mauser. It had only just occurred to him that he hadn't reloaded it since yesterday's incident. He prayed not to have to fire during the operation, otherwise someone might notice that his magazine was missing a cartridge. Behind them, the cops continued to advance, their weapons likewise drawn.

They herded the men onwards. Some abandoned themselves to their fate, but most ran away. It was as if they were in a fox's den: the foxes fled to the second exit, unaware that a pack of dogs was waiting there too. They had stationed a third truck at Kleiststrasse, by a courtyard that could be reached via the rear exit of *Pille*. A troop of hard-boiled officers waited there, a group that wouldn't shilly-shally for long, as that was where those who knew this underground labyrinth best would be heading. The hard cases.

The music grew louder and suddenly they were standing in a large vault, in which only a few dim lamps were burning. It was brightest on the stage, bathed in the dazzling glare of a spotlight. Two women were embracing and performing something approximating a dance, only their movements weren't always in time to the sound of the band. When they noticed the wall of policemen that had formed by the entrance, they held each other tight, as if they were freezing. Perhaps they were ashamed, although they weren't even completely naked. The place was relatively tame in general, Rath thought. Things had been far more unruly in *Venuskeller*.

The two CID officers calmly positioned themselves in front of the cops and looked around the vault. They were in no hurry to pursue the fleeing men, knowing that no-one could escape. Behind them a door led into the next vault. As far as they knew the room was just as big as the one they found themselves in, only it was divided into a number of private booths. Anyone who wanted to gain access had to cough up a little more money than out front, which was obviously restricted to a rather tame striptease.

Wolter put his weapon away, dug his thumbs into his belt and tried to make himself heard, but his voice was drowned out by the music. It took a moment for the band to grasp the situation. The clarinet was the last to cease playing. Then it needed a little while longer for the general muttering to die down and for Wolter's voice to be heard.

'. . . might I ask you please to remain quiet? This is a police action. We will merely take you to the station, register your personal details and take a short statement. Then you can go. This operation is directed against the owners of this illegal establishment, not its patrons.'

Most of the guests allowed themselves to be led away like obedient lambs. The musicians didn't make any move either. The staff behind the counter likewise remained calm. Only a few ran towards the back, where the men from the passageway had already disappeared. Normally a well-built employee saw to it that no-one strayed into the second vault, but now anyone could go through. From the back room, shouting could be heard. A half-naked woman came through the door, saw the uniformed officers and immediately turned around again.

Gradually, the chaos abated and the area emptied. Rath gave Wolter a sign that he would move towards the back and beckoned four cops over. They weren't interested in the private booths, where men were getting hastily dressed on the beds. The women had disappeared, leaving only a few items of clothing behind. A second door opened onto a long, murky passageway with sewage pipes running along the ceiling. Rath switched on his flashlight. To the right, the way led through a series of winding passageways to the rear courtyard on Kleiststrasse. He led his people in the opposite direction. The end of the vaulted passageway was marked by a steel door, behind which the grinding of an organ could be heard. Now they'd find out if Krajewski was as good as his word.

He switched the flashlight off again. It was impossible to tell if the room was being guarded, and, if it was, the flashlight presented too obvious a target. The door was firmly locked. He landed a well-directed kick at precisely the height of the lock, and the door swung open into a dark room.

The darkness was illuminated only by a single beam of light flickering through the smoke-filled air. An organ was playing bombastic music, a strange mix of the *Marseillaise* and *Heil dir im Siegerkranz*. No-one turned to face the intruders: the organ drowned out all other sounds and the action on the screen had obviously cast a spell over everyone. Even the cops who stepped into the room behind Rath.

The screen was considerably smaller than the one in *Gloria Palace*, though the film would probably have filled the largest theatres in the city, if a legal screening had been allowed. A still sprightly Kaiser Wilhelm, the First this time, was having it off with a woman who bore a striking resemblance to the French Empress Eugenie, while Napoleon III sat on a chair next to them, looking on in chains as he snorted with rage. The Bismarck portrait standing on the bedside table was a nice touch, the unmistakeable thumbprint of Johann König, only this time in moving images. Rath moved over towards the organist, whose eyes were on the film, and tapped her lightly on the shoulder. She gave a start, but played on until he put a finger to his lips.

Once the organ had died, for a brief moment only the occasional groan and hum of the projector could be heard, then the groaning subsided too, before Rath's flashlight prompted a fleeting commotion. Women who had obviously been crouching in the depths of the cinema seats sprang up and adjusted their clothing. They seemed less startled than the men in the theatre, whose faces were bathed in a bizarre light by the beam of the flash. A corpulent, older gentleman, whose erection, caused by the film and the services of the young lady, was still plain to see, hurriedly pulled up his trousers. The other men in the room, around two dozen of them, were concerned with similar matters, either with ladies or alone.

'This is a police operation, gentlemen,' he said. 'I ask you now to place yourself in the hands of the offices of law enforcement.'

'Outrageous!' growled the fat man, who had just managed to pull his trousers over his erection. 'There will be consequences, young man. You can't do this to me!'

'I can,' Rath said, and turned towards the cops. 'Make sure this horny fatso gets locked in a cell.'

The fat man tried to protest, but two uniformed officers had already grabbed hold of him and were leading him outside.

'You'll regret this, I promise you that,' the fat man raging, 'I'm a friend of the Minister of the Interior! This is a scandal!'

'You're telling me,' Rath called after him.

He wasn't the first man tonight who claimed to have prominent friends. They wouldn't find out until next week at the latest if any of them really did have connections in the government or similar circles, when the protests would reach the commissioner. Rath doubted there would be many. Most of them, even if they really did wield any influence, would rather content themselves with a night in police custody which they would never mention again, than admit they had been gadding about in seedy, illegal nightclubs.

It took less than half an hour for everyone to be ready for dispatch, patrons and employees alike. Rath gazed after the two trucks as they rolled away from Motzstrasse towards Alex. The green Opel was still parked on the street corner with the doorman looking out of the rear side window. Johnny, the tranny had called him. According to his ID, his real name was the more respectable Wilfried Johnen. Rath had the impression that the man had grown even paler in the course of the last half hour. No wonder: Johnny had had to reckon that, any minute now, along with all these colourful people being bundled onto the truck, his employers would soon stroll past. It would not be good to be seen in a police car when that happened. But Johnny had probably been lucky: most of them would be waiting for their transport to Alex in Kleiststrasse.

Stephan Jänicke sat on the rear seat with the type of frozen face that only an East Prussian could achieve. There wasn't the slightest trace of emotion in it. Rath knew that the rookie hadn't exchanged a single word with the doorman in the last half hour. Not even the East Westphalians with whom Rath had worked in Cologne could manage that. Jänicke was exactly the right person for a job like this. Nothing made a crook of this calibre so nervous as a cop who didn't say a word. Wilfried 'Johnny' Johnen would be ready to talk before he reached the station.

Wolter gestured towards his wristwatch and held five fingers in the air. Jänicke nodded. Rath followed Uncle into the catacombs of *Pille*, where a single officer was performing sentry duty. With badges raised, they crossed to the other side and out of the cellar, but the courtyard was empty. The engine of the truck in Kleiststrasse was already running, though the tailgate was still open and two officers were fiddling with it. The two CID officers said hello and drew nearer. Rath glanced briefly at the load platform but couldn't see a great deal.

'You're a sweet one,' a female voice said, 'perhaps the two of us could do something later!'

A few women found it amusing, but the giggling was scotched by a rough, male 'shut your trap!' Impossible to say whether it came from a colleague inside the vehicle or a pimp. While Wolter was exchanging a few words with the two cops, Rath stepped a little to the side and lit a cigarette. This raid was their last of the evening. In total, they had swooped on nine illegal nightclubs, and they had been on the ground for most of it, racing from one roundup to the next, according to a meticulous schedule. Now it was over Rath inhaled the smoke of the cigarette deeply, as if it were oxygen.

Bruno stood alongside the officer who was currently sealing the tailgate on the final truck, and who would remain behind on guard duty. After the vehicle had groaned into motion, Uncle said one last thing to the cop and came over, fetching a packet of cigarettes from his pocket.

'We've earned this one, don't you think?' he said.

'Eleventh commandment: never contradict your boss.'

'Glad it's over?'

Rath nodded.

'You look tired.' Wolter examined him. 'Not enough sleep last night?'

The circles under his eyes said everything, but there was nothing to be done about it. Rath shrugged his shoulders. 'An operation like this doesn't come round every day.'

'True. Could have been a complete flop though. But now you can breathe a sigh of relief. There wasn't a single place we weren't justified in taking apart. Not one of them smelled a rat. And we didn't catch old man Lanke screwing either. It doesn't get any better than that.'

Rath couldn't help but grin when he imagined the chief of E Division in full cry with a whore. Bruno was right, there had barely been a hitch. At most a handful of revellers had escaped, but they had managed to snare a few hard cases in every bar to compensate. They also had a decent amount of evidence, as some of the bar owners had kept neat accounts. Nevertheless, Rath still couldn't see the point in an operation like this. Raiding criminal dives, drug stashes, arms caches; all that made sense. But nightclubs? If people wanted to enjoy themselves, then they should go ahead and enjoy themselves.

Wolter clapped him on the shoulder. 'Not so pensive, my boy! I wouldn't have bitten your head off if tonight had been a dead loss. We planned the operation together, and if something had happened then it would have been my thick skull on the block. And Lanke could've spent any amount of time tearing it to shreds, but it's a hardy old thing.'

'It all went pretty smoothly.'

'Yes. And as long as the three dozen odd intimates of the Minister of the Interior, the Imperial Chancellor, and the Emperor of China that we dispatched to Alex today don't complain, we shouldn't get any trouble.' Wolter glanced at the time. 'We should be finished in two hours. Will you be able to stay on your feet until then?'

'Give me a pot of strong coffee, a few cigarettes and I'll grill the toughest of them till the day after tomorrow!'

'Let's not exaggerate. We'll wrap things up by three at the latest. If you want, I'll give you a lift home. The real work starts tomorrow anyway. You need to be well rested. It could be a long day.'

'Stephan won't be too happy.'

'What do you mean?'

'It'll ruin his Sunday football. Aren't Hertha playing in the *Plumpe* tomorrow?'

'*A propos*. We should look in on him. Make sure he's not worried about anything.'

They threw their cigarettes on the pavement and walked past the lookout back into the cellar.

'Lanke was asking about you recently by the way,' Wolter said casually, as Rath's flashlight lit the way back.

'Really?'

'Even rang me at home. The first time I've had the honour. Wanted to know how you're getting on. Sounded very paternal, could give you a real fright.'

It sounded like the commissioner had inquired with the chief of E Division about the son of his good friend. Lanke would never have hit upon the idea by himself. Rath realised that Bruno was also curious about what could be behind it. Did he suspect something?

'And?' Rath asked.

'What do you think? I told him you were the most obstinate provincial cop I'd ever had to train.'

'I mean: what exactly did Lanke want to know?'

'Hard to say with that man, but funnily enough it didn't sound like he was looking for misdemeanours. Quite the opposite. Sounded very pleased when I told him who was responsible for our latest success.'

Of course, Rath thought, Lanke has spied another chance. If Zörgiebel had intimated that he was thinking of pulling a man out of E and transferring him to A, then Lanke would only consent to it if he could bring in a replacement. A replacement from the Criminal Police Office in Köpenick. Perhaps Bruno feared they were going to set Lanke Junior up with a job after all? Rath kept walking, lost in thought, until Bruno finally broke the silence.

'Have you already applied to A Division?' he asked.

'Pardon me?' Could the man read minds?

'Rumour has it there'll be a position free there soon, since our colleague Roeder prefers to spread word of his heroic deeds in book form, rather than doing Gennat's dirty work.'

'Roeder wants out?' Rath asked, and his surprise was genuine. Erwin Roeder was notorious throughout the whole Castle for his vanity, and had written a number of books about his uniformly heroic assignments as a detective inspector, causing more mirth than admiration amongst his colleagues. Especially as Roeder had, like a gimcrack Sherlock Holmes, allowed himself to be photographed in the most idiotic of disguises. He suffered the consequences of his authorhood, which had never been viewed favourably by top brass. Perhaps Zörgiebel and Weiß had presented him with a choice. As much as the commissioner and his deputy valued cooperation with the press, nothing angered them more than a detective inspector who was better known to the public than they were. Moreover, it was said that Roeder had certain anti-Semitic leanings, and since the never-ending *Isidore*-attacks in the *Angriff* the deputy commissioner reacted allergically to such things.

Bruno wouldn't let go: 'So, have you applied?'

'No,' Rath could say with a clear conscience.

'You're not already working for A on the side?'

'What is this? An interrogation?' Rath halted and shone his flashlight in Wolter's face. His mind was working feverishly. What could Bruno know? Had he seen something when visiting Nürnberger Strasse? Had Elisabeth Behnke mentioned something about Kardakov's estate? Or was it Böhm who had spread the equivalent rumour? On the other hand, all that was yesterday's news. He didn't need *Aquarius* anymore. The nightmare on Friday had put an end to all his unauthorised inquiries with one fell swoop. In truth they had been ill-fated from the start. No more secrets, in constant fear of being caught, of breaching the regulations and exceeding his authority. All that was over. Even if it rankled to give up the case, especially now he had taken a big step towards its resolution.

'If this was an interrogation, we'd be shining that light in your face, not mine,' said Wolter and blinked. He seemed to be looking Rath directly in the eye, even though there was no way he could see him in the dark, blinded as he was by the flashlight.

'I'm just wondering how you could possibly think that I'm working for A Division? About two weeks ago I received a photo, just like every other detective at the Castle, and that was it. If that's what you call working on the side, then I hereby confess, but I thought we were through with this a long time ago.'

'You're right,' Bruno said. 'It's already caused one pointless argument, let's not go repeating it.'

'No, let's not.' Rath let the beam fall back on the floor, and they continued walking. 'You know I'd like to work in Homicide and, sooner or later, I'm going to take my chance. My cards are on the table.'

They reached the rear courtyard on Motzstrasse and took their leave from the uniformed officer at the main entrance to *Pille*. Wolter stood for a moment under the dark arch of the courtyard entrance before they emerged back onto the street. He placed a hand on Rath's shoulder.

'Let's not kid ourselves,' he said. 'Operation Nighthawk will be our last joint action for Vice for the time being. If I understood Lanke's call correctly, then you'll be temporarily transferred to Homicide next week.'

Rath couldn't make out his eyes in the shadow.

'If that was the case, I ought to have heard about it a long time ago. No-one's informed me.'

'Informed you? Why, that's not strictly necessary.' Wolter laughed and imitated a rasping parade ground tone. 'You are to do what your superiors tell you, understood?'

'Change division in the middle of our investigation? What rubbish.'

'Rubbish?' Uncle shrugged his shoulders. 'You might just be right, but that's never stopped anyone at the Castle before. If Gennat needs people, he gets them.'

The clock in the large conference room showed half past twelve, and inside the din was on a par with that of the waiting room at *Anhalter Bahnhof*. The room was so brightly lit that the dark night outside vanished into oblivion. Everything had been pushed up against the wall—only eight tables stood neatly in a row, each one occupied by two detectives, one from I Division, the *Erkennungsdienst*, or identification service, usually known simply as ED, and one from E Division, under whose overall control the operation had been carried out.

Those waiting stood in long lines, guarded by a number of officers, revellers from the nine illegal cellar bars the police had visited in the last few hours. Men still in their waiter's aprons stood next to gigolos in elegant evening dress, seedy types in conspicuously expensive suits next to serious men who, to judge by their appearance, must have been director generals or privy councillors. The lines in front of the two tables occupied by officers from G Division, the female CID, were even more colourful. Young stood next to old, black next to white; some girls looked so young they must have still been minors. In one row there were a number of bored-looking women wearing nothing apart from Prussian military jackets from the previous two centuries. That had to be the troop from *Pegasus*. Many were scantily dressed and had only been able to throw on something makeshift, sometimes little more than a man's overcoat—and not always with the agreement of the owner. There were howls of protest when the victim discovered his apparel on the body of the woman with whom he had lain only hours before.

Rath looked at the spectacle. They had only just arrived at the Castle. Bruno and the rookie were still questioning Johnny, the doorman they had caught napping outside *Pille*. They wanted to make sure they questioned him today, while he was ripe. Rath knew the man would talk. Above all, when he learned that he wouldn't be able to join his mates in the cell otherwise. If he didn't appear there, he would seem more suspicious than everyone else put together.

The cells were filling up gradually. Most of their haul was still in the conference room. What seemed like chaos was actually based on a system. When someone reached the front, they were subjected to the same procedure of papers, body search and a few questions. Those who could prove they were respectable citizens with no previous record, those who weren't in possession of illegal items such as narcotics, pornographic images or weapons, were allowed to return home, provided they hadn't aroused suspicion in any other way. Others were transferred to the uniformed officers outside in the corridor, then taken first to the ED photographer and subsequently to a cell in the Castle.

The police machinery was running like clockwork. Here in the conference room they didn't really have a great deal more to do, apart from put in an appearance. That was a point of honour. They were responsible for Operation Nighthawk, which had bestowed a night shift upon the officers in the room, at the weekend at that.

Rath strolled aimlessly through the ranks. It couldn't hurt to keep his eyes peeled, to gather first impressions and think about how to tackle the interrogations tomorrow. They had brought in over five hundred people today, of which, once their details had been noted, roughly a sixth would spend the rest of the night in custody. Eighty to ninety, and they would all have to be interrogated.

'Young man! What a surprise. See what happens to the likes of us when we're not careful! I won't be going to *Pegasus* in a hurry again, I'll tell you that!'

Rath turned round. Oppenberg, the movie producer from *Venuskeller*, was beaming at him. The man who had given him cocaine. The raid hadn't been able to spoil his mood, perhaps he was accustomed to such things.

Oppenberg adopted a confidential tone. 'Don't worry,' he whispered. 'The cops will let us off. The main thing is you've got your papers, and no snow in your pocket.'

Rath didn't have time to answer. The man was just as talkative as the first time they had met.

'Where did they pick you up? Were you back in *Venuskeller*? You disappeared so suddenly the other day, Vivian rather missed you. But, never mind, we still had our fun!'

He nudged Rath in the side as he gazed around. Vivian was nowhere to be seen. Perhaps she had got away from the cops. Rath certainly wouldn't have put it past her.

One of the guards pushed his way to the front.

'Quiet, my friend,' he said, tapping Oppenberg roughly on the shoulder with his truncheon. 'Time to leave the detective inspector in peace!'

The film producer looked first at the cop and then at Rath in surprise. For a moment their eyes met, only for Rath to turn his gaze on the uniformed officer.

'It's OK, Sergeant,' he said. 'This man was drawing my attention to something important.'

Before Rath could feel any more uncomfortable, a loud cry distracted everyone's attention. All heads turned in one direction. At the other end of the room a couple of guards had had to intervene, as two men who obviously recognised each other tried to lay into one another. What they were accusing each other of was unclear, but both their faces were bright red. Pimps, Rath assumed, and took advantage of the commotion to move discreetly away from Oppenberg. The officers separated the pair of squabblers and took them outside. Anyone behaving like that had clearly earned a night in the cells, no further inquiry was needed.

The encounter with Oppenberg reminded Rath of the previous evening again, a night he would like to erase not only from his memory but from his life in general. Bruno appeared next to him, as if out of nowhere.

'A lot going on here, isn't there?'

Rath nodded. 'Not as dull as Zörgiebel's meetings.'

'Finally a bit of life in the place.'

'Has our man started talking?'

'He's a little more stubborn than I thought,' Bruno said. 'Although I've made it clear what's in store for him. Blondie's in there now. Let's see who can keep quiet for longest.'

Rath recognised the next familiar face in due course. In fact, there were two of them, the muscle-bound Russians from *Kakadu*. The ones that had unintentionally put him onto *Café Berlin* and thus onto Kardakov's trail. Even while waiting to be photographed and fingerprinted, they seemed to be inseparable, Scar Face and his burly friend. Rath had assumed he'd run into them again in *Kakadu*, rather than the Castle of all places. It was Scar Face's turn now, he placed his yellow ID on the table, reminding Rath of the papers he had confiscated from the cocaine dealer in *Café Berlin*. It was about time he handed them over to lost property.

Thinking back to that evening, his curiosity was pricked once more. These two Russians had threatened him in no uncertain terms. Two guard dogs that were protecting their countryman from the German police? At any rate, they were closer to Kardakov than anyone else he'd dealt with. Perhaps they all belonged to this ominous-sounding secret political society. As he made his way with Bruno towards one of the female lines, he carefully avoided direct eye contact. They mustn't recognise him here. Time and time again he looked over in their direction out of the corner of his eye while Wolter spoke to a female inspector from G Division, and soon realised that he didn't have to go to so much trouble—because the Russians, for their part, were looking away too, looking away a little too conspicuously, in fact, for them not to have seen him. All the better, Rath thought, the pair of them didn't seem to be too crazy about clashing with him again.

The ED officer meticulously checked Scar Face's passport, added his particulars to the list and leafed through his book of mug shots, while a colleague from Vice patted down his pockets and frisked him thoroughly from top to bottom. He shook his head when he was finished. Negative.

The ED man, however, seemed to have found something in the file and was making a longer note. The Russian was led away. His friend was dealt with likewise. Both accepted their fate with stoic composure. A night behind bars didn't seem to hold any terrors for them.

Uncle was on first-name terms with the Vice officer. Rath had only met him briefly. While Wolter was speaking to their colleague, Rath gazed discreetly over the ED officer's shoulder. A scrawl. The two names on the list weren't so easy to decipher. *Nikita I. Fallin,* Rath thought he could read. That had to be Scar Face. Underneath was a name that he read as *Vitali P. Selenskij* or *Gelenskij.* Both of them had been picked up in *Bar Noir,* a little place near Winterfeldplatz. The raid had run parallel to the one in *Pille.* Rath couldn't read the notes in the comments column, nor the addresses. Never mind, he thought, and turned away. Bruno seemed surprised by his curiosity.

Rath allowed his gaze to wander over the confusion in the conference room once more. All he needed now was to see Kardakov in one of the lines. Anything was possible; sometimes fate had a strange sense of humour. But instead of the missing Russian, he spied another old acquaintance. The man was strolling calmly through the ranks, arms folded behind his back. In his evening dress he could scarcely be distinguished from the more sartorially elegant of the revellers, it was only his keen vulpine features and hunched gait that marked him out, a gait that had earned the man the nickname *Crooked Lanke.* No doubt about it, Superintendent Werner Lanke, head of E Division, was inspecting the parade in person, and had obviously interrupted his weekend festivities to do so.

Rath gave Wolter a nudge and gestured surreptitiously towards their boss. 'I'm not surprised that we didn't catch Lanke in one of those dives,' he whispered. 'He knew about it.'

'It was probably me that spilled the beans. It can happen when the boss rings you at home.'

When Lanke spotted them, a smile crept across his face, and he interrupted his wanderings to make for the two vice detectives. Rath felt uncomfortable. It was unpleasant to see the man smiling, almost as unpleasant as being yelled at by him.

Superintendent Werner Lanke genuinely seemed to be in the best of spirits.

'Well, gentlemen,' he greeted them with Prussian brevity, 'everything's going swimmingly. Like old times!'

'Yes, Superintendent,' Wolter knew what was good and proper and gave an interim report. 'Operation Nighthawk has proved a success.'

'You've picked up a lot of trash. A few big fish too, Kronberg just told me, and from the worst kind of criminal dens.'

'Depends, sir, there are lots of respectable citizens here too. Hope above all that this operation's put a damper on the deplorable custom of illegal nightclubs. Some of the gentlemen here will no doubt suffer heavy financial losses thanks to tonight.'

'So they should! Give vice no dice!'

Rath, who as the lowest ranking officer had thus far maintained a modest silence, almost gave a start as the superintendent suddenly turned to him and, to top it all, assumed a confidential whisper.

'Well, young man, you've settled in well here haven't you?' *Young man!* Lanke had never called him that before. Crooked Lanke had probably never called anyone that before. Rath nodded, and gave a bemused smile, as the Division Chief placed a hand on his shoulder and took him to one side. 'Your part in all this hasn't gone unnoticed, I can assure you!'

They were now standing by one of the windows that looked onto Alexanderstrasse, a distance apart from the excitement in the room. His boss's unexpected friendliness made Rath shudder.

'People have started to take notice of you upstairs,' Lanke said. The way he rolled his eyes upwards, one might have thought that for Werner Lanke *upstairs* could only mean God. 'I know you haven't been with us for long,' he continued, 'but what would you think if you were assigned a job in a different division with perhaps a little more responsibility?'

'I don't quite understand, sir . . .'

'Next week, you will be working in Homicide,' Lanke said. 'As you are perhaps aware, from time to time E Division places a few officers at Homicide's disposal. On a four-week cycle.' He made a circular motion with his index finger. 'Rotation, you understand?'

Rath nodded eagerly.

'But this time, things will be a little different.' Lanke sounded like a godfather who was about to pull a present from his pocket. 'The commissioner has asked if I can recommend an officer who is in a position to take on responsibility should the situation arise. There is currently a shortage of staff in A. They need someone with experience, perhaps permanently.'

Rath sensed what was coming. Crooked Lanke was passing off the strings Engelbert Rath had pulled a long time ago as his own work.

'Naturally I thought of you straightaway,' Lanke continued. 'You and your skills. You should know that Bruno Wolter has a very high opinion of you. But I said to him that people like Inspector Rath are difficult to keep hold of, they are needed in other divisions.'

'You can actually arrange for me to take on an assignment in Homicide?'

Lanke nodded. 'My word counts for something here. I hope you realise what an honour it is to be given an assignment in Homicide. Gennat takes only the best!'

'But I've only just got used to working in your division, sir, I can hardly leave you and DCI Wolter in the lurch.' Rath gratefully seized the opportunity to get on Crooked Lanke's nerves. 'You know how much work we have ahead of us. Operation Nighthawk only started today. There are still interrogations to be carried out, then everything needs to be evaluated and reviewed for the public prosecutor.'

'There are enough people in E for that. And you don't need to worry about Wolter. He understands.'

Rath continued in a sceptical vein. 'Perhaps I should sleep on it. Once Operation Nighthawk is complete, then we can always tal . . .'

'I'm afraid you haven't quite understood.' As if he had flicked a switch, Lanke slipped back into the tone that Rath was accustomed to. 'I am your superior, my dear inspector, and if I say that you are the best man that I can give to A Division, then that's that. Report to Superintendent Gennat on Monday morning at eight on the dot. Understood?'

'Yes, sir.' Only with difficulty was Rath able to suppress a grin, adopting instead an expression that was typical for a Prussian officer: disappointment masked by absolute obedience.

Lanke seemed to like it. He put on a smile. 'There, you see,' he said and clapped Rath on the shoulder. 'We are in agreement. And by the way . . .' The chief of vice leaned over towards Rath a final time, and spoke in a whisper once more: 'I'm not expecting any thanks. You can rejoice in silence. Tomorrow is your last day in my department. I don't want to see you in E Division again, my friend.'

His colleagues looked at him expectantly as he returned to the table. No sooner had Lanke moved far enough way than Bruno gave voice to his curiosity.

'So?' he said. Lanke was already making his way towards the exit with his hunched gait. 'When's the big day?'

'Sorry?' Rath threw his colleague a questioning glance. What the hell was that supposed to mean?

'When are you two getting married?' Uncle asked, completely serious. Then burst out laughing. The two other officers joined in.

19

Another short night. He had fallen into bed around half past three and been awakened at half past seven by a tremendous crash somewhere in the flat. Elisabeth Behnke started screaming. Maybe Weinert had forgotten to shoo his ladies out of the house on time? Truth be told, it took a lot less to make old Behnke hot under the collar. His landlady's mood had grown increasingly volatile in the last few days and even little things were making her go berserk.

He didn't have to be at the Castle until ten and tried to get back to sleep, at least for half an hour. It was pointless. Just as he was on the point of nodding off, the screaming started again. He admitted defeat and got up. A quick glance in the mirror told him he didn't look any better than yesterday, the circles under his eyes were still there. Still, at least he *felt* better. The ghosts that haunted him had disappeared and the clearer he recalled the events of yesterday, the better his mood became. *Report to Superintendent Gennat on Monday morning* was the first order from Lanke that he was happy to obey.

Naturally they had spoken about it the previous evening as Bruno drove him home. Uncle had simply nodded when he heard about Lanke's instructions. *I told you so,* no doubt it was supposed to mean. Rath had remained in his seat for a moment when the black Ford came to a halt in Nürnberger Strasse. Saying goodbye at the door of the car had felt like saying goodbye to E Division, like saying goodbye to a colleague, the like of whom he would struggle to find in A Division.

'If those bastards in A get on your nerves, just come and see me,' Bruno had called after him, as he drove down Nürnberger Strasse.

The sky was an outrageous shade of blue, and Rath had no desire to have his morning spoilt by a foul-tempered Elisabeth Behnke. Just the right weather for a spot of breakfast at *Josty* on Potsdamer Platz. In the mornings the sun shone through Leipziger Strasse directly onto the café terrace.

His attempts to avoid Elisabeth Behnke backfired when he almost tripped over her. What was she doing at such an hour in her tenant's bathroom of all places?

She flashed her eyes furiously at him as she crouched by the open flap of the boiler and busied herself in the ash with a poker.

'So,' she hissed, 'sleep well, Inspector?'

He ignored her tone. 'Oh yes, thanks, very well,' he replied, knowing that his exaggerated friendliness would provoke her even more. 'Only, I was awakened a little noisily . . .'

She flung the poker into the ash so that it threw up a cloud of dust.

'Would the gentleman also like to take a bath and complain that the boiler isn't clean?'

So that was the reason there had been trouble this morning. Rath couldn't imagine that Weinert had been looking for it.

'But Elisabeth . . .' he began.

'Don't give me Elisabeth!' She was seriously angry. 'Just tell me, what is the meaning of this mess?'

He still didn't understand what she meant. She crouched in front of the boiler again, poked around furiously with the tongs and finally pulled out a long, only partially burned strip of fabric. Rath gave a start. The last remains of his suit!

'Perhaps you can tell me why you've put cleaning rags in the boiler? And don't tell me it wasn't you! Weinert couldn't get the boiler to work thanks to this rubbish, and left for work unwashed and in a foul mood. But it's all the same to you! The pair of you don't give a damn about anything, and so it's always left to old Behnke to do the dirty work!'

'I'm sorry.' He did genuinely regret it. Why hadn't he taken a closer look at the boiler yesterday? 'Come, allow me, I'll clear it up.'

He reached out his hand for the fabric. Suddenly she began to sob and covered her face with her soot-blackened hands. The suit rag fell to the floor and he realised that she was embarrassed to cry in his presence. He'd have liked nothing more than to take her in his arms and comfort her, but that was the worst thing he could do in this situation. He stood next to her helplessly.

'Elisabeth, it's OK. I wasn't thinking, I needed to throw the old rag out and . . .'

She stood up and looked at him out of tear-swollen and black-smudged eyes.

'Why can't you just be an arsehole?' she said, and disappeared through the door.

He looked at the mess in front of the boiler and sighed. Then he started to clean.

He was at the Castle earlier than usual. With no-one else in the office he used the time to study the lists in peace. It seemed that some of the women to whom they owed the success of Operation Nighthawk in the first place had fallen back into their clutches. They had picked up Squealing Sylvie in *Bar Noir*, and Red Sophie in *Blauer Holunder*. The ladies obviously felt safe following their release and had already started working again. Rath could have bet they were already back posing as models for pornographic snaps, although not in Johann König's studio, as he was still awaiting trial in Moabit.

Squealing Sylvie spat at Rath when she recognised him. He had plumped for the troop from *Bar Noir* to start with. Not because he set great store by a reunion with Sylvia Walkowski, but rather because there were two names on the list that had aroused his curiosity.

Nikita Ivanovitsch Fallin and Vitali Pjotrevitsch Selenskij were their full names. More instructive were the comments that ED had added to their particulars: Fallin, the first name on the list, Scar Face therefore, had attracted attention in February 1926 due to a count of grievous bodily harm. In the column below, the officer had only needed to write *ditto* after Selenskij's name. Even then the pair had been inseparable, and hadn't hesitated in bringing their physical strength to bear.

He acquired a stenographer and an interrogation room, and had the various characters brought in, in the order they appeared on the list. He didn't want to let anyone know about his particular interest in the Russians and so had to work his way through a procession of small-time crooks and more or less innocent family men, as well as being spat at by Squealing Sylvie, until the list was down to the two men.

At last.

However, when he telephoned the officer in the holding cells to request that the first of the two Russians be sent through, he received a surprise. At first he thought he had misheard.

'What's that supposed to mean: *is no longer there?*'

He was almost shouting down the receiver, which didn't seem to unsettle the warder. Rath heard papers rustling as the man leafed through his documents.

'Nikita Ivanovitsch Fallin was released this morning,' the warder said. 'Along with another Russian . . .' Another rustle of paper. '. . . Vitali Pjotrevitsch Selenskij.'

'Him as well?' Now Rath was *really* shouting. 'Who the hell authorised that?'

'The commissioner.'

'You're trying to tell me that Dörr . . . , that Herr Zörgiebel personally came by to release prisoners?'

'Of course not. His signature and stamp are enough.'

'And who brought you these release papers?'

'They were in the in-tray this morning. As is normal in a case like this.'

'What do you mean?'

'Special treatment. You haven't been working here long, have you?'

'The only thing I know is that two important witnesses have vanished!' Rath was becoming louder and louder. *Ignorant Prussian rabble!*

'Don't get so worked up. You have the address. You can go and visit the witnesses at home. That's how your colleagues normally do it.'

Rath slammed the phone into the cradle before he could be charged with insulting a police official.

He stormed out of the interrogation room, snorting with rage. Uncle was talking to a man whose top hat and tails looked significantly worse for wear following a night in police custody. Both men looked up in surprise as he stormed through the door.

'Can you break off for a moment?' Rath asked.

Wolter ordered the officer in the corridor outside to keep an eye on the man in the tailcoat and went outside with him. Uncle pulled him into a niche that led to the atrium.

'Have you lost your mind?' he hissed when they were alone. 'You can't just storm into my office and interrupt an interrogation.'

'It's still *our* office.'

'Let's not split hairs! This had better be important.'

'I'm sorry, but I can hardly believe what goes on in this place!'

'Calm yourself down!'

Rath told him what had happened.

'Special treatment, you say?' Wolter laughed. 'Then you're out of luck!'

Rath didn't understand.

'Someone's bailed out one of their stoolies. The two of them must be working as police narks. That's normal here, we don't want our informants sitting in the can. They're not much use to us there. That's probably why someone's made sure they were released.'

'But who?'

Wolter shrugged his shoulders. 'No idea. Political police. CID. Could've been anyone.'

'There must be some way of following this up. When I catch the knucklehead who let these guys out . . . well, they're in for a rude awakening!'

Wolter shook his head. 'Follow it up? I'm afraid you'll be banging your head against a brick wall. Our colleagues keep things close to their chest when it comes to informants. All it usually takes is a confidential letter to the commissioner, who issues the release papers, and hey presto.'

'But Zörgiebel isn't even on duty today.'

'The commissioner is always on duty, remember that. He has the most urgent documents delivered to his house every morning, even at the weekend, which he signs at breakfast time.'

'So, at breakfast time the commissioner releases the people we've bust our balls to catch during the night?'

'Now, wait a minute. No-one's released any criminals here. We detained people who were in the wrong bar for a night. Without a warrant, we can't keep them longer than twenty-four hours anyway.'

'They weren't even locked up for ten hours. We didn't let them go home last night for good reason. They've both got police records!'

'If you think you're onto something, then you can go and visit them at home.'

'That's exactly what they told me in the holding cells.'

'Well, there you go.'

'I still don't understand. Why didn't our colleague just warn his informants before the raid? Instead of pulling a stunt like this.' He couldn't help thinking back to how he had advised Krajewski against going out on Saturday night in *Haus Vaterland* a few days before.

'Warn them? How do you think that would work? Narks are fundamentally untrustworthy. The very fact they're working for you is proof that they have no principles. And you want to give someone like that confidential information? I'd far sooner pull a stunt like that, as you call it.'

That stood to reason. Rath decided it was best not to tell Bruno anything about his meeting in *Haus Vaterland*, about how he had warned Krajewski.

'Believe me, it's not such a bad idea to nab these guys once in a while. You remember how we searched Kaiser Wilhelm's house? Something like that gets you respect. Every so often, these people need to be reminded that they're on thin ice, otherwise they get cocky. Besides, narks are more credible with their own people if they get hassled every now and then by the cops.'

'But not when they're released prematurely.'

'Who's going to find out? To their pals in the cells, it just looks like they're being led away for a good grilling. And after their unexpected premature release, they owe their friendly local officer a few favours again. That's how it works. You have to bring your informants to heel. It doesn't take long for them to get fresh. That's when you have to show them who's boss, that it's you who decides whether they're in trouble or not.'

A little while later, Rath was back in the interrogation room working his way through the list one name at a time. No-one else from their haul at *Bar Noir* had been released early; he had them brought to him one by one from the cells. The interrogations weren't particularly fruitful, but he was nevertheless able to pass a few characters on to different departments. All of them small fry. There weren't any criminal masterminds in that motley crowd. Rath's last day in E Division was also one of his most boring. He was finding it harder and harder to concentrate, and noticed himself gradually taking mental leave of Vice squad.

His thoughts were already revolving around A Division. That is: they were already revolving around a particularly beautiful face in A Division.

He had had no choice but to wait, but it wasn't only his patience that was being sorely tested. People were looking at him curiously, as he stood by the construction hoarding, gazing at the brick mountain that was police headquarters. He viewed it as fitting punishment for his idiotic behaviour yesterday, but then his waiting was rewarded as she strode energetically between the hoardings which guided pedestrians through the maze of construction sites towards the station at Alexanderplatz. Rath withdrew into a corner and waited until she had passed. She hadn't noticed him. It wasn't so easy to keep pace with her; several passers-by grumbled as he jostled past. But finally, he caught up with her, and was holding the bouquet of roses, purchased at the train station scarcely half an hour before, under her nose as they walked.

He could have embraced Charly on the spot as her face reflected her various states of mind in quick succession. First surprise, then, when she recognised him, something approaching indignation, and then a smile tugged at her mouth, which she nevertheless tried to repress, and which had soon entered into a duel with her indignant expression. He followed her, waving the roses and putting on his most charming 'deep down all men are just little boys' grin. When he saw her dimple forming, he knew he had won. He could have shouted 'hurrah' out loud, but managed to pull himself together. She stood still once more.

'And there I was beginning to worry this could turn into a marathon,' he said and handed her the flowers.

'Did you have a good sleep?' she asked. She smiled as she spoke, and inside he jumped for joy.

'Why? I'll sleep at the end of the month.'

At last she took the flowers. 'They're lovely,' she said. 'Pick them yourself?'

'Fresh from the evidence room.'

'And what am I supposed to do with them? I don't see any vases anywhere.'

'We'd better eat them here.'

She laughed and, at last, he put his arm around her.

A short time later they were standing in front of Weinert's Buick in Dircksenstrasse. The journalist had granted the favour after Rath promised him a few pieces of exclusive information about yesterday's raid. The press still didn't know anything about the operation. Weinert hadn't hesitated in bringing Rath the keys. The exchange hadn't taken place at the

Castle, of course. They had met for a beer in the *Letzte Instanz* and afterwards they had returned to their jobs, Weinert to his office in Kochstrasse and Rath, car key in pocket, to the station. He had worked his way through the rest of the names on the list in no time.

And now he was standing in front of Weinert's Buick, jangling the keys and savouring her big eyes.

'Yours?' she asked.

'When I want to impress women, I always get hold of a car.'

He opened the passenger door like a practised chauffeur.

'Thank you Johann.' She stretched her chin out and sounded strangely nasal. 'You can finish work a little earlier today, and when you've washed the car please come to my bed chamber.'

'Very good, ma'am.'

'Please, I'm not married.'

'Unmarried? Well, I'd never have . . .'

'Don't get fresh!' She shook her head indignantly. 'Tsk, tsk. Such impudence. It wouldn't have been like this under the Kaiser!'

She was right about that. The chauffeur took it a step further by giving the young lady a kiss, a long one at that, before starting the engine and driving off. First port of call was Moabit as the roses needed to go in water. He didn't mention that he was also curious about where she lived. He took the tourist route, chauffeuring her past the castle and via Unter den Linden through the Brandenburg Gate, past the Reichstag and victory column and over the Spree. They drove with the top down, and such was his joy that he felt like he could spread his wings and fly as she sat next to him, her black hair blowing in her face.

Unfortunately, it took less than quarter of an hour for them to reach Spenerstrasse. And he had to wait in the car.

'It's better this way,' she said. 'Greta still doesn't know anything about you. We don't want the poor girl to have a stroke. She isn't too keen on men at the moment.'

A short time later she was back in the car. He wasn't sure, but he could almost believe she was freshly made-up. And she was wearing a different coat.

'Where to now?'

He glanced at the time. 'Nearly eight. I think it's time for a nice dinner.

And since we already have a car, then we should really take a drive into the country. It's Sunday after all.'

The restaurant *Bellevue* was situated on Lake Tegel. They sat on the terrace and watched the sun go down.

'Nice new suit you've got there,' she said.

Rath shrugged his shoulders. 'Do you think so? I needed something new for work. I've got my first day in a new division tomorrow, you see.'

Her face was priceless.

'No!' she said.

'Yes!' He enjoyed her surprise. 'I have to report to Gennat at eight on the dot. That's an order from Lanke himself.'

'That's going to be hard. We'll be running into each other the whole time.'

'I can think of worse things.'

'You know what I mean,' she sighed. 'No-one can see us together. Officially, we barely know each other. We'll have to address each other formally.'

'Then we'd better toast our friendship pretty soon. In front of all our colleagues I mean.'

'My God, Gereon. I don't know if I can do this.' She appeared genuinely dismayed.

'You're not even in work tomorrow.'

'Luckily! That way I've got a few days at least to mentally prepare myself for the new situation.'

'It's only temporary. I've no idea how long a stint like this usually lasts.' He didn't want to tell her everything, above all the role his father had played in the transfer.

'Once I've got used to the fact that you belong to us, then you should stay.' She took a sip of Riesling. 'It'd be a good thing for our division. You wouldn't believe how many idiots there are in A.'

'Maybe, but there are idiots in E too.' He thought of Lanke. 'Probably all over the Castle.'

'Well, at least one of them's going now. Vain little toerag.'

'Erwin Roeder.'

She nodded appreciatively. 'You're well informed! Are you eating in the canteen more often now?'

'People know about Roeder's story at Aschinger's too.'

'Do they know that he's not just leaving A, but quitting the whole force?'

'I've been wondering whether I should apply.'

'It'd be nice if it worked out, but it's probably pointless. I've heard that Dörrzwiebel already has someone lined up. Probably another arselicker or someone with connections. At any rate, they say Gennat isn't best pleased.'

Rath was now certain he would apply. He didn't want her to think he was an arselicker. Or someone with connections.

'I thought Gennat only takes the best.'

'He does, but he can only choose from the candidates the commissioner puts forward and Roeder's already been relieved of his duties. We need people urgently.'

'Sometimes I have the impression that A Division devours CID officers like Cronos did his children.'

She raised her eyebrows. 'I say, classically educated.'

'People from Cologne know their way round the antique Gods. We're all ancient Romans after all.'

'We're using up a huge number of officers at the moment. Take *Aquarius*, the case I told you about last time—we have detailed knowledge about how the vehicle ended up in the canal with the corpse, we know the cause of death, and the places on the body where the injections were given . . .'

'Injections?'

'Yes. They gradually pumped him full of drugs. We can almost completely reconstruct the poor devil's last hours. It's taken unbelievable commitment to find all that out, and yet we still don't know what the poor guy is called. Let alone why he had to die.'

'And Zörgiebel still keeps on?'

'He still calls, but less often than last week. If the press forgets about a case, at some point it becomes less important for the commissioner.'

'Then drop it.'

'That's what Böhm suggested to the boss. He thinks there are more important unsolved deaths for Homicide to be concerned about. But Zörgiebel doesn't want to know, so, for the time being Böhm has to keep going.

And gather together informants who aren't bringing us any closer to solving the case.'

'You've probably amassed a mountain of files?'

'Yes. It's slowly becoming confusing. And it's mostly superfluous, if you ask me. The number of people we've asked in the area around Tempelhofer Ufer! Countless statements, but none that point to a possible perpetrator.'

She was talking herself into a real rage. When he saw her in her element like this, he could have eaten her alive on the spot. Instead he sipped on his coffee and continued to listen.

'At least we have two witnesses, who observed the same thing independently of one another, two men helping a third into a cream-coloured vehicle that was parked on Möckernstrasse, not far from the bridge.'

Rath's ears pricked up. 'Two *men?*' He asked, almost as a reflex. His curiosity in all matters Kardakov hadn't run dry. In his mind an image appeared of Alexej Kardakov and Svetlana Sorokina disposing of Boris's corpse after they had relieved him of the Sorokin gold.

'That's what the statements say, two men. Why?'

'Strange that one always assumes that criminals are men. The possibility that it could be a woman is all too hastily discarded.'

She considered briefly. 'There's something in that,' she said. 'Women really are constantly being discriminated against. In every field, even crime.'

The house in Nürnberger Strasse was dark when he arrived home. Charly had insisted that he take her back to Spenerstrasse, even if they wouldn't spend the night together. Instead they had sat in the car for a long time outside the house and kissed. Rath could have bet that Greta, had she chanced to look out of the window just once, would have seen more than if he and Charly had actually gone up to the flat. But she had her principles and he wanted to respect them.

He removed the key after he had parked the Buick in front of the main door, and snapped the hood shut. There had been so many thunderstorms these last few nights that you just never knew, and there was an unpleasant closeness in the air.

In the house, all was quiet. He knocked quietly on the door to Weinert's room. No reaction. Perhaps he was still at the office? A second knock also went unanswered. Rath opened the door. Weinert would have done the same. The gleam of light from the hall fell on an empty bed. The journalist really wasn't at home. Maybe *he* had a girlfriend with whom he could spend the night. Rath sighed as he thought about Charly, lying all alone in her bed.

He groped for the light switch beside the door. If there was no-one at home, then there was no reason for him to bang his shin against a chair that might be in the middle of the room. The light from the bulb told him that everything was in its rightful place. Weinert's room looked the same as always. The empty bed at the side, by the window the desk and chair. Weinert's wardrobe appeared just as enormous as Rath's. The most noticeable difference in the furnishings was the desk and the large bookshelf.

Where to put the car key? The chaos on the desk seemed too great to put anything else on top. His gaze fell on the typewriter. What if he were to place the key on the keyboard? A journalist couldn't fail to see something like that. There was still a sheet of paper in the machine, which was almost completely covered in writing. It looked as if Weinert had forgotten about it after his argument with old Behnke this morning. Perhaps he had missed it in the office?

He was just about to turn away to find a more suitable place to leave the keys, when two words from the heading above the article caught his eye.

Red Fortress.

It took a moment for him to remember. Of course, that was the organisation that Major General Seegers had mentioned. The *Red Fortress.* The secret communist society.

What does the Red Fortress want? read the whole title above the article in the typewriter.

Rath was amazed. How was it that Weinert was preoccupied with the same communist sect that Rath had encountered during the course of his investigations into Kardakov? That was a strange coincidence, but then the penny dropped.

Berthold Weinert had known Alexej Kardakov.

The journalist had been living at Nürnberger Strasse for more than a year. And for all that time, he had been the neighbour of the missing Kardakov. Rath was prepared to bet that Berthold Weinert knew more about his neighbour than Elisabeth Behnke did. The man was a journalist.

20

So, there he was sitting opposite the legend. Because that's exactly what Superintendent Gennat was. The chief of homicide was known as *Buddha*, partly on account of his stoic calm, but more because of his corpulence, which had also earned him the nickname *The Full Ernst* from less respectful colleagues. Gennat's passion for cakes was known throughout the city. In the past, he had often made the murder wagon stop at the bakery *en route* to an investigation, and only with an ample selection of cakes would they proceed to the crime scene. That was a few years ago. Now, Gennat seldom drove out himself. It wasn't necessary anymore because the Homicide division he had set up at Alex was staffed with hand-picked officers and boasted one of the best detection rates in the whole of the Castle. For the most part, Gennat remained in his office, its furnishings more akin to that of a living room, eating cakes and pulling strings. He knew about every single investigation and still undertook particularly tricky interrogations himself. His psychological astuteness was infamous. He had made even the most hard-bitten customers pour their hearts out.

Rath could see very well how, too, now that he was sitting opposite this man whose reputation preceded him. Gennat appeared friendly, almost sleepy, and carried his double chin with a certain pride. But Rath wasn't about to be fooled; out of this gentle face blazed two eyes on high alert. Two eyes that were currently examining the new inspector with curiosity.

They hadn't sat down at his desk, but rather at a living room table, round which were two green chairs and a worn, green sofa. The door to the outer office opened where Gertrud Steiner, Gennat's long-serving secretary, balanced a tray with tea. A lavish selection of cakes was already laid out on the table. While she poured, Gennat assumed the task of doling out the cakes. Rath asked for a nut cake; all he could tolerate at this hour. Gennat meanwhile shovelled an enormous slice of gooseberry tart onto his own plate.

'Thank you, Trudchen.' Gennat sank back into the green cushions. 'Tuck in, Herr Rath,' he said and took a sip of tea. 'You haven't been in Berlin long, I understand?'

'Barely two months.'

'In which division?'

'E.'

'And before that you were in Cologne?'

'Yes.'

'Have you ever been part of a murder investigation?'

'Many times. In Cologne we don't have a permanent Homicide division like here, but there are specialists. It was usually me they consulted following a suspected homicide.' Sell yourself as best you can, he thought.

Gennat didn't seem impressed. 'Yes. I've heard all about your previous service. You know the commissioner from before?'

'That's right. I worked under Herr Zörgiebel when I was in Cologne. He entrusted me with the lead on several investigations.'

Gennat nodded and took a forkful of cake. Rath used the pause to take a bite of his nut cake, nodding in appreciation. The best he had eaten in Berlin so far. Gennat knew where to shop.

'Now, Herr Rath, you will initially be deployed in a team that has already been operational for some time. We need every man possible on investigation *Möckern Bridge*.'

Investigation *Möckern Bridge* was the official name for *Aquarius*. So much for a position of responsibility, that would have been too good to be true. So, it was donkey work after all. Rath tried to swallow his disappointment, and reached for his teacup.

'This case is currently causing us a lot of trouble,' Gennat continued. 'An unidentified dead man. You will have heard about it, as we informed the other divisions last week. The thing was in all the papers . . .' Rath correctly sensed what was coming next. '. . . I'm afraid even that has scarcely provided our colleague Böhm with any clues. But he is an experienced man. You can learn a lot from him.'

So, it seemed good old Zörgiebel had led his pal Engelbert Rath up the garden path. The commissioner was only interested in putting as many men as possible on a case he had become fixated on.

'Believe me, sir, it is a great honour to be able to work in Homicide.'

'No need to speak so loftily, my dear Rath! It's not an honour, it's a bloody grind, you should be aware of that. You can forget about finishing at a regular time . . .'

The door flew open and Gertrud Steiner stormed into the room without a teapot. Gennat looked up in annoyance.

'What's the matter, Trudchen? I did say no interruptions!'

'That's why I'm here, sir! Because I *had* to interrupt! There's a call for you, I think you should take it!'

'Well, put them through.' Gennat stood up, and the secretary returned to the outer office. No sooner had she closed the door than the telephone on his desk sounded. He picked up.

'Yes?'

His gaze, which moments before had been mourning the plate of cakes he had left behind, grew suddenly serious.

'Where?' he asked, and pulled out a pencil.

'When?' The pencil scratched against the paper.

'No. We can't bother Böhm with it. He has enough on his plate. He's got Zörgiebel on his case every day.'

A scratch of the pencil and then Gennat fell silent. It wasn't clear if he was listening or thinking.

'Pull Henning and Czerwinski off the stakeout, and inform ED. I'll take care of the rest.'

He hung up. Slowly, he returned to the table and sat down at his plate of cakes. Silently, he shoved a forkful of gooseberry tart into his mouth and chewed on it slowly. He still appeared to be thinking. Then he placed the cake fork on the plate.

'My dear Rath, forget most of what I've just told you.' Gennat looked him in the eye and asked, 'Do you think you're capable of leading a homicide investigation?'

The murder wagon was waiting with its engine running as Rath and Jänicke stormed into the atrium. He had requested the rookie from Gennat, and Lanke had provided. He needed at least one familiar face in his homicide team, and unfortunately Bruno was out of the question. But, an assistant detective from the old troop, at least that was a start. Rath had sensed the mistrust confronting him as soon as he stepped into the car. No wonder: for three of the four men in the vehicle, he was a stranger. The driver and the two CID officers examined him defiantly. Not even Jänicke gave him a friendly look. The stenographer was the only one who smiled. Luckily her name was Christel Temme, and not Charlotte Ritter.

'Good morning, madam. Good morning gentlemen,' Rath said as he fell onto the well-cushioned back seat. 'Shall we then?'

He hadn't even managed to close the door when the driver stepped on the gas, and they shot out through the exit onto Alexanderstrasse.

Now he was sitting between Stephan Jänicke and the man who had introduced himself as Detective Paul Czerwinski, a small overweight man with the beginnings of a bald patch. He must have been roughly the same age as Rath but looked a little older on account of his thinning hair—and was two ranks below him in the police hierarchy. In the passenger seat in front was Assistant Detective Alfons Henning, whom Jänicke had addressed by his first name, a tall, gangly young man, whose eyes danced behind his glasses. The two assistant detectives obviously knew each other from police academy. Perhaps the atmosphere might yet improve.

The journey wasn't a long one. The address hadn't meant anything to Rath at first, but now that the murder wagon was approaching *Schlesischer Bahnhof*, the area seemed more familiar. The vehicle made a few turns before reaching Koppenstrasse, coming to a halt in front of a wide gap in the row of houses. A plaque revealed that the not-for-profit housing cooperative NOVA was throwing up a light and modern tower block complex. A hoarding blocked the view of the building site.

The ED vehicle was parked at the side of the road. Otherwise the only sign that anything had happened here was the presence of two cops who were chatting by the entrance to the construction site. Barely a single passer-by paused at the scene. No wonder. The standard phrase that every police officer reeled off to protect a crime scene from rubberneckers—*please move on! There's nothing to see here!*—held true in this case. Apart from a site fence and two cops, there really was nothing to see.

The uniformed officers saluted as the various members of CID climbed out of the vehicle. One of them stayed where he was, the other escorted the officers to the building site. At the moment there was nothing doing. To the left was a digger without a driver. Some of the workers had settled on a sunlit stack of planks, while others were standing around, hands in their pockets. The majority, however, had gathered on the other side of the construction pit at an embankment made out of excavated March of Brandenburg sand and were gazing into the depths. Down at the foundations a group of cops had also taken up position, though clearly there was more to see than just blue uniforms. Next to the construction pit, the men from ED had already started their work. They were mixing plaster of Paris in a little tub to pour into the footprints.

A thickset man detached himself from the group of construction workers and came towards them.

'This is the site foreman,' the cop said, 'he can show you everything.'

The foreman greeted them with a nod when he reached them. He was wearing white overalls, and a blue wool pullover covered in plaster and cement. His hair was greying. He had to squint against the sun as he examined first Czerwinski and then Rath.

'Come with me then, gentlemen,' he said, in a thick Berlin accent.

Even though the sun was shining, the ground was still slippery from the rain of the previous nights. The men cursed as the foreman led them across the site. Mud, sludge and puddles everywhere. They had almost everything you could think of in the murder wagon, even a mini chemistry lab, but no-one had remembered to bring gumboots.

The uneasy feeling accompanying Rath intensified as they approached the other side of the excavation. The south-side of the site was also blocked by a hoarding. In the background the brick walls of a dreary rear courtyard rose up against the sky.

'Where did you find him?' he asked the foreman, who was walking directly in front of him.

'What d'you mean find? I just saw that the lads had messed up the foundations, the whole base was like hill country, so I says open it up again, we need to re-pour it. And then suddenly a leg appears in the concrete. Naturally, we called you straightaway, Superintendent.'

'Detective Inspector.'

'Whatever you say.'

It wasn't until they had walked around the construction pit and were standing on the embankment that they saw something black peeking out from the concrete: crinkled fabric, full of cement, unmistakeably a trouser leg.

'At first we just thought it was an old pair of trousers, thrown in as a joke. But there's someone in there.'

Rath nodded and climbed into the excavation, no longer paying attention to where he stepped. He could forget about his shoes, the second pair he'd chucked inside a couple of days.

The cops saluted him.

'First Sergeant Stürickow, 87th precinct,' said the highest-ranking officer. 'Suspected male corpse in the concrete, sir.'

'Not yet recovered?'

'Not yet recovered, sir. Waiting for CID first.'

Exemplary. The realisation that forensics was an important aspect of police work was gradually seeping through to even the beat cops. Here of all places he had to meet one who seemed to have understood.

A pitiless anxiety slowly but inexorably took hold of him. He was almost trembling, but there were men gazing at him, mesmerised, and awaiting instructions. Detective Inspector Gereon Rath was here to issue orders. Very well, he didn't want to disappoint them. He would keep them so busy they didn't have time to think.

'Henning, bring the camera down here,' he cried. 'Before we start uncovering everything, we need photographs of the *status quo*.'

The assistant detective had strapped the camera round his shoulders and was labouring down the embankment, almost slipping in the damp topsoil.

Rath turned to the foreman. 'Is there somewhere we could talk in private?'

Shortly afterwards they stood in the neighbouring rear courtyard in front of a trailer that had been secured with a new padlock. Two kids were playing hopscotch on the pavement.

'Had to park it here,' the foreman explained. 'No space on the site itself. And what happens? 'Course: it gets broken into.' The construction worker fiddled awkwardly with the key in the lock. 'Wouldn't surprise me if it was one of the low-lives around here. Anti-socials, all of them.'

He nodded disgustedly in the direction of the two children. Rath didn't have to ask him to continue. 'A bike was nicked, and about ten marks are missing from our drinks kitty. Your colleagues were already here on *Sonnabend*, but they didn't find anything.'

Rath felt uneasy at the small, rickety table. The foreman sat opposite, with the stenographer between them. Christel Temme was approaching fifty and had nothing in common with Charly. Nevertheless, she took her job seriously, which consisted of taking everything they said down in shorthand. Beyond that she wasn't concerned about anything; she left the thinking to the horses, or in this case, the CID.

First, Rath took down the man's details—Edgar Lauffer, 57 years of age, resident in Danziger Strasse—then the real questioning could begin.

'So,' he said. 'Let's start again at the beginning. How and when did you discover that something wasn't right with the construction site?'

The foreman scratched his head. 'Well, this morning, of course. I hope you're not after an exact time?'

'If possible, yes.'

'We start at six. First I go through what needs to be done that day with the team and then I divide them up. So that everyone knows what they should be doing. Don't want anyone to be standing around looking stupid in the corner, do we?'

Rath fiddled with his pen and looked up at the trailer roof, while the stenographer tirelessly noted every syllable.

'Should I carry on?' Lauffer seemed a little confused.

'Please do.' Rath could sound about as merciful as a Grand Inquisitor. Lauffer began to stutter.

'Well . . . I think it must have been around quarter to seven when I went down to the excavation and saw the whole mess.'

'What did you see?'

'It was the concrete . . . it was all . . . how can I put it . . . it looked more like the High Alps than a foundation.'

'And when did you actually pour the foundation?'

'Friday. I know that for a fact. It was after the public holiday.'

'And on Saturday . . . I mean *Sonnabend*, the concrete was still fine?'

Lauffer began kneading his hat. His face told of his guilty conscience. It wasn't just that he had used the break-in to pocket the contents of the drinks kitty; Rath suspected that the construction workers had spent most of their Saturday drinking beer and playing skat. At any rate, they hadn't made great strides with the building. It was the only way he could explain the foreman's embarrassment.

'So?' Rath probed. 'Was the concrete OK on *Sonnabend*?'

'I don't know.'

'But you were working here.'

'Yes. But there was the break-in, the whole kerfuffle.'

'You didn't take a look at the foundation?'

'I looked to see if the concrete had set. It had rained the previous night, remember?'

'But the whole mess, as you just called it, you hadn't noticed it by then?'

'No, I suppose not, but . . .'

'So the corpse could have been deposited in the concrete on Sa . . . *Sonnabend*, or even Sunday.'

Lauffer shrugged his shoulders. 'Don't know. Only if someone opened that corner back there up again, chucked the corpse in and re-poured. It was already beginning to set on *Sonnabend*.'

'But it's possible. You just said you didn't notice anything about the concrete on *Sonnabend*.'

'No, that's right. Didn't see the whole mess until this morning.' The relief on Lauffer's face was palpable. 'It wasn't one of my lads. It was a murderer who ripped up all our good work. They stop at nothing these days, these criminals!'

Rath felt pleased with himself as he left the trailer to take a look at the progress of the salvage operation. The conversation with the foreman couldn't have gone any better. In the excavation they were still retrieving the corpse from its concrete grave. Rath had assigned the task to Jänicke, and he was directing the cops, who were making a mess of their uniforms as they went. They had to make sure they didn't damage the corpse, and were going about their business carefully with hammer and chisel. From time to time there was a suppressed curse. The concrete was hard but still damp, and it was leaving ugly stains on their blue uniforms. The construction workers looked on, grinning furtively. The body of the deceased had already been uncovered; next would come the head. Slowly but surely, they whittled away the scraps and lumps of concrete.

Rath joined the others and once again had the uncomfortable feeling that all eyes were focused on him. *That's completely normal,* he told himself, *after all, you're the one who's leading the investigation.* For a brief moment, all eyes were averted as a man in a grey coat, holding a leather bag in his right hand and a hat in his left, made his way across the site, teetering through the mud like a stork. Dr Schwartz was recognisable from a long way off. The pathologist hadn't thought to bring gumboots either.

'Good morning, Doctor,' he greeted the pathologist, the latter gazing round searchingly, no doubt on the lookout for a familiar face from Homicide. Rath proffered a hand and came towards him. 'Detective Inspector Gereon Rath. I'm in charge of the investigation.'

Schwartz examined him closely. 'Haven't we met?'

'Only briefly. Hannoversche Strasse. I brought you two victims of the May disturbances.'

The penny dropped. 'Ah, yes,' he said, not showing the emotion this memory aroused. 'Then you enjoyed seeing those corpses so much that you just had to find some more?'

'It's good to enjoy your work.'

'You said it, my friend, you said it.'

Schwartz climbed into the excavation whistling a funeral march. A strange customer, Rath thought, and followed suit.

Despite the traces of concrete, the face of the deceased was now visible, even if the concrete had played havoc with its physiognomy, and the missing left eye made it seem like a grotesque mask.

Nevertheless, one of the uniformed officers who had helped dig him up seemed to recognise the dead man despite his disfigurements. Stürickow, the first sergeant from the 87th precinct, was flabbergasted.

'Well, I'll be damned,' he cried and took a step back. 'If it isn't Saint Josef! No wonder, he was always going to come to a sticky end!' He shook his head in disbelief. When he noticed the curiosity and surprise on the faces of those around him, he shrugged and added by way of explanation: 'I've known him since primary school.'

Saint Josef. That was the name Josef Wilczek had been given, since he wasn't just known as a highly versatile crook, but also as a devout Catholic. He didn't have any family, but Sergeant Stürickow and Wilczek's landlady could both identify him beyond any doubt at the morgue. By the time Jänicke provided the news from Hannoversche Strasse, Rath had long since got hold of Wilczek's file from the records office, and spread its contents across Erwin Roeder's abandoned desk. Ironically, it was exactly the same office that Charly had pulled him into a few days before. It wasn't especially big, but it had a distinct advantage over Rath's old office in E Division. Namely, he had it to himself. Even the outer office was abandoned, as Roeder's secretary had gone on holiday, most likely to type up the ex-policeman's new manuscript.

ED had photographed Wilczek from all sides. At the time, this peculiar saint had sported a moustache. The photographer had clearly forgotten to say *smile, please,* and Wilczek was gazing into the lens like someone who was about to gobble up small children as soon as the photo call ended.

Rath stared at the file as if it had landed on his desk from a bad dream. He had suspected it ever since he'd set foot on the site that morning. A single glance had been enough to dispel all doubt: it was the same construction site. On that fateful night, he had simply approached from the other side. From the south, and the rear courtyard where the trailer stood.

The realisation had hit him square in the face and he hoped that no-one noticed how nervous he was. Or at least that they had put it down to the fact that Detective Inspector Gereon Rath had been plunged in at the deep end when Buddha charged him with leading the investigation. Rath still couldn't quite believe it. Was that fate he could hear laughing behind the nearest door? His first official homicide case in this city, the case he had been waiting for—and a corpse that Detective Inspector Gereon Rath himself had buried. Well, congratulations!

Even in the seclusion of Roeder's tiny office, the thought persisted that the whole thing could be a trap. Why had Gennat sent him, of all people, out to the dead man? Was it really just because of a shortage of people in A Division? Or had everyone known about it for a long time and were simply waiting for him to make a mistake? Whenever he considered it more closely, however, he always came to the same conclusion: no-one could know anything. He just had to calm down and bring his paranoia under control.

His thoughts were interrupted by the ringing of the telephone. Either it was Gennat, or one of his colleagues reporting from the field. No-one else could have access to the new number. Sullenly, he reached for the receiver.

'Yes?'

'Good afternoon, Inspector! Herr Heinrich was kind enough to give me your number. It's Michael Lingen from *Tageblatt* here. I have a few questions if you don't mind . . .'

Which fucking idiot had given the press his number?

There was no reason to be friendly. 'And what if I do mind?' Rath said. 'It just so happens that I'm rather busy.'

'Please pardon the interruption, Inspector. Naturally you still have work to do during your final days at the station. But I thought—well, ultimately it's in your best interests.'

Your final days at the station? What the hell was that supposed to mean? Was the guy trying to blackmail him?

'What do you mean by that?' Inside, Rath had put up his fists.

'I mean exactly what I said.' The journalist didn't sound like he was trying to take him for a ride. Actually he sounded rather offended. 'Ultimately,' the man continued, 'you must want *Tageblatt* to bestow a favourable review on your new book, Herr Roeder!'

Rath didn't have to think long before alighting on a suitable response.

'Do you think a Prussian official can be bought?' he intoned. The *faux* outrage came easily to him. 'Do you think I'm going to say a damn thing to a hack like you?'

Rath slammed the receiver into the cradle. The new book by his ex-colleague Roeder was unlikely to come off too well in *Tageblatt* now.

The picture on his desk hauled him back to reality. Josef Wilczek was gazing at him furiously, as if reproaching him for his violent death. The face on the photograph seemed familiar somehow. It was easier to make out than the disfigured profile of his corpse; easier, too, than the face Rath had seen that night under the shadow of the brim of his hat.

Perhaps it was the moustache that made the difference. At any rate, Rath had the feeling that he had encountered the man before the fatal incident, but no matter which way he examined Wilczek's features he couldn't for the life of him say when and where their paths might have crossed. On Marlow's patch, perhaps? Or even before that? Rath pushed the thought aside.

It wouldn't get him anywhere right now. He had probably just dreamed of the dead man once too often.

There were more urgent things to worry about. One way or another he would have to be damn careful. He couldn't afford to make a mistake, which, paradoxically in this case, meant making as many mistakes as possible. Mistakes that made solving the case impossible without putting him in a negative light. If Rath wasn't going to solve this case, then he needed to do so in an intelligent way, that is, in a plausible way so that no-one thought he was a rank amateur, or worse still, became suspicious and began to surmise the truth.

He gave a start as the telephone rang.

'Inspector Rath, CID,' he said.

'Nibelungen publishing house,' he heard a woman say in a voice that seemed to brook no argument. 'Doctor Hildebrandt, outer office, I'm connecting you now . . .'

Before Rath could say anything, he was put through. The male voice on the other end of the line was one he hadn't heard before.

'Well, my dear fellow! Still hard at it these last few days? I'm sitting here with the final proof. The part where you mention the Jewification of the police force . . .'

Rath broke him off. 'Doctor Hildebrandt I presume?'

Silence at the other end of the line. The publisher needed a moment or two to compose himself.

'Who am I speaking to?' he asked after clearing his throat.

'CID, Berlin. If you want to report a crime, then you've telephoned the right place. If not, I recommend you use another line . . .'

Dr Hildebrandt hung up.

Rath let the receiver click back into place. The face on his predecessor's desk was staring at him as if to say: Hey! Forget Roeder! Concentrate on me! This is *my* file we're talking about!

Saint Josef. Why did it have to be a saint he'd buried, of all people?

For the most part the Berlin underworld was in the habit of naming its members after other distinguished characteristics, with the result that safe-breaker-Willis and razor-Edes were far easier to find than saints. But when it came to names, Wilczek would have made things difficult for an American

222 | VOLKER KUTSCHER

Indian tribe. The truth was he did everything, but nothing properly. His file gave no clear indication of what it was he specialised in. He had made a splash in various fields during the post-war years, always with something illegal. And he had always ended up getting caught. Indeed, the word 'rag-bag' might have been invented to describe Wilczek's rap sheet.

The list started with petty larceny and ranged from breaking and entering, perjury and falsification of documents right through to grievous bodily harm. All told, it amounted to two years in prison and five years' hard labour, and no doubt served as sufficient recommendation for *Berolina*, which was the most interesting thing he had gleaned from the file. Josef Wilczek belonged to Red Hugo's *Ringverein*, which, in turn, was in thrall to Dr M.—further proof that Johann Marlow must have put the man onto him.

Officially, of course, the Wilczek file pointed to a different conclusion, that the murderer moved in criminal circles. First of all, they would have to sound out *Berolina*, the perfect assignment for the rookie. Rath sent Jän-icke to the Barn Quarter, to *Mulackritze*, a known criminal hang-out, which was also a favourite of Red Hugo's men. He was almost certain that Johann Marlow would never show his face in a place like that. At most, he would send his Chinese bodyguard to haul the head of *Berolina* into a car waiting outside. No great danger, then, that the rookie would get in Dr M.'s way.

A convincing red herring—what more could he have asked for? Well, for one that Czerwinski and Henning got as little as possible out of the people in the tenement houses between Koppenstrasse, Münchebergstrasse and *Schlesischer Bahnhof.* But that was to be expected. The people in this district weren't especially talkative, particularly not to the police. He hoped to keep the two experts from Homicide pointlessly scouring the apartment houses for as long as possible. That way, they wouldn't get any big ideas, start reconsidering things and drawing their own conclusions.

He charged Christel Temme with making a neat copy of all the statements made by the construction workers. For the time being, that angle posed no danger. Even the interrogation of the site foreman couldn't have gone better. Lauffer's statement made it almost impossible to specify a timeframe when the corpse could have been deposited in the concrete. The workers had been even more vague than their foreman. According to their statements, the time of the incident was more likely to have been Saturday or Sunday than Friday. If push came to shove, he had an absolutely watertight alibi for both evenings, which could be confirmed by various police officers as well as a stenographer. He hoped he would never have to make use of it, but as matters stood there was still evidence out there that pointed to him.

The telephone on Roeder's desk rang again.

'Alexandria *Ringverein*. Services of all kinds. Who might I kill for you this time?'

'You could start by killing the jokes, Herr Rath! They're so old they should be given the *coup de grace*.'

It didn't seem to be a journalist, or a publisher either. The voice seemed familiar to him. 'Who am I speaking to, please?'

'Schwartz here. Can you spare a little time and come down to Hannoversche Strasse? Or would you rather keep playing the fool?'

The pathologist. Rath took a deep breath. At least it wasn't someone from the top floor. 'That was quick, have you finished the autopsy already?'

'No, but I thought you might like to attend. That way you'll have the initial results by this evening.'

Some sort of test of courage, no doubt. The pathologist wanted to see how the newbie reacted. Was he soft or could he handle it?

Rath decided he could handle it.

'I'll be with you in an hour, Doctor, if that's OK?'

Not even two weeks had gone by since he last passed through this door. Rath took a deep breath before entering the yellow-brick building in Hannoversche Strasse. This was where everything had begun. He gave the door that led from the foyer to the showroom a determined push and entered. On the way to the autopsy rooms, he went past a glass wall behind which Berlin's unidentified dead were laid out as in a macabre waxwork. This was where they had displayed Boris for three days, and yet there was no-one who knew the man, or at least no-one who would admit to it. In the meantime, he was certain that there were people in this city who were aware of both the first and last names of the dead Russian, and who nevertheless had good reason not to get in touch. People like Alexej Kardakov, for instance, or Svetlana Sorokina—and most likely Johann Marlow too.

The autopsy room was still sealed. Rath waited outside the door. What could he expect to find behind it? Did Schwartz merely want to shock him, or had he found something he could spring on the unsuspecting inspector? He tried to shake off this latest attack of paranoia. The darkness, the rain. No-one could possibly have recognised the men in the courtyard below.

His thoughts were interrupted by Dr Schwartz emerging energetically into the corridor, his lab coat waving behind him.

'Good day, Inspector,' the doctor said and shook his hand. 'Shall we, then?'

The keys jangled loudly as he opened the door. Rath followed him into the room, and saw that the corpse was already on the marble table, covered by a sheet. He watched Schwartz carefully wash his hands at the basin. There were only a few blood spatters on his white coat. Somehow the pathologist's elegant appearance didn't quite fit with his profession, or his primitive sense of humour.

'My first job as a concreter,' he said, as he approached the autopsy table.

'I dare say. Corpses encased in concrete are rather rare, aren't they?' Rath hoped that Schwartz hadn't noticed how nervous he was.

'I wouldn't bet on it, my friend,' Schwartz replied. 'There's a lot of building work in Berlin; and not everyone is granted a proper burial.' He winked at Rath. 'I wouldn't like to know how many new buildings have been erected on bones. But that's something for the archaeologists in a thousand years' time.'

He pulled back the white cotton sheet. Wilczek looked significantly cleaner than he had done in the excavation.

'I've taken the liberty of preparing something,' Schwartz said. 'So that you don't have to give up too much of your time.'

Wilczek's head looked like a beer stein with an open lid. Schwartz had sawn a perfect circle in the top of the skull to get to the brain. That was bearable. At least he hadn't expected Rath to deal with the sound of the bone saw. He had always found that to be the worst, much worse than all the blood, for example, or the sight of a face that had been skinned, the eyeballs gaping in their sockets like two glass marbles.

'Fortunately, most of the concrete was stuck to his clothing, so that contamination of the body was limited,' Schwartz said. 'I did find a lump in his mouth, but it entered *post mortem*. Likewise, some concrete also penetrated the skull, through this hole here.' He gestured towards the empty eye socket that gave Wilczek's opened head an even more sinister expression.

Rath breathed a sigh of relief. Dr Schwartz hadn't just done a little preparatory work; clearly he had already examined the corpse in detail. The doctor had most likely been trying to give the newbie in A Division a little scare.

'Can you say anything about the cause of death at this stage?' he asked, reeling off the routine questions a homicide detective asked a pathologist to conceal his nerves.

'It wasn't concrete poisoning, even if it looks that way,' Schwartz said. He opened a tin can and showed Rath a projectile smeared with blood. 'He got this in the eye, and it did him no good, I'm afraid.'

Rath nodded absent-mindedly and felt himself burning up. The goddamn bullet! He had seen it coming. Of course it had still been in his head, and the doctor had found it.

'It's a little deformed, could be a ricochet. So, probably an accident rather than a well-aimed shot,' Schwartz said and dropped the bullet back into the can. The *plink* was muffled by the smear of blood and brain. 'Something for your colleagues in Ballistics,' the doctor said, before screwing the can closed and handing it to the inspector.

'Are you one hundred percent sure about the cause of death?' Rath asked, as he accepted the plain tin can.

Schwartz shrugged. 'I've never known anyone to survive having a piece of metal like that in their brain, and I can't see another possible cause of death. The concrete came later, poor guy. He was already dead when he was buried. Nothing points to suffocation, and I haven't been able to find any other injuries that might have been fatal. The only thing was a badly healed nasal fracture. You don't die of something like that, and it's a few years old anyway.'

'Can you rule out all other causes of death? Poisoning, for example?'

'Young man, if you absolutely insist upon it, then I can open up the stomach. But believe me, it doesn't smell too good.'

'I know,' Rath said. 'But perhaps it is necessary.'

Schwartz laughed. 'I like you, you don't shy away from anything! Well, you can rest easy, Inspector. I've taken care of that already.' The pathologist pulled the sheet down past the navel. There were fresh incisions on the breast and stomach of the dead man, which had been hastily sown up again. 'I've examined the state of the vital organs, the contents of his stomach too. Nothing unusual, just beer and *bratwurst* leftovers.' He pulled the sheet back up. 'But there's something else that might interest you!' Schwartz lifted Wilczek's right wrist and turned it slightly. 'Before his sudden death it seems likely that our friend here also fired a gun. These powder burns suggest there was a shoot-out. Don't get too fixated on the idea, it's just a possibility.'

'And when did our man die?' Rath asked, rattling out the questions the same way he used to get through the Lord's Prayer: automatically, without listening to his own words, let alone what Dr Schwartz said in response. His mind was on other things.

The bullet.

As far as the case went, the piece of metal he was holding in his hand was the best lead so far. It was only a matter of time before word got out that the bullet Dr Schwartz had fished out of Wilczek's brain had come from the service revolver of Detective Inspector Gereon Rath.

'I hope that's sufficient, Inspector.'

'Pardon?'

Schwartz was gazing at him over the rim of his spectacles.

'Naturally you will also receive a written report of my findings, my good man, but I do expect you to listen. I am speaking to a detective inspector and not a medical student, am I not?'

'Sorry, Doctor.' Rath cleared his throat. 'I wasn't quite with it. Could you please repeat what you've just said?'

'I wouldn't do it for a student, so I hope you appreciate it.' Schwartz pushed his glasses up and suddenly sounded very officious. 'As already mentioned, I am afraid I cannot determine exactly when the death occurred, due to the heavy contamination of the open wound. A precise statement is further complicated by the fact that the corpse was embedded in concrete, which could conceivably have delayed the body's decomposition.'

Rath nodded. At least the spur of the moment decision to bury the body in concrete had achieved something.

'It is nevertheless certain,' Schwartz continued, 'that the corpse was not in the fresh air for long. The poor man was placed in concrete shortly after his death. Exactly when he came into contact with the concrete cannot be established on the basis of this forensic report. That could still take a few days, even a week.'

'Thank you, Doctor.'

'You will receive the written results tomorrow,' Schwartz said, before covering the corpse once more. 'There you will also find details pertaining to the state of the vital organs, the contents of the stomach and similarly appetising things . . .'

The bullet clattered in the can, as Rath walked through the showroom back towards the foyer. Each clattering sound reminded him that he was carrying a ticking time bomb.

Could be a ricochet.

Misdirected bullets seemed to follow him around in this city. First Krajewski on the scaffolding, then the two women in Neukölln, the ones who had brought him to the morgue in the first place, and now Wilczek. The last of these bullets was now threatening to bring him down.

He came to a halt in the lobby, just a few metres shy of the main door. A thought was racing through his mind, and he had to stand still to capture it. More a flash of inspiration than a thought, it felt almost as if it had sprung up of its own accord. The porter gazed at the inspector in amazement as the latter removed his wallet from his coat and looked inside, only to replace it and head for the porter's office.

'Where's the toilet here?' he asked.

'That way,' the porter said, pointing towards the swing door in the showroom.

A series of small signs coyly pointed the way. When Rath opened the door, all was quiet in the tiled room. He locked himself in one of the cubicles and opened the toilet lid. Soon he had opened his wallet and was examining the bullet from the Lignose. The projectile had long since become a sort of symbol for his friendship with Bruno, who had saved his life above Hermannplatz. But now there was a better use for it.

Rath opened the tin and let the bullet from the Mauser drop into the toilet bowl. There was a harmless splash, then a low click as the metal came into contact with the ceramic bowl. Streaks of red weaved their way through the water, gradually dissolving into pale red clouds. Next he dipped his index and middle fingers into the blood-smeared tin and rolled the bullet from the Lignose between his fingertips. When it looked bloody enough, he dropped it into the tin. Although Ballistics would certainly wash it before any examination, the bullet should at least appear as though it had been removed directly from a brain. Carefully, he screwed the lid tight and put the tin back in his pocket. After flushing he waited a moment or two until the swirl had died back down. There was no sign of the bullet, which had disappeared into the Berlin sewerage system. Perhaps a rat would swallow it by mistake, perhaps it would end up in a sewage farm, or perhaps it would simply disappear into the bowels of Hannoversche Strasse. At all events, it would never wind up under the microscope of a ballistics officer in ED.

Nor would there ever be a comparison sample for the bullet that was currently clacking around inside the can. The weapon it had been fired from had been taken out of circulation by Bruno, as part of the deal they had struck with the informant Krajewski. The ballistic examination in the Wilczek case would therefore, alas, come to naught.

This thought was an immense source of comfort, and Rath's mood improved straightaway. When he emerged from the cubicle, he would have liked nothing more than to whistle a tune, but he managed to restrain himself. Better not to attract attention. He couldn't hear anyone in the other cubicles, and he certainly hadn't seen anyone, but you could never be too sure. He cleaned the blood from his fingertips, and exited the toilet. There was no-one in the corridor, so he went back through the foyer and waved goodbye to the porter on his way out. Dusk was already falling.

21

Rath had divided his people into groups. Czerwinski and Henning, Plisch and Plum, as they were called at the Castle, were still knocking around the Stralau quarter, combing the tenement houses around the construction site. They appeared inseparable, and it was best to deploy them as one. Meanwhile, Jänicke was trying his luck with the honourable members of *Berolina*. Marlow would be nervous when he learned the cops were scoping out his favourite *Ringverein*. Perhaps the rookie would expose some sort of criminal squabble, which could conceivably serve as a motive. Of course, such a lead would come to nothing, but it was better to have a lead that came to nothing than to have nothing at all. If he had to begin his stint in A Division with an unsolved case, he wanted at least something to show for his efforts.

He sat at his new desk, thinking; brooding more than he would have liked. The telephone rang. Probably some reader or newspaper journalist for good old Herr Roeder! Well, he'd get rid of the lot of them for good!

'Plötzensee detention centre. Cellblock for delinquent authors and CID officers,' he answered.

'Kling, Zörgiebel's office.' It didn't sound as if the female voice on the other end of the line had a sense of humour. Dagmar Kling, also known as the Guillotine, guarded the commissioner's outer office like a Cerberus. 'Is that you, Inspector Rath?'

'Speaking.'

'The commissioner would like to see you in half an hour, Inspector.'

Rath knocked on Dagmar Kling's door promptly at nine, but was obliged to wait. She invited him to take a seat on a bench. The padded door to Zörgiebel's office was closed, as the commissioner was still in a meeting. Kling hadn't needed to say anything because, despite the padding, voices penetrated the door. The Guillotine carried on typing as if none of this concerned her, and yet they were bellowing so loudly in there that it was possible to hear almost every word. Rath pretended not to listen, playing instead with his hat and examining the engravings of old Berlin on the wall. Even if he had wanted to be discreet, the voices were impossible to ignore.

'. . . but we are doing everything humanly possible, Commissioner!' said the unmistakeable voice of DCI Wilhelm Böhm. The man seemed to be under a great deal of pressure; his barking sounded almost desperate.

'Then what is humanly possible is not enough!' Zörgiebel responded in the singsong Mainz accent Rath remembered from his Cologne days. The angrier the man became, the higher the pitch. Woe betide you if he moved from tenor towards alto, or even broke into soprano. 'The press wants to see some results! You don't have to solve the whole case but, heavens above, you must have *something* new!'

'Nothing that would interest the press, Commissioner. Numerous tiny details, maybe significant, maybe trivial. For the moment I can't decide, and I don't want to leave the choice to the press.'

'But you are there to make such decisions, DCI Böhm! By now you should have at least *something* approaching a lead, damn it! You can't stand here and tell me you're investigating all avenues. What lines of inquiry are you following right now? That's enough! We don't have to tell them anything more. The last press conference was over a week ago. I can understand why they're impatient. It's when we don't give them anything that speculation runs wild.'

'Then let it run wild. With all due respect, Commissioner, I am not some sort of media clown. I am trying to do my job.'

'Then kindly do it in such a way that it yields results. Do we understand each other?'

'My first duty is to the law, Commissioner, not to these newshounds! Let them write whatever they want. Good day!'

The door flew open and a bright-red Wilhelm Böhm shot out of the chief's office, past Rath and Dagmar Kling, who continued typing unmoved. What an exit, even if it wouldn't do his career any favours.

'Inspector,' Dagmar Kling said, gesturing towards the open door, 'the commissioner will receive you now.'

Zörgiebel had composed himself quickly. When Rath entered, he stood up and stretched out his arms like an opera singer.

'Young Inspector Rath!' He offered a fleshy paw. 'How have you settled in, my friend?'

Rath felt as if he had been ambushed. He would have preferred if the fat man had remained behind his desk and invited him to take a seat on one of the uncomfortable chairs. He certainly didn't want to be the commissioner's friend.

'Thank you. Berlin is no Cologne, but . . .'

'You said it! You said it!' Zörgiebel appreciated the truism, without being interested in further details.

The telephone rang and he picked up angrily.

'I said I didn't want to be disturbed, Fräulein Kling.' He listened for a while. 'I have already given the Interior Ministry my answer. The Berlin police will treat this case like any other. A normal missing person's case. Most of them turn up again after a few days. Now, please, no more disturbances.'

He hung up.

'A member of staff at the Soviet embassy has gone missing,' he said to Rath. 'The communists are already making a song and dance about it. I'd bet the guy has been enjoying a few good days—and nights—in our city, and will be back outside the embassy in no time. He wouldn't be the first to succumb to the temptations of capitalism.'

Zörgiebel led Rath to a seating area. The suite was relatively new, its chairs not as worn as the green monstrosities in Gennat's office. 'Please make yourself comfortable.'

Comfortable? Rath took a seat in one of the beige-coloured chairs, feeling anything but comfortable. At least there was no cake. 'Thank you, Commissioner.'

Zörgiebel offered him a cigar, which Rath turned down, took one for himself and placed the carton back on the table. 'So,' he said, 'What progress are you making with your homicide case?'

Good question, Rath thought. *I know who it was, but I'm not going to say!* 'The evidence points to an altercation in criminal circles,' he said, as bureaucratically as one might expect from a Prussian officer.

'That's something!' Zörgiebel beamed, probably hoping that this case, at least, would be quickly solved.

'The victim was a small-time crook, a member of the *Berolina Ringverein*,' Rath continued, 'the bullet a possible ricochet. Could have been an accident, therefore, or it could be that our man was involved in a shootout. There were powder burns on his right hand.' He broke off and shrugged his shoulders. 'But we still don't know anything else.'

'You don't know anything else? But that's already an awful lot, and in such a short space of time! Believe me, there are other detectives out there groping in the dark after weeks of investigations!'

The commissioner seemed to have lined Böhm up for the kill. Sometimes the right people got hit after all.

'A murder investigation is never easy.' He was slowly becoming more relaxed. Time to take a few precautions. The day would come when Detective Inspector Rath would also have to disappoint the commissioner, and soon. Would Father's old friend receive him quite so warmly then?

'Is anything easy?' Zörgiebel made a dismissive gesture of the hand. 'Up here, you have to deal with politics. Believe me, sometimes I envy the officer on the street for his tough but honest duty.'

Rath preferred to keep his counsel. He doubted whether the commissioner had even the slightest idea of what being a beat cop these days entailed. He shrugged his shoulders. 'I'm happy for the chance to work in Homicide again.'

'I'm glad, young man, I'm glad!' Zörgiebel seemed in very high spirits. 'I thought we could call a press conference for this morning. What do you say?'

Rath was horrified, but didn't let it show. 'A press conference?' He tapped an Overstolz out of the packet and lit it. 'Do you think that's necessary, Commissioner? We don't have to make a big deal of this case. It's probably just a shoot-out amongst crooks.'

'Don't be so modest!' Zörgiebel took a puff on his cigar. 'Or do I detect a little a publicity shyness? Have no fear, young man, I know how badly the press treated you in Cologne, but this case offers you the perfect introduction to the Berlin press corps. Take the opportunity, these things are important and I'll be by your side. After all . . .'—he paused for effect and took another drag on his cigar. The air was gradually becoming thicker—'. . . it's not as if it's your bullet in the corpse this time, is it?'

Rath gave a forced smile.

'So, it's agreed,' Zörgiebel continued. 'Eleven on the dot in the small conference room. Collate all breakthroughs in the investigation by then, and submit a copy to me half an hour before the start. Perhaps you could also enlist the general public. Say we're looking for witnesses, you know the drill. That sort of thing always goes down well, and you'll have the press on your side.'

'Does it really make sense for me to hold a press conference as a homicide detective?' Rath inhaled cigarette smoke. 'My department is still E Division, Commissioner. I'm only working on a homicide case temporarily.'

'My dear Rath, that Vice squad isn't right for you is something we both agree on. I need the best men available for A Division. Do your job well, and I'll see what I can do for you.'

Rath raised his eyebrows and feigned surprise. He stubbed out his half-smoked cigarette and took out the letter he had drafted the previous evening.

'May I present this to you in person, Commissioner? I wanted to send it internally, but since you've already received me . . .'

'What's this?'

'An application, Commissioner.'

'I see.' Zörgiebel nodded and took the letter, and a smile flashed across his face. He looked deep into Rath's eyes.

'Do you know what, my young friend? You really are your father's son!'

Had it been right to apply for Roeder's position at that moment? While he was working on a case that was going to be shelved with the other wet fish? Rath was at odds with himself as he strolled back to Roeder's little office. It wasn't perfect timing, granted, but would there be a better chance? There was a post free in A Division and the commissioner was well disposed towards him; all he had to do now was show what he was made of.

And that was precisely the problem. He couldn't.

On top of all that, he had to appear before the press with the damned Wilczek case. The commissioner needed good press like a morphine addict needed his next shot. Hopefully this time he wouldn't be forced into any ill-considered promises.

Rath reached the end of the corridor, A Division's appendix, so to speak, where the solitude of Roeder's office received him like an old friend. Only the outer office had a typewriter, so he sat at the abandoned secretarial desk, inserted a sheet of paper and started to think.

Fortunately, he had taken care of the most important things in the Wilczek case already. His greatest concern, the projectile, had been eradicated. The results of the ballistics report, which would be available in the coming days, would only confirm the theory that he was about to expound, namely that it had been a fatal quarrel between criminals. All that remained was to whisk the inquiry into a nice story, taking care to work in the activities of both the rookie and his two colleagues from A Division, and the press would have their fodder. *Shoot-out in criminal underworld*, was an everyday occurrence in the East. Readers in the more sheltered Western districts, meanwhile, loved stories which got them all shivery in the safety of their drawing rooms, while at the same time confirming what they had always suspected: that Berlin was a match for Chicago in every way.

The pack had smelt blood. At this precise moment, Rath wouldn't have wanted to change places with Zörgiebel as he raised both hands in appeasement. His attempt to keep the crowd at bay seemed more like a gesture of helplessness.

'Gentlemen, please!'

There were so many questions being thrown that his words were scarcely audible. A pack of hungry press-wolves surrounded him as he stepped down from the podium in the small conference room. He raised his hands a second time, and for a moment it seemed as if the noise did in fact momentarily subside.

'Gentlemen, I have answered all your questions,' he said. 'There's nothing more. If you'll excuse me, I have an important meeting.'

He tried to take a few steps towards the exit, but didn't get far as the pack surged forward and the questions rained down for a second time.

'Is Berlin becoming dangerous again, Commissioner?'

'How can a killer still be at large weeks after the event?'

'Do the police still have the situation under control?'

'Will there be an internal investigation into bloody May?'

The pack wouldn't let go. Zörgiebel was like a bull amongst a pack of wolves: big and strong but with no hope of survival. A camera bulb flashed and he held a hand to his face. Rath decided to score some points with his boss. He jumped back onto the podium and raised his hands. The gesture appeared less defensive than Zörgiebel's; indeed it made it seem like he actually had something to say.

'Gentlemen, please!' The first reporters turned towards him. 'Let the commissioner leave. If you have any questions, direct them towards me!'

Zörgiebel moved towards the exit where he was ushered out of the room unharmed. Rath gazed after his boss until he disappeared.

Zörgiebel had miscalculated. The press conference had been a disaster, and yet everything had started so innocuously. He had told them about the dead man in the concrete and handed over to the investigating officer. Rath had presented the facts soberly and objectively, without drawing any conclusions. Instead he had outlined the investigation in such a way that the press couldn't bypass the story of a gangland shoot-out. The pack had dutifully swallowed it, exactly as Zörgiebel intended. Everything had gone according to plan until Rath invited questions from the floor. They had come thick and fast, only not one of them was directed at the investigating officer or focused on the Wilczek case. Instead they were all directed at the commissioner, and focused exclusively on *Aquarius*. Finally, they had turned to the May disturbances. In seconds, the whole press conference had been tipped on its head and Zörgiebel confronted with precisely the topics he had been hoping to avoid. His evasive answers did nothing to appease the reporters, and, in the end, he had shut down the press conference.

That was when they had really decided to go for him.

Now they were looking at Rath expectantly. The room had fallen silent, and the pack had been at least partially tamed.

'Please, ask away,' Rath said.

A reporter raised his hand, but one of his less well-brought up colleagues beat him to it.

'Over a week ago in this very room we were shown photos of a mutilated corpse that police had dredged from the Landwehr canal. We dutifully published these photos and now we have a right to be informed about the progress of the investigation.'

'Exactly! There must have been some progress.'

'Here, here! You can't just . . .'

Rath raised a conciliatory hand.

'I must disappoint you. I know nothing about this particular homicide investigation. Nevertheless, I am happy, as far as possible, to answer any questions you might have regarding the Wilczek case.'

The noise level rose again as Rath smiled pleasantly but firmly into the room. He could be as slippery as an eel when he wanted, and this gang of crazed telltales didn't deserve anything better.

'You can't fob us off like that!'

'I'm afraid that I can only reasonably answer questions on the case that I am working on. I apologise for any inconvenience, but let's not get carried away.'

He heard a few isolated murmurs of protest, which merged increasingly with a more general chuntering. The reporters pushed off towards the door, and the room emptied quicker than a bathtub whose plug had been pulled.

In no time, they all disappeared and the calm in the conference room seemed almost eerie. He climbed down from the podium. Only Berthold Weinert had remained by the door, and the journalist grinned as he greeted his neighbour.

'Congratulations, Gereon,' he said. 'I haven't been fobbed off so artfully in a long time. First you smuggle the commissioner out of the room and then you play the fool.'

Rath didn't take the bait. 'Aren't you a political journalist? Since when are you interested in criminal investigations?'

'Crime, politics, what's the difference? All jokes aside, at the moment I'm also working as a police correspondent. You have to be flexible in this job.'

'I was surprised there were so many here.'

'True, we weren't informed until less than two hours ago. Bit of a liberty when you've been working on the case all through yesterday. Since information about the dead man from the Landwehr canal has been blocked, I suppose a lot of journalists wanted to grab the chance to take another pop at Zörgiebel.'

'They managed it too.'

Weinert shrugged his shoulders. 'Yeah, well, at the end of the day everyone's gone home empty-handed.'

'At least you've got a really good story from the criminal underworld. I thought your lot loved stuff like that.'

'That stunt won't have made you many friends among my colleagues.'

'So? I've still got one journalist friend. Right?' He held out his hand to Weinert.

'Let's call it a business associate,' the latter said, before shaking.

They said their goodbyes outside the conference room, after Rath had turned down Weinert's invitation to lunch. First he needed to think things through in his little office.

The chief of the Berlin police had a problem, and it might just provide the perfect spring board for the promising young Detective Inspector, Gereon Rath. After such a disastrous press conference, he knew he had to keep working on the case, even if he wasn't part of Böhm's team. He was, at least, part of Homicide. It was a good thing that Roeder's office was so quiet; a good thing, too, that Wilczek had links to *Berolina*. It meant that he could perhaps construct a link between the two cases that presented a halfway decent explanation for his having gathered so much information on *Aquarius*: namely, that in the course of his investigations into the Wilczek case, he had stumbled upon a mysterious hoard of gold and a fugitive Russian named Alexej Kardakov, and could thus present the team working on investigation *Möckern Bridge* with the decisive breakthrough that DCI Wilhelm Böhm had thus far failed to achieve.

The telephone rang, either a publisher or the commissioner. He let it ring. It was almost twelve, time for lunch. Just this once he would spend it in the canteen rather than at Aschinger's. He glanced at the time. It would take him half an hour to reach Schöneberg by train. Weren't musicians in the habit of taking breakfast at midday? Perhaps he'd be able to cadge a cup of coffee.

'Inspector! What a surprise!'

Ilja Tretschkov still seemed pretty drowsy when he opened the door. Nevertheless, the musician recognised Rath straightaway. The trumpeter's hair was tangled and sticking up on his head, and he was wearing an embroidered dressing gown which would have done the Byzantine emperor proud. He was yawning, but his alert eyes were darting to and fro.

'Can I come in?'

'Of course.'

The flat was tidier than Rath had expected, and bigger. Tretschkov seemed to have more money than his former singer. He led him into a small drawing room, gentle rays of sun slanting through the pale curtains. On the table were a few sheets of music and a pencil which he cleared away.

'I've just started working,' he said, before leaving the room with the paper. 'Would you like something to drink?'

'Well, if you're making coffee . . .'

'Tea.'

Of course, the man was Russian. 'Fine,' Rath said. When he was alone he looked around. A nice room, everything in its rightful place. Tretschkov seemed to be a disciplined man, not a Bohemian even if he slept late. A bust of Tchaikovsky sat on the bookshelf. Most of the spines were adorned with Cyrillic letters, but there were a few German names too. Nothing political, as far as he could make out, and no sign of the phrase *Krasnaja Krepost* either, whether in Cyrillic or Latin. There was the rattle of crockery from the door, and Tretschkov returned bearing a tray containing two steaming cups of tea.

'Ready so soon?' Rath asked in surprise.

'Doesn't take long with a samovar,' said Tretschkov. 'Most Russians in Berlin aren't here of their own free will, and everyone tries to keep a little something of their homeland.'

He placed the cups on the table and they sat down.

'Excuse my appearance,' Tretschkov said, 'but I wasn't expecting visitors. My friends know that I get up late. If the band has an engagement, I usually don't make it home until four.'

The tea was very strong.

'What can I do for you, Inspector?' The musician presented the same cooperative impression as in *Café Europa* but Rath couldn't shake the feeling that he knew more than he was letting on.

'Countess Sorokina, you remember?'

'Of course.'

'Has she turned up since we last spoke? Have you heard anything from her?'

'Unfortunately not.'

'You've been looking after her flat?'

'I'm still looking after it. I have a key. Didn't I tell you all this?'

'I think so.' Rath paused. What was the man hiding, and why? 'You watered her plants, is that right?'

Tretschkov nodded.

'Did you take anything out of her room?'

'Do you mind? I'm not a thief.'

Rath decided to change tack. There was no reason he couldn't give the musician a bit of a grilling. Unlike during their first conversation, he was now officially a member of Homicide.

'Herr Tretschkov. This is the second time I've spoken to you about Frau Sorokina and you still haven't asked why I'm looking for her.'

'I assumed that someone reported her missing.'

Rath shook his head. 'Aside from you, there doesn't seem to be anyone missing her, and *you* haven't been to the police. So, there is no missing person's case.'

'Then why are you looking for her?' Tretschkov's calm manner couldn't fool Rath. He was becoming increasingly nervous, his eyes betraying him. It was time to go on the attack. Rath sent two words his way. Tiny, venomous arrows that served only one purpose: to provoke a reaction, with a bit of luck perhaps even a careless one.

'The gold,' he said.

Tretschkov sat up straight, his eyes dancing a Charleston. Rath registered the change with satisfaction and fired his next arrow. 'You know what I'm talking about,' he continued. 'One man had to die because of the gold, another has disappeared—and the Countess with him.'

Tretschkov's unflinching calm took on an air of stiffness. Only his eyes were moving. 'I don't know what you're talking about,' he said.

Was it time to intimidate or should he play the sympathetic cop? No, he had to keep going; he'd have him any minute now. He decided to lose his patience. Abruptly, he stood up and leaned forward, supporting himself on the table.

'Listen to me, pal!' Rath sounded as if he was only barely holding it together. Tretschkov shrank back involuntarily. 'It's time you stopped playing hide-and-seek! You're digging a pretty big hole for yourself and things are going to get nasty.'

The musician sat as if turned to stone. 'I don't know what you mean.'

'You know something that could aid a murder inquiry, but you remain silent. I can't see what you hope to gain. If you think the Countess is in danger, you should cooperate. We can protect her.' Rath looked Tretschkov in the eye. 'If you are concealing a murderer . . . Are you aware of what the consequences might be?'

'Svetlana, a murderer?' Tretschkov exploded. He was on his feet now. 'Absurd!'

'If you're so sure about it, I can't understand your attitude.'

'Perhaps you should consider your *own* attitude, Inspector Rath!' The musician was talking himself into a rage. 'The police are getting nowhere in a murder investigation, and decide to blame a foreigner. A foreigner who, for good reason, is residing *incognito* in your country. Do you seriously believe I could trust you? You've already condemned Svetlana.'

'I don't condemn anyone. It's the judge who does that, but someone has tortured and killed one of your fellow countrymen. I'd like to know who it was, and you can help.'

'A countryman?' Tretschkov seemed genuinely astonished. 'What are you talking about?'

Rath showed him the photograph of the wet, dead Boris. 'Do you know this man?'

Tretschkov shook his head vigorously. 'The one they fished out of the canal a week or two ago? He's Russian?'

'An acquaintance of Alexej Kardakov.'

'Kardakov you say!' Tretschkov sank back into his chair. 'I might have known!'

'Known what?'

'That this man would bring Svetlana misfortune.'

'They were a couple, weren't they?'

Tretschkov nodded. 'She met him about six months after she joined the band and suddenly she became a different person.'

Because she no longer wanted to share a bed with her band leader, Rath suspected. 'How do you mean?'

'She became so serious. She used to laugh a lot. I fear he might have infected her with his arcane political ideas.'

'Which you don't have any time for . . .'

'I've had it with these starry-eyed idealists! You can see where it's led Russia!'

'Kardakov was a communist?'

'No idea what he called himself. He couldn't stand the Bolsheviks at any rate, that was something all three of us could agree on for a change. I never talked to him about politics, he was unbearable on the subject. In fact, I never talked to him much at all.'

'Have you seen him since the Countess disappeared?'

'No.'

'Did her disappearance come as a surprise?'

'What do you mean?'

'Were you surprised when you suddenly no longer had a singer, or had you been expecting it?'

Rath sensed that he had touched another sore point. 'She told me about it,' Tretschkov said finally.

'And she asked you to get something from her flat . . .'

The musician looked at him wide-eyed. 'How do you know that?'

'I looked in her wardrobe. You removed something from the coat lining and took it with you.'

'She asked me to. It was about four weeks ago. She had been late for rehearsal. I wanted to scold her, but then I saw her eyes with such fear in them . . .'

'What was she afraid of?'

'She didn't say. She just gave me her key and asked me to unstitch the lining of her winter coat, take what I found and make sure it was well hidden.'

'So, that's what you did?'

'She disappeared as soon as she'd given me the key. She just said "farewell" and told me to look for another singer. Out of the question, I said. We'll wait for you! We can manage without a singer for a while.' He hesitated, overcome by the memory. 'It was just so . . . strange. She sounded so odd. As if she was leaving forever. It broke my heart to see her go.'

'But you looked after her room.'

'She asked me to. Told me to check everything was OK, water the plants. To make as if she'd only left town for a while.'

'You didn't believe that.'

'I honestly didn't know what to believe.'

'Do you think you'll see the Countess again?'

Tretschkov shrugged his shoulders, a picture of misery. 'I hope so,' he said, 'but I fear the opposite.'

'Aside from you, has anyone else been in the room these last four weeks?'

'Who?'

'The Countess herself? Kardakov? Stalin's spies? You just said she was afraid, and you told me Stalin was after her.'

'That's just a hunch . . .'

Rath realised he was losing his patience, but pulled himself together. 'Did you notice anything?' he asked calmly. 'Did the room ever look different to how you left it? Like someone had been rummaging around?'

'How did you know? I cleared the whole mess up. Almost nothing was where it should've been.'

'When was this?'

'Maybe a week after she disappeared.'

'You said just now that suspecting Countess Sorokina of murder was absurd. Does the same apply to Kardakov?'

'Him?' Tretschkov's voice was full of disdain. 'He'd do anything for his political ideas. Kill anyone who stood in the way of his ever so just cause. Including himself!'

'Could he have the Countess on his conscience?'

'You mean . . .'

'I don't mean anything for the time being, but Kardakov has disappeared. Do you think it's possible?'

Tretschkov's face told Rath that he had voiced the musician's worst fears. He stood up. It was time to head back to the Castle.

'Very well, Herr Tretschkov, but there's one final thing I must ask you. What was it you found in the coat?'

The musician went to the shelf that Tchaikovsky was guarding, returning with a music notebook. It didn't look like jazz. The musician exited the room once more, returning with a knife.

'I play classical too,' he said when he realised that Rath was studying the music. It sounded almost apologetic. 'You earn more in this city with dance music.' He cut open the thick pasteboard. A thin, white envelope fell out and landed next to Tretschkov's teacup.

The musician passed it to the inspector.

'I haven't opened it yet,' he said. 'I haven't dared.'

22

Bülowplatz was still one of the shabbiest parts of the city. All it had in abundance was space. A wicked wind blew across the enormous, bare expanse, the only resistance provided by the people's theatre, whose unadorned structure stood like a steamer stranded in the desert. Twenty years ago now they tore down the narrow, old streets of the Barn Quarter, but still the new buildings hadn't materialised. The triangle surrounding the people's theatre was largely formed by construction hoardings and shacks; little wooden huts selling cigarettes, beer and soda; and a hairdresser offering ladies and gentlemen the latest Parisian styles at knock-down prices. The desert was testimony to the failed plans of ambitious city-planners, although they had succeeded in creating space, in cutting a swathe through the winding crush of the Barn Quarter.

An old newspaper blew past Wilhelm Böhm as he entered the square. It was a wretched area. No wonder the communists had their headquarters here, he thought. Karl-Liebknecht-Haus resembled a political advertisement pillar, so heavily was its façade plastered with slogans and portraits of Lenin, Luxemburg and Liebknecht.

In front of the house an abandoned lectern was being taken down amongst discarded sandwich papers and empty beer bottles, the remains of a rally. The communists weren't exactly a tidy lot.

Two cops were on guard duty in front of the shack. *Cigarettes at cost price* proclaimed a faded red advertisement above their heads, its colour starting to peel. Two rusty enamel boards advertised *Engelhardt Biere* and *Engelhardt Special Hell.* The guards in front of the entrance looked uneasy. This was not a good place for men in police shakos.

Böhm looked around as he reached the shack. The murder wagon still hadn't arrived. He knew he'd be quicker on foot; he should have made that bet with Gräf after all. The construction sites on Alex were currently the worst traffic hazard in the whole city. Even for a police car.

'Afternoon,' Böhm snapped at the cops and showed his badge. 'You haven't touched anything, I hope.'

'No, sir! Crime scene exactly as found.'

'Who discovered him then?'

The older officer shrugged. 'No idea. Someone phoned in anonymously. Probably a bum surprised to find someone in his bed. Or his toilet.'

'A bum who calls the cops? Because the emergency number's free? Perhaps you're right. You came straightaway?'

'Depends what you mean by straightaway. We've got other things to do, you know.'

'Wait for the end of the rally, did you?'

Since the events of May, uniform was avoiding the communists. The officer grew surly.

'You here to give us grief or to solve a murder inquiry?'

Inside the shack was dark; a strong smell of urine hung in the hair, daylight penetrating only in thin strips. Böhm switched on his flashlight. The corpse was lying against the wall, head forward. Above average height, thin, blond hair. He squatted to look at the face but could scarcely make anything out. There, where the nose had been, was a gaping, bloody wound. The blood had run down the man's collar and coloured his shirt red.

Outside, he heard the wagon arrive and the voice of the cop: 'The DCI's already at the crime scene.'

Gräf appeared in the door, camera over his shoulder.

'Let's hope he's got his papers on him, eh, sir?'

'Your job is to shoot photos, not wisecracks. We can check what's in his coat after.'

For a split second the darkness was illuminated by the flash.

'Everything's in the can,' Gräf said when he had finished. 'Won't be enough for a decent profile shot, though.'

That wasn't necessary either, since the dead man had proof of identity in his pocket. Straightaway Böhm knew that this would be a red letter case; that he could assign the *Möckern Bridge* file to the wet fish. The DCI looked at the passport photo, the serious young face staring back at him, and breathed heavily.

In his hands, he was holding a Prussian police ID.

The letter that Tretschkov had given him was a disappointment. So far, Rath had only managed to suss one thing out, that it wasn't a letter at all. The envelope contained a single, thin sheet of paper, home to a muddle of letters that he had spent the entire evening brooding over, without making any headway. At least there weren't any Cyrillic letters—though it wasn't any more intelligible for that. Everything pointed to the fact that it was some sort of encoded message, but Rath couldn't even begin to figure out what the cipher might be. There wasn't a single clue, nothing that made any sense, just a series of different-sized letters, drawn—yes, the letters appeared to have been drawn, rather than written—at varying intervals, either side by side or one below the other.

He had fallen asleep over the paper, only to wake up in the middle of the night, blinking into the light that still burned in his room. The whole right side of his head was in pain from the hard table surface. He had given his face a quick wash and hauled himself off to bed. Just before he fell asleep, he realised that he had forgotten to call Charly again. It was also his first thought on waking.

This morning he had tried a few times from his office, once his team were out and about and he was alone again, though of course no-one had picked up. Greta was probably at work, and Charly must have been sitting in some lecture theatre, boning up on articles. Whatever. She'd be back at the Castle tomorrow.

He would address her formally.

The telephone rang. Rath was surprised to hear the voice of Wilhelm Böhm rasping down the receiver.

'You need to come to Bülowplatz,' he said, 'I'm here with one of your colleagues, Assistant Detective Stephan Jänicke.'

'Why can't Jänicke talk to me himself?'

'If only he could.' This time Böhm sounded nothing like a bulldog. Rath almost had the impression the fat man was sighing. 'Inspector, I was called out because someone found a corpse. Stephan Jänicke is dead.'

The DCI was waiting for him as he made his way across Bülowplatz barely ten minutes later. A large contingent of uniformed officers was guarding the shabby wooden hut where Jänicke's body had been found. Serious faces. No sign of the quips that were usually wheeled out to combat the horror of a crime scene. When one of their own was murdered, the Prussian police didn't stand for any nonsense. Still, that wasn't the only reason a hundred officers were sealing off the area. A growing crowd had gathered to chant slogans. Clearly the communists regarded the appearance of police on their patch as a provocation. *'Ar-beiter-mör-der!'* it echoed in time, *'Zör-giebel-knech-te!'* Murderers, slaves to Zörgiebel!

Böhm greeted him with a handshake. Rath had never seen him so becalmed.

'Come with me, Inspector,' said the DCI. 'Schwartz is taking care of Jänicke. Have you any idea why someone would want to kill the poor guy? Could it be something to do with your current case?'

Rath shrugged his shoulders. He hadn't been able to shake the thought since making his way over from Alex. Had he sent the rookie to his death when he put him onto the *Mulackritze*? The place wasn't far away. Perhaps Jänicke had rocked the boat a little more than Red Hugo liked. In this neighbourhood it was easy to stir up a hornets' nest. Even when you had no idea; especially when you had no idea.

Rath kept his thoughts to himself as he followed Böhm into the hut. A spotlight illuminated walls adorned by posters that were long out of date. On the back wall, a damp bloodstain still glistened. Beneath it a man was crouching on the floor in a pale, light summer coat, head hunched over something on the wall. Dr Schwartz appeared more serious than usual. Today, he had left his infamous sense of humour at home.

'Your colleague?' he asked as he stood up. Rath nodded. He wasn't looking at the doctor but at the bundle on the floor, the fair hair smeared with blood, the face likewise. There was barely anything left of the nose. If he hadn't known who it was he wouldn't have recognised Jänicke. What a lousy way to go, in a hovel that reeked of piss.

'Must have happened three, four hours ago,' Schwartz said, wiping his hands with a white handkerchief. 'Contact shot. You don't need to be particularly handy with a gun for that. Seems to have shoved the barrel right under his nose.'

'He was shot here, right?' Rath asked and pointed to the bloodstain on the wall.

'Everything points to it. Of course, we still need to examine whether it's really his blood,' Schwartz said.

Rath shook his head. 'Shooting off his nose,' he said. 'What sort of person does that?'

'It's what some of the new *Ringvereine* do with traitors,' Böhm said. 'Just blast away their noses. But they don't normally blow the person's brains out too.'

'The Black *Reichswehr* used to have it in their repertoire too, back in the day,' Dr Schwartz said. 'Just like the Red Front. In the wild years, that was.'

Maybe the wild years are about to return, Rath thought. 'Are there any witnesses?'

Böhm shrugged his broad shoulders. 'No idea. We don't have any yet. The man who found him preferred to remain anonymous. I'd be willing to bet those troublemakers out there know more. Thälmann's lot were holding a rally this morning in front of Karl-Liebknecht-Haus. Perhaps one of them saw something.'

'Or fired the shot.'

'Or fired the shot, but it looks as if the young man knew his killer, given how close he let him get. As far as I know Jänicke was no Red.'

'Perhaps two people held him, while a third took the shot.'

'Let's stop speculating and start gathering clues.' Böhm's tone was brusque once more, as Rath had grown to expect. 'Why don't you tell me what the assistant detective was doing at Bülowplatz in the first place?'

So Rath told him about Saint Josef and Red Hugo, and how he had put Jänicke onto *Berolina* to pursue a possible lead in this farce of an investigation he had staged to distract from his own guilt. A farce that had suddenly become deadly serious. The DCI listened in silence.

'Very well, Inspector,' he said finally. 'I think in that case I should take a look at your files from the Wilczek case. Perhaps you could look out any records of statements taken by Jänicke.'

Rath felt uneasy about letting someone else sniff around a case that he regarded as a private matter, so to speak.

'If there's a link,' Böhm continued, 'we should merge our investigating teams. Under my leadership, of course.'

'If you gentlemen would excuse me,' Dr Schwartz raised his hat. 'My work here is done. You'll learn the rest in Hannoversche Strasse. I'll call you, Böhm.'

In the narrow door the pathologist almost bumped into a powerfully built figure, whom he greeted briefly. Bruno Wolter came in. Uncle looked pale and harried, as if he had run all the way from the Castle. So Böhm had also called E Division. Logical really. When a police officer was murdered, it seemed reasonable to assume it might have something to do with his work. But with the König case, of all things?

'My God,' Bruno stammered, when he saw the corpse. His gaze wandered from Böhm to Rath, before he sat down beside Jänicke's body. Rath had never seen Uncle so agitated. He had always thought of him as a tough old so-and-so, but that was how it was with lots of police officers. Often they seemed cold-blooded because they didn't allow things to get to them, but some things got to you whether you liked it or not. Rath placed a hand on his colleague's shoulder.

They were silent. Outside, the communists were still bellowing their slogans.

'If these commie arseholes don't put a lid on it soon, I won't be responsible for what happens,' he heard Bruno say through gritted teeth.

The news of Stephan Jänicke's death spread through the Castle like the shock wave of a bomb, furiously quickly and to devastating effect. For the majority, the issue of guilt was already resolved. If a police officer was killed at Bülowplatz, it had to be the communists. An aggression took hold, worse than the uncertainty of two weeks before. Back then most people had simply been afraid of a revolt. Now, however, a desire for revenge threatened to push every rational thought to one side.

Scarcely had Zörgiebel heard Böhm's report than he rounded up all senior-ranking CID officers. Everyone knew what it was about before Zörgiebel even entered the room. The Jänicke case was being made number one priority. Two weeks after the communist riots, the commissioner began, police simply could not allow one of their own to be viciously murdered. Zörgiebel made no bones about where, in his opinion, the guilty party was to be found: amongst the members of the now banned RFB and, with that, he captured the mood in the room perfectly.

Rath thought it unwise to add more fuel to the fire; and indeed the commissioner immediately back-pedalled, calling for the utmost caution and reserve. 'We must not give the press any occasion to launch a fresh attack on the Prussian police, who are only performing their duty. Therefore, please see to it that you proceed as carefully and as scrupulously as possible. As a matter of principle, interrogate all parties in the presence of an additional officer, who will then countersign your statement in case any communists accuse us of conducting third degree interrogations!'

Third degree interrogations. That was the name given at the Castle to an interrogation where officers had used their fists as a means of establishing the truth.

As expected, Böhm would lead the investigation. In the meantime, every other homicide case was to be put on ice, while CID concentrated all resources on the Jänicke murder. Böhm approached the lectern to say a few words and distribute papers detailing his instructions, like a school teacher handing out worksheets. Apart from CID, Section 1A would also be pressed into service. Rath had difficulty imagining that Böhm had been responsible for that. Clearly, the commissioner believed it was a politically motivated murder and hoped to use the political police's network of informers.

Zörgiebel remained in the conference room with Böhm, while the officers set to work. Outside, the reporters were already waiting, the same ones the commissioner had only just condemned. This time they wouldn't bother him with the usual hogwash, he could be sure of it. A policeman, murdered at Bülowplatz, while the communists were lamenting the May dead . . . Even for the Berlin press, that was no everyday story. Rath barely registered any hostile glances, and those he did see were directed not at the commissioner, but at him. Weinert was right, some of them hadn't taken kindly to the inspector's appearance the day before.

'Bloodthirsty mob,' he heard Bruno curse quietly under his breath. They soon pushed past the journalists, and were surrounded by colleagues in the corridor outside. Since Jänicke was their partner, there were words of comfort raining down on all sides. Some of them even went as far as to express their condolences, as if it had been a close relative who had died. The majority, however, declared that they 'would get the swine that did this,' or that it was time 'to do away with that Bolshevik rabble.' In short, they swore bloody revenge. Rath hoped the daily grind would soon bring them back down to earth.

He accompanied Wolter into their old office. The two former partners were to examine Jänicke's desk.

'Who'd have thought we'd be working together again so soon,' Bruno said.

Rath gave a forced smile. 'I wish it was under happier circumstances.'

He didn't really think they'd find anything new. He was familiar with Jänicke's statements, which had all been logged in the Wilczek file, but you never knew. The assistant detective had completed all his paperwork in the old Vice office, since there was no room in A Division. Roeder's old office was that of a lone wolf; during Rath's early morning briefings with Henning and Czerwinski, one of them always had to perch on the edge of the desk, even after fetching an additional chair from the abandoned outer office.

As predicted, they didn't find much in the drawers. A folder in which the official regulations of the Prussian police had been filed, the plan of action for Operation Nighthawk, the sports section of *Vossische Zeitung*, a few pages of handwritten notes on the König case, a few porn photos, on which the faces were circled in marker pen—the prints they had used to identify the various actors.

'Not very fruitful,' said Bruno, once the contents were spread across the table.

Rath nodded, but there was something missing. Something that he had seen only that morning in Jänicke's hand.

'Didn't Stephan have a black notebook?' he asked Bruno. 'It would be interesting to know what he wrote in it.'

'He always took it with him. It was his most prized possession—he never left it lying around. Böhm must have picked it up.'

'We should let him know anyway.'

Bruno nodded thoughtfully. 'Then let's get all this junk packed up and sent to Böhm,' he said. 'We'll add a little report so that Homicide knows why the kid had porn in his drawer. In case they get any daft ideas.'

'Can you draft it?' Rath asked. 'I've got to update the Wilczek file.'

'Do you think it has something to do with his death?'

Rath shrugged his shoulders. 'If it does, then it's on my conscience. It was me that sent him to the Barn Quarter.'

Bruno laid a hand on his shoulder. 'Come on, don't be too hard on yourself. It's a dangerous job. Besides, who says it wasn't the communists?'

'Do you really think that?'

'They're capable. The Red Front might be banned, but that doesn't mean it no longer exists. The ban has just backed them into a corner like a wild animal. And when an animal gets backed into a corner, it bites.'

'I hope you're right.'

'Head up, my boy! It's bad enough to lose a colleague. Don't go blaming yourself for it too!'

By that evening the police murder had already become a major news story. Rath bought the evening edition of *Tageblatt* in Alexanderplatz station and read it on the train. Zörgiebel was clearly using Jänicke's death for his own ends, and skilfully avoided giving voice to any suspicion. Officially, police were still pursuing all avenues. Nevertheless, the way he described the crime scene and the circumstances surrounding it left little choice but for journalists to conclude that a police officer had fallen victim to a communist attack.

The sensationalist papers at the newsstand hadn't taken any half measures and had come up with correspondingly sensational headlines on their title pages. Although *Tageblatt* had left it at a simple *police officer murdered*, under the dry headline they had still listed all the details circulated by Zörgiebel at the press conference, not least the fact that communists had gathered that morning in the vicinity of the crime scene outside Karl-Liebknecht-Haus and that at lunchtime Prussian police had been described by the same group as murderers.

Bruno was right. Blaming yourself was pointless. The only one responsible for Jänicke's death was the person who had pressed a pistol to his nose and squeezed the trigger.

How well he had been served by his former boss was something Böhm had unwittingly confirmed when Rath brought him the Wilczek file. Rath had added a page with a few observations as to why he had asked

Jänicke to investigate on *Berolina*'s patch. Partly it had been a way to justify his actions to himself.

'What's this?' Böhm had asked, looking at the page as if Rath had just handed him a piece of used toilet paper.

'A few pointers regarding the course of the investigation . . .' Rath had begun, before Böhm interrupted him.

'Young man, I don't know if this has been made sufficiently clear,' Böhm had bawled, 'but *I'm* the one leading this investigation. I don't need pointers!'

Rath had slammed the file on the table and left without saying goodbye.

What an arsehole! Even now he was still annoyed. Was he really going to let himself be treated like that?

Böhm could push other people around if he enjoyed it so much, but Gereon Rath wasn't going to stand for it. Whenever he thought of the arrogant homicide detective, Rath looked forward to the day when he could show him up with the *Aquarius* case, on ice for now, like the Wilczek case. Both wet fish for the time being. But Zörgiebel couldn't keep it up for ever. Rath didn't think that Superintendent Gennat agreed with all A Division officers being concentrated on a single case. True, a murder investigation was also a race against time, and experience told him that the first day or two were the most important. If you hadn't achieved a breakthrough by then, the whole thing would drag on for weeks and become an exercise in painstaking drudgery.

The evening didn't quite pan out as Rath had imagined it.

As he was climbing the stairs to Nürnberger Strasse he saw his suitcase standing outside the door to the flat. Next to it was a large cardboard box with a cord tied round it. Rath unlocked the door and lifted the suitcase, surprised at how heavy it was.

Elisabeth Behnke must have heard him. She was waiting in the corridor, examining him as if she were on break duty in a convent school and he'd just urinated in the yard.

'Why are you still here, Herr Rath?' she asked. 'Take your things and leave!'

She was addressing him formally again. It seemed to be serious. Only, he couldn't take it seriously.

'The suitcase might be deceptive, but I wasn't planning on going anywhere,' he said. 'I happen to live here.'

'Hardly, Herr Rath.'

'Is this some kind of joke?'

'I can assure you that a tenant breaking house rules is no laughing matter!'

'What's the matter this time?' Rath wasn't aware of having done anything wrong.

'You should read your rental contract more closely! Female visitors are expressly forbidden and can lead to the immediate termination of the lease.'

So that's how the wind was blowing. But why now? If she had seen Charly then why hadn't she made a scene about it last week?

'I don't know what you're talking about.'

'Don't try and fool me, Inspector!' She laughed aggressively and hysterically. It sounded like she was braying. 'Or perhaps it's *you* who wears this sort of thing?' She lifted an artificial silk stocking in the air. Rath recognised it as the one Charly had been wearing last Thursday. Where on earth had old Behnke found it?

'How dare you go snooping around my personal things?'

'Snooping around? I was changing the sheets! Like every Wednesday! This was in your duvet cover. Can you tell me how it got there?'

'I don't think that's any of your business, my dear Frau Behnke!'

This quarrel had been coming for days. Like a storm that finally breaks and dispels the oppressive humidity.

'I'm afraid it is very much my business when you take a woman to your room—despite the strict ban!'

'I didn't realise this was a convent!'

'It's not a convent, Herr Rath, but it is my flat! And if you don't stick to *my* rules, then you must bear the consequences!'

Rath wasn't just bearing the consequences but the weight of the suitcase. He laid it down.

'So this is my notice.'

'Yes.' She rummaged in her purse and held a few notes out towards him. 'Here.'

'What's this?'

'The rent you get back. You've already paid for this week.'

'Keep the money.' He made a move to get past her.

She stood in his way. 'Where are you going?'

'To my room.'

'It's not your room anymore.'

'And my things?'

'Already packed.'

'Then at least let me say goodbye to Herr Weinert.'

'He's not home. Please go now!'

There was no point arguing with a hysterical Elisabeth Behnke. He shook his head, picked up the suitcase again and made for the door.

As he dragged the heavy suitcase and bulky cardboard box onto Nürnberger Strasse, he heard a window above him opening. *His* window. Elisabeth Behnke was looking out. Banknotes were fluttering down onto the pavement, a lady's stocking sailing in their wake. Without a word, she banged the window shut.

Clearly, she wanted to give as good as she got.

He collected the banknotes, stuffed the stocking into his coat pocket and stood at the side of the road with his belongings and waved for a taxi.

My God, what a lousy day!

Bruno was flabbergasted to find Rath outside his door in Friedenau, loaded like a donkey.

'Do you always bring so much stuff when you visit?'

'Let me come in first.' Rath explained the situation as they sat a short time later in the Wolters's living room, interrupting his story only when Emmi Wolter came in and placed their drinks on the table. Bruno shook his head.

'Should I have a word with Elisabeth?' he asked. 'Maybe it can still be sorted out.'

Rath waved him away. 'Nah, leave it,' he said, 'it's probably better this way.'

Being booted out had finally put an end to the painful comedy of the last few weeks.

'I can stay in a hotel until I find somewhere new,' he said. 'Do you mind if I use the telephone?'

'A hotel? You must be crazy! Out of the question.' Bruno turned his head to the side and shouted: 'Emmi!'

Emmi Wolter poked her blonde head through the door.

'Can you prepare the guestroom? Gereon is staying for a few days.'

'Of course.' Bruno's dutiful spouse disappeared once more.

Rath protested. 'No, it's fine, I don't want you to go to any trouble.'

'Trouble? You must be joking. There's more than enough room. And the larder's full, so don't make a fuss. You'll stay with us until the weekend, and if you still haven't found something by next week, then I can always start collecting rent.'

Bruno raised his cognac glass. 'So,' he said, 'and now let's drink to Stephan Jänicke, and to catching his killer.' They clinked glasses and for a moment no-one said anything, as both men dwelled on their thoughts.

'Me, you and Jänicke, that could have been some team,' Wolter said after a while. 'Nonsense,' he corrected himself, 'that *was* some team.'

'I always liked the kid, even if I barely knew him,' Rath said.

'Stephan was alright.'

'Even wanted to take me along to the football. I didn't go.'

'Do you think he was lonely?' Wolter asked.

'He'd left his family and friends back in East Prussia, and whether he had any here . . .'

'But Berlin welcomes every new citizen with open arms!'

'Yeah, and with clenched fists.' Rath couldn't help thinking back to his own arrival in this cold, alien city.

Wolter grinned. 'You just need to strike back.' He took another sip. 'It's funny though,' he said suddenly. 'I don't know either Stephan's parents or any of his other friends, but now that he's dead, we're going to meet them all.'

'At the funeral?'

Wolter nodded.

'Have you got enough people?'

'Brenner's with us . . . with *me* in the office. And then Gregor Lanke's arriving on Tuesday.'

'My sympathies!'

Wolter forced a smile. 'Thanks,' he said, 'but better save your sympathy for next week. A funeral with flags, uniforms and a salute. Zörgiebel wants to deliver the eulogy himself.'

'I can't think about it,' Rath said. 'How am I supposed to look Stephan's parents in the eye? If I hadn't loaned him he might still be alive.'

'You don't know that!' Bruno sounded peeved. 'Maybe he was just in the wrong place at the wrong time, and Bülowplatz *is* the wrong place for a police officer when the commies are banding together. It doesn't matter if you work for Vice or Homicide!'

He stood up and moved towards a dark-coloured cupboard, behind the glass door of which the drinks cabinet was located. He returned with the bottle of cognac.

'Better it's on the table,' he said.

'Wilful drunkenness is what we're doing here.'

Bruno shrugged his shoulders and poured. 'If you can't get wilfully drunk on a day like today, when can you?'

23

When he awoke the next morning, Rath didn't know where he was. His head throbbed when he sat up until, gradually, his memory started to return. He had stayed at Bruno's. They had got drunk, drowning their grief at Jänicke's death in cognac. At least, that's what he thought. Only to realise that it wasn't grief he was feeling, but rage allied with fear. Rage that didn't know where it was directed; fear that didn't know what it was afraid of.

He hoped he hadn't told Bruno too much, but couldn't remember.

In a corner of the room, next to the chair where he had thrown his clothes, stood his suitcase and a large cardboard box, a reminder that old Behnke had chucked him out and he had no home. Since he didn't want to impose on the Wolters for too long, he would start looking for a new flat today.

Emmi Wolter knocked at his door. 'Herr Rath? Are you awake? Breakfast is ready.'

Bruno was already sitting at the table when Rath entered the dining room, freshly showered but still hungover. The smell of coffee hung in the air. Bruno grinned broadly, apparently without a hangover.

'Sleep well?'

'The sleep was OK. Waking was the problem.'

'Sit down, have a coffee and eat something. Then you'll feel better.'

Breakfast did him good. Emmi Wolter made even better coffee than Elisabeth Behnke.

They took the Ford to the Castle, and it felt almost like the old days. They didn't talk much during the drive, but Bruno made Rath feel like he wasn't alone in this city. They parked in the atrium and went together to the conference room where Böhm had arranged an eight o'clock briefing. The room slowly filled until, at eight on the dot, Böhm emerged like a school master sweeping into a classroom, followed by his team. Rath's heart almost stood still when Charly entered last, closing the door behind her. She took her seat at a table on the platform at the front and laid her pen and paper out. Realising that he wasn't the only man in the room stealing a glance at her legs, Rath felt a pang of jealousy.

Was she deliberately ignoring him? In vain he tried to catch her eye. She was looking almost constantly down at her pad, and when her dark eyes did gaze into the room they didn't fix on anything.

Böhm summarised their findings, but Rath was barely listening. The image of Charly kept running through his brain, Charly, Charly, Charly, as he observed her discreetly out of the corner of his eye. He had almost forgotten how good she looked. He rummaged in his coat pocket until he found her stocking, exactly where he had stuffed it yesterday, and couldn't help but smile.

A sudden bustle of activity interrupted his thoughts. Böhm had finished and people were getting ready to leave. Chairs were being shuffled as a burble of chatter started up and Charly handed leaflets to people on their way out. Rath's heart pounded as he walked past her and their hands briefly touched. Her gaze was so remote it almost hurt.

'Thank you, Fräulein Ritter,' he said.

He almost forgot to say goodbye to Bruno. His colleague grinned as he made his way back to E Division. Hopefully, he hadn't said too much last night when he was drunk.

It was only when he was sitting in his little office that Rath took a closer look at the piece of paper. There were a few names on it but he had no idea what he was supposed to do with them. He should have paid more attention, but even now he couldn't get Charly out of his head. The names were arranged alphabetically, all beginning with the same letter: I.

There was knock on the door. He sat up.

'Yes.'

'DCI Böhm would like to return these documents.'

Charly was standing in the door, smiling and offering the Wilczek file.

'Oh, why don't you come a little closer? And shut the door behind you.' She entered. 'My secretary isn't here today, so I'm alone and . . .' But she had already pressed her lips onto his mouth. The Wilczek file crashed onto the desk and fell to the ground.

They looked at each other for a time in silence. He could have got lost in those eyes.

'I'm sorry about your colleague,' she said.

'I guess it's just a lousy job.'

'Was he a close friend?'

'I barely knew him. He was a pretty taciturn guy. An East Prussian.'

'He was younger than me, wasn't he?'

'Twenty-two.'

'There are too many people in this country who think they can settle their affairs with guns.'

He nodded. 'And it's our job to teach them that's no solution. Or at least one that'll land them in jail.'

'It's nice here. A few potted plants and you could almost call it cosy.'

He took her in his arms. 'We have to see each other more often,' he whispered. 'I missed you.'

'If you're pining for me, there's always the telephone.'

So, she had taken offence.

'Guilty as charged,' he said. 'But whenever I rang there was no-one there. Maybe I'd be better off writing letters.'

'Real love letters!' She sighed theatrically and rolled her eyes upwards. 'Yes please! I'll disconnect my telephone!'

'I'm afraid I'm not very good at stuff like that. Interrogation records and reports are about the only things I write normally.'

The need to bestow numerous caresses on your person shall henceforth be seen as unavoidable. I don't have a problem if you write like that. I read sentences like that every day.'

'I like it when you're goofy.'

'Goofy? I'm not really goofy, just in high spirits.'

A thought occurred to him. He went to the coat stand and fetched the stocking from his pocket. '*A propos* high spirits,' he said, waving the rayon stocking. 'To this *corpus delicti* I owe my temporary homelessness.'

Her eyes almost popped out of her head. Even then they were pretty.

'My landlady discovered this while she was changing the sheets and gave me summary notice to quit.'

'No?!'

'Yes!'

She stood there so dumbfounded that he couldn't help but grin until they both exploded with laughter.

When they had calmed down, her fingers began to play with his tie. 'Gereon,' she said, 'I have to tell you something.'

'What is it?'

'I . . . Well, you hadn't been in touch, so I thought I'd try at yours. By telephone, I mean. And . . . you didn't pick up, so I let it ring a little longer, and then . . . then finally someone did pick up. A woman.'

He sighed. 'A Frau Behnke . . .'

'Yes, Behnke. I asked for you and she said you didn't live there. So I asked whether it was Nürnberger Strasse 28, and all of a sudden she got mad and started bawling like one of the Furies, saying if I dared set foot inside her house again . . . hers was a respectable house and I was a little tart.'

Rath could picture Elisabeth Behnke changing the sheets in his room; first she finds a lady's stocking, and then its owner rings.

'And then?'

She shrugged her shoulders. 'I was so shocked at her screaming that I couldn't think of anything to say. So I hung up. She called me a little tart and all I wanted was to say hello!'

'Grr . . . I should bite your head off. You've made me homeless.'

'Where are you staying now?'

'They say the best spots are under Victoria Bridge, but I'm not sure if I'll stay there. Berlin's got so many nice bridges it's hard to decide.'

'And for real?'

'For real, a colleague has taken pity on me. At the moment I'm living with Bruno Wolter in Friedenau. No chance of female visitors there either. That's what you get!'

'But I'd rather like to pay you a little visit,' she said and began stroking his chest.

'Let's see, there must be a key for this door somewhere,' he mumbled and was searching the drawers when the telephone rang. Both of them gave a start. The feeling of tenderness had gone west, his erection too.

'That's probably Böhm,' she said and started barking: *Take your filthy hands off my stenographer and get on with your work!'*

She kissed him and left, blowing him an extra goodbye kiss at the door.

He let the telephone ring until she was outside, took a deep breath and picked up, fists mentally raised to parry Böhm's barking.

'Rath, Homicide.'

'Weinert, *Abendblatt*. What's this I'm hearing? You've moved out? Just like that?' The journalist sounded dismayed.

'Moved is the wrong word. Old Behnke *threw* me out.'

'You didn't get yourself caught did you?'

'A stocking got itself caught. A lady's stocking in my bed.'

Weinert laughed. 'Sorry, but you're not serious? That's enough for her to boot you out?'

'I'd be careful if I were you. Tell your women they should start wearing men's socks when they come to visit.'

'Thanks for the tip.'

'My pleasure, but I'm sure that's not the reason you called.'

'I'd like to get together to exchange some ideas. I tried yesterday evening but you didn't come home. Or at least that's what I thought—until I realised Frau Behnke had stuck her oar in.'

That suited Rath, he needed to speak to the journalist anyway.

'When and where?'

'Should we say right now, at ten in *Moka Efti*? Near Friedrichstadt underground. It's far enough from Alex that you won't run into any cops, and close enough to Kochstrasse.'

'*Moka Efti*? The new place? Isn't it a bit expensive?'

'Publisher's treat. It's all going on expenses.'

Weinert was already at a table when Rath entered. An escalator led to the first floor and straight into the bar. The dances began here in the afternoon and lasted long into the night, and had already made *Moka Efti* a staple of the Berlin party scene. In the morning, however, it was mostly dominated by shoppers from Leipziger Strasse, taking a break after visiting Wertheim or Tietz. Then there were a few journalists like Weinert from nearby Kochstrasse, as well as the idlers who liked to combine their newspaper reading with a good cup of coffee.

And the coffee really was good. The smell alone was enough to make you wide awake. To wash it down, they had ordered a large bottle of sparkling mineral water. Rath lit an Overstolz and listened.

'It's about the dead policeman,' said Weinert.

'You weren't at the press conference.'

'To hear Zörgiebel pedalling shit about bloodthirsty communists? No thanks!'

'So your paper didn't publish anything?'

'A colleague was there and we published the same crap as the rest. Only, the communist papers see it differently. For them it's a revenge killing by Nazis or the Black *Reichswehr*. Politically motivated killing seems pretty doubtful to me. The dead man wasn't in the political police.'

'No, the dead man was my colleague. First in Vice, and then in Homicide.'

'My sympathies.'

'We weren't exactly close.' Rath drew on his cigarette. 'So, what do you want to know?'

'The avenues you're really investigating. Who has the victim on their conscience?'

'Wish I knew. I'd have solved the case and earned myself a few brownie points.'

'Only if you serve up a communist. Zörgiebel's already homed in on Thälmann's lot.'

'I'll see what I can do for you. We're still at the start of our investigations. I can only say we're pursuing all avenues, and the communist lead is simply one of many.'

'Call me when you know more.'

'If you leave my name out of it. And if you do me a favour.'

'The Buick's still in Kochstrasse.'

'It's not about the car. I wanted to suggest a deal. It could result in more exclusive information for you. You can tell me about a man who also moved out of Nürnberger Strasse.'

'Alexej Kardakov?'

Rath nodded. 'And everything you know about *Krasnaja Krepost*.'

'The *Red Fortress*? Why are you interested?'

'Could be the key to solving a spectacular case. If you help me, you'll get exclusive information.'

'Don't talk in riddles. What case?'

'The one that's driving Zörgiebel mad because your colleagues are all on his back and he doesn't have any answers. The dead man from the Landwehr canal.'

'That's over since yesterday at the latest. We've got a dead police officer now. *That* is spectacular!'

'Only a few days ago you just about lynched the commissioner because he didn't want to cough up any new information about the corpse from the Landwehr canal.'

Weinert laughed. 'Journalism is a day-to-day business. People forget quickly.'

'Then you need to make sure they remember! Whether a case makes the headlines or gets tucked away on page fifteen is still something the free press decides.'

'You want me to go against what everyone here in the press is writing and build up a case that no-one's interested in anymore?'

'Isn't that the real scandal? That the commissioner's frozen all current homicide investigations and has CID working at full capacity to solve the Jänicke murder? An unknown corpse is dredged from the canal—nothing happens. A police officer is shot dead—and the commissioner applies a completely different set of standards.'

Weinert whistled through his teeth. 'You should have been a journalist. Or a politician.'

Rath had known Weinert would bite the moment he saw how the journalist reacted to the phrase *Krasnaja Krepost*. They ordered another round of coffee.

'So, Alexej Kardakov,' Weinert began. 'When I moved into Nürnberger Strasse about a year and a half ago, he was already there. As a neighbour, I saw him even less than I see you. I always had the feeling he was deliberately avoiding us Germans. He was still living in Russia, really. Played host to a little Russian colony most evenings. Things got pretty lively.'

'That's what El . . . that's what Frau Behnke said.'

Weinert hesitated for the briefest of moments before continuing. 'If she'd known the heads of the *Red Fortress* were meeting under her roof, she'd probably have called the police.'

'Kardakov was one of the leaders of the *Red Fortress*?'

'I'd never have thought him capable of it either. I always assumed he was a hard-working but unsuccessful author. The typewriter was always rattling away. I only discovered two months ago that he was involved in politics.'

'Just before he moved out?'

Weinert nodded. 'We knew each other pretty well by then, even if it was about half a year before we had a coherent conversation. He ran out of paper and knocked on my door to see if he could borrow some. We chatted for a bit, mostly about writing. He speaks excellent German, by the way, but writes in Russian.' Weinert paused and took a long drink of sparkling water. 'Well, and then—it must have been sometime in March, it was bitterly cold anyway—I overheard something by chance. For the first time since I'd been living in Nürnberger Strasse, German was being spoken in the next-door room. I have to say it made me curious.'

'You eavesdropped on the conversation?'

'Curiosity is an occupational disease. Besides, they were discussing interesting things, money and politics. From time to time they switched to Russian, but mostly they spoke in German, even if some had trouble understanding. I think the Russians had a couple of German visitors and were making an effort. The only Russian words I heard again and again were *Krasnaja Krepost.*'

'The *Red Fortress*. That was when you knew they were commies?'

'I didn't discover all that until later and didn't give it much thought at the time. Incidentally, I'm pretty sure it wasn't the first time they had met.'

'What kind of Germans were they? Politicians?'

'I wondered that myself. Businessmen, I suspect. The Russians were talking about percentages at any rate. The Germans wanted fifty percent, but the Russians were only willing to give ten. Finally, they agreed on forty.'

'So we can safely assume that the Russians weren't businessmen . . .'

'As they were getting up to go, I had a look through the keyhole. Couldn't see a great deal though. One of the men was rather short and stocky and wearing an expensive fur coat. That is, he didn't look anything like a politician, and he definitely wasn't a communist. Seemed more like a director general. And strangely, there was a Chinese man there too. Pretty international crowd really.'

Marlow, the thought flashed through Rath's mind. The man in the fur coat could only have been Johann Marlow! Marlow and his Chinese shadow in Nürnberger Strasse! But why was the underworld boss visiting a small-time coke dealer, a tiny wheel in his organisation? Forty percent could be lucrative. Forty percent of eighty million marks!

'Well,' Weinert continued, 'like I said, curiosity is an occupational disease. I wanted to know what this *Red Fortress* was all about.'

'And Kardakov told you?'

'Of course not, and I didn't ask. Far too risky if he discovered that I'd been eavesdropping on his meeting. The *Red Fortress* operates underground. I kept quiet and did my research elsewhere. There are other ways of getting information. Yielded some pretty interesting findings too.'

'The *Red Fortress* wants to overthrow the German government?'

'The *Soviet* government.'

'You're joking.'

'I'd known since that evening in March that they had nothing good to say about Stalin. That night they moaned so much about the Moscow government that I'd never have guessed they were communists. But they are, hardliners at that. The name tells you everything you need to know. The *Red Fortress* regard themselves as the guardians of true communist doctrine after Lenin's death.'

'So do Stalin and Thälmann.'

'So does just about every Red. That's the problem with the Left: they spend more time fighting themselves than their opponents. For Thälmann's followers, being called a *Trotskyite* is worse than being called a *Nazi.*'

'Does Trotsky belong to the *Red Fortress* then?'

'Difficult to say. There are rumours, but Trotsky himself has never said anything about it. Perhaps he's just waiting for the *Red Fortress* to succeed before revealing his true colours.'

'So, what does the *Red Fortress* want?' It wasn't until he'd asked the question that Rath realised he'd quoted the title of Weinert's article.

'Their ultimate goal is world revolution, of course, but first they want to get socialism in the Soviet Union back on the right track. For that to happen they need to overthrow Stalin.'

'Of course. Am I mistaken or are this lot a little power crazy?'

'They're just ambitious. They're realistic about the fact that idealism isn't enough for a *coup d'état,* you need lots of money too. I just wonder where they're going to get it. What sort of businessman supports the communists? Even the ones launching an attack against their own?'

'I think I can tell you that,' Rath said.

Weinert had told him a great deal, so he decided, as far as possible, to tell him everything he had learned up to that point: about Kardakov's connection to Countess Sorokina; her family's gold, which had allegedly been smuggled into Berlin from the Soviet Union; and about Marlow and Red Hugo's *Ringverein,* both of whose roles were still unclear. Yet, having listened to Weinert, Rath now had a better idea of what their roles might be. Together with his girlfriend, Kardakov was intending to smuggle the Sorokin gold into Germany and use it to achieve his ambitious political aims. Marlow's job was to take this conspicuous supply of gold, which Stalin's people were also trying to locate, and convert it into inconspicuous Reichsmark bills and bank statements. Kardakov was using his boss as a fence—for forty percent.

'Interesting, interesting,' Weinert said. 'Why didn't you announce that in the press conference?'

'Because it would've have compromised ongoing investigations,' Rath lied, without going into any further detail. The tried and tested killer blow that thwarted every journalist.

'So why are you telling me?'

'Because, thanks to your help, I've just taken a giant leap forward. Just please don't publish anything I've told you yet. I promise you'll be the first to get the story. You'll have it going through the rotary printer while the others are still attending the press conference. I'll give you the green light in a day or two.'

'Green light?'

'Just like at Potsdamer Platz. Be ready and, when the light switches to green, step on the gas!'

The morning was getting on by the time he returned to his desk. In fact, it was almost lunch. He'd give it a miss today. He hadn't even started looking for a new room yet.

First of all, he had to bring his view of the *Aquarius* case up to date. He was finally making some headway. True, he still didn't have anything that would stand up in court, but collecting evidence was Böhm's job, not his.

By now he could at least present a coherent argument, provide an additional line of inquiry. That was all Zörgiebel had asked of Böhm; it was just that he hadn't managed to deliver. Not so Rath, who could hand the commissioner a murder suspect, perhaps even two. If not exactly on a silver platter, since Kardakov and Countess Sorokina had disappeared, at least it was a start. Something would be stirring with *Aquarius* again, for the first time since the evidence had been secured, Rath suspected. It felt like Böhm had been going through the motions ever since.

The telephone rang. Rath picked up and stated his name.

'How far have you got with that list?' Speak of the devil. Böhm's list! He hadn't even properly looked at it yet, let alone worked out what he was supposed to do with it.

'The list, sir? Well, I think tomorrow . . .'

'Tomorrow? How long do you need to follow up on a few alibis? Do you want to give the Red Front time to go underground? I want to see your report on my desk by the end of the day, is that clear?'

'Yes, sir!'

Rath hung up noisily. What an arsehole.

At least he knew what he had to do now. Böhm must have obtained a list of RFB members from Section 1A and divided the names amongst the officers.

He examined the sheet of paper. Six names, all beginning with I. No addresses. He would have to head to the passports office as it was unlikely any of them would own a telephone. That meant he would have to drive out to see them, to Wedding and similarly unappetising districts. He had imagined his Thursday afternoon differently, but at least the drive would give him time to think. He called the motor pool and reserved an Opel.

A little while later he was standing in the passports office.

'You're late, your colleagues were all here this morning.' It was the same official who had got on his nerves the last time. At least the old boy didn't seem to recognise him.

'Well, I'm here *now!* So get your lazy arse going. It's only six addresses.'

'Don't you tell me how to do my job, young man! It wouldn't hurt you youngsters to take a little more care over things.'

The old man put on his glasses and marched over to the roll-front cabinets, comparing the names at least ten times with the index cards he pulled from the drawers. Once he was convinced he had the right addresses, he returned to Rath at the wooden barrier.

'Here you are.' The passports official laid the index cards on the table. Rath put them in his jacket and made to leave.

'Where are you going?'

'Back to my office, if it's all the same to you.'

'You can't take the cards with you.'

'Just for a few hours.'

'Sorry, but it's the rules. You're only allowed to look at them. Make a note of them instead.'

Rath pulled out his pencil and notebook and began to transfer the addresses. When he was finished he could only count five. So much for taking a little more care over things.

'Hey, over here!'

The man was offended. 'I'm not some sort of *maître d'*,' he protested. 'Remember that!'

Rath ignored him. 'You've only given me five addresses,' he said.

'Of course.'

'There are six names on my list.'

'Only five Germans, though. This one here . . .' He pointed to the fourth name down. 'We don't have him. Must be a foreigner.'

'A foreigner in the Red Front?'

'Why not? Ivanov. Sounds Russian, don't you think? And there are plenty of red Russians.'

'So I need to go to the foreign passports office?'

'The alien passports office. You'll find it . . .'

'. . . left at the end of the corridor, room 152,' Rath completed the sentence.

The passports official examined him wide-eyed, his reading glasses still perched on his nose. By the time a flicker of recognition spread across his face, Rath had already disappeared.

The official in room 152 was more straightforward and less concerned than the old boy about sticking to the rules, though he wasn't any cheerier. If anything, he was grumpier.

He had things to do, he had scolded, when Rath lodged his request. 'Take a look yourself. I'm sure you can open a cabinet.'

So there he was, standing in front of the same roll-front cabinet that the old man had used two weeks ago to locate Kardakov's index card. He couldn't resist the temptation. Before going through the letter I, he turned his attentions to K. Perhaps he had renewed his identity card in the meantime . . . but now that he was holding the index card he saw that everything was exactly the same as before. The last registered address was Nürnberger Strasse 28, which meant that Kardakov's documents were no longer valid. Perhaps he didn't need them anymore, because he had long since acquired false papers, along with a new name. Rath put the card back. He thought of two more names, Russians with whom he still had a score to settle, the pair that was surely linked to Kardakov, and who thus ought to be included in the file he would present to Zörgiebel. Fallin lived in Yorckstrasse, while the second address was in Kreuzberg; the entry must have been changed only recently. When Rath realised what the entry said, the pencil almost fell out of his hand.

Vitali Pjotrevitsch Selenskij lived on Luisenufer!

Most likely in the rear building with the good old German name *Müller* on the doorplate. Now Rath was certain that the Russian heavies were with Kardakov and the *Red Fortress*. They were probably his bodyguards, one of whom had been detailed to protect the boss's girlfriend, smuggled into her tenement under the name Müller. Not exactly very original, but it had worked. Until now.

He noted the addresses. Two more tiles in a mosaic that, though still far from complete, was beginning to take shape. It was about time he shared his knowledge. He smiled contentedly, and almost forgot to look for the addresses he had come for in the first place.

24

Dear Herr Zörgiebel, is the Berlin police force neglecting its duties?

Several incidents from the recent past give us cause for concern. It is the duty of the police to maintain law and order, solve crimes and, above all, to ensure that justice prevails. We ask you: is the Berlin police force still up to this task?

Imagine, my dear Zörgiebel, that you are sitting in a concert hall. Suddenly police storm the building and fire machine guns into the audience because it is alleged that two pickpockets are seated among them. An overreaction, you cry? And yet that is precisely what is happening in your city. Not in a concert hall, but on the streets, in Wedding, in Neukölln, in the heart of Berlin.

Your police force, whose duty it is to maintain law and order, is in breach of the very same. Rather than protecting its citizens from violence, it has inflicted violence upon its citizens.

You gave us renewed hope when the victim of a violent crime was salvaged from the Landwehr canal, and you faithfully promised to do everything in your power to catch his killer and make the city's inhabitants feel safe once more.

Having promised us this, Herr Zörgiebel, why have you withdrawn all officers from the investigation?

I'll tell you why: because a police officer was shot dead and the Berlin police force is concentrating all its resources on finding his killer. At your behest, Commissioner!

A dead officer, that is regrettable, it is true! But does it give you the right to operate a double standard? Is a civilian murder victim of lesser importance than a victim in police uniform? We ask you, Herr Zörgiebel, are all non-police officers second-class citizens? Can the police force be allowed to neglect its duties and ignore unsolved cases whenever one of its own falls victim to a crime?

Rath pushed the paper contentedly to one side. The journalist had done a good job in softening Zörgiebel up for his next visitor, Detective Inspector Gereon Rath, bearing glad tidings in this, the commissioner's hour of need.

Rath had got hold of the eight o'clock edition of *Abendblatt* in the foyer downstairs and taken it to his room. From his window he could look onto Askanischer Platz and the nightly illuminated *Anhalter Bahnhof*. He had spent his first few nights in the *Excelsior* too, before he had moved into his room at Elisabeth Behnke's when *Anhalter Bahnhof* had lain under a carapace of snow and ice.

He glanced at the time. Already nine. She should be here any minute.

In the bathroom he used both hands to splash cold water on his face. The man in the mirror looked a little worn out, but satisfied all the same.

No wonder he was tired. After his visit to the passports office, the afternoon had dragged on and on. It had taken time for Rath to canvass all six names on his list as he had had to call on four of the addresses several times before finally getting hold of someone. A good thing he had use of the car, since three of them lived in Wedding, two in Friedrichshain and one in Prenzlauer Berg. None in Kreuzberg, where Rath would have liked to pay another two men a visit, but there was still time for that.

All six men on his list had an alibi for Wednesday morning. They had been at the rally outside Karl-Liebknecht-Haus and could each name a dozen witnesses who had also taken part. Rath imagined that his colleagues, who had also been checking the alibis of former Red Front members, had fared likewise. What was the point? An endless list of names with dubious alibis would scarcely help them solve the murder, and if there was one thing Rath couldn't stand, it was tedious assignments that made little or no sense.

Did Böhm hope the perpetrator would react carelessly if police suddenly turned up? Rath suspected that these former Red Front members were only being checked for Zörgiebel's sake, while Böhm was off pursuing a completely different line. People like Gereon Rath were making fools of themselves for the commissioner, while Wilhelm Böhm would bask in the glory of a successfully solved case.

Rath had drafted the report quickly and indifferently, the most frequently occurring word being *ditto*. No wonder, what with six practically identical statements. If he didn't see the point in an assignment, then he completed it in a correspondingly lacklustre manner.

He had still been sitting at the typewriter in Roeder's outer office when Charly came in to collect the report. The fact that she was acting as messenger quickly improved his mood, likewise the imminent prospect of spending the evening with her. The *Excelsior* was huge, respectable and relatively inexpensive, in other words just the ticket. When he had first booked the room over the phone, Charly hadn't really seen the attraction, but since she categorically refused to take Rath back to hers, she didn't really have much of a choice.

'We need to make our relationship more official soon, Gereon,' she had said. 'We can't go on playing hide-and-seek in hotels!'

'I wonder if Zörgiebel will let us keep working in the same department?'

'Then I'll transfer to G Division. It's where I'll end up if I become a police officer anyway,' she had said before disappearing with his report.

He had telephoned Bruno to say he wouldn't be coming out to Friedenau later, not mentioning that he was staying in a hotel—nor had he said anything about his companion.

It was almost eight when he finally left the Castle and took the underground to Potsdamer Platz. He re-emerged directly in front of *Haus Vaterland*, night-time Berlin receiving him with its boisterous revellers and gleaming neon signs. The walk via Königgrätzer Strasse took him past *Europahaus*, where he stood outside the cinema watching patrons stream inside. Exactly one week ago he had stood here waiting for Charly, kissing her for the first time in *Café Europa*. Filmgoers jostled past and he set off once more. The *Excelsior* was only a few steps away.

There was a knock on the door. It had to be her. He folded the copy of *Abendblatt* that still lay open on the table and hid it under the bed. For some reason he had a guilty conscience about it, even if he couldn't say exactly why.

'Open up,' she called through the door, 'I don't have a hand free!'

She beamed at him as he opened the door. In her right hand, she was holding a little suitcase, in her left several paper bags bearing the names of department stores. She pressed a kiss onto his cheek.

'This time, I've come prepared,' she said. 'I don't want to have to go to work again wearing the same dress as the day before. And you . . .' She threw a Tietz shopping bag onto the bed. '. . . for you I've brought some fresh underwear and socks.' A third bag flew onto the bed. 'Whether the shirt will fit or not, I'm not sure, I had to guess your collar size. But the tie should match your suit at any rate.'

He took the bags from the bed in amazement. 'Not bad! Should I try it on now?'

She hung the DO NOT DISTURB sign on the door.

'Try it on? Think again, Inspector. This is not the time to be trying things on. It's the time to be taking them off!'

He obeyed, but first he saw to her, covering each area of exposed flesh in kisses, her arms, her shoulders, her slender neck. When he bit into the nape of her neck, she let out a quiet groan. She wanted to turn him towards her, kiss him, embrace him, but he motioned for her to keep still. He took off her shoes and rolled her stockings slowly down her legs, first the right and then the left. As the dress slid from her shoulders, he could hardly stand it any longer but maintained the slow tempo. She shivered slightly, as his hands clasped her breasts and his mouth reached for her neck once more. Only then did he slowly turn her towards him. For a brief moment they looked each other in the eye, breathing heavily.

Then they fell upon each other as if starved.

Afterwards they lay next to each other for a long time in silence. He gazed at the ceiling lost in thought, Charly wrapped in his arms. He hadn't been this happy in a very long time.

You're in love, my friend, he told himself.

Charly was right, it couldn't go on like this. Still, things would soon be different. He'd have a permanent position in Homicide, no more secrets, a professional, not to say personal, future in this city at last. He would have been only too happy to move in with her straightaway, especially since he was already looking for somewhere to live. True, he didn't want to spring it on her, but—for the first time he could feel it—with a woman like Charly by his side, he could be happy in Berlin.

'You know what you're into?' she asked suddenly, stroking his chest. 'Delayed gratification.'

He laughed. 'Sounds like a criminal offence, do you learn phrases like that in the Faculty of Law?'

'It's not a crime, it's something very arousing.'

'Are you trying to say we should always take a week's break?'

'Absolutely not!'

And this time they got straight to the point.

He was first to rise in the morning, and it was lovely to wake next to her. How peacefully she lay. He stroked her face gently so as not to wake her, stood up and went to the window. The rain was drumming on the immense roof of *Anhalter Bahnhof*, but there was still lots going on below in Askanischer Platz. The Whitsun traffic had begun and umbrellas were streaming towards the station.

To the left, Möckernstrasse led into Königgrätzer Strasse. A few hundred metres on, it continued over the Landwehr canal, where Boris's corpse had been found.

He'd put an end to this business today. Pass everything over to the commissioner, sell his story as best he could. Zörgiebel would have no choice but to give him Roeder's desk, and all this secrecy would finally be over.

Smooth arms wrapped themselves around his chest. Her warm body nestled up to his. He hadn't even heard her.

'Lousy weather, isn't it?' she mumbled, still half-asleep.

'And we didn't even bring an umbrella.'

'The sort of weather that makes you want to stay in bed all day.'

'Only I fear that good old Wilhelm Böhm wouldn't allow it. He's got a lot of work to delegate at the moment.'

'Get back to bed,' she whinged.

'What did Böhm do with your old case? Has it been closed?'

'The file's with the wet fish. Now, come on.' She pulled him towards the bed.

'Hey!' he protested. 'What's the big idea? I don't have much more than a quickie in me.'

'Well, I am impressed by your vocabulary, I have to say. You can tell vice cops are well versed in this sort of thing . . .'

Before she could carry on, he had thrown a pillow in her face.

They skipped breakfast but were still late for work. They didn't say their goodbyes until they had reached Alexanderplatz station. While Charly walked into the station, Rath chose to have a browse at the newspaper kiosk. A few papers had reacted overnight and jumped on the bandwagon that Weinert had set in motion. Zörgiebel had angered too many journalists for them to pass up the opportunity to get their own back. Rath didn't think that a single one of them would have checked that Zörgiebel had frozen all other investigations for the sake of the Jänicke case. They had just cribbed it from Weinert.

He only entered Roeder's office to hang up his coat, then he was on his way again.

The wet fish were located in the Central Homicide Archive, which Gennat had set up and cultivated as if it were his own child. That was also why he had housed it in a room next to his office, a big room whose longitudinal wall was completely blocked by filing cabinets. In the middle of the room was a reading table with eight chairs, which could also be used for smaller meetings. The card-index cabinet was located under the window with a thriving rubber plant on top. It was probably looked after by Trudchen Steiner.

The files were categorised according to mode of death with only a small cabinet reserved for unsolved cases—testament to the unflinching self-confidence of A Division. Böhm must have felt great when he deposited the *Möckern Bridge* file here. No homicide detective liked putting anything in this cabinet. The Wilczek file was a different matter, of course, Rath would be only too happy to dump it with the rest.

In the space of two weeks Böhm had managed to fill not just one ring binder with information but four, an astonishing disparity between effort and outcome.

Rath wedged all four files under his arm, intending to bury himself in the *Möckern Bridge* case until late afternoon. Then it would be time to tell Zörgiebel—while they were already starting up the rotary press at *Abend-blatt*.

Unfortunately when he returned to Roeder's office with the ring files, there was a new sheet of paper on his desk. Charly must have brought it.

Another six names, the letter P this time. They'd soon have covered the whole alphabet. Rath decided to ignore the list. What he was planning to do today would be as good as declaring war on Böhm anyway, and none of this would make any difference. He opened the first file and set to work. Any number of witnesses interviewed, and someone—probably Böhm himself—had circled and marked the more interesting sections. At ten he telephoned Weinert before carrying on, working through lunch.

There were no more sightings of Charly. He tried not to think of her too often, but it wasn't easy as some of the statements he was reading had come from her. At half past four he telephoned Zörgiebel's outer office and requested a meeting with the commissioner. Dagmar Kling tried to offer him a slot after Whitsun.

'I'm sorry, but this is an urgent matter. I need to speak to the commissioner today.'

The Guillotine was merciful. 'I'll see what I can do.'

'It is extremely urgent.'

Scarcely five minutes later, Dagmar Kling called back. 'The commissioner will see you in twenty minutes. He's not in the best of moods.'

'Believe me, I'll cheer him up.'

He didn't have to wait, the Guillotine waved him straight through.

Zörgiebel seemed overcome with remorse. The press coverage today certainly hadn't been to his liking.

'Good day, Commissioner.'

'Good day, Herr Rath. What can I do for you?'

'I hope it's me who can do something for you, Commissioner. Do you remember the dead man who was found in the Landwehr canal two weeks ago?'

'Everyone keeps reminding me.'

'I think I've found a new lead that might help us solve the case.'

Zörgiebel's eyebrows rose sharply. 'Why are you talking to me, Inspector Rath?' he asked. 'DCI Böhm was leading the investigation.'

'*Was leading*, Commissioner, *was leading*. But then he was given the Jänicke case. Since it currently has priority, I thought the best thing to do was to consult the Commissioner directly. You can decide how best to proceed. The case has already been assigned to the wet fish.'

Zörgiebel nodded. 'It's probably not the worst idea, coming to me. So what have you got? And how did you come by it?'

'That's a long and complex story . . .'

'Then give me the abridged version. You can put the rest in your report.'

'The dead man they found in the canal is Russian. First name Boris, I don't know his surname. Anyway, he belonged to a communist splinter group that calls itself *Red Fortress*—or at least worked for them. On their orders, he smuggled a large amount of gold out of the Soviet Union, gold that belonged to the noble family Sorokin.'

Rath watched Zörgiebel closely. The word Sorokin didn't elicit any reaction. It seemed the story of the Berlin gold wasn't quite as well known as Major General Seegers thought.

'The head of the *Red Fortress* is a man named Alexej Kardakov, whom I strongly suspect of Boris's murder,' he continued. That the Russian had once lived in Rath's flat was none of Zörgiebel's business. 'Kardakov has gone underground, likewise his accomplice Countess Svetlana Sorokina, whose family concealed the gold from the Bolsheviks.'

'Wait a minute!' Zörgiebel interrupted. 'Why would they kill the man who brought them the gold?'

'Because he wanted to clear off with it. According to my information, the money was to be used to finance the underground work of the *Red Fortress*.'

'You mean weapons?'

'They weren't planning to print pamphlets! The gold is alleged to be worth eighty million marks.'

'Difficult to find someone who'll cough up that much.'

'Which is why Kardakov had already established contact with a *Ringverein* in advance, and how I hit upon the connection in the first place. It was *Berolina*, the *Ringverein* Josef Wilczek belonged to.'

Zörgiebel gave him a questioning look.

'Wilczek, the dead man in the concrete,' Rath continued. 'His *Ring-*

verein was supposed to turn the gold into cash for the *Red Fortress*. Clearly it never reached either the *Fortress* or *Berolina*.'

'And this smuggler—Boris—is supposed to have embezzled the gold?'

Rath nodded.

'How did *he* turn it to cash?'

'I suspect with the help of another *Ringverein*. Perhaps he made a deal with Stalin's people and collected a reward. There are a number of possibilities.'

'How did such a large amount of gold make it across the border undetected in the first place?'

'That's a question I still can't answer, Commissioner.'

'And I imagine you don't have any conclusive proof either?'

'That's the problem, Commissioner. There's hardly any evidence. At least DCI Böhm knows which direction to take his investigation in now, and Kardakov ought to have a lot to say, once he has been found.'

Zörgiebel glanced at the time. 'This is most irritating, Herr Rath.'

'Irritating, Commissioner?'

'The worst possible time to inform the press. We won't get it in the evening editions.'

A good thing too, Rath thought, *since I've given Weinert my word.*

Zörgiebel appeared pensive. 'First we should put out a warrant for this . . . what's his name?'

'Kardakov.'

'Right. Do you have enough evidence to justify a murder charge?'

'He's going to be very important for the progress of the investigation. If not as a suspect, then as a witness. The Countess too.'

'We'll wait a few days. We can inform the press after Whitsun.'

Rath cleared his throat. 'I'm afraid that's not possible, Commissioner.'

'Pardon me?'

'We need to inform the press immediately. Otherwise it won't reflect well on the Berlin police.'

'I'm not sure I follow.'

'I only got the decisive information from a journalist today, someone who knew Kardakov personally and has done research on *Krasnaja Krepost . . .*'

'On who?'

'The *Red Fortress*. Some of the things I've just told you, above all the stuff about the *Red Fortress* and the Sorokin gold, will appear in *Abendblatt* tonight.'

'That smearsheet . . .'

'Which is why I thought it was my duty to inform you right away, Commissioner.'

'You're right, you're right.' Zörgiebel waved his fat hands gruffly. 'And you can't stop this muckraker from . . .'

'Afraid not, Commissioner. The man invoked the freedom of the press and believed he had performed his duty by informing the police.' Rath reached into his jacket. 'He did, however, provide me these pictures. These show Kardakov, while this is the Countess. She was working under a false name as a singer.'

Zörgiebel examined the pictures, resting his massive chin in his hands.

'If we go to the press with this story today, then we have to be careful, I hope that much is clear. There's far too much speculation.'

'Of course, Commissioner, but we can at least announce a breakthrough.'

'Good, I'll discuss the matter with Gennat and Böhm, and get the necessaries underway. You should be present at this meeting, Inspector.' He reached for the house telephone. 'Dagmar? Please ask Gennat and Böhm to join us. Let's say in ten minutes, and notify the press. Tell them I'll be holding a press conference in one hour.'

He hung up and fished a cigar from the case on his desk, offering one to Rath. He turned it down. Bad enough to have to sit opposite Böhm, but with a cigar in the corner of his mouth, it would just be plain embarrassing. He tapped an Overstolz from the red packet.

'I prefer cigarettes, if you don't mind sir.'

Zörgiebel leaned forward and gave him a light.

'My dear Rath, it's not that I'm displeased with your findings, but you really should have gone to Böhm with them. How long have you known that a *Ringverein* was mixed up in this?'

'The connection wasn't clear until today, Commissioner, after I'd spoken to the journalist. I asked to see you straightaway.'

'Which journalist is it?'

'I had to assure him absolute confidentiality. The article will appear under a pseudonym. Revealing secrets like this is not without danger.'

'Will he be available as a witness in that case?'

Rath shrugged his shoulders, fished a piece of paper out of his pocket and placed it on the table. 'I also have the addresses of two Russians, most likely colleagues of Kardakov. They could lead us to him.'

Zörgiebel took the piece of paper and cleared his throat. He looked as though he'd had a tough day.

'I'm indebted to you, Herr Rath,' he said. 'A breakthrough in this investigation was long overdue.'

'I'm only doing my duty, Commissioner.' *Modesty doesn't get you anywhere,* Rath thought to himself, but it wouldn't be the first time Zörgiebel had heard that line and he'd know how to interpret it.

'You are aware, I hope, that I can't promote you, Herr Rath? Even if you personally were to put Stalin behind bars. The Interior Ministry has issued a moratorium on promotions.'

'I know, Commissioner.'

'So, what is it you want?'

'My own office, with my name on the door, and my own secretary at last.'

Zörgiebel smiled. 'Very well, Inspector! I think that can be arranged.'

'Thank you, Commissioner.'

'If I could give you one piece of advice, young man, it would be to take some time out over Whitsun. You've accrued a lot of overtime.'

'And the investigation? I thought Böhm needed every man.'

'If I were you, I'd be avoiding the DCI for a few days. The meeting in a moment will be bad enough and I can't promise that he will keep his calm. You've been conducting an investigation behind his back, no matter how you try to spin it. If you're lucky, he'll have just about calmed down again by Tuesday.' Zörgiebel shook his head. 'My dear Rath, you should remember one thing. If you carve a career for yourself at the expense of others you're going to make enemies. There's an old saying that you always meet twice in life. Well, I can guarantee that you'll run into DCI Böhm more often than twice.'

The press conference went famously. Zörgiebel introduced Rath as the man who had made the decisive breakthrough in the *Möckern Bridge* investigation. Admittedly he neglected to mention that Rath didn't actually belong to the investigating team, or that the team had been disbanded. It was meant to look as if the press had been wrong to suspect Zörgiebel and the Berlin police of dropping everything to expedite the Jänicke case. The commissioner never tired of expressing his indignation at this assumption.

'Gentlemen,' he said. 'You now have the opportunity to atone for your error.'

At first, Rath hadn't seen Charly, but she must have been standing next to the door for a long time. She was looking on with a sceptical gaze, arms folded in front of her chest. Had Böhm sent her? The DCI had stayed away from the press conference, even though Zörgiebel had wanted to take him onto the platform with them. During the short meeting just now in Zörgiebel's office, the homicide detective had stormed out in a rage, slamming the door behind him. Clearly, he was accustomed to making such exits. Gennat hadn't come either, not believing they had enough to go to the press. He had told Zörgiebel as much in no uncertain terms.

Thus the commissioner had staged the conference with Rath alone, after they agreed on what information to disclose. It seemed to be enough for the press. The reporters busily noted it all down.

Charly remained by the door after the conference was over, the reporters pushing past her into the corridor. In truth, there was no reason to hurry, since the evening editions were already on sale and the extras hadn't carried the story either. She stayed where she was until the whole crowd had moved past. Rath was last to leave with Zörgiebel, whom she greeted politely, reserving a hostile gaze for Rath which he put down to their agreement not to act like a couple at the Castle.

He didn't realise ignoring him was the last thing on her mind until she spoke.

'You really are an arsehole, Herr Rath,' she hissed, so loudly that the commissioner could hear, and left him standing like a daft schoolboy.

25

Well then, happy Whitsun!

Charly wasn't answering her telephone. He had tried the whole of Friday night and, on one occasion at least, had managed to get her friend on the line. Greta had informed him tersely that Charly was away over the holiday and hung up.

He couldn't believe it. Charly wasn't free until Sunday, when they had been planning to take a drive out to the country together. Thinking of the holiday plans they had hatched in *Excelsior* cut him to the quick and he gave up dialling her number. It was late by the time he left the Castle and rode out to Friedenau. Bruno was already on his way to bed, but sat drinking with him for a while. It was becoming a habit, but not even the alcohol could banish the thought of Charly.

There was no sign of her when he arrived at the Castle on Saturday, even though he wasn't working. In A Division he found only an exceedingly bad-tempered Wilhelm Böhm, who didn't say a word and looked at him as if he were a disgusting insect. He hadn't thought it possible, but it was almost worse than having the man yell at him.

Zörgiebel had been right, there was an icy atmosphere in the whole of A Division. Still, Rath was sure he could handle it, even if the business with Charly had hit him hard. She seemed to despise him for what he had done, for his secrecy, for the humiliation he had inflicted upon Böhm but, most of all he suspected, for the fact that she had fed him exclusive information about the *Möckern Bridge* investigation. He hadn't told her anything about his plans, let alone his findings. He had sucked her dry, squeezed her like a lemon.

But, what was he supposed to have done? By the time he'd met her he was already up to his neck in it and he *needed* this success. He, Gereon Rath, needed a personal success, a success that he didn't want to, couldn't, share with self-righteous superiors such as Böhm.

His parents had called on Friday evening and congratulated him. Zörgiebel had probably notified his old friend, and mentioned Gereon's days off too. Didn't he fancy coming to Cologne for Whitsun, Engelbert Rath had asked. 'It would make your mother so happy.'

Gereon didn't have an excuse to hand. He had arranged to meet friends, he said, and besides, he had to look for a new flat. Weak excuses. His father naturally assumed there was a girl behind it and began to tease his son. The old man could believe whatever he wanted. Gereon couldn't deal with his family right now, with the exception of Ursula perhaps, his younger sister. He missed her sometimes, but the rest of them could go hang. The silence over Severin; and then the speeches in Anno's honour, so skilfully delivered by Engelbert that Gereon always felt like a failure. There was no way he was ever going to measure up to Saint Anno.

The only person who could cheer him up now was Bruno, although Rath had thought about going away over Whitsun to give the Wolters space. Bruno had just given him a serious look and said, 'You're not imposing at all. It's great to have you here, Gereon. You're the son Emmi and I never had.' It had taken Rath a moment to realise that Bruno was teasing him. Uncle was only twelve years older than him, and Emmi Wolter at most seven or eight. He must have a pulled a great face, because Bruno had burst into laughter.

The Wolters had invited guests to stay over the holiday, a couple they were friendly with, Rudi and Erika Scheer, as well as Agnes Sahler, a friend whose husband had died two years before. Though the invites had been sent out long before Rath had been made homeless, and there couldn't have been any intention of pairing the two off, a strange atmosphere developed between them. Whether by accident or design, neither made much of an effort with the other, preferring to keep to the existing couples in the room. A few times Rath had stolen away from the company and tried to ring Charly. No-one picked up.

On Whit Sunday, the three men had sat in the garden drinking, long after the women had retired to bed. Rudi Scheer, a quiet, friendly man of about fifty, had talked about the old days on the firing range and how Bruno had taught the new recruits how to shoot. For the first time, Rath heard something about the time that had brought Bruno the nickname Parabellum. Scheer was still responsible for the armoury at Alex, but Bruno didn't

want anything to do with weapons. Rath asked why he had been transferred to Vice.

'Ach, the accident,' Scheer had said, only to fall silent immediately when
Bruno cast him an angry glance.

'There are things it's best not to talk about,' he had said.

He had changed the subject to the Kardakov case. Rath talked about
the progress of the investigation, despite having been more or less cut off
by Böhm. Zörgiebel had reassigned the case to the DCI, even if the latter
had never officially relinquished it. Rath knew they hadn't found Kardakov yet, and that the Countess was still missing. The two Russian heavies
had been arrested and brought to Alex on Friday night, but turned loose
again on Saturday morning. He didn't tell Bruno it was the same Russians
he had tried to arrest after the raid, hoping they hadn't been released in the
same manner as the week before. Special treatment! Just thinking about it
made him angry. He ought to have given the pair a good grilling when he
had the chance. Kardakov would have been theirs long ago.

Rath learned why the two Russians had been released when he was back at
his desk on Tuesday morning, reading through the interrogation statements. Both Fallin and Selenskij had affirmed that they held no truck with
communists, nor did they maintain any ties to an organisation called *Red
Fortress*. They had never heard of Alexej Kardakov. Above all, their claims
were substantiated by still having in their possession documents indicating
that they had been officers in the *Ochranka*, the Tsar's secret police. They
were colleagues then, after a fashion. Was that why they had originally been
released from police custody?

Rath gazed in annoyance at the interrogation statements. He'd have
liked to have put these Russians through the mill himself, but Zörgiebel
hadn't allowed it. It was Böhm's case again, and that was that!

Gennat himself was looking after the Jänicke case. The team dealing
with the *Bülowplatz* murder had been slimmed down, though perhaps
'slimmed down' was the wrong expression, given that it was Buddha heading the inquiry. The man weighed in at a minimum 300 pounds.

Thus Rath wasn't sure what he was supposed to be doing when he returned to his desk after an enforced three-day break. The events of Friday

had rather shaken things up in A Division. Was he still assigned to the Jänicke case? Or should he reopen the Wilczek file, which he'd sooner have snapped shut and shelved? The only thing Zörgiebel had made abundantly clear was that from now on his involvement in the Kardakov case would be restricted to what Böhm asked of him—no more operations carried out under his own steam. Only, the DCI hadn't asked for anything. He wasn't even speaking to Rath. Not about the weather, and certainly not about the ongoing investigation.

Nevertheless, he was determined to knuckle down. After yesterday, the bleakest Whit Monday of his life, the whole day spent thinking gloomy thoughts, after a day like that, where even the evening binge with Bruno had done nothing to lift his spirits, he knew that the only way to stop himself thinking of private matters, of Charly, of what would happen when next they met, was to drown himself in work. At least he wasn't the type who joined the foreign legion because of a woman.

He decided to call Gennat. Perhaps he would take Rath onto the *Bülowplatz* team. That still seemed like the most meaningful assignment A Division had to offer. Jänicke's killer couldn't be allowed to escape unpunished. Besides, there was probably a lot he could learn from an old fox like Gennat.

Rath had the receiver in hand, but didn't get as far as dialling.

There was a knock. A man in white work trousers stood at the door, in the one hand a wooden case, in the other a piece of paper.

'Yes?'

'Detective Inspector Gero Rath?'

'Gereon!'

'The sign writers, Inspector.'

The sign writers? Despite his best efforts, Rath could only make out one. 'Good. Please just get started,' he said. 'But remember: it's Gereon.'

'That's what it says here.' The sign writer waved the piece of paper.

Gingerly, he unpacked his colours, brushes and stencils and positioned himself in front of the open door.

'Can't you close it?'

'Fraid not, the light here is better. It'll only take a few minutes.'

The man started daubing away, as calm as you like. Sometimes Rath envied such people, even if they also made him nervous.

The sign writer was almost forced to start over when a man hurried through the door and barged into him. Kronberg, from ED, was carrying a brown envelope.

'Working on the door already?' he said. 'Is this going to be your office?'

'Looks that way. Small, but at least it's mine. Just need a secretary now. What can I do for you?'

'Other way round,' Kronberg said and waved the envelope bearing the stamp of the Berlin police. 'Wonders will never cease!'

'Have Hertha won the league?'

'No.' Kronberg gazed at him uncomprehendingly. No sense of humour, the man. 'You requested a ballistics report last week. Forgotten already?' he continued. 'And this here is the result. You'll be amazed. Could be a big lead, and not just in your case!'

Now it was Rath's turn to gaze uncomprehendingly. The ballistics report from the Wilczek case? Rath already knew whose weapon the bullet came from, which was precisely why he'd been expecting it to be a dead end. How could it have turned up a lead? ED had only examined the souvenir from Krajewski's pistol. Did that mean the porn Kaiser had been fiddling around with it before the incident on the roof?

'We've taken a close look at the projectile—and found a reference sample, also submitted last week. There is a more than ninety percent chance that both projectiles were fired from the same weapon, a Lignose one hand. Popular with communists and small-time crooks.'

Yes, a Lignose, I know, Rath nearly said. 'Which reference sample are you talking about?' he asked instead.

'The *Bülowplatz* case. We examined the bullet last week, priority you know, on the orders of the Commissioner.'

'Yes, yes!' Couldn't he just come out and say it? 'Out with it, man!'

'The bullet that killed Assistant Detective Stephan Jänicke came from the same weapon as the bullet found in Josef Wilczek's body.'

Rath said nothing as Kronberg looked on triumphantly, like a Roman commander on victory parade.

'That's foxed you, hasn't it?'

It had indeed. The revelation had left him flabbergasted.

'That's me finished,' a voice interrupted his thoughts.

'Sorry?'

'Finished.' The sign writer stood in the door and gestured towards the name he had painted. 'Still not dry though. Be careful.'

'Thanks. Can you close the door behind you?'

The sign writer nodded and closed the door so carefully it might have been made of sugar.

Rath sat at his desk and stared at the door, his name emblazoned on it. However, it wasn't the door that was bothering him, but the brown envelope. Was it really possible? He opened it. He needed to see it in black and white, it couldn't be true!

But deep down a voice was telling him that it had to be.

No matter how much he turned it over in his mind, there was simply no other solution: Bruno Wolter had shot Stephan Jänicke.

PART III

THE WHOLE TRUTH

21st May—21st June 1929

26

He rang three times without a response, turned the key in the lock, entered the flat and closed the door gently. The clock at the end of the hall showed half past three. It felt strange to be here in broad daylight. What if Emmi Wolter suddenly appeared? What if she had been taking a nap and hadn't been able to make it to the door in time? He could tell her he had forgotten something, she might still believe him. But once he started raking through her things? How would he explain that? Perhaps it had been a silly idea to drive out here, but Rath had to know for sure.

Gennat had pinched the report, along with the Wilczek file. The chief of homicide was now certain that Wilczek's killer had Jänicke on his conscience too. According to his theory, the assistant detective had most likely rumbled the Wilczek killer during his investigations into the city's criminal underworld.

Under normal circumstances, Rath would have been delighted about having his own desk in A Division, about belonging to the legendary Buddha's team, and about the fact that Gennat would have to assign the Wilczek case to the wet fish.

Under normal circumstances he would have been delighted, but nothing seemed normal anymore.

He had pretended to get on with his work, but his mind was on other things. Realising that he was actually looking for explanations that exonerated Bruno, he wondered if Uncle had perhaps returned the Lignose to Krajewski? Or simply flogged it?

And why would he shoot Jänicke?

Unable to think of anything else, he had got hold of a car and driven to Friedenau and now, here he was, loitering in the Wolters's flat, not even knowing where to look. If Bruno still had the pistol, then he must be hiding it somewhere. Rath didn't think Uncle told Emmi all his secrets, and certainly not secrets like this.

It therefore made little sense to look downstairs, where the Wolters had their kitchen, as well as their dining and living rooms. He went upstairs, which was where the guestroom was situated. He didn't need to look there, nor in the Wolters's bedroom, even if it did contain an enormous wardrobe where loads of things could be stored. Where then?

Rath tried to imagine he was married to Emmi Wolter and wanted to hide something from her.

Bruno had a study, a realm in which Emmi never set foot. When she wanted to clean, she had to ask permission. Rath had only been inside once, when he had been looking for Bruno a few days before. He'd barely had time to poke his head round the door before his host rose from his desk and ushered him outside. Downstairs in the living room they had enjoyed a beer together, as so often in the last few days.

At first glance, the room seemed like a normal study: a desk, a few roll-front cabinets, framed photos on the wall. No gun cabinet. Rath gazed at the photos. There were uniforms in almost every one: soldiers' uniforms, police uniforms. In one he thought he recognised Major General Seegers, albeit in captain's uniform, shaking the hand of a still relatively slim Lance Corporal Bruno Wolter. A second picture showed Wolter wearing his sergeant's stripes and staring proudly into the camera beside another sergeant whom Rath didn't recognise, but guessed was Helmut Behnke. Another picture that must have been taken just after the start of the war showed three lance corporals in the trenches, marked by dirt and the strain of slaughter, but smiling nevertheless. Rath recognised Wolter and the man from the previous picture straightaway. The third soldier was Rudi Scheer, the Wolters's guest over Whitsun, in his younger days. A rectangular patch on the wallpaper showed where another picture must have hung until recently.

He tore his gaze away from the pictures and began to examine the cabinets. Typical roll-front cabinets, just like those at the Castle. He slipped on a pair of gloves and examined the first. Locked, as were the rest. He rummaged through the desk drawers for a key. They weren't exactly tidy. In the top drawer there was some change, a few ten pfenning coins, the odd Reichsmark, a rubber, a few pens, a letter opener, and paperclips everywhere, clinging to the rest of the junk like ticks. The next drawer down was a muddle of all sorts of papers: bills, taxes, letters, postcards, a few newspapers. *Die Standarte, Der Stahlhelm.* The chaos in the lower drawer was even greater, with all kinds of odds and ends packed into a wooden box. Rath removed it and tipped its contents out. Ammunition packs fell onto the parquet flooring and different calibre cartridges rolled out, little *Stahlhelm* badges, a pair of pincers, a little hammer and all sorts of rubbish. The ammunition had given him hope, but there was no pistol to be found.

If Wolter really was Jänicke's killer, then he'd have disposed of the weapon long ago. Perhaps he had returned it to the unsuspecting informant Krajewski? That would be plausible. Assistant Detective Jänicke had located the missing member (a fitting description, Rath thought) of König's porn troupe, Franz Krajewski, who had killed the rookie for fear of being discovered. All Wolter would have to do was leave an anonymous tip-off and send a team of uniformed officers to the porn Kaiser's to find the weapon. The weight of evidence against poor old Krajewski would be overwhelming, enough for any public prosecutor.

Rath began to pack everything away, including the small black book he was holding in his hand. Wait a minute, a black notebook!

It didn't necessarily mean anything, there were any number of books like it. But when he opened it and read the name on the first page, he knew for sure. He had found the notebook belonging to the late Stephan Jänicke.

The missing notebook Gennat was looking for.

All of a sudden, Rath didn't care about the pistol, the book amounted to the same evidence.

Bruno Wolter was a murderer!

Still, that didn't answer the decisive question. Why had he killed a colleague who had never done anyone any harm, an innocent lad fresh from police academy?

Rath leafed feverishly through the thin pages. There were no entries at the back, but a few pages had been ripped out. Jänicke had probably needed a few scraps of paper and plundered the book. At the front were his notes on the Wilczek case, revealing nothing that Jänicke hadn't already mentioned in his reports. Nevertheless, the book was more than a simple notebook; Jänicke had also used it as a diary. Not that Rath could make much sense of the entries. Apart from the date and time, Jänicke had used abbreviations that were open to all kinds of interpretations.

1505/900/I at B

The date of his death, but what did the letters mean? Was Jänicke intending to give information to a B at nine? To Bruno? What kind of information? Or did it stand for something completely different?

He had heard a key turning in the lock, the jangling of a bunch of keys, followed by the resounding thud of the Wolters's heavy front door snapping shut.

Shit!

He put the junk back in the box, before instinctively pocketing the book, crept over to the stairs and looked down. A red ladies' hat was hanging on the coat stand and Rath recognised Emmi Wolter's blonde locks. He jerked his head back as she turned round. She didn't appear to have seen him; he heard her hang her coat up and disappear into the flat.

Rath listened, hoping she would go into the kitchen to prepare the evening meal, but no such luck. He had already started to descend the stairs when the living room door opened and Emmi Wolter stepped into the hallway, a shopping bag in her hand and a popular song on her lips. Rath quickly disappeared into the guestroom. If she caught him, at least let it be there.

He closed the door quietly and listened. She came up the stairs and went into the bathroom. Perhaps this was his chance. Quickly, but without making a noise, he opened the door, slipped outside and closed it once again. In the bathroom he could still hear her singing and whistling.

He had just reached the stairs when the bathroom door opened and Emmi Wolter emerged singing into the corridor, in the one hand a half-full toothbrush glass, in the other a bottle of vodka. Her face froze in the middle of the song. She stared at him.

'Oh,' she said inadvertently.

Rath said nothing. He thought about what he should tell her. In the meantime, he hid his hands behind his back and discreetly removed his gloves.

'Well, this is a surprise, Herr Rath,' she said, her voice trembling slightly. 'Finishing so early!'

Only then did he realise it was she who felt as if she had been caught. Emmi Wolter drank in secret and he had caught her in the act!

'Good afternoon, Frau Wolter,' he said. 'A bit of thought would save a lot of legwork . . .' he patted the breast pocket of his jacket. 'Important notes.'

'Ah, yes.' She was frozen to the spot, looking like a rabbit before a fox.

'Having a little drink?' Rath asked, gesturing towards the bottle.

'My God, Herr Rath . . .' she stammered. 'It's just . . . You mustn't . . .' She swallowed. 'Bruno can never hear of this!'

For a moment he gave her a stern look, as if he was considering whether his conscience would allow him not to tell his friend about his wife's secret.

'Hmmm . . .' he said, 'everyone has their little secrets, I guess.' He gave her a conspiratorial look. 'Then please don't tell Bruno how forgetful I am. No-one at the station can find out I was here in broad daylight.'

He placed an index finger to his lips and she nodded zealously. He left her standing and descended the stairs.

'Then . . . see you tonight, Herr Rath,' she cried after him, her voice still trembling.

He was dreading the evening when he arrived at the Castle. He would probably be able to avoid running into Bruno at the station, but it was inevitable that their paths would soon cross. At the very latest, it would happen tonight in the Wolter household.

Rath also avoided Gennat, as well as his other colleagues. After dropping the car off at the motor pool, he withdrew to his solitary office and pretended to continue on the Wilczek/Jänicke case.

Which he did, after a fashion, trying to make sense of Jänicke's notes. Most of the diary-like abbreviations concerned an ominous-sounding *W*, whom Jänicke had met a total of five times from the middle of April, long before the Wilczek investigation. The phrase *SG*! was heavily underlined after the first entry.

Who was *W*? It could hardly be Wilczek. Wolter? At any rate there was no meeting with *W* on May 15th, only the entry Rath already knew about: *1505/900/I at B.* Whatever that meant. Did *B* stand for Bülowplatz?

A sixth meeting with *W* was obviously still to take place: *2405/830/W in P*, a meeting on May 24th, in three days, at eight thirty. In *P*, wherever that might be. Potsdam perhaps, where Jänicke had been at police academy?

Did *W* know that Jänicke was dead? Probably, given how widely it had been reported in the press.

Rath spent the rest of the afternoon brooding over the entries, always ready to shove the black book into the open top drawer of his desk if he received an unsolicited visitor. One of Gennat's people for instance, or perhaps even Bruno Wolter. Rath had taken the precaution of closing both doors, the one leading to the outer office and the one leading into the corridor.

He scanned the whole book for further entries containing the letter *W*. Jänicke had met this person so often that he must have noted more than the simple time of their appointment. Then again perhaps not. What if *W* was a woman? What if this ominous-sounding *W* was simply a Wilhelmine or a Waltraud whom the shy East Prussian idolised?

Rath continued leafing through the book. In the first part, Stephan Jänicke had entered a series of telephone numbers: the service numbers of E Division, just below them Bruno's private number, and a little further down Gereon Rath's former extension in Nürnberger Strasse also made an appearance. Elisabeth Behnke would answer the phone now. He mustn't forget to have it disconnected. He didn't want old Behnke using his private line.

The numbers were arranged neither alphabetically nor by any other discernible system. Suddenly Rath came across an entry that made him wonder. There was no name next to it, just a telephone number, one of many, barely noticeable in the mass of numbers and letters: *Westend 2531*.

Perhaps it was a lead. He reached for the receiver.

'Fräulein? Berlin-Westend please. Extension two-five-three-one. Thank you, I'll wait.'

It took a moment for someone to pick up at the other end. A woman's voice answered.

'Wündisch,' she said.

Rath was so confused he forgot to hang up.

'Hello?' he heard the woman ask, 'who's there please?'

Rath decided not to hang up after all.

'Böhm,' he barked into the receiver. 'Your husband, please!'

'My husband? Sorry, he's not at home. You'll still be able to reach him at the station.'

Rath muttered something incomprehensible and hung up.

Well now! Jänicke's notebook contained the private number of Deputy Wündisch! The head of Section 1A, the political police.

Not all division chiefs had his private number, such was the man's secrecy, but a simple assistant detective, who had only just finished his training, kept the number in his notebook as if it were a matter of course.

Now Rath knew what *W* stood for. He also knew the meaning of *SG: streng geheim. Top secret.*

The politicals had recruited the rookie for their own inscrutable purposes, Wündisch enlisting him, probably at police academy. Rath leafed through Jänicke's notebook and saw his suspicions confirmed. The first meeting with *W* must have taken place as far back as February: *1102/1700/W in P.*

The political police had recruited Stephan Jänicke before he worked for E Division. That could only mean one thing. They had selected a dedicated and eager police trainee and deliberately placed him in E Division.

Whom he had been spying on was obvious, his boss and future killer. Rath couldn't help thinking back to that Sunday when he had unexpectedly come across Jänicke in their office at E Division. Jänicke had been snooping around Wolter's desk.

That still left one question. What had Bruno Wolter done that made him so interesting?

As far as Rath knew, Uncle didn't have any political leanings, at least none that went so far as to make him a person of interest for 1A. He certainly wasn't the only member of the police corps to have a soft spot for his wartime comrades. Or perhaps it wasn't about politics, but corruption? The snoops from 1A were deployed by the commissioner for internal investigations of all kinds, but why should Wündisch have been personally responsible for Jänicke if it was simply a question of a corrupt vice cop?

There had to be more to it, and Rath wanted to know what. He wanted to know why Stephan Jänicke had to die, and what had made a murderer of Bruno Wolter.

Before he left the station, he considered what he should do with the little black book. Initially he had toyed with the idea of copying the most important entries and placing the original back in Bruno's desk, only to think better of it. He had to play safe.

If Jänicke's book turning up on Wolter's private desk was simply a coincidence—which Rath doubted—then he wouldn't miss it, since he didn't know it was there. If, however, Bruno Wolter did have something to do with Jänicke's death, then he would have drawn his own conclusions by now, particularly after the ballistics report. Rath had to keep the book as security. He would have handed it over to Gennat long ago if chance had allowed, but he was too deeply involved for that now. He had destroyed evidence when he exchanged the bullets.

Rath didn't drop by E Division when he left the station. Although he couldn't avoid meeting Wolter, he wanted to put it off for as long as possible. Besides, Fregestrasse was accessible by public transport too. Before taking his place in the Wannsee train, he deposited the book in a locker at Potsdamer station, placing the key in a Prussian police envelope which he then carefully sealed and franked. Next he looked for a letter box amongst the evening throng. He found one right by the station exit, a dark-blue mailbox belonging to the *Reichspost*, and dropped the letter inside. When he stepped onto the platform a quarter of an hour later at Friedenau, he took a deep breath, as if he were about to dive through a long underwater cave. He had to close his eyes and swim through or, better still, keep them open.

Bruno had appeared to dinner strangely on edge, while Emmi seemed conspicuously nervous on account of their shared secret. Rath himself had lost his appetite but was choking down the sauté potatoes and fried eggs as best he could.

His conversation was limited to isolated compliments regarding the food, which he nevertheless picked away at fussily. On one occasion he asked Emmi Wolter for the salt. She passed him the sugar and was inconsolable over her error.

'Don't worry about it, Emmi,' Bruno said, 'it happens. Even CID officers get things mixed up from time to time, don't they Gereon?'

Suddenly Rath was wide awake.

Had Wolter drawn the right conclusions? That would mean they were wise to each other, even if neither knew all the details. Uncle no doubt suspected that the investigation into Josef Wilczek's death was full of inconsistencies, and that somewhere along the line a certain Detective Inspector Gereon Rath had to be involved.

Still, perhaps Rath was just imagining things and Bruno's comment hadn't meant anything. He decided to ignore it. 'Thank you,' he said, accepting the saltcellar that Emmi Wolter passed him.

'How is your investigation going?' Wolter continued. 'Any idea who might have killed Jänicke? Or that crook, what was his name again?'

'Wilczek.'

'That's right. Killer's the same man, that's what people are saying.'

'Looks like it. The bullets came from the same weapon.'

Wolter nodded.

'If we find the weapon, then we'll find the killer too,' Rath said. The sentence was a trial balloon, but the DCI was too hard-nosed to show his hand.

'Not so easy to find a weapon in a city of millions,' he said.

'If Jänicke's notebook were to turn up it would be a step in the right direction. His killer probably took it from him. It could contain the motive.'

He knew that Bruno still hadn't looked in his study. He couldn't have realised the book was missing—unless Emmi Wolter had telephoned him about Rath's visit and Bruno had had her search his desk. But it didn't seem like it. He doubted whether Emmi Wolter could even follow their conversation.

'If you ask me, it was one of those fucking communists,' Wolter said emphatically. 'Wilczek was shot in a communist area as well.'

'If only it were that easy. Sometimes the culprit's not the person you bargain on.'

'Sometimes homicide cases remain unsolved.'

'Not with Gennat.'

'Even he must have given up on a case.'

'It's the curiosity that drives you. You know that,' Rath said. 'The question why someone had to die, you can't get it out of your mind.'

'Sometimes it's better to let the dead rest. Not everyone who solves a murder gets their own office. Sometimes all they get is trouble.'

'Jänicke knew his killer,' Rath said, watching Wolter's face as he spoke. 'You'd have to be pretty cold-blooded to blow away a friend at such close range, don't you think?'

Wolter shrugged his shoulders. 'Life isn't always as simple as you think.

Besides, what does friendship even mean? Not every acquaintance is a friend. A friend is someone who never leaves you in the lurch, who sticks by you even when times are tough.'

Now it was Rath's turn to shrug.

'I've found a new room,' he said after a pause. 'I won't be in your hair after tomorrow.'

'Oh,' Bruno appeared surprised. 'Why the rush? Can't wait to get away from us? We had almost got used to you, hadn't we Emmi?'

'Yes, darling.' Emmi Wolter wasn't quite with it. The conversation just now had obviously confused her, and it seemed she was still troubled by her guilty conscience.

'I can't take advantage of your hospitality any longer. I've outstayed my welcome here already.'

He placed his serviette on the table and stood up.

'But Herr Rath, you will come and visit us, won't you?' Emmi Wolter said. Clearly she hadn't failed to notice the tension between the two men.

Rath said 'good night', and went upstairs to pack his things.

27

Just before seven the next morning, Rath found himself standing in the large foyer of the Hotel *Excelsior* which, with its lush botanical arrangements, reminded him of the palm house at Dahlem. He had reserved a single room by telephone the day before, prior to leaving Alex and driving out to Friedenau. He'd sooner spend five marks than another day in Fregestrasse. The concierge at reception greeted him cheerfully, before adopting an expression of acute regret as he looked down the reservation list.

'Herr Rath, I must confess that we weren't expecting you so early. I'm afraid the room is still occupied.'

'Would it be possible for someone to look after my luggage?'

'Of course.' The concierge glanced disapprovingly at Rath's cardboard box and waved a boy over.

'Thank you,' Rath said, as the boy heaved the heavy suitcase and box onto a luggage trolley. 'I'm going to have breakfast first.'

The concierge replied with a sour smile.

A short time later, Rath was in the breakfast room, feeling almost at home. The coffee did him good.

He had barely been able to sleep, not only because he was sleeping under the same roof as a murderer, but because his restless mind kept asking the same question over and over again. Why?

He ought to have left straight after dinner, but for some reason he had wanted to keep up appearances, to avoid making the rupture quite so open. Perhaps he was still clinging to the hope that it could yet turn out to be one big mistake.

He had left a message on the dining table, subdued but friendly, in which he thanked the Wolters and explained his early morning departure by saying he was keen to move into his new room. He neglected to mention that it was a hotel room. He had placed a twenty mark note on the message, money that neither Bruno nor Emmi would otherwise have accepted. He didn't want to be in the Wolters's debt, not even for the telephone call he had made to book the taxi.

Thus he left as he had arrived, laden with a suitcase and a cardboard box. An hour passed by before he made his way back to reception.

'Ah, Herr Rath,' said the concierge. 'Good news! The key to your room . . .' he fished it off the hook. 'The previous guest has left. I arranged for it to be made up as soon as possible.'

'Much obliged.' Clearly the concierge was expecting some sort of tip for the extraordinary lengths he had gone to. Rath ignored him.

'If you would be so kind as to take care of the formalities . . .' The concierge pushed a registration form across the counter.

'I'm sorry, but I have things to do. If we could take care of that at lunch . . .' He placed the key on top of the form and passed both items back across the counter.

'It's not usually how we do things, but I'm sure we can make an exception for our regulars.'

He arrived late, but still before nine. He found a young woman at the desk in the outer office, playing languidly with her pen. Strands of blonde hair hung over her eyes, and a nose that was too big protruded over lips that were too thin. She leapt to her feet.

'Erika Voss, Inspector,' she said eagerly, proffering a hand. 'I'm your new secretary!'

Rath hung his coat on the stand.

'Did you work for Herr Roeder?' he asked.

She shook her head. 'I'm new here, Inspector.'

Who the hell had Zörgiebel sent him? She couldn't have been more than twenty and exuded the unmistakeable scent of *eau de cologne*. Charly smelt better. 'I see. Well, it doesn't matter. Has anyone called?'

'No, Inspector. Is there anything I can do, Inspector?'

'Do you know how to make coffee?'

She did, and soon there was a steaming hot mug on his desk. He had closed the door to the outer office, needing some quiet to think things through. As absurd as it might sound, it was time he resumed with current investigations. Erika Voss needed something to do; and he couldn't let Gennat discover that he was chasing a phantom, that there was no *one* killer who had both Jänicke and Wilczek on his conscience.

It wasn't long before his peace and quiet were disturbed by a commotion in the outer office. A loud voice. 'I *must* speak with the inspector.'

Fräulein Voss was obviously trying to ward him off. There was a knock before she poked her blonde head through the door.

'Inspector, there's a Herr Roeder outside claiming this is his office . . .'

What did Roeder want here?

'Send him in.'

Erika Voss nodded and waved Erwin Roeder through. Rath's predecessor held his hat in his hand and gazed around the room. The man was smaller than Rath had expected.

'Well, everything looks the same,' he said. 'Roeder,' he said, stretching out his hand. 'Erwin Roeder. I used to work here.'

'Rath, Gereon Rath. What can I do for you, Herr Roeder?'

'My departure from the police service came rather suddenly and I've had a lot to do in the last few weeks. Being an author is a very time-consuming business, you know, and . . .'

'Please get to the point, Herr Roeder.'

'I don't know how long you've been here, but I can see your name's already on the door. If you've moved your things into my desk I'm sure you'll have found it by now.'

'What?' The man was beginning to get on his nerves.

'I left a few photos in my desk that I'd like to pick up.'

Rath couldn't remember there being any photos, but he hadn't looked through the drawers particularly thoroughly.

He shrugged. 'I don't know what you're talking about.'

'Could I just . . .' Roeder took a step forward and made a move to open one of the desk drawers.

'Don't you dare!' It came out sharper than Rath intended. Roeder looked at him indignantly.

'This is *my* office now, and *my* desk,' Rath continued, quieter now, but firmly. 'I'd be happy to see if you've left anything behind, if you'd like me to.'

'If you wouldn't mind,' Roeder said, gazing to the side like a slighted tenor. 'The pictures should be in a black box.'

Rath rummaged quickly through the desk. In the upper drawer he found only his own things along with a few notes on the Wilczek case, pens and paper. However, a big surprise awaited him in the lower drawer. There was a big, heavy cardboard box as Roeder had said, and hidden behind it a small pistol. He wouldn't have noticed it if he hadn't been intending to lift the box out of the drawer.

It was a Lignose.

He knew straightaway which pistol it was, and rapidly deduced that Bruno was trying to frame him. He had probably realised the notebook was missing and drawn his own conclusions. If Rath already had the book, he only had to plant the gun on him and he could present Gennat with the perfect murder suspect. *If we find the weapon, then we'll find the killer too,* Rath had said, and Wolter had gratefully seized upon the idea.

There was barely time to think. He removed the lid from the box, wrapped the pistol in a charge sheet from the drawer and slid it under a pile of photos. They weren't personal photos; Rath could see they were the work of a professional as he hastily shoved a few on top of the pistol. Under different circumstances, the image lying on top might have coaxed a smile. It showed Roeder as a safe-breaker, complete with flat cap, fake moustache and blowtorch, wearing a grim look on his face. Instead Rath closed the lid and lifted the heavy box out of the drawer before Roeder noticed anything.

'Is this what you're looking for?'

Roeder nodded eagerly and took the box. Rath hoped in vain that he wouldn't look inside.

'May I?' He lifted the lid and leafed through the glossy prints at the top. He seemed satisfied. 'Very nice,' he said. 'Thank you.' Roeder put his hat back on. 'I must be going. Pressing engagements. Please see it to that A Division's detection rate improves, young man. From what one hears, it currently leaves a lot to be desired.'

'Goodbye, Herr Roeder.' Rath couldn't bear the man any longer. He ushered him past Erika Voss to the door, almost colliding with Ernst Gennat on the way. Buddha gazed at Roeder in surprise.

'Well, I never, what are you still doing here? I hope you haven't been arrested for murder!'

'Don't worry, Superintendent. That won't be happening. This is the last time you'll see me in these halls. Just wanted to get to know my successor. Adieu!'

Roeder wedged the box firmly under his arm and set off towards the stairwell.

'Good morning, sir,' Rath said. 'Please come in.'

'Good morning, Rath. I see your secretary is already here.' Buddha tipped an imaginary hat. 'Good morning, Fräulein Voss.' He took Rath to one side. 'I need to speak to you privately, Inspector.'

They went into Rath's office.

When they reached the door Gennat turned for a second time. 'Fräulein Voss, would you be so kind as to go to my office and ask Fräulein Steiner for the Jänicke file?'

He closed the door. 'Just a precaution. Erika Voss has only been with us three weeks and is therefore still very curious, no doubt. Trudchen will keep her occupied for a while. As long as we have a little quiet here.'

'Is it something confidential, sir?'

'Strictly confidential.' Gennat paused thoughtfully before continuing. 'I won't beat around the bush. I've just received an anonymous tip-off about the Jänicke case, a call in which a fearful suspicion was voiced.'

'An anonymous tip-off. Since when do we take them seriously?'

'That's something you always have to weigh up, Inspector. In this case, the caller seemed so extraordinarily well informed that I'm afraid we have to take it seriously. He knew for example that we were missing Jänicke's black notebook, and that the assistant detective was killed with a Lignose.'

'What suspicion are you talking about?'

'A fearful suspicion, which I can scarcely credit, but which I must investigate. Herr Rath, the caller claims that the pistol used to kill Stephan Jänicke belongs to you.'

'That's ridiculous!'

Rath had sensed it from the moment he had found the pistol in the drawer. Bruno had gone on the attack.

'If this man is so well informed,' he said, 'then perhaps it was the murderer himself, trying to lead the police up the garden path.'

'That's what I suspect too, Herr Rath, but I have to be sure.' Gennat cleared his throat. 'Inspector, do you agree to let me carry out a search of your office?'

'If you insist on it, sir, then of course.'

Rath felt a lump in his throat but didn't swallow until Gennat got on the phone to ask for his men.

Of all people, it was Detective Paul Czerwinski and Assistant Detective Alfons Henning who came through the door minutes later, Plisch and Plum. Rath's former colleagues were now doing Buddha's legwork. Gennat didn't let Rath out of his sight while the two men scoured his office. He stood at the window, smoking and looking out on the street below, doing a good job of feigning offence. Outside a train was emerging from the station, slowly picking up speed. In a few moments it would reach the windows of E Division. Would Bruno be observing the same train? What thoughts would be going through *his* head?

Plisch and Plum needed fewer than ten minutes, having also combed Erika Voss's abandoned office.

'Nothing, sir.'

Gennat nodded. 'Good.'

He seemed genuinely delighted not to have to arrest Rath, but no wonder. A murdering cop was even worse than a murdered cop. Perhaps there was also some sympathy for his new colleague—even if Rath knew that had never stopped Gennat from handing his clients, as he affectionately knew them, over to his father at Plötzensee jail.

'Good,' Buddha said once more. 'Then we just need to pay your flat a visit, and we'll be done.'

Rath swallowed. His flat too.

'I've just been given notice on my flat,' he said. 'I'm staying at a hotel.'

'We'll be discreet.'

Later, the four CID officers were standing in the foyer of the *Excelsior*. The concierge was terribly friendly.

'Inspector, would you take care of the formalities now?'

'Later. The key, please. I need my room for a little meeting.'

'As you wish, Inspector.' The concierge passed the key across the counter. 'Room 412. Should I have drinks sent up?'

'Thank you, that won't be necessary. Is my luggage already up?'

'Of course. Have a pleasant stay.'

A short time later, Gennat's colleagues had searched the hotel room. Although Rath explained that he hadn't even set foot inside, they searched not only his luggage but all the cupboards. Rath positioned himself at the window. This time he wasn't looking onto *Anhalter Bahnhof*, but a treeless rear courtyard.

'Please excuse the fuss, Inspector,' Gennat said after Plisch and Plum had completed their search with another, 'Nothing, sir!'

'It's fine,' Rath said. 'I'd have done exactly the same.'

'You're right. We have to pursue every lead that seems halfway plausible, no matter how perplexing it appears. Not that this will be of any comfort, Herr Rath, but it wouldn't be the first time a police officer had murdered a colleague.'

Rath nodded. *If only Buddha knew how close he was to the truth.*

After the fruitless search, they went back to being four colleagues discussing a case.

Since it wasn't lunchtime yet, Gennat invited them to nearby *Café Josty* for coffee and cake. Everyone was still a little embarrassed by the operation, and Buddha was trying to restore the peace. He ordered an ample selection of cakes, rich ones at that, and after the first slice Rath sensed he would be skipping lunch. Czerwinski and Henning seemed to think likewise. All three turned down the second slice that Gennat tried to shovel onto their plates. Buddha just shrugged his shoulders and helped himself to a piece of *Schwarzwälder Kirsch*.

'So, gentlemen,' he said at last, after he had polished off a fourth slice, 'we earned that! What a lot of work, just because of some joker.' He made it sound as if Rath had been working alongside them, instead of being the subject of their investigation.

'I don't think it was some joker. I think it was the murderer,' Rath said.

Gennat nodded. 'Maybe, but he wasn't able to laugh at our expense. We were so discreet that no-one noticed anything.'

Buddha must have agreed with Henning and Czerwinski that the operation was to be carried out in the strictest confidence. No-one would dare go to the press when there were so few people aware of it.

It was almost twelve when they returned to the Castle.

'Let's get back to work,' Gennat said, when he took leave of the three men outside his office door. 'See you tomorrow at the funeral.'

Rath had almost completely forgotten that Stephan Jänicke was due to be buried at the *Georgen* Cemetery on Greifswalder Strasse tomorrow morning at eleven.

For the rest of the day he had free rein. Gennat hadn't dared force a new assignment on him. Thus he had time to brood once more. Why was Wündisch after Wolter? What had Jänicke discovered?

He played with the idea of phoning the head of the political police and asking, but 1A was legendary for its secrecy. Even when someone died during an undercover investigation, it was unlikely the politicals would cough up any information. They would keep the whole thing under wraps, and perhaps that was what Wolter was counting on. What he needed was more information about Jänicke's operation, which he hoped to find in the notebook. Perhaps he had overlooked something. He would have to go through it again and it was a pain he couldn't get to it right away.

On the other hand it was a good thing Plisch and Plum hadn't found it on him. He just needed to be patient.

Shortly after three Roeder called, as expected.

'In with your photos, you say? I've been looking for it everywhere. It must have fallen inside.'

'Inspector, you surely don't think I'm going to *deliver* your pistol to you! I'm afraid you'll need to come here. I swore I'd never set foot inside the station again!'

'I'm just happy it's turned up at all. I'll pick it up straightaway, if that's alright with you.'

'Nothing doing, I'm afraid, but you might come to the *Imperator* café at five. I have a meeting with my publisher.'

'In Friedrichstrasse?'

'Exactly. That way you don't have to come all the way out here. If I could give you one more piece of advice, young man . . .'

'Yes?'

'Keep your office tidier! Order is the alpha and omega of our profession. You ought to be more careful, especially with a firearm. Now, if you don't mind, I have things to do!'

When Rath entered the *Imperator* at just after five, Roeder was sitting with a fat man wearing glasses, presumably Dr Hildebrandt. He had wrapped the Lignose in newspaper so that no-one would notice it changing hands. By now Roeder's fingerprints would probably be the only ones on the pistol, Rath thought, as he said thank you courteously and stowed the bundle in his coat. From Friedrichstrasse he went directly to the *Excelsior* where the concierge was waiting with eager anticipation.

'Ah, Inspector!' He pushed the registration form across the counter and appeared relieved when Rath finally began filling it out.

'One more thing . . .' The concierge waved an envelope. 'Something just came for you in the post.'

Rath took the letter and moved towards the lift, but only after he had closed the door to room 412 did he open the envelope and let the small silver key drop out.

Before Rath went to bed, he strolled to Potsdamer station and looked inside his locker. He placed the pistol inside and fished out the little black book before closing the locker once more. Right now Jänicke's notebook was the most exciting bedtime reading he could imagine, even if he didn't understand a single word.

28

The church could scarcely contain the crowd. A huge police contingent had arrived for the burial of Stephan Jänicke, with the plain-clothes officers clustered around the back rows. The violent death of a young officer had affected many Berliners. Nearly all the papers had sent reporters, and there were a number of men with cameras at the back of the church.

Rath gazed around. Some pews were filled entirely by the blue of police uniform. The plain-clothes officers were no less uniformed either, dressed in black to a man with their top hats resting in folded hands. Rath was wearing the same suit he had worn for the funeral of Alexander LeClerk Jnr. Unhappy memories, he sensed them rising.

The coffin was draped in the sober black and white of the Prussian flag, and flanked by two officers in parade uniform with gleaming buttons and highly polished boots. In the front row, next to Zörgiebel, stood a man and a woman, both white-haired although they weren't much older than fifty. Stephan Jänicke's parents had travelled from Allenstein. As far as Rath knew, it was the first time they had crossed the Polish Corridor, the first time, in fact, they had ever left their East Prussian homeland.

How would they react if they had known that their son's killer was seated only a few rows behind? Rath couldn't make out Wolter's face from his seat further back, but he had worn a serious expression as he entered the church. He wanted to avoid Uncle if possible; even the sight of him was unbearable. Would their son's killer look the Jänickes in the eye at the grave? Would he shake their hands and offer his condolences?

The dead man's book hadn't provided any answers and, this morning, he had thought about throwing it in the canal along with the pistol. Still, he didn't want to abandon hope so quickly. If he knew the motive, he could produce the necessary evidence, and the ballistics report would testify that Bruno Wolter had also executed Josef Wilczek. Rath wouldn't contradict it. No, he wouldn't have any scruples there, not since Wolter had tried to plant the murder weapon on him.

The service was sober, without pomp. Rath's first visit to a Lutheran church almost felt like a disappointment. As the mourners set off from Greifswalder Strasse, he maintained a distance from Wolter, which wasn't difficult since Wolter clearly had no interest in encountering Rath. He fell to the back of the cortege while Rath remained at the front with the homicide detectives, beside Gennat and Böhm.

He hadn't seen Charly, but she was probably back at the Castle, holding the fort. It was better that way. Jänicke's funeral wasn't exactly the ideal place for their first meeting since their memorable encounter at the press conference. *You really are an arsehole, Herr Rath!* Whenever he recalled that moment, he realised that her eyes were no longer filled with love, but disappointment and contempt.

Six young men, colleagues of Jänicke's at police academy, removed the coffin from the hearse and took it on their shoulders. They passed through the entrance to the cemetery just behind the priest, with the funeral cortege in tow. All was quiet, except for a finch sounding its call over the graves. Police colleagues strode silently side by side, accompanied by a light rain. Nevertheless, it seemed to be getting warmer. Rath wasn't the only one sweating in the greenhouse-like heat. Zörgiebel wiped his brow with a white handkerchief. It would be no easy task accompanying the parents of a dead police officer to their son's grave. The commissioner walked alongside the Jänickes.

The coffin bearers followed the main avenue for some time, before turning right onto another main road, eventually reaching a brick wall. A few metres beyond rose the façade of a tenement house, next to it a brick building, most likely a school and, beside the wall, was a freshly dug grave.

The priest stood still; the coffin bearers took a few more strides until they were exactly positioned on both sides. They were just about to lower the coffin onto the wooden beams that had been laid across the grave when the peace was shattered by a brief but violent cry.

Surprise or horror? Rath couldn't say, only that it had come from one of the coffin bearers. The six young men froze, and the coffin tilted precariously. After almost losing their composure, the six men were soon gazing as stoically as before. As police officers they had learned to control themselves, but Rath knew they must have seen something terrible and, suddenly, all sense of normality was lost.

The coffin was still hanging in mid-air, as if the coffin bearers couldn't decide where they should set it down. They exchanged uncertain glances, before shouldering it once more and carrying it slowly back, away from the grave. The priest moved aside, confused, and Zörgiebel reacted immediately. Leaving the Jänickes where they were, he moved quickly but with dignity to the open grave. His eyes widened for a fraction of a second. He removed his top hat, and wiped his brow. Seizing the Jänickes by the arm he pulled them away and motioned discreetly to Gennat, who had remained a few metres ahead of Rath. Despite his corpulence, the head of A Division moved with astounding speed, waving Böhm and a few colleagues over. Rath wasn't sure if the gesture was intended for him or not, but made his way across anyway.

A sense of uneasiness set in amongst the mourners, and a few rubbernecks moved towards the front. The murmur rose to a clamour and Stephan Jänicke's funeral was suddenly devoid of all ceremony.

Rath pushed past the coffin bearers. An unbearable odour was rising from the damp earth—and then he saw it.

There was already a corpse in the newly dug grave. Clods of earth hung to a stained, rotting grey suit. Hands and feet were reduced to a bloody pulp, and the body was in an advanced state of decomposition.

Suddenly there was a flash, momentarily bathing the corpse in an eerie, dazzling light.

A few reporters had taken out their cameras and instinctively began to snap. Gennat bellowed his orders, uniform pushed them to one side and a chain of blue uniforms surrounded the grave.

Rath stood between the uniformed officers, gazing at the corpse in disbelief. Though the face of the deceased had also been marked by decay, his features were still so clearly recognisable from the mug shots that there was no room for doubt. He didn't have to wait for the official identification to know that this corpse was going to bring him trouble. For in the grave that had been dug for Stephan Jänicke lay the mortal remains of one Alexej Ivanovitsch Kardakov.

Remains was the appropriate word, Rath thought as, barely half an hour later, he watched two men from ED pour plaster of Paris into the footprints right next to the stinking bundle that was all that was left of Kardakov. A third man was carefully examining the pockets of the mouldy suit with the aid of a stick and a pair of tweezers. All three had handkerchiefs around their noses and mouths, but were still wearing their top hats.

The rain had abated, but the humidity was becoming unbearable. The ground was steaming and muggy air carried the smell of decay in billows across the graves. It was bad enough up here, Rath thought. God knows what it must be like below.

They had begun the police work immediately, as most of the specialists were already on the scene. Dressed as they were they had set to work without complaint. Gennat had to send for Dr Schwartz and the forensic equipment from the Castle, but that hadn't taken long, since Alex was close by.

The coffin containing Stephan Jänicke's corpse was now in the cemetery chapel. As long as the forensics team was still working on the grave, the burial couldn't take place. Rath would've liked to know how Zörgiebel was planning to explain that to the parents.

Whoever had deposited the corpse in the grave, one thing was for certain. He had not only disrupted the ceremonial funeral of a policeman killed in the line of duty, but utterly destroyed it.

Uniform had dispersed the mourners, ushering them from the cemetery as delicately as the situation allowed. Now only officers from Homicide and ED moved between the graves. With their black top hats, the men looked like a disorientated company of mourners. At the Greifswalder Strasse entrance, meanwhile, police were making sure that no-one set foot inside the cemetery for the time being. The little gate on Heinrich-Roller-Strasse was closed anyway.

Above all, the men from ED were looking for footprints—but they had their work cut out. Hundreds of shoes had trampled on the ground where moments earlier mourners had passed behind the coffin. It was pointless to even look there. At first glance, things didn't look much better by the grave, as it wasn't just the coffin bearers and priest who had lingered there.

Zörgiebel, Gennat's men and the officers who had sealed off the area had also left their tracks, to say nothing of the rubbernecks and press photographers. Fortunately Gennat had been quick to react and ensured that all those involved had their particulars taken down, so that any subsequent comparison of footprints, though laborious, was still possible.

The press photographers had initially refused to give their names, as they feared reprisals. Nevertheless, uniform hadn't taken possession of a single camera. The last thing anyone wanted was to provoke a scandal, as Zörgiebel himself had invited the press. Rath didn't believe any more than Gennat that a newspaper would publish a photo of a decomposing corpse. The pictures, which by now would be lying fully developed in the papers' offices, would be securely locked away, but they would achieve at least one thing. The Berlin police wouldn't be able to whitewash the facts. The photos would tell an interesting story. Namely, that the freshly dug grave of murdered CID officer Stephan Jänicke contained the corpse of Alexej Kardakov, a murder suspect for whom they had recently issued a search warrant. Taking this information and a few rehashed details from the previous week, a resourceful journalist could fill an entire front page, without needing a press conference or any exclusives from indiscreet police officers. Besides, it was pointless trying to keep an incident like this, where there had been so many eye-witnesses, under wraps. Zörgiebel must recognise that too.

Forensics emerged from the grave, and Assistant Detective Reinhold Gräf hauled his camera down to take some close-ups. Gräf tied a handkerchief around his face and turned up the collar of his jacket. Rath doubted whether it would do much good. The assistant detective appeared almost as pale as the corpse.

A man from ED was showing Gennat what he had found in Kardakov's jacket, an astonishingly well-preserved packet of cocaine, a *Berolina* membership pin and a yellow identity card, *valid until 16th May 1929.*

Gennat leafed through the document, using a handkerchief to avoid leaving fingerprints. 'Looks like we've found your killer, Herr Rath,' he said. 'Afraid he looks pretty dead. No good arresting him now.'

Rath nodded silently, feeling humiliated. Gennat had said it in a relatively harmless way, but the gaze of his colleagues had been less forgiving. Kardakov's corpse had made a complete fool of him. The man whom Rath had taken for a killer, for whom he had initiated a police search warrant, had clearly been the victim of a violent crime himself.

'When was he supposed to have killed this man?' Gennat asked.

'About three weeks ago.'

'I'd say that three weeks ago he looked pretty similar to how he does now.'

Precisely the same thought was going through Rath's head. Kardakov was not a murderer, he was a victim of the same person who had Boris on his conscience. He had known the moment he had seen the corpse and the treatment doled out to the hands and feet.

'I fear the warrant was a little rash, sir,' he said.

Gennat nodded. 'It was even more rash to suspect the man of murder without any proof. Still, this corpse is something of a result for you. Imagine if the poor devil was still alive. If he'd just gone to the Baltic Sea for a few weeks, only to be arrested by police on his return to Szczecin station after seeing his picture in the papers. It's tantamount to character assassination. You'd have had that to answer for, Inspector!'

Not just me, the commissioner as well, Rath thought. Zörgiebel had ignored Gennat's protests, had issued the warrant for Kardakov and had gone public with Rath's theory. The commissioner had made a fool of himself too—and Rath knew Zörgiebel would never forgive him for it.

He had made a whole host of enemies at the Castle. Böhm was standing with Kronberg and a few members of ED a little to the side by the cemetery wall. Not so much to avoid the stench, but Rath himself. To Böhm, I'm a decaying corpse too, Rath thought. Strictly speaking, he didn't have a single friend left at Alex. The one remaining person he had counted as a friend was the worst of all. Uncle: Bruno Wolter.

A red haze on the edge of his field of vision made him look up.

It was Charly.

She came striding across the cemetery in her red dress, past the men in black, holding a folded umbrella in one hand and a shorthand pad in the other. Rath felt a stabbing pain as she surveyed him briefly, only to move on without so much as a word of acknowledgement. It didn't stop her greeting the superintendent all the more cheerfully.

'Ah, Fräulein Ritter,' Buddha said, sounding almost relieved, 'good that you're here!' He sent her straight over to Kronberg, who was debating something with Böhm by the wall. 'Take down Forensics's findings first. Then we'll turn to our friend Dr Schwartz.'

Charly continued on her way, while Rath gazed after her.

Had Gennat noticed the tension between them? Buddha gave nothing away but continued to look pensively at the corpse.

'He's been dead for at least four weeks if you ask me.'

Dr Schwartz arrived shortly afterwards to confirm Gennat's estimate. The doctor shook his head again and again as he examined Kardakov's corpse. Schwartz appeared to be the only one who didn't mind the smell, even while he was right next to the corpse.

'Looks like he was buried and then dug back up,' he said, when he was standing next to the CID officers again. 'Forensics will be able to tell you more.'

'How did he die?'

'I don't know yet. There are clear parallels to another corpse I've examined, but there appear to be some striking differences too.'

Gennat nodded. 'You're referring to the case Böhm worked on?' He whistled loudly through his fingers and waved the DCI over. Böhm was still with Kronberg and Charly by the cemetery wall. He couldn't avoid Rath any longer, but approached Gennat without deigning even to look at him. As far as that went, he seemed to have struck up an agreement with Charly.

'Sir?' Böhm barked.

'You should listen to what Dr Schwartz has to say,' Gennat said. 'It's about your case.'

'It wasn't my idea to search for the man who is mouldering away down there!'

'I appreciate rivalry in my division, Böhm, but make sure you don't poison the atmosphere. We can only make progress if we work together.'

He hadn't been looking at Böhm when he said this last sentence, but Rath.

'I think it would be advisable for you both to shake hands,' Buddha continued. 'You haven't even said 'good morning' to each other yet.'

'Is that right?' Böhm stretched out a paw, and Rath grasped it. He would have preferred a reconciliation with Charly, and gazed across at her while Dr Schwartz continued with his explanation.

Half an hour later, Rath had already botched his first chance at making up with Charly. Gennat hadn't forced them to shake hands, but had sent the pair of them off together. The division chief had detailed around twenty officers to question the inhabitants of Heinrich-Roller-Strasse, which bordered directly onto the cemetery, and allocated number 17 to Gereon Rath and Charlotte Ritter.

If it was supposed to have been a peace-making manoeuvre, then it had backfired horribly. Yet how Rath's heart had leapt when Gennat assigned her to him, whether through joy or nervousness he couldn't say. Her proximity alone made him euphoric, the chance to work with her even more so. Only for her behaviour to sober him up.

Cold and impersonal, she had walked beside him like a stranger, barely saying a word and addressing him formally when she did. Nor was it just for appearance's sake. The look in her eyes told him she hadn't forgiven him.

'What do you suggest, Inspector?' she asked, when they were standing on the other side of the cemetery wall, outside the five-storey tenement. Their colleagues had long since disappeared into the neighbouring houses.

'We can drop the titles, nobody'll hear us,' he said.

'I have no intention of creating professional difficulties for myself by being too familiar with an inspector, especially one who hasn't earned it.'

She was a lawyer, a pretty good one too by the sound of it.

'That was exactly what I wanted to talk about. Don't you at least want to . . . ?'

She cut him off. 'I don't recall the superintendent giving you orders to discuss anything with me.'

If that was how she wanted to play it, Rath could be just as clinical.

'Very well, Fräulein Ritter. So that there is no danger of our becoming over-familiar with one another, I suggest that we question the witnesses separately. You do one half, I'll do the other.'

He had actually addressed her formally, and didn't get the feeling she was too upset. Clearly the whole concept rankled more with him.

'As you wish, Inspector.'

'Then you take the two upper floors and I'll take the three below.'

Her long legs were already flying up the stairs.

Rath shrugged his shoulders and set to work.

He was finished quickly. You couldn't even see over the cemetery wall from the ground floor flats, and no-one had noticed anything suspicious, neither the caretaker nor the teacher who lived opposite. As for the flats higher up, there was no-one home except for Elfriede Gaede, a deaf old lady on the first floor. Though Frau Gaede had a prime view of the cemetery, she only had eyes for the numerous cats that prowled through her rooms. It took some time for Rath to realise that Frau Gaede was not only deaf but almost completely blind. And he was happy to leave the stench of cat piss behind.

Downstairs, he stepped onto the street and looked around. There was still no sign of Charly. To the left of the tenement, by the corner of a red-brick house, he could see Plisch and Plum, each with a cigarette. Rath joined them and lit an Overstolz. At least the pair hadn't run away as he approached.

'You finished too?' he said, placing the cigarette carton back in his pocket.

'It's a school,' Czerwinski said, 'huge building, but only the caretaker and his wife live there.' He drew deeply on his cigarette. 'Neither of them saw anything.'

'It's a crackpot idea, if you ask me,' Henning said. 'What are the people here supposed to have seen? Whoever dumped the body came via the cemetery. Clambering over the wall would be far too obvious, with a corpse at that. It must've been someone who knew the cemetery staff, someone who knew a police officer was being buried here today.'

'It was in all the papers,' Rath replied. 'There can't have been too many freshly dug graves at *Georgen Cemetery* this morning.'

'Strange business,' Henning said. 'Why would someone throw an old corpse into a fresh police grave?'

'It is odd,' Rath agreed.

The killer hadn't allowed Kardakov to surface for no reason; that was certain. Perhaps they wanted to put one over the commissioner? Or Rath? Was it even the killer who had dumped the corpse? There was something artificial about the whole thing: the cocaine in the jacket pocket, the identity card, and to top it off the *Berolina* pin. Was Marlow involved? Was someone trying to tell them that Dr M. or Red Hugo had killed the two Russians? Perhaps a rival *Ringverein*, one that was trying to create trouble for *Berolina* and make a fool of the police at the same time? The *Nordpi-*

raten weren't on good terms with *Berolina* at the moment. Perhaps it merited a closer look.

The three men finished smoking and Rath decided to accompany Henning and Czerwinski back to the cemetery. He wasn't going to wait around for Charly, only to be treated like dirt.

Despite their cigarette break, the trio were among the first to report back to Gennat, but without much to go on. A man from number 19 had seen two men that morning dragging a cart across the cemetery's main avenue, but couldn't remember the exact time. Officers were gradually returning, even those who had questioned the cemetery staff. Buddha listened patiently to all the reports, barely making any notes. He was said to have a phenomenal memory.

They were slowly building a picture. The cemetery gardener had only dug one grave yesterday, that of Jänicke. Just before ten today, the man had assured, there had still been no corpse inside, as that was when he had checked the beams for the coffin. That meant the pair—if it was indeed the two men that the witness had seen—must have completed the job between ten and eleven. It was something to go on at any rate.

It wasn't until the last of the officers returned from Heinrich-Roller-Strasse that Charly re-emerged, walking alongside Reinhold Gräf, smiling and chatting animatedly.

Without warning, Rath was overcome by a severe pang of jealousy.

C'mon man! He thought. *You've got enough problems as it is without worrying about her! Forget Charly, put her out of your mind! Don't let her treat you like this!*

For the time being their work was done. The first CID officers were already on their way back to the Castle to write their reports. Two undertakers had removed Kardakov's corpse from the grave and placed it carefully in a zinc coffin. Then they had set off. The mortuary car was already waiting for them at Greifswalder Strasse.

From the grave to the mortuary car, Rath thought to himself, as he watched the men. Usually it's the other way round.

He had seen the storm coming. Erika Voss was waiting with the news.

"The commissioner would like to see you, Inspector."

Rath knew it would be no ordinary meeting, and he was right. He had never seen the fat man so furious. Zörgiebel rose from his desk to pace up and down the room, his voice operating in the higher registers.

The door to the outer office was closed but Rath knew that Dagmar Kling could hear every word.

'Do you have any idea of what you've got me into?'

Rath's instinct told him it was best to remain silent.

'You've made a mockery of me and the entire Berlin police force. In front of everyone!'

Rath still said nothing. Let Dörrzwiebel tire himself out. At least no-one could say the commissioner was his best friend anymore.

'We issued a warrant for a man, stated he was the prime suspect in a murder inquiry, and it turns out the man has been dead longer than his alleged victim! How d'you think that looks?'

'I'm sorry, Commissioner, but it wasn't me who dumped the body there!'

'It was you, Herr Rath, who set the entire police force on the wrong track! We've gone to enormous lengths to search for a man who's been dead for weeks. Every paper published his photo, just like every paper is now going to publish this unspeakable story. What other surprises do you have in store for us? Whose corpse is going to turn up next? The Countess?'

Rath shrugged his shoulders. 'I hope not, Commissioner.'

'I'll give you I hope not! I'm not sure you quite understand, Inspector. If you weren't the son of Engelbert Rath, you'd be packing your case right now for Köpenick! There's a vacancy there at the moment. You can go back to finding lost cats, and be glad I'm not making you dust court exhibits for the rest of your days!'

That was how easy it was to fall out of favour with Zörgiebel.

Only yesterday he had been feted as the man who would bring glory to the commissioner. Now he was the police dunce, the sole reason why Zörgiebel cut a sorry figure in the press.

'I'd like to put things right, Commissioner.'

'That's rich. How do you propose to do that?'

Rath had an inkling why Zörgiebel was so incensed. The SPD had arranged to have its party conference next week at Magdeburg, and the commissioner would not only have to justify the bloody May riots to his fellow social democrat party members, but also his force's record on law enforcement in the imperial capital. Given the recent headlines, Zörgiebel could hardly expect to make a good impression. Now, on top of everything else, there was the incident at the cemetery. An unparalleled embarrassment, a clear loss of authority. Zörgiebel must be afraid his party would tear him to pieces.

'I just meant that if I can help in any way, I will do so, Commissioner. At least give me a chance.'

'I'll give you one final chance, young Rath, and I urge you to take it. Bring me the people responsible for these awful crimes, these brutes who have so brazenly made fools of us, so that we can finally put them away. I want to see results in five days at the latest.'

'That isn't much time, Commissi—'

'If you want to keep your desk in A Division, you ought to make use of it!'

'It's actually DCI Böhm who's been working on the case, and Superintendent Gennat . . .'

'I don't care how you do it! If Böhm doesn't want you, then you'll have to work alone. It's what you do best after all.' Zörgiebel was standing behind his desk now, motioning towards the door. 'Now get out! Get to work! The next time you walk through that door, I expect you to have something for me. A killer, and this time with evidence that's admissible in court. Do we understand each other?'

Rath nodded and opened the door. Yes, he understood and he was willing to bet Dagmar Kling had understood every word too.

Dr Schwartz had worked like never before. Even the autopsy report on the Jänicke case hadn't been ready this fast.

It was an effort for Rath to keep his eyes open as he ploughed through the medical jargon. It was already late and he lit another cigarette to keep himself awake. The ashtray on the little table inside Gennat's office was already overflowing. He and Buddha were the only ones still working in A Division.

Trudchen Steiner had been the last to leave. The secretary had just had time to bring them the evening papers, almost all of which had accorded the incident at *Georgen* Cemetery a big spread. Most had dug up the old picture of Kardakov and placed it next to a photo of Jänicke's funeral. Speculation was running wild, as Rath had expected. Buddha likewise, it seemed, as the reports didn't faze him in the slightest. The superintendent sat at his desk, puffing thoughtfully on his cigar.

'Don't you want to go home, Inspector?'

Gennat seemed genuinely concerned.

'No, sir. I've made a mess of things, and I'd like to sort it out. I'll work through the night if I have to.'

'I have a bed here so I don't have to go home,' Gennat said, 'but I am *not* going to share it with you.'

Rath laughed. 'That won't be necessary, sir. If you want to go to bed, just tell me. I'll take a taxi back to the hotel.'

'Are you still at the *Excelsior*?'

'I haven't had time to find myself a place.'

'Remind me tomorrow. Perhaps there's something I can do.'

As ill-disposed as many of his colleagues at the Castle were to him at the moment—Böhm and Charly in particular—Gennat was treating him well. He had made it clear that he wanted Rath on the case, for his insight into Kardakov's character. Irrespective of whether he had been wrong in the past, Buddha still believed that Rath could be of assistance whether Böhm liked it or not.

He immersed himself in the autopsy report once more. Truth be told, he had expected the results to be similar to the *Möckern Bridge* case but, though there were many parallels, there were also some surprising differences.

As was the case with Boris, the abuse Kardakov had suffered hadn't caused his death. It was probably the same torturers, professionals who knew how to hurt their victims without injuring them fatally and used drugs in a calculated way. They alternated between torturing their victims and nursing them back to health, administering pain-killing injections for any appropriate response. That was how you coaxed information out of your victims, not through pain alone. Dr Schwartz had also detected traces of heroin in Kardakov's body and found injection sites, as with Boris before him. Nevertheless, it *wasn't* the heroin that had caused Kardakov's death.

The man had died of cyanide poisoning. Dr Schwartz found the remains of the poison in his mouth, as well as thin splinters of glass, which suggested that Kardakov had bitten down on the capsule himself. Suicide, then? Or had his tormentors forced him to swallow the capsule? Had they planned to do that with Boris too? Was his heroin death an accident? Had he been given an overdose by mistake?

Two deaths that were almost identical. Only, one had died of a heroin overdose, while the other had succumbed to cyanide poisoning.

The case was more puzzling than ever.

Gennat pushed the papers to one side and was studying the forensic report again.

'Where do you think our friend was buried before they decided to dig him up?' he asked, chewing on his cigar.

Rath had just read the document. Kronberg's people had found pine needles in the soil on the dead man's clothing. There weren't any pines trees in *Georgen* Cemetery.

'Suggests a forest floor, don't you think?'

'Exactly what I was thinking. Let's have a list made up of all pine forests in and around Berlin. We might just find his old grave.'

29

Rath was at the station by dawn, taking refuge in his secluded little office. Gennat had actually slept at the Castle; Rath had interrupted him shaving as he fetched the interrogation records from Buddha's office. Apart from the two of them, A Division was still completely empty. Rath had barely slept. He was taking Zörgiebel's threat seriously and time was precious right now.

He had ploughed through yesterday's statements page by page, but found barely anything they could use. Perhaps the one given by the man from Heinrich-Roller-Strasse 19, who had witnessed two men pulling a cart across the main cemetery avenue. It had looked like an ordinary coffin cart, he had said, and he knew what he was talking about since he often saw them from his window. Unfortunately, Rath's colleagues hadn't asked what was on the cart. It was clear, however, that it couldn't have been the staff pulling it, as the cemetery gardener had said that, after finishing the preparations for the Jänicke funeral, they had gone to the memorial service in the church. After all, it wasn't every day they saw a ceremonial funeral. That meant the two unknown men must have entered the cemetery chapel, where the coffin carts were usually kept. Yet the chapel was locked up, and Forensics hadn't found any signs of forced entry.

A witness from Greifswalder Strasse claimed to have seen two men dragging a carpet across the street. A cart, a carpet—perhaps the men had transferred the corpse. Either way, they had chosen a means of transport that was in accordance with the surroundings. Neither witness had thought anything of what they had seen until a few hours later when the police came knocking. Nor could they describe the two strangers. Both agreed it had been two men in grey hats and coats, but they couldn't give any further details, no facial features, nothing that stood out. They weren't even sure of the colour of their hair.

Rath studied Charlotte Ritter's interrogation records particularly thoroughly. They were more carefully composed than his own, but she clearly hadn't been able to discover anything more. There had been no witnesses in Heinrich-Roller-Strasse 17, or at least none that she had encountered.

Erika Voss arrived shortly after eight, surprised to find him in his office. 'You're not normally here so early, Inspector!'

'But you are, I hope, Fräulein Voss.'

She put the coffee on without his having to ask. Up until now, he had been smoking cigarettes to keep himself awake, and was glad to have a steaming mug of coffee placed in front of him. In vain he tried to order his thoughts. On the one hand because they still had too little information to put together anything meaningful; on the other because his mind was haunted by the image of a woman. A woman who had no business being there. A slender, pretty face with a resolutely curved mouth and dark eyes you could disappear inside. The dimple on her left cheek when she smiled; *if* she smiled. He had to get out.

When he returned the statements to Gennat's office Gertrud Steiner was in her place, while Henning and Czerwinski stood alongside the superintendent at his desk. Before them lay various maps, on which wooded areas were marked. Gennat gave a few brief instructions, enough for Rath to infer that the day would begin with police combing the pine forests around the city.

Nevertheless, Gennat agreed to what Rath had in mind. Indeed, Rath thought he discerned something approaching respect in the superintendent's eyes, or at the very least approval. Whatever the case, Buddha seemed to like him and in A Division that was what mattered. A certain Wilhelm Böhm could be as awkward as he liked.

Even so, Gennat hadn't spared him the morning briefing. Once again, he felt a stabbing pain when Charly appeared, although at least she had greeted him this time. 'Good morning, Inspector,' she had said. The briefing didn't last long; there wasn't a great deal to discuss. For the most part it was a question of summarising their findings to date, as well as discussing the pine forest operation, in which several hundred police officers were to be deployed. In addition to Henning and Czerwinski, Buddha had tasked other members of CID with overseeing different patches of wood. Mostly they would work in pairs. For a moment Rath feared (or perhaps hoped, he couldn't be sure) that Gennat would send him off again with Charly, but Buddha let him work alone.

By nine Rath was finally underway. He drove to the cemetery again to verify the statements, and perhaps get a few more. Above all, he wanted to have a look round the school. So far they only had the unhelpful statements made by the caretaker and his wife, but today things would be different. No other house in Heinrich-Roller-Strasse could come up with as many potential witnesses as the school.

Around 300 young lads were arriving at the 58th *Volksschule* for boys, as Rath called politely at the rector's office shortly before nine. He could have spared himself the bother because when he expressed a desire to visit all the classes whose windows looked onto the cemetery, the principal, whose name was Edelhard Funke, gave him a good dressing-down. It was unnecessary, he said. No-one had seen anything!

'Our pupils do what their teachers tell them. They don't gaze out onto the street,' the rector said succinctly. When Rath tried to protest, the slippery man met him with a question of his own: 'When did you say this was supposed to have happened?'

'Between ten and eleven, but most likely after half past ten.'

'Well, there you are!' Rector Funke said triumphantly, as if he had just successfully derived Pythagoras's theorem. 'That's when second recess is. At that time every pupil is in the schoolyard, which goes out to the back. No-one could have seen anything from there!'

With these words, Rath was ushered outside, and by quarter to ten he was back on the street. He had barely spent half an hour inside the school and most of that had been spent waiting to see the rector. What a good start to the day!

He decided to question August Glaser, the witness in number 19, a second time. Perhaps he had a little more to say than his present statement. A second visit could work wonders, Rath had often found. This time, however, it didn't work anything: Glaser wasn't at home.

Rath knew that ninety percent of police work consisted of fruitless endeavour, but right now he didn't have the patience. Time was pressing and his lack of sleep wasn't doing much for his state of mind.

So back to number 17 it was then, this time without Charly, to the people they hadn't found at home yesterday. Charly had also rung one doorbell in vain, at least that's what it said in her report. Rath had made a note of the name.

Inge Schenk was still in her dressing gown, but invited him in nevertheless. She was extremely kind, offering him both coffee and liquor. Rath decided on coffee.

She led him into the living room, asked him to take a seat and returned shortly afterwards carrying a tray. He was given his coffee, while she poured herself a glass of something stronger.

She didn't even pour him half a cup, more like a puddle. By the time Rath had asked his first question, his cup was already empty.

She didn't respond. 'Another?' she asked.

He nodded, and she reached for the coffee pot. As she topped him up, she leaned so far forward that her ample breasts almost spilled out of her dressing gown. This procedure repeated itself so many times that Rath began to discern the method behind it. Each time she topped him up she drew a little closer, providing an ever more generous view of her décolletage. Soon she was splashing two or three drops of coffee onto his lap and rubbing his crotch with a serviette, by which time Rath had had enough. He left his hospitable surrounds quick-sharp, sprinting down the stairs as he went.

On the first floor landing, he encountered the old lady whose army of cats he had so admired the day before. Elfriede Gaede. She was beaming at him.

'Inspector! Good that you're here!' She waved him in. What now?

'Sorry, I don't have any time,' he said, trying to move past her. She didn't seem to hear. Her thin fingers reached for his arm and pulled him into the flat. He had no choice but to follow: Elfriede Gaede wasn't as weak as she looked. Besides, the last thing Rath wanted to do was get involved in a wrestling match with an old woman.

'What is it?' he asked, louder this time.

She looked at him. At least she seemed to have heard him.

'No,' she said, shaking her head energetically, 'on the ledge!'

Rath remembered a similarly absurd conversation from the day before, and rolled his eyes to the ceiling. The flat still smelt like one big cat pan. The old lady led him to the open window.

'There,' she said and pointed outside. 'He just went out, and now he can't get back! Poor Napoleon!'

Rath leaned out of the window. Five or six metres to his right, a great fat tomcat was sitting on the ledge of the façade, spitting at him.

Wasn't rescuing cats what Zörgiebel had said lay in store for him in Köpenick?

'Isn't there a local policeman who can help you?'

'This morning? What do you think?'

She seemed genuinely incensed. Rath didn't know quite why, but realised he wasn't going to get out of here until a fat cat named Napoleon was rubbing back against the legs of an old lady named Elfriede Gaede.

He took off his hat and coat and climbed onto the narrow ledge. Clinging to the wall like a limpet he edged his way towards the cat. The animal seemed less than enthused, arching its back and recoiling.

Stay where you are you little bastard, Rath thought to himself, not daring to say it out loud. Not because of Frau Gaede—who wouldn't have heard him anyway—but in case Napoleon recoiled any further, or fell onto the street out of shock.

He was slowly making progress. The distance between him and Napoleon was decreasing. He had almost reached the tom when he heard the husky, metallic rattle of the school recess bell.

Napoleon gave even more of a start than his would-be rescuer. The fat tom leapt forward, somehow managing to get past Rath's legs, disappearing through the window in the blink of an eye.

The inspector needed a little longer to get back. As he was trying to manoeuvre himself backwards through the window, he spied five boys on the street below, eleven, twelve years old at the most. They were climbing over the brick wall of the cemetery.

From this vantage point, he had an excellent view of what they were doing. They were under a shrub near Jänicke's closed off grave, where one of them seemed to fetch something from the ground and share it out amongst the rest. Moments later, white clouds of smoke were swirling from the branches of the shrub. The boys were puffing away on cigarettes. It looked like a well-rehearsed ritual. Indeed, it seemed almost as if the smokers spent every recess there.

Rath ignored Elfriede Gaede's thanks, as she held Napoleon in her arms, stroking him, grabbed his hat and coat and went out into the street.

The best way to judge how long it takes to smoke a cigarette is to smoke one yourself. Rath positioned himself against the cemetery wall and fumbled around for an Overstolz. He had just trod it out when the first of the boys came over the wall: straw-blond hair, freckled, cheeky face, eyes wide open in surprise. He made to escape, but Rath grabbed him by the scruff of the neck.

'Don't try to run away,' he said. 'I only want to talk to you. If you answer a few questions for me, everything'll be dandy. If you make trouble, I'm going to have to tell your rector what you get up to in the cemetery during recess.' He pulled out his badge. 'I'm a policeman, you see, but one you can talk to.'

A puzzled face appeared on the wall above.

'Incidentally, that applies to your friends too. Tell them to come over here and nothing will happen, I promise.'

The boy stood as if paralysed. His friend on the wall clearly didn't know whether to give into his instincts and run, or let common sense prevail.

'Come on, quickly! Recess'll be over soon,' Rath said.

Finally the boy sprang to life. 'Kalle, come on,' he said to the next boy, hesitating on the wall. 'Hanke, Zerlett, Froese, you too! Or else we're in trouble.'

A moment later the five boys were standing around Rath looking abashed. He told them what had happened the day before.

'We know! We're not stupid! It's in the paper!' Kalle said. 'Besides, we . . .'

He was silenced by a poke in the ribs. The freckle face seemed to be in charge here.

'Listen here, boys! I'm investigating a murder. The fact that you smoke only interests me in so far as I'm hoping you were here during recess yesterday as well.'

'And?' Freckle face asked.

'You could be important witnesses.'

'You see, Hotte! I told you we should have gone to the cops,' Kalle said to freckle face. 'Now we're in a right mess!'

'Oh, shut up,' Hotte moaned.

'If you've got something to say to the police, it's still not too late,' Rath said.

The four boys looked at Hotte. Clearly, they wanted to leave the decision up to him. He was still humming and hawing a little, but pulled himself together.

'Well,' he said. 'We were in the cemetery, Inspector. Yesterday too.'

'And you saw something?'

Hotte nodded. 'There were two men heading straight for our bush with this cart. We'd just buried the fags and were about to leave. Stayed in our hideout, of course.'

'Two men with a cart?'

'Exactly, it was the cemetery cart, we recognised it. But the men weren't from the cemetery.'

'How do you know?'

'The people from the cemetery are either in tails and top hat, or going about in their work clothes. These wore normal grey hats, suits and coats.'

'Could you see them?'

'Hardly. They turned off somewhere, away from the bush. Besides, it was raining. They were pretty powerful-looking though.'

'Was there a carpet on the cart?'

'No, 'course not. They had a perfectly normal coffin.'

'I see,' Rath nodded. 'Everything as usual, then.'

'No, actually,' Hotte said. 'The coffin wasn't nailed down. And when they reached the grave that'd been dug, they tied handkerchiefs around their mouths, opened the lid, got rid of the beams, and tipped the coffin out.'

'Tipped it out?'

'Tipped it into the grave. It all happened pretty fast. We didn't realise it was a dead body 'til we saw it in the paper. Otherwise we'd have gone straight to the station. Promise!'

'And then?'

'Then they were off. Beams back over the grave, close the lid on the coffin and away.'

'What about you lot?'

'Us as well, man! We were already late for school!'

'You didn't look inside the grave?'

'No, promise. We didn't have any time.'

Rath wasn't sure whether to believe him, but it didn't really matter now. 'Thanks for the help, lads.'

'You're alright, Inspector. At first I thought old Funke had put the fuzz onto us.'

Rath considered for a moment whether he shouldn't give the boys away after all. He thought about how much fun one could have with the help of a wet sponge, a chair and a clueless school principal, but ultimately decided against it. No doubt Rector Funke would have his work cut out with these boys anyway.

'So none of you could make out a face? To describe to our sketch artist?' Shakes of the head all round. 'Still, one of you ought to make a statement. I promise I won't say anything to your principal or your parents.'

'I can do it,' Hotte said bravely.

'Good, I'll take you straight after school. Tell your parents you have to take care of something important. Won't take long, and there'll be cakes besides.' Rath knew he could count on Gennat for that.

'If you'd asked yesterday, we'd have told you all this, Inspector. Promise.'

'You could have told one of my colleagues as well. They were here yesterday. Did no-one question you?'

More shakes of the head.

'You don't live on this street then?'

'Heinrich-Roller, no!' It sounded almost as if Hotte was offended. 'We're all from Winsstrasse.'

'I see,' Rath gave a knowing nod. He took the police photos from last week out of his pocket. 'Have you seen this man around here?' he asked. He had to leaf through the pictures like a pack of cards until he found the image of Kardakov. 'Must be a few weeks ago now.'

Each of the boys looked at the photo in turn and shook their heads. Rath put the photos away again. Kardakov could have gone underground in this area before his tormentors caught up with him.

On the other side of the road, the school bell trilled. The five boys set off. At the entrance to the school they stopped for a quick discussion. One of them turned round. It was Kalle.

'Inspector!' he said. 'Can you show me the man again?'

Rath fished out the picture of Kardakov.

'Not him, the other one.'

At first Rath wasn't sure which one he meant, but then he showed him the old mug shots of the two Russians.

The boy's gaze fell on the picture of Selenskij.

'Him,' Kalle said after considering briefly. 'He was the one pulling the cart yesterday. Hundred percent.'

Shortly afterwards, Rath was in a green Opel on his way to Kreuzberg. Before collecting Horst Jezorek and Karl-Heinz Urban, that is, Hotte and Kalle, from school and bringing them to the station, he wanted to pay a visit to an old acquaintance.

Selenskij!

As so often in this case, the pieces of the puzzle were rearranging themselves in his head. Selenskij, whom they had let go of once already, did have something to do with Kardakov after all! Only, he wasn't his bodyguard. He was the one who had deposited Kardakov's corpse in Jänicke's grave, whatever the reason. Perhaps he also had Kardakov on his conscience.

At any rate, it was no coincidence that he lived in the same house as the missing Countess.

Was the Russian working for Marlow? Rath was now almost convinced he'd seen one of Marlow's people on Luisenufer before: Josef Wilczek.

At that time, Saint Josef had still had his moustache. Rath had assumed he was a tenant and questioned him innocently on Kardakov, only for Wilczek to fob him off with some nonsense or other.

Josef Wilczek had been there because he was visiting Vitali Selenskij. The Russian must be one of Marlow's people, likewise his scar-faced friend. Rath was willing to bet that scar face Fallin had been the second man at the cemetery, even if none of the boys had recognised him.

If they really were Marlow's people, it begged the question why Dr M. should want to dig the corpse back up and place it right in front of their noses.

Or were the Russians part of the *Nordpiraten Ringverein*, who were currently at loggerheads with *Berolina*?

The one thing that certainly didn't fit into the picture was that the pair were working as police informants. Informants were hardly colleagues, of course, but why should they want to disrupt a police funeral and make a fool of the entire Berlin police force?

Who were they working for at the station? The politicals? That they were linked to Wündisch's mystery men seemed the most likely explanation.

The light at Moritzplatz showed red. Rath examined his pistol. He would need it if Selenskij turned nasty, and that was a real possibility. Rath didn't think the Tsar's secret police had exactly treated people with kid gloves back in the day.

On Reichenberger Strasse, there was a mortuary car coming towards him. Another dead person. One hundred and twenty-four Berliners died every day, five of them violently, mostly as the result of an accident, according to the statistics Rath had consulted in Cologne in preparation for his new posting. Police investigated a new murder or manslaughter case every four days; he wouldn't be short of work in A Division.

Already from the street he could see that something was wrong on Luisenufer. There were three police bicycles leaning against the wrought-iron fence that enclosed the meagre front garden. A cop from the 106th precinct was standing outside the door to the rear building; Rath showed him his badge.

'Homicide? What are you doing here, Inspector? It was only an accident,' the man said.

'Routine,' Rath mumbled and pushed through the door. Herr Müller's flat was open. Rath went inside—splashing into a great pool of water. The entire hallway was submerged. Margarete Schäffner was crouched on the floor wringing out a cloth. The water was splattering into the pail. She still had a lot of work to do.

The flat seemed unusually light and welcoming given it was in a rear building. It was so sparsely furnished that the water hadn't caused too much damage, even if it had spread to every corner. Rath followed the puddle and ended up in the bathroom. Three men were standing next to the bathtub: two cops and a man in grey work overalls. All three looked at him in surprise. Rath didn't even have to ask to know that the man in the overalls was Hermann Schäffner. This time he wasn't out with the SA.

He showed them his badge.

'An accident, Inspector,' Schäffner was quick to say. 'An unfortunate accident.'

'What the hell happened here?' Rath asked brusquely. 'Start at the beginning.'

Schäffner stood to attention. That was the good thing about these hobbyist soldiers. They still treated Prussian officers with respect.

'Well, Inspector,' Hermann Schäffner began. 'When the electricity cut out, I didn't think anything of it at first.' He swallowed before continuing.

'I changed the fuse and was surprised when it blew again straightaway. So I went through the building, checking if everything was in order with the electrics. And it was, at least in the front building. It was only when I got to the rear building that I saw the water coming towards me on the stairs. Immediately I thought something's not right here, and went in.'

'So you have a key?'

'Of course! They're always hanging in my little workshop in the yard.'

'What did you see?'

'I was just about to say. Water everywhere, more than now, Margarete has got rid of most of it already. And then I heard water splashing and went into the bathroom. Well, there he was inside the tub. Dead as a doornail.'

'Who?'

'Müller, the one who lives . . .' he corrected himself: '. . . lived . . .'

'And where is he now?'

'The undertaker's collected him already,' said one of the cops. 'We didn't know that Homicide would be coming out. It happened hours ago.' He cleared his throat, as if embarrassed by the justification. 'We had the corpse examined by a doctor, Inspector. Everything by the book. When he confirmed the man had died from an electric shock, we didn't see the need . . .'

'Electric shock?'

The cop pointed towards the electric hairdryer lying on a wooden stool. 'This was in the bathtub . . .'

'I pulled the plug,' Schäffner explained when he saw Rath's questioning gaze, 'as soon as I saw the mess. I also turned the water off, the tub was already overflowing.'

Now the bathtub was empty, and there was only a tidemark to show that Herr Müller/Selenskij had used it from time to time.

'So if an appliance like this falls into the water, it can kill you?' Rath asked.

'Modern times, modern accidents,' the second cop said with a shrug of the shoulders.

'I probably dealt him a second blow when I changed the fuse,' Schäffner moaned, 'but how was I to know!'

'Now don't go blaming yourself! We've talked about that already,' the cop comforted him. 'The man didn't survive the first electric shock.'

'Isn't this a little unusual?' Rath asked.

'What?' the cop asked. All three looked at Rath quizzically. Somehow he had the impression that Schäffner and the cops were old friends, which wouldn't be too surprising. The 106th precinct was located on Luisenufer too, just a few houses further along.

'That a man was using an electric hairdryer,' Rath continued. 'Aren't they more women's things?'

'I knew Herr Müller pretty well,' Schäffner said hastily. 'He's always used one, ever since they've been around. Not that he was a queer; he just wanted to impress the ladies. He always wanted to look chic.'

Chic? Rath remembered Selenskij differently. The tide mark in the bathtub told a different story too.

'You say you knew him pretty well,' he asked. 'Then you must have known that Herr Müller wasn't actually called Müller, but Selenskij, and that he was Russian?'

Schäffner looked at him wide-eyed.

'What? Don't talk nonsense.'

'He's even registered at this address under the name Selenskij. As caretaker, surely you must have known that!'

Schäffner gazed at the two cops uncertainly. 'What does your colleague want from me?' he asked. 'It's not a crime to know your tenants, is it?'

'I'd like to speak with you in private, Herr Schäffner,' Rath said. 'Should we go to your flat? Or would you prefer to come down to the station?'

Hermann Schäffner preferred to remain in his flat.

He didn't lead Rath into the living room with its enormous yellow chairs. Instead, they sat in the kitchen on hard stools. From his perch, Rath could keep an eye on the courtyard. The cops had remained outside, likewise Margarete Schäffner. He had requested a few people from Forensics and forbidden the caretaker's wife from wringing any more of the bathwater into the pail. Through the kitchen window he watched her talking and gesticulating animatedly with the three police officers whom Rath had likewise ordered into the courtyard to await the arrival of ED. She probably didn't have a good word to say about that arrogant upstart of a detective inspector, who had upset the peaceful order of her tenement block.

Hermann Schäffner rocked back and forth on his stool, clearly uncomfortable. Rath didn't say anything for the time being, but simply lit a cigarette.

'You knew Herr Selenskij for a long time, then?' he asked suddenly.

Schäffner hummed and hawed. He didn't know what to do with his hands.

'Herr Schäffner, if you've got nothing to hide, then I suggest you talk. Otherwise, you'll only make yourself a suspect in a murder inquiry.'

'A murder inquiry?'

'Herr Selenskij alias Müller was murdered.'

'What are you talking about?'

Rath knew it was no accident the moment he had seen the hairdryer. A PROTOS hot air shower: the same model he had seen a week or so ago a few floors further up, in the Countess's attic flat.

'The hairdryer that fell into the bath didn't belong to Herr Selenskij, and you know it.'

'Hardly means I'm the murderer now, does it? Not when I got him the flat in the first place! Why would I want to kill him?'

'What do I know? You wouldn't be the first caretaker to have a run-in with his tenant.'

Schäffner could have got hold of the hairdryer. He had a key for every flat. Mind you, the Countess's flat had been sealed off for a week, and the police seals were still in place; Rath had made sure of that before entering the Schäffners's flat. Nevertheless, it was a murder the perpetrator had wanted to stage as an accident, and for some reason both Schäffner and his police friends were anxious not to challenge that assumption.

At any rate Rath's accusation had worked. Schäffner was becoming agitated.

'That's just nonsense,' the caretaker grumbled. 'If I want someone out, then I chuck 'em out on the street, like Brückner, the red swine. I don't have to kill anyone!'

'You said you were the one who got Herr Selenskij the flat?'

'That's right.'

'So you have known him for a while?'

'I got him the flat, yes. But I didn't know him.'

'Why?'

'I'm not sure what you mean, chief.'

'Why did you get him a flat when you didn't know him?'

Schäffner hesitated. The conversation had taken a turn he didn't like, and it was too late for him to do anything about it.

'Come on then! Talk! I can always take you in.'

'What do I know? I'm a philanthropist.'

'Don't talk rubbish. Why?'

'Well, if you really must know, because a friend asked me to.'

'A friend. From the SA?'

Schäffner nodded.

'Who?'

'You won't know him!'

'Who?'

'*Sturmhauptführer* Röllecke.'

The name didn't mean anything to Rath. Likewise the rank. *Sturmhauptführer*? It didn't exist either in the police force or the *Reichswehr*, only in the private army of the Nazis. Sounded like someone pretty high up. Schäffner claimed not to know Röllecke's address. Well, he'd get hold of it somehow.

'Why?' Rath asked again, after he had made a note of the name.

'Why what?'

'Why was Selenskij to move in here? Did Röllecke tell you the reason?'

'No, he didn't. But I don't refuse a comrade anything! He probably just wanted to do a favour for a friend.'

Rath nodded. He thought back to Gennat's promise of the night before. The superintendent had wanted to help him look for a flat. Perhaps he didn't need to anymore.

A vehicle rolled through the entrance gate and parked outside the rear building. Two men from Forensics climbed out, and one of the cops pointed towards the kitchen window.

'So, Herr Schäffner, that's it for now. Many thanks. Might I ask that you continue to place yourself at our disposal?'

'Of course, Inspector.'

Rath issued brief instructions to the men from Forensics, before climbing back into the Opel.

———

He just managed to reach Heinrich-Roller-Strasse in time for the end of the school day. The bell rang as he parked the Opel by the cemetery wall directly opposite the school gate. He leaned against the vehicle, lit a cigarette and waited for the pupils to emerge. Only a few seconds after the bell had rung a horde of yelling children poured out onto the pavement. The five smokers were the last to appear. Horst Jezorek casually approached the vehicle, his four co-smokers close behind.

'Here I am, Inspector!'

'Good.' Rath opened the car door. 'Kalle, it would be good if you could come too. You ought to have a look at our rogues' gallery.'

'Really?' Kalle beamed.

The pair were the envy of their classmates as they climbed into the vehicle.

'Hey Froese,' Hotte called to his smoking buddy. 'Tell our parents we're out running a few errands for old Koslovski, earning a few pennies.'

The boys even found the drive exciting. Rath took a little detour to make it worthwhile. That way, he could also avoid the traffic chaos at Alex. He crossed Frankfurter Allee and approached the Castle via Kaiserstrasse.

A little later, parked in the atrium, Hotte was amazed by the enormous glass roof. Meanwhile, Kalle's eyes followed a riot squad as they raced through the central portal, and out onto Alexanderstrasse at breakneck speed.

'It looks just like a train station,' Hotte said.

'So this is what the *Red Castle* looks like inside!' Kalle said appreciatively. 'And me right in the middle.'

Rath had promised the boys cake, and so he delivered them to Gennat.

'I have two important witnesses for you here, Superintendent,' he said. 'The matter is to be dealt with in the strictest confidence.' Rath winked at Gennat, who seemed to understand.

'In the strictest confidence. Well, of course,' he said. 'Now, lads, take a seat. Do you want a slice of cake?'

Had anyone been listening at the door, they wouldn't have been surprised. Buddha spoke to dangerous criminals in exactly the same way— and yielded astounding results.

While Trudchen Steiner served the cakes, Gennat took Rath to one side.

'Strike lucky in the school, did you?'

'Next to the school actually. The pair of them were smoking in the cemetery. We can't tell their parents or teachers. I promised.'

Gennat nodded. 'Leave the two of them to me, Inspector. I have a different assignment for you. You know the *Delphi*, don't you?'

'That's where Countess Sorokina sang. As Lana Nikoros.'

'That's right. The place is still closed for renovation. About two hours ago, we received an anonymous tip-off that Countess Sorokina was hiding there. Could be a stupid prank, but head over there now with a few people from the 122nd precinct and take a look.'

Rath nodded. 'OK, Superintendent.' He hesitated a moment.

'Was there something else?' Gennat asked. 'I don't want to keep my young guests waiting too long.'

'There was another fatality this morning, sir. Vitali Selenskij, the Russian we questioned a few weeks ago as part of the Kardakov case, and then released. I was just about to pay him a visit, because one of the boys I brought you claims he saw him in the cemetery. But the man was already in the mortuary car. Electric shock in the bath, a hairdryer.'

'Strange.'

'I thought so too. Police from the local precinct were already on the scene when I arrived, but the officers didn't think it necessary to notify CID. I don't believe it was an accident, so called Forensics out as a precaution.'

'That ought to have been the responsibility of the officers on the scene. Bloody idiots! Every unnatural death has to be investigated by CID, even an accident! The inquiries of a few amateurs in uniform aren't enough!'

Clearly, Gennat didn't think much of the local constabulary.

Rath gave a brief report on what he had learned from Schäffner. He didn't mention that it was the Countess's hairdryer in Selenskij's flat. For some reason he felt uneasy about it, maybe because all too often this case had left him feeling that someone was deliberately trying to put police off the scent.

When Rath stopped by his office briefly, it seemed that Erika Voss was desperate to see him.

'There you are, Inspector. Superintendent Gennat has called at least a hundred times, and . . .'

'It's been taken care of.'

'. . . and Administration would like to speak to you,' she continued, 'a Herr Rossberg. Finance Department. I've had him on the line at least twenty times as well. I've taken a note of his number.'

Rath was shocked. Was he supposed to take responsibility for the unnecessary search for Kardakov? The idiots from Finance would be better off talking to the commissioner, the search had been Zörgiebel's idea.

'Thank you, Fräulein Voss. Please put me through.'

The man on the other end of the line made it clear straightaway that it was best not to tangle with him.

'Good day, Inspector! Can you please inform me why your telephone bill has suddenly rocketed?'

Rath couldn't. Was Erika Voss using his continual absence to make private calls? Even if she was, how was that any of these idiots' business?

'My telephone bill? I'm sorry but I don't have to justify any calls that are being made from my offi—'

'I'm not talking about your office. Your private line. In case you've forgotten, the Free State of Prussia bears those costs as well!'

'I've got no idea what you're looking for! I haven't had a private line for more than a week now!'

'I haven't received any notice of cancellation, and neither, clearly, has the *Reichspost*.'

'I've moved out! I'm currently staying at a hotel. I forgot to cancel, but that's not usually necessary when the telephone's no longer being used.'

'No longer being used? Then how do you explain all the calls? In the last week alone your telephone bill has trebled. Fortunately, the *Reichspost* notified us of this development in good time. The Prussian police has to make savings, Herr Rath, this is unacceptable! We will be sending you an invoice for the share of costs exceeding your normal allowance and then deducting it from your wages!'

On his way out west, Rath took a little detour past Yorckstrasse. In vain: Nikita Fallin wasn't at home.

Likewise the operation in *Delphi* seemed doomed from the start. The cops in Kantstrasse weren't exactly champing at the bit to help an officer from Alex. Before setting off, Rath tried to notify the landlord, but only got his secretary on the line, Felten. Rath recalled their first encounter. A slippery customer.

'A criminal! In our building? What makes you think that?'

'I didn't say anything about a criminal,' Rath corrected the man. 'It's about an important witness.'

'I see. That's why you want to proceed on the quiet.'

'How I choose to proceed is up to me. Can you provide us with a key or would you prefer us to kick the door down?'

'I will, of course, support the police in this matter, Inspector.'

He was already waiting on Fasanenstrasse when the police arrived. Rath posted an officer at every entrance to the building before going in with Felten and two other cops. The secretary led them though an unprepossessing door towards an iron staircase.

'It goes downstairs.'

'Are you sure she's hiding downstairs?'

'I wouldn't know where else. It's just props and other junk in the cellar. No-one's been down there for weeks. There's work going on upstairs. We're renovating at the minute.'

In the end props and junk were all they found. No Countess for miles around; nothing to indicate that anyone had been hiding. Just one big expanse of rubble. Next to all manner of bits and pieces made out of plaster, wood and cardboard, almost all of it broken, were the remains of a sofa, feathers coming out of its cushions, a curved bedstead and a torn mattress.

Felten gazed at the scene wide-eyed.

'Would you look at this mess!'

'Doesn't look much like a hiding place.'

'But someone must've been here,' Felten said. 'Everything's broken. All these things were in good nick when we put them down here.' He gazed about him, still stunned. 'I think you should leave an officer here,' he suggested, 'in case she returns.'

'And *I* think you'd be better off calling the Refuse Department and asking them to clear all this rubbish away,' Rath said. 'There hasn't been any Countess living here, maybe vandals at most. If this is an attempt to get your establishment onto the front page, then you can consider it failed.'

'I don't know what you're talking about.'

'It was *you* who called us, my dear Felten,' Rath shouted at the secretary. 'Just as surely as you say amen in church. Well, you can thank God that I can't prove it! The Prussian police don't stand for people giving them the run around.'

He was still in a bad mood when he parked his car in Nürnberger Strasse shortly afterwards.

Weinert opened the door.

'Well, what a surprise,' the journalist said, grinning. 'The man who palmed me off with a murdering corpse.'

'Come on, you thought it was a plausible theory too.'

'Very plausible, even. Still, doesn't seem to have been right.'

'Well, now we know. Can I come in all the same?'

'Of course.' Weinert stepped to one side. Everything looked the same; they sat at the empty dining room table. 'Still a little early for supper. Would you like tea?'

'I'd prefer coffee.'

Weinert went to the kitchen unit, put the water on to boil and started fiddling with the coffee grinder.

'What brings you here?' he asked. 'New revelations? If so, I hope they're right this time.'

'Come on. You didn't do too badly out of it. All the papers published it—it's just that *Abendblatt* was a day early.'

'You're right. A canard that everyone prints is hardly a canard anymore.'

Rath looked around. There was no sign of Elisabeth Behnke.

'Has my room been let already?' he asked.

'No, it's barricaded up like the *Reichsbank*. You'd think old Behnke was looking after the British crown jewels.'

The kettle began to whistle. Rath watched Weinert as he tipped the boiling water carefully into the coffee filter.

'So where is our dear old landlady?'

'Should be here any minute. Just running a few errands. Perhaps you could have supper together—if she's forgiven you, that is, you old dog. Receiving female visitors, just imagine! Tsk, tsk!'

'I bet you're still at it every night.'

'Every night? I couldn't possibly at my age. But that doesn't mean I'm about to let some old landlady spoil my fun.'

'Just make sure you don't get caught! The consequences can be dire.'

'Sometimes I think she's known for a long time, but doesn't dare throw me out. Perhaps she's afraid of appearing on the front page of *Abendblatt*.'

'She wasn't afraid of being arrested by CID, I can tell you that.'

The men laughed. Weinert poured the coffee. Rath felt the hot liquid flowing through his body, dispelling the fatigue that was constantly threatening to take hold of him.

'What do you want from her?'

'It's private, which in this case means work-related. Nothing to concern the free press.'

'Normally that's something for the free press to decide itself.' Weinert finished his coffee. 'Still, you're in luck. I'm in a hurry, so there won't be any eavesdropping.' He stood up. 'Nice to see you again. Let me know if you have anything interesting in future.'

'You're not going to leave me alone, are you? I'm a stranger these days!'

'You're a policeman . . .' Weinert hesitated. 'But you're right, it's irresponsible. I'm going to lock my room.'

'I promise I'll be good and wait here. If she takes too long, I'll leave a note.'

Weinert left the room. Rath heard the journalist slam his bedroom door, probably after retrieving his hat and coat, and then the heavy front door clicked to.

Rath poured himself more coffee and stared into his cup. The clock on the wall was ticking loudly. He shifted back and forth impatiently in his chair. He had more important things to do than to wait for his former landlady. In truth, it would probably be enough to take the telephone with him; then he could leave right away.

Rath went to his old room and shook the door. Weinert had been right: it was locked.

Where did Elisabeth Behnke keep her keys?

Probably in her private chambers, and he had already seen that the door was ajar.

He felt even more uneasy in her flat than he had done in the kitchen.

If she caught him here he really would have some explaining to do. As he searched the drawing room, he listened intently for any noise, above all the turning of keys in heavy doors. After a quick tour through her bedroom, he finally found what he was looking for.

Rath had only been in her living quarters once before, about six weeks ago when he had signed the rental agreement. On that occasion, she had led him straight into this strange drawing room, on the one hand a fairly normal, plush living room of the sort that had been modern during the Kaiser's reign. On the other it was a kind of military shrine, in the centre of which stood a large oil painting depicting Helmut Behnke in the uniform of a Prussian sergeant, underneath it a sabre with black and white tassels, which had been presented to his widow upon his death, and any number of photos showing Helmut Behnke during the war. In front of this memorial wall stood the bureau where she had fetched the keys to Rath's room.

Rath stared at this morbid display, which took up an entire wall. Instead of looking in the drawers for Elisabeth Behnke's keys, he decided to examine the photos, his gaze coming to rest on a picture that was familiar to him. He had already seen it once, in an office in Friedenau. It showed the newly appointed sergeants Helmut Behnke and Bruno Wolter. Bruno Wolter, Helmut Behnke's old comrade, looking slim and gazing proudly into the camera. The picture must have been hanging here during Rath's first visit too, only on that occasion he hadn't noticed, as he had been studiously ignoring this altar to a fallen soldier. Indeed he had barely even looked across, since he didn't want to show his new landlady just how much the display had unsettled him.

Wolter could be seen elsewhere on other photos, always with Helmut Behnke. The pair really did seem to have been inseparable. Until, that is, a French grenade had ripped off both of young Sergeant Behnke's legs at Soissons, and he had succumbed to his injuries a few days later. *Höllenschlacht an der Aisne* a military film would later dub it: *Slaughter on the Aisne*.

Rath tried to tear himself away from the pictures, but they drew him into the past, into the war, reminded him how different things might have been if he had only been born a few years earlier. Like Anno . . .

Then he saw a face that prompted a flash of recognition in his brain. A face he hadn't been expecting to see in this gallery, which suddenly jerked him wide awake.

Was it possible?

Five men by an artillery gun, looking tired but gazing proudly and confidently ahead. A captain and four lance corporals, a picture like a thousand others.

On the shaft in front sat the captain, left hand leaning imperiously on a cane. Alfred Seegers. To the left next to the cartwheel was Lance Corporal Rudolf Scheer, while directly behind the captain stood Lance Corporals Behnke and Wolter.

To the right of Wolter stood a man whose moustache reminded him of a police mug shot. The man was a few years younger, and the ends of his moustache were twirled upwards in the manner of Kaiser Wilhelm, but it was him, no doubt about it: Josef Wilczek!

Saint Josef!

The man from *Berolina* had been one of Bruno Wolter's former comrades!

30

Friday night, and there were still tables to be had in *Venuskeller* without bribing a waiter. It was just before ten and the revellers wouldn't be arriving until later, the band was playing its heart out and the first guests were trying to match the noise with their chatter. In place of last time's American Indian routine, Rath was treated to a performance by harem girls, two rather plump women in pastel-coloured, semi-transparent veils undressing one another. Not very erotic, but they were probably saving the edgier routines for later.

Rath never thought he'd be back here of his own accord. Yet here he was, fighting back his fatigue. The noise merged in his ears to form a single, soothing slur. He didn't even bother to order when the waiter came to his table.

'I need to see Dr M.'

'I'm sorry, but I don't know what doctor you're referring to, sir. Can I get you something to drink?'

He seized the man by the collar. A few guests looked round.

'Listen to me, my friend. If you're getting cold feet because someone's asked for the doctor, fetch Sebald to take the decision out of your hands. But do something. Believe me, Dr M. wants to see me; he *doesn't* want me to have a drink here.'

'Very well, sir.' The waiter seemed unperturbed as he disappeared with his tray. Rath gazed after him and lit a cigarette. The man didn't go to the counter, but instead opened a discreet little door beside the sparsely populated dance floor. Well, what do you know! How was it that every time he learned something new about this case, he understood less than before? Every insight gave way to disenchantment. The knowledge that Josef Wilczek was in cahoots with Bruno Wolter had once again thrown up more questions than it had answered.

His discovery just now in Nürnberger Strasse had sent the adrenaline pumping through his body. He had felt like a chemist who had chanced upon a new element, albeit one he was unable to classify. He must have stood in front of that picture as if in a trance, his gaze rigid while the thoughts raced through his mind.

Outside on Nürnberger Strasse a car horn had sounded almost right outside the window, and it was this noise that had taken him back to the present, and reminded him what he was actually there for. He had opened the drawer and removed her keyring, tried the keys one by one until he opened the door to his old room. It looked exactly the same as before, only the bed wasn't made. With a tug, he pulled the telephone cable out of the wall.

Once he had put the keys back, he simply lifted the picture off the wall.

Before dropping the Opel off at the Castle, he had driven to Potsdamer station. He couldn't think of anything better than to stow the picture and the telephone in his locker alongside the pistol and notebook. Its contents increasingly resembled a curiosity cabinet, and he wondered whether anything inside would be admissible as evidence.

He had taken the car back, but avoided Gennat's office. Erika Voss had already finished work for the evening when Rath spread the contents of the Wilczek file across his desk. He almost had the impression he was avoiding his secretary, and perhaps he was. He leafed through the file that he himself had put together. Above all, he was interested in the older cases that had been transferred to the file in note form: Wilczek's prior convictions. Rath noted the dates and got hold of the old case files. Had Bruno Wolter ever had any official dealings with Saint Josef? All his efforts were in vain. There was nothing. No arrests, nothing at all. Not even a premature release from custody, an instance of special treatment as with Selenskij or Fallin. Yet Rath was certain that Wilczek had worked as a police informant for his former comrade-in-arms Bruno Wolter, even if such details were kept off the record.

Fallin's flat in Yorckstrasse was near the *Excelsior* and Rath had taken a little stroll there before freshening up for the evening in his hotel room. When no-one came to the door, he had picked the lock and taken a look inside. He didn't have much time to scrutinise the flat, but at least the Russian wasn't lying dead in his bath. Rath had left again before he ran the risk of being caught. He told himself not to immediately expect the worst.

Perhaps Fallin had gone into hiding because he had got wind of his friend's death.

'Benno's already informed me that you're unarmed, Inspector. I hope you haven't been snorting any cocaine this time.'

The voice brought him back to the *Venuskeller*. Sebald's balding head gleamed over the shiny table-top like the moon over the Wannsee.

'Take me to your boss, then you can get back to enjoying your dancers,' Rath said. 'Maybe you should have a think about your stage programme while you're at it. This veil dance would be an impertinence even somewhere legal.'

'I wouldn't use that tone with Herr Marlow if I were you,' Sebald said.

They didn't even have to go over the road this time, as Marlow had made himself comfortable in one of the back rooms. He was sitting at Sebald's desk with a few figures hanging around the darkest corners of the room, all of them in evening dress. Liang was standing behind Marlow's chair.

'Good evening, Inspector,' the crime lord greeted him, just as friendly as during their first encounter. 'Excuse me for making you wait. You mustn't think that your presence had escaped our notice. I wanted to see if you were keeping to our agreement . . .'

'What agreement?'

'Not to visit *Venuskeller* on your own time.' Marlow drew on his cigar. 'Believe me, I know how difficult that is. And secondly . . .'

Right on cue a side door opened and a naked girl entered, lighting a cigarette with the table lighter on Sebald's desk before disappearing as quickly as she had emerged. Rath recognised the well-built performer from the American Indian routine. The men in the room grinned suggestively, all of them, that is, apart from Marlow and the Chinese man.

'. . . secondly I had things to do.' Marlow was grinning now too, though it was almost charming when he did it.

'Patience is one of my greatest virtues,' Rath said. 'You need it in my job. The same goes for staying power.'

'Then let's hope you have that too.'

'I wouldn't be sitting here getting on your nerves otherwise.'

'Oh, is that what you're doing?'

'I hope so.'

'And *I* hope you have more to offer than last time.'

'Why don't we see? But I'll only speak to you in private.'

Marlow laughed. 'I don't think this is the place for *you* to be imposing conditions. Besides, you can never speak to me entirely in private, you should know that by now.' He waved his left hand limply through the air as if swatting a fly. 'Sebald, take your men for a little stroll. I'm sure Liang is more than capable of catering to our friend's needs.'

He said it in a very friendly manner, but it sounded like a threat. Sebald left the room with four men. Three remained behind.

Marlow came straight to the point.

'I've been reading about your exploits in the papers recently, Inspector,' he said. 'I see you're investigating murders these days. So far without much success, or am I wrong?'

'I've just told you I'm patient. You have to be able to wait for success too. For the moment, for example, when you are escorted into a Black Maria by two police officers.'

Marlow's voice changed immediately and the temperature in the room grew icy. 'You certainly are brave, Inspector. I recommend that you think carefully about how much bravery you can afford to show in this room.'

'Is that supposed to be a threat? You wouldn't dare kill me as well!'

'*As well?* What's that supposed to mean?' Marlow raised his eyebrows. 'Whatever ideas you might harbour about my business, I haven't killed anyone.'

'Then *had* killed. Let's do some straight talking for once. What's your role in all this? How many people do you have on *your* conscience?'

Marlow flicked the ash from his cigar.

'Don't get carried away now. If we're going to do some straight talking, then why don't we start with *you*. I've always been open and honest; you on the other hand would have me believe you were after the Sorokin gold. An outright lie. So, what game are *you* playing?'

'I'm looking for a murderer.'

'Then you should damn well look somewhere else!'

Marlow slammed his fist on the table so suddenly that Rath gave a start.

'When you showed up just now in *Venuskeller*, I thought perhaps you'd realised that cooperating was in your interests too. Now here you are again, talking big!'

'You're always saying how much you want to work with me. Yet after our last conversation you tried to have me killed!'

'Where do you get such ridiculous ideas? Believe me, Inspector, if I really wanted you out of the way, you wouldn't be sitting here now.'

Marlow seemed genuinely appalled.

'Why should I work with you?' Rath asked.

'Finally, a sensible question!' Marlow's voice sounded just as warm and friendly as it had at the start of their conversation. 'I'm going to offer you a very simple deal. I'll help you arrest your killer, you help me find the gold.'

'That's only going to work if you tell me everything you know, including your role in all of this.'

Marlow smiled his smile, which inspired more fear than confidence.

'Of course,' he said. 'But first, two things. One: if the gold turns up, leave it in the care of Marlow Imports, without the police making any trouble.'

'As long as you guarantee me free rein to catch the killers, even if it means arresting someone from *Berolina*.'

'I'll provide reinforcements if you like.'

'Let's not get carried away,' Rath said. 'The second point?'

'That you don't use anything I have said or am about to say in court.'

Rath only needed a moment to consider. 'Fine,' he said. 'So, who goes first?'

'I've already told you so much, Inspector. Now it's your turn.'

Rath took a cigarette from his pack before he began.

'You know that one of your men is working for the police?' he said, waving the match out. 'Was working.'

Marlow raised his eyebrows in surprise. 'I hope you have a name.'

'Josef Wilczek.'

'Saint Josef!' Marlow blew a cloud of smoke across the table. 'Of all people! That rat would've snuffed it years ago if it wasn't for me.'

'You saved his life?'

'I removed a bullet from his bloody guts. He was one of the people still playing war in 1919.'

'So you really are a doctor?'

'Let's say that I have certain medical skills.'

'So Wilczek was part of the *Freikorps*?'

'An armed group at any rate, one that wore field grey and rifle slings.'

'An ex-front soldier who couldn't help himself. That fits. Wilczek was working in tandem with an old war comrade at the station. Bruno Wolter, DCI in Vice.'

'Well, well! Your old boss?'

Rath was amazed. 'You're well informed.'

'Normally it's the police who work for me, rather than the other way round. I made a few inquiries after you dropped by so suddenly two weeks ago.' Marlow gave the Chinese man a wave, and Liang poured whisky into two glasses. Rath sniffed at the glass and nodded appreciatively.

'From Scotland,' Marlow said. 'Better than the hooch that Sebald serves out there.' His head gestured towards the door leading to *Venuskeller*. The noise from the bar was barely audible in the back room. 'So,' he said, raising his glass, 'let's drink a toast.'

The men drank.

'I had a feeling the police were in on it,' said Marlow finally. 'I thought there was something funny about Wilczek's death. It was a cop that did for him. Yet your first thought is to make *Berolina* nervous.'

'I'm still working on the assumption that it was a gangland shoot-out.'

'Nonsense. Saint Josef was taken out. Probably by his boss. By Wolter!'

Rath said nothing. Let Dr M. believe what he wanted.

'The fact that it's a vice cop, now that surprises me. What does he want with the gold? To open a whorehouse as big as the *Reichstag*?' Marlow stubbed his cigar out. 'This is about politics, and the arms trade. How is a vice cop supposed to get hold of weapons?'

Through his old army friend Rudi Scheer, Rath thought. Scheer was in charge of the Berlin police armoury. That gave him plenty of opportunity to buy more weapons than necessary and divert them through dubious channels. Perhaps he had even misappropriated the odd weapon from police reserves. Was that why 1A had put Jänicke onto Wolter? That meant Rudi Scheer was most likely under observation too. Still, Jänicke's cover had been blown, and Wolter had almost certainly warned his old friend Rudi long ago. The two of them wouldn't be laying themselves open to any more attacks from 1A. Then there was the link to the *Reichswehr*, to Major General Seegers, who was so well informed about the Sorokin gold. Bruno had some damn good options when it came to trading weapons, even as a vice cop.

But none of that concerned Marlow. Rath decided to muddy the waters. 'Maybe it's got nothing to do with weapons,' he said.

'It's about weapons, you can be sure of that! Kardakov wanted to use the money to buy weapons and someone stopped him. Still, that was only the first part of the drill. The second is to get hold of the gold and arm the troops. That's just as true for Stalin's people as it is for the Black Hundred. Just don't ask me what a vice cop is doing mixed up in all of it.'

'Stalin's people?'

'Do you remember the story about the missing Soviet embassy worker that made the papers last week?'

Rath remembered. The Soviet embassy at Unter den Linden had submitted a protest note to the commissioner. They suspected counter-revolutionary forces at work. Typical of the Soviets to use any opportunity to fire an ideological broadside. Zörgiebel had refused to prioritise the case at the expense of other missing person cases.

'The man was a Chekist, a member of the Russian secret police,' Marlow continued. 'He was trying to recover the gold for the fatherland of all workers. He wasn't very successful.'

'*Wasn't?*'

'I fear he won't be seeing Mother Russia again.'

'Did you . . . ? I mean your people . . . ?'

'No. I imagine the competition saw to him. I only know he's out of the race. Just like his helpers from the local Red Front. Thälmann's boys like nothing better than crawling up Stalin's arse. Serves them right. They won't be bothering us anymore.'

'What about the *Red Fortress*?'

'Pardon me?'

'Are you still working for Kardakov's organisation or were they bothering you too?'

'I don't work for anybody. I had a business arrangement with Alexej Kardakov, and now he's dead.' Marlow took a sip of whisky. 'But I think I've said enough. It's your turn again!'

'I can give you two more names.' Rath took his time stubbing out his cigarette in order to keep Marlow in suspense. 'Vitali Selenskij and Nikita Fallin.'

'More Russians? Where do they fit into all this?'

'Two first-rate arseholes who used to work for the Tsar's secret police. They're the ones who staged the whole thing with Kardakov's corpse yesterday. If they dumped him in the grave then they most likely killed him too . . .'

'Black Hundredists,' Marlow cried inadvertently.

'What did you say?' That phrase again. Rath had never heard it before today.

'You don't know? Well, I'm not surprised.' Marlow laughed. 'I only encountered it when Alexej Kardakov was giving me some political pointers. You need to know who you're dealing with in an operation like this, and Kardakov was more afraid of the Black Hundredists than he was of Stalin's Chekists.'

'With good reason perhaps, given his current condition. What can you tell me about them?'

'Tsarist terrorists, if I can put it like that. Pretty nasty bastards. Similar to the SA, only this lot make the SA seem like a bunch of uptight boy scouts. Kardakov knew they were after the gold as well.'

'I thought the two Russians were working for the *Nordpiraten*.'

'Don't get me started on those pimps. The pirates don't know anything about the gold, the idiots!'

'But they're at war with *Berolina*. Kardakov didn't just have all his papers on him when he was found, but a *Berolina* membership pin too. Looks as if someone's trying to make trouble for *Berolina*.'

'Seems to be working too. Your people are giving Red Hugo hell again. Poor guy, his nerves are shot at the moment.' Marlow gave the Chinese man a nod and he refilled their glasses. 'Believe me, Inspector. If Fallin and Selenskij have anything to do with Kardakov's death, then they belong to the Black Hundred. The way Kardakov and that other poor swine . . .'

'Boris.'

'. . . the way those two were tortured, so brutally yet at the same time so insidiously, that's the trademark of the Black Hundred.'

Rath took a drag on his cigarette and thought for a moment. What

Marlow was saying might just make sense. Ex-secret police who couldn't help themselves, and who still knew how to inflict pain.

'And?' Marlow was growing impatient. 'What else do you know?'

'Not much,' Rath said. 'Selenskij's dead.'

'Murdered?'

'Probably.'

'By who?'

'Good question. There are several possibilities: either by a competitor in the race for the Sorokin gold, or by an accomplice because he had made a mess of things and become a security risk. Or perhaps it was just revenge.'

'This damn gold has killed a lot of people, without making a single one of them rich,' Marlow said.

Rath nodded. Clearly a whole lot of people knew about the gold: Marlow and his men, Wolter's wartime comrades and their informant Wilczek, the communists, the Black Hundredists, the Countess Sorokina and the now leaderless *Red Fortress*—no wonder they were all getting in each other's way.

'What about Fallin?' Marlow asked.

Rath shrugged his shoulders. 'No idea. He hasn't turned up as a corpse at any rate.'

'Let's hope he's still alive. If he's the one who put Kardakov through the mill, then he probably knows where the gold is too.'

'Then why hasn't he picked it up?'

'Because it's being closely guarded.'

'By who?'

'By my people.'

'What the hell is that supposed to mean? You're telling me you don't know where the gold is but are having it guarded all the same? I think you've got some explaining to do!'

'It's best if you come with me. I'll show you.'

A few minutes later the three men were walking across railway lines in the dark, having cut across Marlow's office in Rüdersdorfer Strasse, the converted former *Ostbahnhof* warehouse, and wound up in the *Ostbahn* goods station. Unlike the passenger terminus, it was still in use.

They came to a halt at a goods shed where, by the weak light of the electric lamp, they could make out the words *Marlow Imports Ltd* on the shed wall. As they stepped onto the loading ramp, a shadow emerged from the dark of the shed. The man was clearly carrying a machine gun under his coat.

'OK, Fred, it's us,' Marlow cried and raised his arm.

'Evening, boss. All quiet,' said Fred.

Another man emerged from the shed and two more climbed down from the goods wagons, which had been parked on the track by the ramp. All three men were carrying weapons.

'It's alright,' Fred said, 'go back to your posts.'

Rath gazed after the men as they disappeared into the darkness.

There were four tank wagons on the siding. The rust from numerous locomotives had dyed the white lacquer of the bulbous tanks grey and turned their logo a dirty red.

Vereinigte Ölmühle Insterburg, Rath read. Insterburg Consolidated Oil Mills.

'Rapeseed oil?' he asked. 'Do you own a margarine factory too?'

Marlow grinned. 'Margarine from these would be hard to digest. Three tanks contain hydrochloric acid, the other contains nitric acid, around 150 hectolitres per wagon.'

'So where is the gold?'

'That's precisely the question,' Marlow said. 'These wagons were part of a goods train that started for Berlin four weeks ago. The one Kardakov was using to smuggle the gold out of the Soviet Union.'

'But the wagons here are from East Prussia.'

'The wagons, yes, but not the cargo. Russian goods trains are reloaded at the border because their rail gauges are almost ten centimetres broader than ours.'

'Why did Kardakov decide on a train to smuggle the gold? You can't even prepare the cars.'

'That's precisely the question we've been asking ourselves for weeks. Kardakov and the Countess didn't appear at the station on the evening the train arrived, as agreed.'

'Boris came instead.'

'Right. He was the train's escort, but also Kardakov's contact.'

'Then he must have said something to you.'

'That would've been nice, but the man didn't speak a word of German. Besides, he thought something was amiss when he didn't find any of his fellow countrymen, only my people. We tried to calm him down, but then he panicked and ran across the tracks. The next I saw of him was his photo in *Abendblatt*.'

Rath considered briefly.

'Perhaps Kardakov duped you,' he said. 'Gives you some train full of chemicals while he makes off with the gold.'

'I don't think so. Without me, he wouldn't have been able to do much with the gold.'

Marlow lit a cigar and indicated to Fred that he should return to his post. 'Incidentally,' he continued, as he smoked, 'do you know what you can make with three parts hydrochloric acid and one part nitric acid?'

'I'm no chemist.'

'Aqua regia.'

'Never heard of it.'

'Literally, king's water. A very aggressive mix. One which even dissolves gold.'

'What are you trying to say, that the gold is in the acid?'

'No, in fact. We only have hydrochloric acid and nitric acid in the wagons. Neither acid alone can dissolve the gold. Only the mixture can do that. The gold has to be somewhere else.'

'It's not in the wagons?'

'We've searched every millimetre, even though we knew we wouldn't find anything.'

'Why not?'

'How could the gold have remained hidden while it was being reloaded in East Prussia? Quite impossible really. Unless you bribed all border officials and station workers and prepared not only the Russian tank wagons, but the German ones too. Don't forget that we're talking about a huge amount of gold here, several *tons*.'

'Maybe it's coming with a second consignment: an innocuous cargo, scrap metal or something, in which the gold is concealed. Then you use the king's water to dissolve it.'

'That's exactly what I suspect will happen. Only, there's been no talk of a second consignment. I only ever spoke to Kardakov about this shipment. He prepared all the paperwork and I signed—he needed someone above suspicion to request the delivery from the chemical company in Leningrad.'

So, Marlow had played the serious businessman to avoid arousing communist suspicion.

'And did it work?'

'I had a visitor from the Soviet embassy—this Troschin, who's now missing—and that was it. Since then I've known that the Cheka are on standby. I showed the man the delivery and how corrosive the combination of hydrochloric and nitric acid could be, before he left.'

'He was probably glad your men didn't use him to demonstrate.'

'Perhaps.'

'There's one thing I don't understand, Herr Marlow,' Rath said thoughtfully. 'If I've been correctly informed, you were supposed to convert the gold into cash for Kardakov. So how come you're groping around in the dark like the rest of us?'

'No-one's privy to everything. Only Kardakov and the Countess knew how the smuggling operation was going to work.'

'If he was tortured then he must have betrayed the secret.'

'No, because he only knew half of it. The Countess alone knew all the ins and outs of the operation. The whole thing only worked in combination.'

'Some combination! Kardakov's dead. And if the Countess has been carried off too, she'll take her secret with her to the grave.'

'Not if the documents turn up again.'

The documents! Rath couldn't help thinking back to his visit to Tretschkov's. He knew where one of these documents was, but didn't say.

'What documents?' he asked instead.

'A kind of map. Kardakov and the Countess hid plans that reveal the secret somewhere—two thin documents that only make sense when you place them on top of one another and hold them against the light.'

Rath whistled quietly through his teeth. 'If it really was the Black Hundred that tortured Kardakov, they could have taken his half.'

'So Fallin has it!'

Rath shrugged his shoulders. 'Perhaps. Or Selenskij's killer.'

'I suspect they're one and the same.'

It was long past midnight when Rath looked in the mirror of his hotel room and barely recognised the man staring back at him. He splashed cold water on his face.

Fatigue had overcome him at some point while they were still at *Ostbahnhof*. Back in the comfortable chair familiar to him from his first visit to Marlow's office, he was scarcely able to keep his eyes open. Marlow had noticed it too. He reached into his desk and waved a little paper bag in the air.

'Inspector, you seemed a little sharper last time. Could it have been because of this?'

Rath had looked on in confusion. Then Marlow threw him the little paper bag and he stowed it in his pocket. He hadn't taken any—that was something, at least. Still, he thought, a little stimulation for the next few days couldn't hurt. He had so much to do and there was barely any time for sleep.

He hadn't stayed much longer at Marlow's, but managed to hail a taxi at Küstriner Platz. The driver looked at him as though he were an apparition. The lights in *Plaza* were out; he had been too late for the final round of theatre-goers, and was eating a sandwich when Rath disturbed him.

No wonder he had taken him for a ghost, Rath thought, as the cold water dripped from his reflection. He rubbed his face with a towel and lay down on the bed. The thoughts were racing through his mind, chaotically, without rhyme or reason.

Bruno Wolter and Josef Wilczek: the unholy alliance. It was easy to imagine them as arms dealers, given Bruno's numerous links to his old comrades. Were they after the gold too? If they were, they hadn't a hope. Even if Wilczek hadn't died, Wolter would have been in over his head against the competition, consisting as it did of the secret service, and career and politically motivated criminals. Unless, that is, he could count on other allies, more black sheep in the force or the *Reichswehr*. Even so, in the race for the gold, there were others who currently had their noses in front. Not the owner of the gold, Countess Sorokina, nor the intimidated *Red Fortress*, nor even Marlow. All he had were a few tank wagons full of acid. Two men had got closer to the gold than anyone else. One was a scar-faced Russian named Nikita Fallin; the other was a Prussian CID officer named Gereon Rath. The Countess no longer had her map. Even if she was in Fallin's clutches, she wouldn't have been any use to him. Rath knew this, and yet he had chosen not to allay Marlow's greatest fear. Namely, that the Black Hundred could still get its hands on the Countess's map and uncover the location of the gold.

Knowledge is power.

He stared up at the ceiling, as if the solution to the riddle was to be found there. Outside he could hear the first sounds of the dawning city. Yet he was still lying here, incapable of sleep, even though he hadn't touched the packet of cocaine. It was resting between the pages of the bible on his bedside table, just in case.

He would have been better off asking Marlow for a sleeping pill, he thought, as his eyes finally fell shut.

He didn't feel as if he had been asleep for long when the sound of the telephone awoke him.

The friendly voice of the concierge. 'Good morning, Herr Rath. Your wake-up call. It is precisely half past six.'

His fatigue disappeared as soon as he recalled the events of yesterday evening. Adrenaline tingled through his veins. He didn't need any cocaine; he needed a cold shower.

He was out on the streets before seven, walking down Möckernstrasse. At the bank of the Landwehr canal the warped shore fencing had been replaced, and freshly painted metal gleamed in the morning sun. The scraped tree bark was all that was left to remind him of the accident. Thoughtfully, Rath moved on.

In Yorckstrasse he spied the green Opel already from afar. Gennat had obviously heard about Selenskij and placed Fallin's flat under surveillance. He wondered whether Buddha had also placed the dead man's closest friend on the list of murder suspects.

Plisch and Plum were sitting in the car, there was no mistaking it even if Rath couldn't see their faces. Detective Czerwinski had fallen asleep, his head slumped over the wheel. Rath couldn't quite make out what Assistant Detective Henning was doing. He proceeded at a blind angle until he reached the car.

'Morning, gentlemen,' Rath said and tapped the green tin roof. Henning spun round and looked at him wide-eyed. Czerwinski gave a start and banged his elbows. His hat rolled onto Henning's lap.

'Rath, what the hell are you doing?' Czerwinski sounded genuinely upset. 'We're observing a suspect here! Do you want our cover to be blown?'

'You're not observing a suspect, but a flat,' Rath countered. 'If the man was at home, you'd have hauled him off to Gennat long ago. Am I right?'

'It'd be good if you made yourself scarce,' Czerwinski moaned.

'Maybe you could stop snoring too,' Rath said, giving the roof of the car a final tap as he went.

At Möckern Bridge, he caught a train and rode out to Luisenufer.

'What do you want now, Inspector?' Hermann Schäffner asked as he opened the door, breakfast serviette still tied around his neck. 'Don't you think you and your colleagues have asked enough questions?'

'Just one more,' Rath said. 'When is the flat in the rear building available to rent again?'

Schäffner looked at him in astonishment. 'Well, if your colleagues get their act together, Monday we hope.'

'I assume you already have a new tenant?'

'Why?' Schäffner still didn't seem to understand.

'How much did Herr Müller or rather Herr Selenskij pay?'

'Not a lot. Fifteen marks a week. Is that important?'

'Furnished?'

'Of course.'

'Good. I'll take it.' Rath stretched out a hand and Hermann Schäffner shook on it, still a little baffled.

'I don't want to take up any more of your time. I'm sure you have things to do. See you on Monday.' Rath tipped his hat. He had already turned round when he stopped dead in his tracks. 'Ach,' he said, turning to face Schäffner once more. The caretaker gawped through the crack in the door like a rabbit through its wire mesh. 'One more question: I don't suppose *Sturmhauptführer* Röllecke's address has occurred to you in the meantime?'

Of course it hadn't occurred to him. Still, after a moment's thought Schäffner had at least mentioned that Röllecke probably came from Steglitz, even if he couldn't say for sure.

It was a start, Rath thought, as he requested the address shortly afterwards in the passports office. This time he didn't run into the old grouch but rather a helpful, young woman who brought him the card files he required with a smile. There weren't too many Rölleckes registered in Steglitz; one spelt their name with a 'k' only, while two others were under thirty. Rath set them aside for the time being. That left Heinrich Röllecke, resident in Ahornstrasse. Forty-one years old, and therefore probably an ex-serviceman. That was how Rath pictured an SA *Sturmhauptführer*: as a man who couldn't help himself and had to continue playing soldiers. He noted down the address and proceeded to the records office.

He was looking for the old Selenskij/Fallin file that Böhm had gone through the week before when he had had the two Russians sitting in the interrogation room. Their previous convictions obviously hadn't been enough for the bulldog to detain them any longer.

Now Selenskij was dead and Fallin had disappeared.

'Sorry, Inspector!' The records office worker returned. Not as young as the woman in passports but just as friendly. 'The file isn't there.'

'Does Böhm still have it?'

The woman looked through the index files she had brought back with her. 'No, it was requested again yesterday evening. My colleague must've given it out.'

The file was with Gennat.

He would have to speak to Buddha, even if he felt more like hiding away in his office and raking through files. It couldn't hurt to feign a little interest in the work of others; at least then he wouldn't appear like such a lone wolf.

'Good morning, Inspector,' Buddha greeted him. 'Been at Yorckstrasse I understand?'

So Plisch and Plum had snitched on him.

Rath nodded. 'Wanted to check on Fallin, but the flat is already under surveillance.'

'You should have told me yesterday that we'd already interrogated

Selenskij's friend as part of the Kardakov case,' Gennat said. 'I only found out belatedly from DCI Böhm.'

'Sorry, Superintendent, I didn't think of it right away either,' Rath lied. 'It was DCI Böhm who questioned them, not me.'

'Stop taking cheap shots at Böhm. He's going about his duties at least as conscientiously as you! It was your mistake that cost us valuable time in the search for Fallin!'

'Yes, sir.'

'Good, then I hope you take it to heart. Now get on with your work. Briefing in one hour in my office.'

Rath cleared his throat.

'What now?'

'Could I ask you for the Selenskij/Fallin file, Superintendent?'

12. February 1926.

Rath read the file in his office completely undisturbed. The two Russians had got into a fight with communists on the day in question and really filled their boots. One of the Reds had been in a wheelchair ever since, the other had needed his arm amputated. Selenskij and Fallin had admitted their involvement in the fight but denied responsibility for the injuries sustained by the victims, thereby escaping with a mild sentence. No wonder Böhm had shelved the file. Ex-Tsarist secret police who beat up Reds were the last people you'd suspect of belonging to a communist splinter group.

Whether you'd suspect them of abducting, torturing and killing their fellow countrymen in the name of the Black Hundred was an entirely different matter, however.

Rath leafed through all the police reports on the case, all of which seemed to support the judge's sentence. It wasn't until he saw the signature beneath the interrogation records that he began to wonder. They were written in a hand he recognised.

Shortly afterwards Rath was sitting in the briefing like a cat on hot bricks. As expected, there were no new findings. Although Selenskij was a strong suspect following the witness statement made by the schoolboy, he was also

sadly dead. The search for Fallin hadn't yielded anything, nor had the combing of the pine forests, which was still taking place at great expense. That
left their inquiries into the activities of *Berolina*. Red Hugo's people, otherwise good for a tip-off, tended to keep mum as soon as they became the
subject of an investigation. Rath was finding it hard to listen properly and
present his findings on his fruitless search of the *Delphi*. At least Gennat
praised him for getting hold of the decisive witnesses. But none of that mattered to Rath now; even Charly's presence left him cold. The thing he
most wanted was to storm into Bruno Wolter's office, grab him by the throat
and shake him until the bastard finally came out with the truth.

Instead he intercepted Gennat straight after the briefing.

'If you're here to complain about your assignment today, you can forget
it,' Buddha said. 'Nothing like a bit of discipline.'

'No, sir, it's something else. DCI Wolter. Did he ever work for A
Division?'

'I see you've been reading the file.' Gennat nodded and seemed to think.
'Must've been one of his final cases for us. Before the accident.'

The accident! Rath's ears pricked up. Scheer had also spoken of an accident.

'They were colleagues. Has he never told you about it? Come to think
of it, I'm not surprised. A nasty thing, it was.' Gennat took him to one side.
'Bruno Wolter is one of the best shots on the force. He used to train people
on the firing range.'

'I know. Was he still working for A Division at the time?'

'Of course. He's always been a CID officer, just one with a specific set
of skills. Whenever things threatened to get a little dicey and we needed
someone who could shoot, Wolter was brought in. He was a marksman during the war, belonged to a special unit by the end of it.'

'Shouldn't a police officer avoid using his service weapon whenever possible? There are procedures for that sort of thing, aren't there?'

'I don't need procedures, young Rath. There's nothing I hate more than
bullets spraying everywhere. Which is precisely why it's important to have
someone who knows what they're doing.'

'That someone was Bruno Wolter?'

'Yes. He was calm, didn't matter if chaos was raging all around him.
Sometimes a single shot was enough for it all to be over.'

'And for the perpetrator to be dead . . .'

'Wolter never killed a single person in the line of duty. He neutralised the bastards who insisted on waving weapons around. Very precisely. It was more like a surgical incision than a simple shot. Once you've got a hole in your hand, you can't shoot anymore, it's as simple as that. After that my men could pick up the gun-toting wailers.'

'What about the accident?'

'That's the tragic thing. It didn't even happen during an operation. Everyone would've been sympathetic if something had gone wrong there. But no, it was on the range. A young officer caught a bullet, Thies his name was, if memory serves. The best shot in his year. It was clear he ought to be working with Wolter together on the range.'

'And then?'

'The circumstances were never entirely clear. It was probably Thies's fault. He was already helping out on the range, taking care of some of the smaller maintenance jobs. One day a troop of young officers were practising with their rifles, and suddenly there was a body twitching behind the target, streaming with blood.'

'Thies.'

'Somehow he must've got into the line of fire. By the time the doctor arrived he was already dead. Killed by his own colleagues. They removed five bullets from his body.' Gennat paused, as if the memory still made him shudder. 'As I said, it was probably the boy's fault. But Wolter took responsibility and arranged for his own transfer to Vice. That's where he was least likely to have to shoot. No-one's seen him on the range since.'

Accident my arse, Rath thought. He couldn't help thinking of Jänicke's death. Had 1A already tried to place Wolter under scrutiny? The parallels were clear: a young man straight from police academy who is supposed to be working with Wolter dies a violent death.

'He never said anything to me.'

'No-one likes to talk about it at the Castle. A tragic case. Besides, the police lost their best marksman.'

'He wasn't the best officer in those days though.'

'You mean the interrogation records?' Gennat asked. 'Have you noticed how sloppily he conducted them? Still, we can hardly hold that against him now.'

Rath nodded, lost in thought. He couldn't help thinking back to his own investigation into the Wilczek case. Behind Wolter's alleged sloppiness, there appeared to be a system at work. It was as if he had let the two Russians get off deliberately.

The storm yesterday evening hadn't dispelled the humidity, and the muggy air was making his fatigue even more unbearable. Rath was sweating, even though he had wound down the window. Gennat had sent him to Yorckstrasse to take over surveillance duties from Plisch and Plum. The pair smirked when they saw who was relieving them. Next to Rath sat Reinhold Gräf, one of Böhm's people.

'What have you done to end up here?' Rath asked the assistant detective. 'Did you steal a slice of Gennat's cake?'

'I'm an assistant detective. This kind of dirty work's an everyday occurrence,' Gräf said. 'Since when were inspectors deployed for surveillance?'

'Only when they've been misbehaving,' Rath said and lit a cigarette. His last. 'I'd offer you one but . . .' he showed Gräf the empty carton.

'That's OK. I only smoke when I drink.'

'I see. Well, I'm afraid I can't conjure up a hipflask as well.'

Gräf laughed. 'So you've been misbehaving?'

'Ask Gennat.'

'I'm surprised. If you'll pardon my saying so, Böhm thinks you're the sort of person who crawls up the boss's arse.'

Rath was astonished. Hats off to the young man, speaking to an inspector like that. 'Böhm's clearly at great pains to keep that rumour in circulation.'

'He doesn't have a very high opinion of you anyway.'

'You're very open about these things. Aren't you worried about damaging your career?'

'I've always been open and honest with my colleagues, doesn't matter if I'm speaking to a superintendent or a stenographer.'

'That does you credit.' Rath flicked away a little ash from his cigarette. 'Who else is gossiping about me? Fräulein Ritter, no doubt?'

'Charly? Why would she?' Gräf seemed genuinely surprised. 'She doesn't even know you.'

They sat together in silence for a time. Finally, Rath flicked his cigarette stub through the open window onto the road. He opened the door.

'I'm just going to stretch my legs, and buy some more cigarettes. You hold the fort in the meantime.'

'Understood, Inspector.' Gräf tipped his hat. 'You go on. That's why there are two of us here.'

Rath proceeded down the street a little. The exercise was better for his fatigue than the numerous cigarettes he had smoked. He glanced at the time. Eleven past eleven. *Kölle Alaaf!* Up Cologne! He had only been in the car for an hour and already it felt like an eternity. He had better things to do than sit warming his arse in a Prussian police vehicle. Finally taking Bruno Wolter to task, for one. They wouldn't be relieved until six o'clock; it was going to be a long day.

He turned right into Grossbeerenstrasse at the first crossroads. With the green Opel out of sight he felt instantly freer. Somehow he had the feeling that Gennat had sent Gräf to keep an eye on him.

He found what he was looking for just round the corner: a branch of *Loeser und Wolff*, typically enough located right next to a pharmacy. Inside the tobacconist's was dimly lit and sedately appointed. Rath had to wait to be served, and spent the time looking at some nice table lighters. It was his father's birthday soon; it couldn't hurt to start thinking about his present. The shop assistant seemed almost a little disappointed when in the end Rath purchased only cigarettes—even if it was a few cartons of Overstolz as well as a pack of matches.

He was just taking his change when he thought he saw a familiar face on the pavement outside, amongst the hordes of pedestrians streaming past the display window.

The short blonde hair confused him; he remembered the face under the midnight-blue hat differently, framed by dark hair. The face of Lana Nikoros, or Countess Svetlana Sorokina. He stuffed the coins into his pocket and rushed outside, unconcerned by the surprise on the face of the assistant.

She had gone towards Victoria Park. At the end of the street rose the green of the Kreuzberg, before it the heads of passers-by bobbing up and down like heaving ocean waves. He tried to discern her blue hat in the throng. There were a lot of hats. Although he could no longer see the midnight blue, he continued in the same direction. At Kreuzbergstrasse he could just make out a blue hat disappearing into the park. The path wound up the mountain and past a waterfall, until finally he saw her sitting on a bench. Her back was turned to him. Quietly, he drew closer.

'Countess Sorokina, I presume?'

She turned round. A woman who was as gaunt as she was ugly stared back at him. A woman he had never seen before.

She gazed at him as if he had lost his mind. 'And who might you be?' she asked. 'Lord Muck or the Emperor of China?'

Rath mumbled an apology, tipped his hat briefly and went back down the path.

Had he pursued a phantom? Was his fatigue making him see things?

He had to get back to the car, he had left Gräf alone far too long already. Hopefully the assistant detective didn't have a weak bladder.

Reinhold Gräf opened the window on the passenger's side to let some air into the vehicle. When the inspector returned, he would ask him to smoke less. He would rather have done this stretch with Charly than the newbie, even if Rath wasn't nearly as bad as Böhm made out. True, he was a little hard to read, but otherwise he seemed OK. Just a little overworked. Smoked a lot too.

Gräf savoured the fresh air and stuck his head out of the window. No-one was paying him any attention anyway. Out on the street there was still no hint of the approaching weekend in the faces of the pedestrians as they scampered past, only the everyday stresses of the working week. Meanwhile, car drivers tooted their horns if progress in front of them was too slow. In truth, it wasn't a day to be sitting in a car observing a house. Still, that was the reality of police work: for the most part it was boring. Charly would have made the boredom easier to endure.

Suddenly, there was something happening in front of the house. A taxi stopped outside the entrance. A powerful-looking man with a scar running across his cheek emerged, suitcase in one hand, and as he handed the driver his fare, he turned to face Gräf.

All of a sudden his boredom had evaporated. Gräf reached nervously for the photo. No doubt about it: the same scar, the same man! Nikita Fallin had arrived home.

What was he supposed to do now? Go after him straightaway? Better to wait, hold his nerve, the inspector would be back any minute. He'd only gone to get cigarettes.

A glance at the time. Quarter past eleven. After what felt like half an hour, he took a second glance. Sixteen minutes past. He couldn't wait any longer. He'd never forgive himself if the Russian slipped through his fingers just because he was waiting for the inspector.

Gräf checked his pistol and pocketed his cuffs, climbed out of the car and went over to the house. He'd just have to arrest the guy on his own. Inspector Rath would be amazed when he returned. While he's off buying cigarettes, the assistant detective goes and arrests a murder suspect!

He removed the pistol from its holster as he entered the house. In the great, shadowy stairwell he could hear rasping voices a few storeys above. Could it be Fallin? He lived on the fourth floor. What was taking him so long? Had he checked his mailbox first, leafed through his post? Gräf took the safety catch off the pistol and began to climb the stairs as quietly as possible. For a few moments, he could hear only the sound of his own breath allied to the low creak of the steps. Slowly he worked his way up to the second floor.

Then came the jangle of a keyring, and a moment later a woman's voice echoed through the stairwell.

'Nikita?'

The voice came from above. Gräf considered whether he should lean over the banister and look to see who had shouted, who had been waiting for the Russian, when suddenly there was a crackling noise like the sound of wood snapping, followed by a short, sharp cry and a low thud. There was a second thud and the cry died away, as if the air had been sucked out of it; then a third, as a heavy body struck the handrail in front of Gräf, fingers clasping a broken chunk of banister as if they might still find a purchase. Gräf heard the sound of bones breaking before the body rebounded and fell further into the depths, arms and legs twisting wildly. One final crash and all was still.

The assistant detective stood flabbergasted, pistol still cocked in his hand. He rushed to the banister and looked down. On the pale stone floor, lay a powerful-looking man in a dark suit, arms and legs strangely contorted. The image almost resembled a swastika. A bright-red trickle of blood was oozing from under the black body, spreading quickly and growing thicker all the time.

The assistant detective put away his pistol and stumbled down the steps.

The man was lying face down in an ever expanding pool of blood, beside him the broken chunk of banister. Gräf leaned over the body and turned the man's head to one side. A scar ran right across the left cheek.

The creaking of the steps made Gräf look up. A dainty woman was gazing upon the dead man and the blood. Eyes wide open, white as a sheet.

'Is he dead?'

Gräf's felt his neck in vain for a pulse. He nodded.

'My God!' The woman was already at the door. 'Stay here. I'll get the police.'

'Stop,' Gräf called after her, 'I *am* the police!' She was already gone, but it wouldn't hurt if she came back with a few cops. That way he could stay with the corpse.

He listened into the silence. Everything was quiet. Had no-one in the house heard anything apart from the young woman?

In the dark of the stairwell, he had been unable to make out her face, but in her appearance and manner, she had almost reminded him a little of Charly. Only, this woman was blonde; and Charly would never have worn a blue hat.

Rath had been away for almost half an hour in total when he finally returned to Yorckstrasse. The green Opel was still parked in the shadow of a tree on the corner of the street. Exactly as he had left it—except for one detail. It was empty.

At first Rath thought that Gräf had simply leaned forward to pick up his notepad or something, but as he drew closer he realised his initial impression had been correct.

Gräf was no longer in the car!

Where the hell had the assistant detective got to? Had he actually no longer been able to stand the build-up of pressure in his bladder and disappeared into the nearest pub to use the toilet? Was he making a relieved face even now?

He hadn't even locked the Opel. Rath shook his head and sat back in the driver's seat. In vain he looked for a piece of paper, any sort of message. He opened a packet of Overstolz and lit a cigarette. Well, the lad would soon be back. Hopefully he had prepared a decent excuse. And hopefully Fallin hadn't slipped through their fingers.

Fallin! Of course! There was another possibility: Nikita Fallin had returned!

Hopefully nothing had happened to the boy. If his past was anything to go by, the burly Russian was capable of anything.

Rath checked his Mauser, pulled his hat a little lower over his forehead and got out of the car. Slowly he moved over to the house, smoking, head bowed. If Fallin was looking out of the window, he didn't want him to recognise a familiar face from *Kakadu*. He trod his cigarette out before opening the front door.

Whatever he had been expecting, it wasn't this.

On the half landing Assistant Detective Reinhold Gräf was crouched over the corpse of a man whose scar face identified him beyond any doubt as Nikita Fallin.

31

It was just after four when he dropped Gräf off at the station. At least the observation had been cut short; Gennat hadn't detailed the relief until six o'clock. Rath had alerted the Castle from the first telephone he could find, and only then called the 103rd precinct in Möckernstrasse. He didn't want to be accused of not giving his division chief enough information this time. Let Buddha come out in the murder wagon to see for himself!

He came too. Gennat hadn't driven out to a crime scene for a long time. It was clear to all officers present that something must be up if Buddha himself was stepping out of the murder wagon.

This time it was one hundred percent certain they were dealing with a murder. Gräf had told them he had witnessed the fall, and the chunk of banister lying next to the corpse clearly displayed saw marks. The suspicion that someone had transformed the banister into a deadly trap was confirmed when Forensics examined the fourth floor. A big chunk was missing from directly opposite the door to Fallin's flat, where his suitcase was still standing. The banister had been carefully sawn into. In his reconstruction of events, which Rath supported, Gräf had claimed it was probably the woman's cry that had enticed the Russian over to the banister in the first place. He had leaned over to see who was calling him, before plummeting to his death.

The identity of the woman and the possibility that she had intentionally lured Scar Face into the trap was just a hunch at first. However, it was corroborated by the knowledge that the woman, whom Gräf had seen, hadn't called the police as promised. Quite the opposite, she had fled from them.

Gräf, who was inconsolable at his *faux pas*, had been unable to make out her face in the dark stairwell. The only thing he had noticed was her blue hat. Rath could imagine whom the assistant detective had encountered, but preferred to keep it to himself. Not only because he wasn't sure if he really had seen the Countess on Grossbeerenstrasse just before, he also believed that a dirty pig like Nikita Fallin deserved his violent end.

Like Vitali Selenskij before him. Two Black Hundredists who for more than three years had been eating out of the hand of an unscrupulous *Stahlhelmer*. Who had tortured Kardakov and the hapless Boris so brutally. Bruno Wolter's sadistic helpers.

Now both were dead and the thought that their avenging angel, Countess Sorokina, might also pick up the trail of Uncle secretly filled Rath with satisfaction.

It was more likely, however, that she had no idea the two Black Hundredists were in cahoots with a Prussian police officer. Only he knew that, Gereon Rath.

After he dropped Gräf off at Alex, Rath drove on to Potsdamer station. The motor pool could wait on the vehicle, Rath still had things to do. The officers at the Castle would just have to make do without him today.

First of all he went to the station and opened his locker. What a hotchpotch of items he had accumulated: a notebook, a pistol, a photo of wartime companions, a telephone ripped from the wall. And a packet of cocaine. All his dirty secrets were here.

He took the cocaine and stowed it in his pocket. Now he needed it. The sleeplessness of the last few nights was beginning to take its toll. Sometimes he couldn't tell if he was awake or dreaming. Was there really someone standing behind him? Or was it just his shadow? He had to be careful he wasn't seeing ghosts.

Before he returned to the car, he locked himself in one of the cubicles in the station toilet. He didn't have much experience when it came to taking cocaine. He tried to remember that night in *Venuskeller*, the generous Oppenberg and the nymphomaniac Vivian. Rath knew he needed a surface that was halfway flat as well as something to snort with, so he used his ID and a twenty mark note. Werner von Siemens gazed at him sternly, almost reproachfully, as Rath rolled him into a little tube. The white powder in the packet was lumpier than the stuff in *Venuskeller*. He cut it with the help of his Mauser until he thought it was fine enough for his nose, then laid a line out ready. He didn't want to take too much, not knowing how strong the dose was. He stuck the paper tube in his nose and snorted the white powder up like a vacuum cleaner.

That numbness again, and then the desired effect. A wreck only moments before from extreme lack of sleep, he suddenly felt immense energy coursing through his veins. Quickly, he stowed the equipment away, splashed a little cold water on his face and proceeded through the station concourse back to the car. He could have uprooted a tree, but he felt more like cutting Bruno Wolter down to size.

Still, one thing at a time. He drove out to Steglitz.

Ahornstrasse was in a nice, middle-class district. Rath parked the Opel and rang the doorbell. It didn't take long for someone to answer.

There was no need to ask if he was in the right place. The man in front of him was wearing a brown uniform, a black belt and the armband that was increasingly common in Berlin these days: blood-red with a black swastika framed by a white circle. Otherwise, he didn't look especially military. More small and slight, like a bookkeeper. Rath had caught him knotting his tie.

'Yes?' he said.

'Heinrich Röllecke?'

'What can I do for you?'

Rath had a flash of inspiration. 'I'm a friend of Bruno Wolter,' he said.

'Bruno? Why isn't he here himself?'

'Lots to do at the moment. Besides, he needs to be careful. He's still under surveillance.'

'The political police should be more concerned with the Red Front than making trouble for their own . . . Blast!' Röllecke began knotting his tie once more. 'Well, get to the point, man! I have to get to a meeting. The *Gauleiter* is speaking. Dr Goebbels doesn't beat around the bush, so the SA need to be there on time. Before the Reds even think about kicking up a stink. I hope you understand. I'd ask you in otherwise.'

'That's OK. I think we can keep it brief. It's about what happens next on Luisenufer.'

'An infuriating business! I said from the start we should have used a German. But Bruno absolutely insisted on this Russian. Now he's dead.'

'At least it was a Russian that died, not a German!'

Röllecke laughed. 'You're right there. I like you, young man. Our country needs men like you!'

'Selenskij's death is being investigated as murder.'

'Well, probably couldn't have been avoided. A stupid mistake. Now the police are snooping around. It'll calm down again, we just need to be a little patient.'

'Don't you think that Hermann Schäffner could be a problem . . .'

'*Scharführer* Schäffner is a reliable man. The fact that the police turned the flat upside down wasn't his fault. Besides, they won't find anything: he's seen to that.'

'If you say so.'

'You can count on the SA, my friend! We're no less reliable than you *Stahlhelmer*. It isn't words that count but actions, and it's time the *Stahlhelm* got that into their heads. Bruno's been talking about a new consignment for weeks, yet nothing's happened. My people are growing impatient. I've given them a few rusty rifles we finagled out of the Red Front. Absolute rubbish, all of it. At some point we're going to need some decent weapons.'

'Of course.'

'I'm glad you see it that way too. Please inform Lieutenant Wolter that if the loyalty of nationally minded fighters isn't to be sorely tested, it's time to put his money where his mouth is!'

'I'll do that Herr *Sturmhauptführer.*'

'Good. Now if you'll excuse me, I need to get ready. My driver will be here in a moment.'

Rath was unable to say goodbye, as Röllecke had already slammed the door.

The vain, self-righteous squirt! Rath was shuddering as he returned to the car. Röllecke had bought his story without a second thought.

It was exactly as he had suspected. Bruno Wolter and his friends in the SA had secured Selenskij the flat on Luisenufer in order to monitor the Countess. The DCI with the affable face was an arms dealer. An arms dealer who would stop at nothing.

He had to take him to task. He wanted to hear it from him. The truth, or the lie. Bruno would have to look him in the face.

He couldn't say what he was hoping to achieve; he only knew that he had no choice. He had to show Wolter there was someone who had seen right through him and his shady deals.

Rath felt his heart beat faster as he turned into Friedenau from Rhein-strasse.

The man was at home. E Division had finished early for the evening. Rath parked directly behind the black Ford. He rang but no-one answered. As he listened to the echo of the doorbell, he became aware of a rattling, clunking noise and gazed round the corner into the garden where they had sat during Whitsun. The garden furniture was still outside, and Uncle was trudging up and down the lawn wearing loose work slacks, a sleeveless vest and a broad-brimmed old hat as he pushed the mower back and forth. A regular citizen going about his evening tasks, it was scarcely credible that this man was a cold-blooded killer. Rath went behind the house.

Bruno only saw him when he reached the lawn. He left the reel mower where it was and took a few steps towards Rath, wiping his sweaty hands on his vest.

'What a surprise,' he said. 'Knocking off already? And people are saying how much A Division have had on recently.'

'They're not wrong. We've just had to scrape a man off a stone floor. Tried to fly through the stairwell. Yesterday a dead Russian, and today more of the same. These people live life on the edge, maybe they picked the wrong fight.'

'Or maybe they're just stupid. That's my theory anyway.'

'There was me thinking you had a high opinion of them. Of Selenskij at any rate. That's what Heinrich Röllecke said.'

Surprise registered briefly on Bruno's face. 'So, you were at Röllecke's?'

'Yes, and he was rather talkative!'

'Doesn't sound like him.'

'You're lagging behind with your consignment. He doesn't like that.'

Although Bruno still had himself under control, Rath could see the little digs and provocations were hitting home.

'You don't look too healthy, Gereon. Can you tell me why your eyes are twitching like that? Have to be careful you don't go to the dogs in A Division. The work doesn't seem to agree with you.'

'We've a lot on at the moment.'

'Then take a holiday.'

'Not while there's a guilty bastard still on the loose.'

'Come on, the case is closed. You solved it: patriotic Russians eliminating a few Reds from their home country. The killers are dead, all is well. Time to let it go, rest on your laurels for a while.'

'Closed, my arse. There are still too many open questions.'

'Who cares?'

'I do, for one. It's just that the killers can't help us anymore.'

'Then you'll have to figure it out on your own.'

'I know more than you think. There's only one thing I don't understand: why did Fallin and Selenskij torture Boris before they packed him off in a stolen car and sent him flying into the canal?'

'Maybe they just messed up. It can happen. First the guy dies on them before they can get anything useful out of him, then they try to cover up the whole thing and start a campaign of disinformation. Only it fails.'

'It was supposed to look like Boris had pinched the gold from the *Red Fortress*?'

'If you say so,' said Wolter with a shrug. 'Sounds plausible to me.'

'I don't think so. It stretches credibility when someone with mangled hands and feet is found in a car he's supposed to have driven himself, don't you think?'

'Not if the car ends up in front of a tree and the driver's already mush. Maybe that was the plan, until the wheel spun out of control at the kerb and everything went tits up. By which stage things were already dead in the water. Or should I say the canal.'

Rath remembered how the vehicle had shaved a tree on its way in.

'Then why did they dig up Kardakov's corpse?' he asked. 'Was that part of another failed disinformation campaign?'

'What do you mean failed? They made the police look pretty ridiculous there. Above all the new hero of A Division. They made him into a laughing stock.'

'Maybe. I'm just wondering why they'd bother. A Division weren't interested in the Russians. On the contrary, they'd released them a week before. So why would they care about making the police look ridiculous?'

'What do I know? I'm a vice cop, not a homicide detective.'

'You know damn well. It was their skipper who'd run into difficulties, a police officer who had murdered a colleague and realised an old friend was closing in on him. An officer who along with everything else was also having problems with a *Ringverein*. So he tried not only to create trouble for this *Ringverein*, but for the police as well—to distract them, above all the new hero of A Division, as you call him.'

'I prefer laughing stock . . .'

'Dumb luck that this laughing stock won't let go then, isn't it? He's hell bent on convicting a CID officer of his colleague's murder.'

'Everyone's entitled to make a fool of themselves. Like I say, I'd recommend you take a holiday. Be satisfied with what you've got. I've just given you some excellent fodder for the commissioner.'

'Would you be prepared to testify to it in court?'

'Why should I? It's all just speculation. An experienced CID officer gives an up-and-coming officer a tip-off. It's up to you to find the evidence. *You're* the homicide detective, I work in E Division.'

'I could use your assertions against you, as proof that you're in cahoots with the Russians, and Josef Wilczek too. As proof that you're after the Sorokin gold, that you intend to use it to buy weapons for the *Stahlhelm*, that you've been trafficking police arms for years with Rudi Scheer, cutting deals with your volunteer army, the SA and God knows who else.'

'With the Red Front too, no doubt?' Wolter laughed loudly. He removed his hat and wiped his sweaty brow with a handkerchief. 'You've got a big mouth for a cop with a cocaine problem.'

'I just want to make it clear that you've reached the end,' Rath countered. 'You killed Jänicke for nothing. Just because it worked with Thies doesn't mean you'll get away a second time.'

'*Me* at the end?' Bruno grinned, but looked as if he'd sooner have lashed out. 'Have you looked in the mirror recently, Gereon? Do you think the court is going to believe a coked-up cop who shot someone and then botched the cover-up?'

'I haven't shot anyone.'

'You shot someone in Cologne, remember? And you killed Josef Wilczek. Why else would you have given Ballistics the wrong bullet? It can only have been you.'

'What you've just told me is as good as a confession. A confession that you killed Jänicke!'

'Ach, would you cut it out!'

'You know that Jänicke was killed with Krajewski's Lignose because you're the one who pulled the trigger!'

'But where's the pistol now? It isn't in *my* possession, Inspector! Make sure you don't dig yourself a hole you can't get out of.'

'Do you even know why you became a police officer?'

'For the same reason I still am one. To maintain law and order and fight against those trying to destroy it. What about you? Why did you become a police officer? Because Daddy told you to?'

Rath ignored the jibe. 'My reason is very simple. I'm a police officer so that bastards like you don't get off scot free.'

'We all deserve punishment. You're a Catholic, you should know that.'

'I can go to confession.'

'Then go.' Wolter smirked. 'Stop pretending you have less to confess than me!'

'You shouldn't brag so much! I can finish you if I want to!'

'Really? If you tell the truth about you and Josef Wilczek then perhaps you'll have something on me. Perhaps. It would, of course, presuppose that you're a credible witness. And there I have my doubts. Still, if you want, you can always take that chance. Tell them what you did with Wilczek! Tell them why Inspector Gereon Rath made no progress on the Wilczek case! Let's see what happens. I won't be doing it. I can promise you that much. I won't be leaving you holding the greasy end of the stick. Don't ask me why. For old time's sake, perhaps.'

'You really are a cynical arsehole.'

'I'm a police officer and a realist. If you just thought about it for a moment, you'd realise I have more on you than you have on me. But that's not what this is about. I want peace. So why don't we just forget about the whole thing and pretend it never happened? Serve up the two dead Russians as the killers, and Zörgiebel will be happy. Why? How? Wherefore? No-one's interested in these questions anymore. You want a career with CID, don't you? Then you have to turn a blind eye occasionally, and not ask too many questions.'

'Don't you dare tell me what I have to do!'

Wolter looked him and up down, squinting. 'Please excuse me. Emmi will be back any moment and I want to be finished with the lawn by then.' He put his hat back on, turned round and trudged back to his lawnmower.

Rath looked at his broad, sweaty back, helpless with rage. When he was back in the car he slammed the flat of his hand against the steering wheel so hard it hurt.

The worst thing about it was that Wolter was right. There was nothing he could do, absolutely nothing. He couldn't even find an outlet for his rage.

32

She was in the middle of tracing her eyebrows when the doorbell rang. It couldn't be him already. Or could it? If he was one of those overly punctual types, then the evening would be over before it had even begun.

'Greta, can you see who it is?' she called from the bathroom door. 'It's almost certainly for you!'

She wasn't expecting him for a good hour. Ten o'clock, she had said. She had got back from the station at eight, needing a little time to recover after such a lousy day.

Gereon Rath had reported another corpse. Every day it was someone new. The murder suspects were dropping around him like flies. Only, *these* dead Russians might actually be the killers. Unlike Kardakov, with whom he had made Böhm look a fool, only for it to emerge that he had been duped himself. She had almost felt sorry for him, the way the whole Castle made fun of him for selling Zörgiebel a dead man as the killer, but she had pushed aside her sympathy. He deserved everything he had coming, a thousand times over. The way he had treated Böhm, the way he had treated *her*. She thought she had finally found a man who might last longer than a week. Much longer, perhaps even the rest of her life. Yes, she had fallen in love. How unforgivably foolish! It made what he had done to her even worse, the dirty swine!

Now at last Herr Rath had his killers. There was no doubt the Russians had tortured their two fellow countrymen, and they had probably killed them too. A storage shed with a cellar had been rented in Nikita Fallin's name on the site of the *Anhalter* goods station. ED had found traces of blood on the concrete floor, in addition to various tools, among them a large sledgehammer, likewise stained with blood. There were large quantities of heroin hidden in a spare tyre, and in the warehouse above they had found a number of cars, all stolen, some with fresh paintwork. The Russians seemed to have been running such a lucrative car dealership that they had been prepared to use one of their own stolen vehicles to plunge their first victim into the canal.

Unfortunately, that part would have to remain a mystery. Zörgiebel wouldn't mind: who needed a motive? The important thing was that the murders were solved!

Nevertheless, it looked as though someone had had a major hand in both their deaths. An electric hairdryer didn't fall into the bath of its own accord; and the banister in Yorckstrasse had been prepared in advance.

Reinhold had been obliged to eat some humble pie for letting the woman escape. He couldn't even describe her properly, because he had only caught a brief glimpse of her in the gloomy stairwell, most of it spent staring into the light. To atone for his error he had stayed at the Castle until Gennat had almost booted him out. Quite unlike Gereon Rath, whose whereabouts were still unknown. The man was taking too many liberties, even for Buddha, who usually gave his officers plenty of leeway.

But reporting a corpse and hanging around the crime scene, only to leave others to do the dirty work, wasn't how to endear yourself to Gennat. Or Böhm for that matter, but he couldn't stand Gereon Rath anyway.

There was a knock on the bathroom door. Greta poked her red head through the crack in the door.

'Charly? Are you decent?'

'Just about. Why?'

'Visitor for you.'

'Who is it?'

'Someone from the station.'

She examined her face in the mirror. Good enough for someone from the Castle. Did Reinhold want to have a cry on her shoulder? The assistant detective could be a little sensitive at times. Especially when he had made a mistake.

She emerged from the bathroom to discover the man she had least been expecting to see standing in the hall. The man who had been missing in action at the station today. Gereon Rath.

He looked a shadow of his former self. Pitiful. Dark circles under the eyes, sunken cheeks, as if he hadn't eaten or slept for days. What was the matter with him? He had tracked down the last of his killers, hadn't he? Even if only as a corpse.

Upon seeing her he smiled in embarrassment, almost apologetically in fact.

'Good evening, Inspector,' she said coldly, and the smile on his face faded.

'I'd forgotten we were addressing each other formally,' he said. 'To be quite honest, I don't want to play these games anymore.'

'Who said we were playing games?'

Greta cleared her throat. 'Charlotte, I'll be in my room if you need anything.'

Now they were alone. What did he want? At least he hadn't brought her flowers; she'd have beaten him over the head with them.

'Can we sit down somewhere? I need to talk to you.'

'I wasn't aware we had anything to talk about, Inspector! I must ask you to leave.'

'And if I don't want to?'

'Then *I'll* leave. And fetch the police. You ought to be familiar with the crime of trespassing.'

She reached indiscriminately in her wardrobe for a coat and stormed past him. The pig-headed fool!

She was already down by the front door when she heard his footsteps behind her on the stairs. Well, if he wanted a chase, he could have one!

He had known it wouldn't be easy, but he hadn't thought she'd actually run away from him. For a moment he thought it was just a stupid joke and she'd be right back, but what if she took a little longer and returned with a few cops? The nearest police station was just around the corner in Paulstrasse. Rath uttered a quiet curse as he ran out after her. When he emerged onto the street he gazed around searchingly. On one side of Spenerstrasse rose Moabit prison, on the other the lines of the city railway. There was no sign of Charly.

Rath ran to the nearest corner. Melanchthonstrasse. The link road to Paulstrasse: the 28th precinct was right on the corner, but she hadn't gone in this direction. He turned round, catching sight of her black coat disappearing into Calvinstrasse. She was running down to the Spree. He sprinted after her, at least now he knew where she was, and caught up with her just before the bridge leading to Bellevue station.

He held her tight so she couldn't get away again.

'Let me go,' she hissed. 'You're hurting me!'

At least she hadn't called him 'inspector'. He almost smiled.

'Now listen to me, dammit!' he wheezed, completely out of breath. She struggled like a wild horse. A few people were staring at them. 'You can't just run away from me!'

'Yes I can! You repulse me!'

'If that's your way of saying I'm the one who messed things up between us—thank you, but not necessary! I'm well aware of it. If I could turn back time, I would. My secrecy was . . .'

'You sounded me out! You used me! Pretended to have feelings for me! Are you surprised that I don't want to see you? Get away from me! It's enough that I have to put up with you at the station.'

'Just listen to me, that's all I'm asking. I shouldn't have treated you like that, I should have been more open with you. That's exactly what I'd like to do now, be open with you! I want to tell you everything! Hit you with so many secrets it'll make you dizzy.'

'If you want me back and this is some cheap trick to talk me round, then forget it!' Her eyes flashed at him.

'I only want to talk to you. It's not about us. It's about me. I don't know what to do anymore.'

'Why do you think I'll listen?'

'I can only ask you to.'

'Why me, of all people?'

'You're the only person in this city I trust. I'm in such a fucking mess. I . . .'

'Don't take this the wrong way, Gereon, but that's how you look too: a fucking mess.'

He must have gazed at her in surprise. For a moment, she was serious. Then, gradually, the corners of her mouth turned upwards, her dimple appeared and he knew she would listen. How long he had waited to see that smile!

In the hotel room he had paced up and down like a caged tiger, feeling himself gripped by fatigue as the cocaine gradually wore off. Yet he found no peace. He still hadn't got over his meeting with Bruno Wolter, his anger at Uncle, at his own impotence. He was at his wits' end. What should he do? Look on from the sidelines as a murderer went about his work at the station as if nothing had happened? Smile as he played the model police officer? Or should he make an accusation against him?

The public prosecutor would demand evidence and Rath would have to incriminate himself. In the end Wolter would fix it so that they pinned the Jänicke murder on the self-confessed killer, Gereon Rath. A motive would be easy enough to find: the assistant detective had figured out that Inspector Rath had buried Saint Josef, and so Rath had killed him too. It wasn't any more far-fetched than the truth. If anything it was more plausible.

Rath was at the end of his tether. He couldn't fight the lone fight any longer. He needed help. There was only one person he knew he could trust, and so he had pushed his pride to one side and driven out to Charly.

As they strolled through the castle grounds on the other side of the Spree, dusk was already falling and they could have been mistaken for a pair of lovers as they walked side by side.

He told her everything.

How he had investigated Kardakov under his own steam, how Wilczek had assaulted him and how he had died; how he had buried the corpse and fudged the subsequent investigation. And how he was therefore the only person who knew that Bruno Wolter had shot Stephan Jänicke.

He told her about the cocaine and the fatal shooting in Cologne, even if the latter had nothing to do with current events. He only omitted a single detail, his bizarre amorous escapade with Elisabeth Behnke.

Charly listened in silence, the smile on her face long since evaporated.

'I think I need a coffee,' she said when he had finished. 'You look like you could use one too. Maybe even three.'

She was actually shocked. In truth, she had thought nothing more could surprise her but what Gereon had just told her had rendered her speechless.

They returned to Spenerstrasse in silence. The streetlights were shining already.

'I was about to report you missing,' Greta said, when they arrived back.

Charlotte could tell just by looking at her friend how curious she was. She waved her away discreetly when Gereon wasn't looking, and Greta disappeared back to her room.

'Would you like something to eat?' she asked, fiddling with the stove as she put the water on to boil. The way he was sitting there, like a soldier wearied by defeat, aroused her maternal instinct. He seemed like he could really use the coffee; he looked as if he was about to fall off his chair.

'Thank you,' he said. 'But I couldn't eat a thing.'

'I hope that's not a dig at my culinary skills . . .'

'. . . which I haven't experienced yet.'

'I could only have offered you a sandwich anyway.'

'Coffee's fine.'

The water was just boiling when there was a ring at the door.

She looked at the clock above the kitchen table. Three minutes to ten. Her date! In all the excitement she had completely forgotten.

Georg Siegert, a colleague of Greta's. She had dragged him out here, said he could be someone for Charly. Charly had given in, but she could really do without him now. Besides, she no longer had any desire to go out.

She ran to the door, before Greta hit on the idea of opening it.

Herr Siegert was standing there, a triumphant smile on his face, proffering a bouquet of flowers.

'Beautiful flowers for an even more beautiful lady,' he said.

The line was exceptionally stupid, but Herr Siegert's cause was already lost.

Charly took no notice of the plants in his hand. Orchids! She hated orchids!

'How dare you!' she said. 'What impudence!'

Georg Siegert clearly wasn't sure what it was he had dared to do.

'Sorry?'

'If there's one thing I can't stand, Herr Siegert, it's people who aren't on time!'

'I don't understand,' the man said, allowing the hand with the bouquet to drop finally. 'I thought we said ten?'

'Then take a look at your watch! You're two minutes *early!* And you rang even before that! Good evening.'

With that she slammed the door in his face.

The water for the coffee was still boiling when she returned, and Gereon Rath was still sitting at her kitchen table, but she should have been quicker with that coffee. His chin was slumped on his chest. He had fallen asleep.

When he awoke, his nose was filled with her scent.

'Charly,' he mumbled, embracing the pillow. His hands reached out for her but found nothing. He opened his eyes. The bedding smelt of her, but she was nowhere to be seen.

He sat up. Where was he? A cosy little room. Charly's room! Rath stretched out. He hadn't felt this good in days. Above all, he felt well rested, and he had slept in *her* bed! It didn't matter that she hadn't slept in it herself. It hadn't stopped her flitting through his dreams, her and her scent. He pressed his nose against the pillow and breathed in deeply.

The memory of yesterday evening returned only gradually. He had told her everything, he could remember that much, that was no dream. She hadn't sent him packing. She had even tried to make him coffee. That was the last thing he remembered, him sitting in the kitchen while she stood at the stove making coffee.

He stood up and went over to the window. The sun was shining. His things lay neatly folded on a chair. She had undressed him down to his underwear.

Slowly he opened the door and peered outside. There was no-one in the hall. He wondered if the bathroom was free. The door was slightly ajar. The coast was clear! He slipped out of the room.

Rath gazed into the bathroom mirror. He could do with a shave, but there was nothing he could use here. He splashed water on his face and washed his upper body, put a little toothpaste on his index finger, cleaned his teeth as best he could, and washed his mouth out with some Odol.

His reflection still didn't inspire confidence, but at least he felt fresh.

He went into Charly's room and got dressed. Using the comb from his jacket he slicked his still wet hair back, and went into the kitchen.

There was no-one here either, but the breakfast table was laid. The clock showed half past nine. He hadn't slept this late for a long time.

He wondered where she could have gone. And her friend, Greta. Then it dawned on him.

Of course! The Castle! Charly worked almost every Sunday.

He put some water on to boil and poured the coffee beans into the grinder on the wall. He wanted to have a coffee and then drive back to the hotel to freshen up. The Opel must still be parked outside. It was time to take it back to the station. He would have to think up a story about why he had kept the vehicle overnight, but that would be easy enough. Some observation or other, pursuit of a suspect . . . police duty was full of imponderables.

He heard a key turning in the door and, a moment later, Charly poked her head round the corner.

'Sleep well?' she asked, waving a paper bag. 'I got us a few bread rolls.'

'Don't you have to work?'

'I asked Böhm if I could use up a few hours of overtime. He said yes.' She sat at the table and opened the bag of bread rolls. 'But *you* ought to put in an appearance at the Castle. Gennat's probably been asking for you already.'

'That'll please old Böhm, won't it? My getting in trouble?' Rath poured the boiling water into the filter.

'I think you two should talk things out. It'd be better if you worked together, instead of trying to do the dirty on each other.'

He placed the coffee pot on the table and sat down beside her. 'Maybe I should tell him what I told you yesterday. If we're going to have a heart-to-heart.'

His tone was plainly sarcastic, but Charly took no notice.

'Why not?' she asked.

'Are you serious?'

'Böhm is perhaps the wrong person, but you should tell someone at the station, perhaps Gennat.'

'*The Full Ernst?* You mean I should buddy up with Buddha?'

'Someone that you can trust at least. The best thing would be to go straight to Zörgiebel. People say you're on good terms with him.'

'In the canteen.'

'I'm serious, Gereon! Wipe the slate. If you want to look yourself in the mirror again without getting the creeps, it's your only chance.'

'Maybe a shave would be enough.'

'I mean it. If you want Bruno Wolter to get the punishment he deserves, if you want all these dirty deals to stop, if you want justice, then you have to tell the whole truth. There's no other way. Or do you want to spend the rest of your life covering for a murderer?'

'I barely have any proof. And I've broken so many rules in the last few days—more than some people manage in a career. It doesn't matter who I tell, my career with the police will be over.'

'That's a possibility.' She said it evenly. 'They'll probably throw you out for good. You have to take that into account.'

'Thanks for the tip! But I'm a cop, I can't do anything else.'

'Then become a private detective.'

'Spy on unfaithful wives? Act as a bodyguard for a UFA film star? Thanks, but no thanks!'

'Sometimes life doesn't give you any other choice.'

'Christ, Charly! What the hell have I gone and done! If I had just told you everything straightaway, things would never have got this far.'

'If, would; they're words I don't like. It is how it is. Look the facts in the eye. What's done is done.'

'That sounds pretty harsh.'

'Life is harsh, Inspector.'

'Are you always such a fatalist? What about us? What's done is done—does that still apply?'

She hesitated a moment before answering.

'I haven't cried over a man since I was seventeen,' she said. 'And I promised myself that it wouldn't happen again.' She surveyed him with that cold gaze he so dreaded. 'I didn't keep my promise, Gereon. I cried over you, you bastard! Do you think I want to put myself through that again?'

He didn't have to explain to Gennat what he had been up to. It was utter bedlam at the Castle.

They had found the grave, and not just the one Alexej Kardakov had been in for weeks before it was dug up in the middle of the Spandau Forest. They had come upon a real cemetery. Under a carpet of yellowing pine needles, the cops had also found a missing Soviet embassy employee named

Vadim Troschin, as well as two German Red Front fighters, whom the police had assumed had gone underground in the wake of the RFB ban.

Underground was about right, joked Henning, who was working on the two men's files. They had actually been in police custody during the May disturbances but had obviously messed with the wrong people on release.

That Selenskij and Fallin had dug the graves was almost certain: the tyre tracks ED had found in Spandau Forest matched a stolen DKW steam car they had taken in the day before at Fallin's goods shed. Kronberg's people had even found the odd pine needle in its tread. Rath would have bet anything the same DKW had spent some time parked outside the cemetery in Greifswalder Strasse three days ago.

Slowly but surely a picture was emerging. Zörgiebel would be pleased. They had the killers, and Gereon Rath had played his part in catching them. They had resolved most of the questions. Now only one remained. Why had the two men died an unnatural death themselves?

Rath had taken the forensics report back to his office to check for parallels in the Fallin and Selenskij cases. At least that was what he had told Gennat although, in truth, it was the last thing on his mind right now. He didn't care who had the two Russians on their conscience. The main thing was that they had the right people, and for the time being that would be enough, even for the commissioner. Certainly for the newspaper readers, two brutal thugs had got their just desserts.

So why not forget the whole thing with Wolter and, after a shaky start, get back to the day-to-day business of being in A Division, wait for his opportunity and make a career for himself? Why not?

Because he couldn't.

Charly's words were still echoing in his mind. *If you want to look yourself in the mirror again . . .*

And he did. She was right. Rath reached for the telephone.

Unfortunately the commissioner was neither in his office nor at home. The man was well guarded. Dörrzwiebel was already packing his case for Magdeburg. The Zörgiebel family lived in spacious police accommodation on the first floor of the Castle, but the commissioner used it more for official purposes, such as when he received prominent guests. For the most part, he lived at his villa in Zehlendorf. Rath decided to drive out there. The Opel was still parked where he had left it in the courtyard below.

He needed almost half an hour. Outside the wrought-iron gate a police officer stood guard. A good sign: Zörgiebel was at home. Rath got out of the car. The cop looked at him suspiciously. The commissioner's guards had been on edge since the May disturbances, when the communists had stirred up a lot of ill-feeling towards him. He showed his police ID to make it clear he was no Red.

'What are you doing out here, Inspector?'

'I have an important message for the commissioner.'

'You can leave it with me.'

'A personal message.'

'The commissioner isn't receiving any visitors today.'

'He'll make an exception for me.'

'I hardly think so. I have strict orders not to let anyone through.'

'Tell him Inspector Rath wants to speak with him.'

'I . . .'

He was interrupted by the beeping of a car horn. The cop moved keenly to the gate and opened both sides. There was a crunch of gravel as the heavy Maybach rolled slowly out of the entrance. Rath could make out Zörgiebel's face in the back as he sat reading through some files. He ran to the still cruising vehicle and rapped on the window. The commissioner didn't react but the driver did. He stepped on the gas.

Rath chased after the car as it began to pick up speed, until a loud cry caused him to stop.

'Halt! Stay where you are! Or I'll shoot!'

He turned round. The paranoid cop had actually drawn his pistol.

'Listen, this is a misunderstanding. I need to speak to the commissioner. Put your weapon down!'

'I'd rather you put your hands *up*, my friend!'

'My God! I'm not a communist! What do you think I'm going to do? Overturn the commissioner's car with my bare hands?'

The cop didn't say anything, just gazed in confusion over Rath's shoulder. The sound of the engine was growing louder. The Maybach braked right next to the inspector. Zörgiebel had lowered the window.

'I thought so! My dear Rath, what are you doing here?'

'Good evening, Commissioner. I think I'm involuntarily testing the speed of your guard's reactions.'

'Lower your weapon, officer. Can't you tell an inspector from an assassin?'

The cop put his pistol away with a hangdog expression. At last Rath could turn his attention towards Zörgiebel.

'I'm here because I have an important message for you, sir . . .'

'Gennat's told me everything already. Good work, man, good work! You didn't have to drive all the way out here! You've taken what I said last week too close to heart!'

'It's not about the Kardakov case, Commissioner. Well, actually it is, about things connected to it anyway.'

'Can't it wait until next week? I'm en route to Magdeburg. The party conference begins tomorrow and we have our first meeting tonight.'

'It can't wait, Commissioner. It's of the utmost urgency. At the same time, I must ask for absolute confidentiality.'

Zörgiebel considered for a moment.

'Do you have enough money on you?'

'Pardon, Commissioner?'

'Do you have enough money to buy a ticket from Magdeburg back to Berlin?'

'I think so.'

'Then what are you waiting for? Get in!'

A moment later, Rath was next to Zörgiebel on the comfortable back-seat of the Maybach. They had the back of the car all to themselves. In front of them sat the driver and a police lieutenant, separated by a thick glass pane which blocked out any sound. The driver pounded the vehicle over the country road towards Potsdam.

'We won't be disturbed here,' Zörgiebel said. He had finished reading and seemed to be in a better mood. 'Can I offer you something to drink?'

Rath was astonished. The commissioner's official vehicle even had a little bar.

'Usually I don't drink when I'm on duty,' he said. 'But right now I could really use a whisky.'

'You're not on duty at the moment, my boy,' Zörgiebel said and poured.

'Depends on how you look at it. This is an official conversation.'

'Come on! We know each other well enough for this to be off the record.' Zörgiebel passed the whisky glass to Rath and raised his own. 'Cheers, Inspector.'

The men drank. The commissioner had poured himself a cognac. He would need it too, Rath thought. And when he was through with his story, he would need another.

Rath took a deep breath then let fly.

Barely a hundred kilometres later, he had told him everything. The Maybach had just passed through Genthin, and the driver had stepped on the gas once more. As the vehicle proceeded along *Reichsstrasse 1* towards the city of Magdeburg, Zörgiebel did in fact pour himself another cognac and fell silent. He obviously needed to chew on what the inspector had just told him.

Rath used the time to lay his badge, his ID and his gun on the black leather.

Zörgiebel looked at him dumbfounded. 'What on earth are you doing? Put your weapon away! Do you want it to go off?'

'I would like to request that you discharge me from police duty, sir.'

'Ha, you're not getting away that easily. Now, take your things off the seat!'

Rath stowed the items in his pocket. Only now did he notice traces of a white powder on his ID. With a casual gesture, he wiped it away.

'I must say, I have some difficulty believing this story,' Zörgiebel said finally. 'A *Stahlhelm* network, a flourishing weapons trade from police reserves, which is also being used to arm the Nazis?'

That one of his officers hadn't baulked either at killing people or having them killed, seemed less of an irritant to the commissioner.

'Call Wündisch,' Rath suggested.

'Oh I will, you can count on that. As soon as I reach Magdeburg. So 1A have been doing their own thing again, have they!'

'Sacrificing an inexperienced officer in the process.'

Zörgiebel shook his head, as if he still couldn't believe it. 'Now, young Rath,' he said, 'none of what you have told me today can ever get out, you understand that, don't you? Neither your own transgressions, nor the arms trafficking within our institution, nor the political aberrations of a single officer.'

'I'm sorry, sir, but I don't see any other way,' Rath said. 'Only when we expose the whole truth can we begin to root out the black sheep amongst us. I am offering to step down from police service in order to appear as a witness against DCI Wolter.'

'Cut this nonsense out! Leave the service? Don't even think about it! I will not allow it!' Zörgiebel was indignant. 'What do you think will happen if this story ends up in the public eye? There's already an investigative committee following the May disturbances. Against the police, not the Reds! What do you think will happen when it gets out that there are people amongst us flogging police arms to the Nazis?'

'You're really prepared to let someone like Wolter get off scot free? Just because it might create political difficulties?'

'Scot free? There can be no question of that happening! We just can't go at it like a bull at a gate! We cannot allow the reputation of our police force to suffer further damage.'

'What do you propose then?'

'That's what I'm trying to work out! And don't go thinking *you'll* be spared either, Inspector!'

33

Half an hour later the official car of the Berlin Commissioner crossed the Elbe into Magdeburg. As the sun set behind the many-towered silhouette of the city, Zörgiebel asked the driver to stop outside the main station.

'You know what you have to do, Inspector?'

Rath nodded. 'I think it could work. What do we do if he takes the bait?'

'Leave that to me, my dear Rath. Just give me concrete proof of Wolter's links to the Nazis, and I'll take care of the rest!'

'I won't let you down, sir,' Rath said as he opened the car door.

'Best of luck!'

'Likewise, Commissioner.'

'Keep me up to date.'

Rath got out. The Maybach turned and came to a halt on the other side of the road outside the Hotel *Continental*. A boy opened the door and Zörgiebel heaved himself out of the vehicle. Rath gazed after the commissioner until he had disappeared inside before entering through the great central portal into the main station. He studied the timetable. Another three quarters of an hour before the next fast train to Berlin. First he bought himself a coffee and counted his change. Then he found the nearest public telephone and dialled.

'Yes,' said the unmistakeable voice of Johann Marlow at the other end of the line. So, it really was that easy to get hold of Dr M.

'I think I've found a way for you to get your hands on the gold,' Rath said.

That was all it took to make Johann Marlow into a patient listener.

The train took two hours to get to Berlin. At Potsdamer station, Rath fetched the pistol from his locker and stowed it in his pocket, making sure no-one saw him do it. On the station forecourt he got into one of the many taxis waiting there and rode back to Zehlendorf. It had been raining while he was away; the streets were glistening wet. The Opel stood outside Zörgiebel's garden gate. The guard had been withdrawn. Rath switched on the engine and turned off the main road into Kolonnenstrasse. Even at this late hour there was a build-up of traffic outside Berlin Tempelhof Airport. Rath weaved his way through the crush and drove on towards Neukölln, before parking the car in Leykestrasse.

Krajewski wasn't home. A good thing, as a little preparation would make the thing seem more believable. Rath had the door open in a flash, groping his way through the darkness into the kitchen. The sugar bowl? Why not? The little pistol fitted perfectly, although there was already a bag of cocaine there. Clearly, Krajewski hadn't learned anything. When Rath left the flat, he didn't go to any great lengths to conceal the break-in. No-one had seen him. He emerged onto the street, got in his car and made himself comfortable. He had a perfect view of Krajewski's front door, and enough time to think over the plan he had sketched out on the train.

It was three in the morning when Krajewski arrived. Rath was happy that he had slept so well the previous night. Otherwise he would almost certainly have nodded off, despite the many cigarettes he had smoked. Once the man had disappeared into the house, Rath climbed out of the car and rang the doorbell like crazy. The fake Kaiser looked surprised to see him.

'You coming in the middle of the night now? I have to sleep too you know!'

'But not right now. Let me in, I need to talk to you.'

Krajewski opened the door, more obliging than his initial griping suggested.

'What's the matter then?'

'I came to warn you. You're in danger.'

'Well, that's new. The fuzz, warning us! The taxpayer's finally getting his money's worth!'

'This flat has been broken into.'

'There's nothing here.'

'The burglar brought you something.'

'That was nice of him.'

'Not exactly. He's trying to fit you up.'

'What?'

'Do you own a pistol?'

'You should know. It was your upstanding colleague who took it off me!'

'Then, why don't you take a look? If you really don't have a pistol, then it was a false alarm and I can be on my way.'

'I'm sure it's nothing,' Krajewski said. Nevertheless, he began opening drawers, gazing suspiciously over to the side, probably trying to make sure Rath didn't find his stash of cocaine.

When he emerged from the kitchen, he had the Lignose in his hand.

'I don't believe it! My little pride and joy's back! To what do I owe the honour?'

'I thought as much,' Rath said. 'It was my colleague.'

'What the hell? Is he trying to give it back discreetly, or what?'

'Hardly. DCI Wolter is a piece of shit. He put a bullet through someone's head with your Lignose and now he wants to pin it on you.'

'Whose head?'

'A police officer.'

'And I'm supposed to believe you?'

'I'm investigating the case. Discreetly of course. It's very hard to prove it was the DCI. We had hoped to find the murder weapon at his home. Unfortunately, we were too late. He was able to hide it here just in time. Don't go thinking he's coming to collect it. Chances are he's about to put a team of cops onto you. If I were you, I'd get rid of anything here that isn't entirely legal. The pistol first of all.'

'Christ! My prints are all over it now.'

'You can wipe them away.' Rath began to doubt that Krajewski was the right man for his plan. Still, he was the only possibility; the only one who would be credible enough. 'Now listen to me,' he said. 'I have a plan for how we can get the bastard, but you need to help me.'

'Shaft a copper?' Krajewski grinned. 'Gladly. I just never thought it would be an inspector who'd ask!'

Rath forced a smile. 'Happy to oblige.'

'What do I have to do?'

Rath fetched the note he had written on the train from his pocket. 'Can you read?'

Krajewski nodded.

'Good. Everything you need's here. Call this number and do exactly what it says. Then you'd best burn the note, understood?'

Krajewski nodded and skimmed the lines. He paused in surprise. 'But . . . this is your number!'

'Not anymore. I work in Homicide now.'

'But you want me to ring it anyway?'

'Correct. Tomorrow morning, early. Just do exactly as it says.'

The concierge in the *Excelsior* seemed almost sad when Rath asked for a taxi and the bill the next morning.

'I hope the inspector will be honouring us with another visit soon,' he said.

'Not too soon, I hope.' Rath was fed up with living in a hotel.

Schäffner seemed to be expecting him when he climbed out of the taxi on Luisenufer with his suitcase and cardboard box in tow.

'You really do want to move in then? I thought you were joking!'

'The Prussian CID never jokes, remember that!'

'Of course, Inspector.'

'Can I move in then?'

'But of course! Your colleagues only released it on *Sonnabend*, but my Grete spent all of yesterday scrubbing like a maniac. Everything's spic and span.'

Rath nodded contentedly, like a Prussian captain. 'Good. I've got a lot on at the moment.'

'Because of all the dead bodies?'

'That too. Then there's supposed to be a big weapons deal going down in the next few days. It's causing us a lot of trouble.'

'I see.' Schäffner could barely contain his curiosity. 'You're going to bust it, are you?'

'I wish. At the moment, we only know that a consignment is expected in the city. We don't have a clue where or when.'

Schäffner grinned. 'Why don't you try the Reds? They're always up for a good beating.'

Rath ignored the comment. His little message had hit home, that was enough. 'Well, my good man, shall we? I must be going.'

Schäffner followed Rath eagerly with his modest baggage. The man hadn't been lying. The flat smelt like a soap factory. Even the tide mark in the bathtub had disappeared.

Only eleven o'clock! Could the clocks at police headquarters be slower than elsewhere? Gregor Lanke could almost have bet on it. He was bored, on Monday morning already. A good start to the week! If only the DCI would head out he could look at the pictures again. That was the best thing about Vice so far: looking at pictures. Occasionally he had taken a few home in the evening. Strictly forbidden in theory; it was evidence after all. But the other divisions at Alex could only dream of evidence like this, and the guys in Köpenick probably didn't even know this sort of thing existed.

The telephone on his desk rang. That didn't happen often. He gave a start.

'Vice squad. Lanke here,' he said.

'Could I speak to Inspector Rath, please.'

'He doesn't work here any longer.'

Brief silence at the other end. 'Then Inspector Wolter.'

'Detective Chief Inspector Wolter,' Lanke corrected and placed his hands over the mouthpiece. 'Sir,' he called to the neighbouring desk, 'there's an oddball who wants to speak to you.'

'What's his name?'

'He didn't say.'

Reluctantly Wolter rose from his desk. He hadn't been in the best of moods these last few days so it was a good thing that Uncle Werner was in charge, that way the DCI was unable to vent his ill humour on colleagues. At least not on a certain Gregor Lanke.

'Give it over then,' Wolter said, snatching the receiver from his hand. 'Wolter,' he said grouchily into the mouthpiece.

For a while he didn't say anything, simply grabbed a piece of paper from Lanke's desk and started taking notes. Lanke tried to see what his boss was writing, but he concealed it skilfully with his hulking frame.

'We can't discuss this on the phone,' said Wolter finally. 'We need to meet. Make a suggestion.'

Ten minutes later, he was on his way and Gregor Lanke was delighted. He could go back to looking at picture.

Rath spent the whole day dealing with trivial matters, getting as good an overall picture of the Kardakov case as possible. Not for the public prosecutor, as there wasn't a lot more he could do, but for Gennat, who hoped to learn more about why the two Russians had to die. If the reason why Fallin and Selenskij had killed and tortured was clear, then perhaps it would also be clear why they had been sent to their deaths.

Most people in A Division thought they already knew the killer's address: *Unter den Linden 7.* The Soviet embassy was the seat of the Chekists whom Stalin had smuggled into the country as embassy employees. People like Vadim Troschin.

Rath had a different idea about who might have the two Russians on their conscience, but preferred to keep it to himself. When he engaged in speculation it was to back the Chekist theory, even if he believed it about as much as he believed in Father Christmas. For most of the time he kept a low profile, hiding in his office to make calls. In Steglitz he could only get hold of the housemaid. The master of the house wasn't expected until lunchtime, nor would he be available at his office. Rath had also tried to call the Hotel *Continental* in Magdeburg a few times, but always in vain. The commissioner had left the building and hadn't yet returned, the friendly concierge informed him.

During the lunch break, Rath didn't go to the canteen or to Aschinger's. Instead he got hold of a car and drove out to Steglitz.

The housemaid opened the door.

'The master is at the table, I'm afraid,' she said.

'Please tell the *Sturmhauptführer* that I have a message from Lieutenant Wolter. An urgent message. I can only discuss individual details in private.'

The girl seemed to be used to mysterious visits like this.

'If you would like to wait in the drawing room.'

She led him into a little reception room. On the wall hung a framed photograph of that Hitler, a strange bird with a Charlie Chaplin moustache, who looked just as devoid of humour as Wilhelm II. On the table lay copies of *Angriff* and the *Völkische Beobachter*. Heinrich Röllecke made no secret of his political views.

It didn't take long for the master of the house to emerge. Rath put the *Angriff* he had been leafing through to one side.

'Ah, it's you! Are you acting as Bruno's messenger again?'

'The lieutenant has an important message for you, *Sturmhauptführer*.'

'You can finally deliver the weapons to the SA as promised?'

'How did you know? So, *Scharführer* Schäffner had reported it.' Rath tried to sound as surprised as possible.

Röllecke smiled arrogantly. 'The SA has ears everywhere. Is the consignment ready?'

'The exchange will take place tomorrow evening at eight, Herr *Sturmhauptführer*,' Rath said in a military tone. 'Report to *Ostbahnhof*, on the site of the goods depot, platform six. In uniform. You'll need a few men for transportation, as well as a van.'

'You don't have to tell me what to do! Do you think this is the first time I've transported arms? I'm well aware I can't use a pram. The margin is still the same as agreed, yes?'

'Of course, Herr *Sturmhauptführer*. And there's one more thing . . .'

Röllecke looked at him impatiently. 'Well?'

'Please bring the money with you.'

Rath drove back to the Castle, retrieved the oldest files on the Kardakov case from Gennat and took them into his office. That was where the evidence Detective Inspector Gereon Rath had contributed to the investigation one and a half weeks ago had ended up, when he handed it to Böhm. The DCI hadn't deigned to look at him or the documents, and had simply left them on his desk without touching them. Nevertheless, the documents had found their way into the file, even if they weren't arranged according to any discernible system. Rath had spent a long time searching for them, and initially feared that Böhm had disposed of them. Then he found what he was looking for. He took the document Tretschkov had given him out of the file and stowed it in his pocket. It would take some time for anyone to notice it was missing as, at the moment, A Division had other concerns.

Rath spent the rest of the day brooding and making calls. Had he really thought of everything? It was such a hastily cobbled together plan. Everything depended on whether Bruno Wolter would bite. There were any number of things that could go wrong, but now that he had set the wheels in motion there was no going back.

Late in the afternoon he finally reached Zörgiebel. The conference must have been taking a break. At any rate, the commissioner was in his hotel.

'I hope the party conference is proceeding to your satisfaction, Commissioner?'

'That rather depends on how things are proceeding with you, Inspector!'

'Tomorrow evening,' Rath said. 'It will be settled tomorrow evening. If he comes, then you can send him packing the day after tomorrow, I promise. It's possible there'll be more arrests. I might need a few men.'

'Fine. I've spoken to Wündisch. He's still feeling pretty embarrassed. Section 1A will give you all the people you need. That way, the operation is guaranteed absolute secrecy.'

'I could use a few armed cops as well.'

'Let Wündisch take care of all of that. He knows what units can be relied on.'

'Is he aware of how risky this operation is?'

'He sent a CID officer into the firing line, and he perished. He has to be prepared to expose his own people to danger too.'

'It's not just his people, it's everyone.'

'I know how dangerous it is for you too, Herr Rath! I did say you wouldn't be spared. See the whole thing as making amends. It'll be alright.'

34

It had grown colder, and a nasty wind was blowing across the tracks of *Ost-bahnhof*. Bruno Wolter knew the terrain and pressed on. He had already searched for the gold in vain a few weeks ago with Selenskij and Fallin. Instead they had stumbled upon four tank wagons. The delivery from the Soviet Union was how Wilczek described them. He didn't know what the wagons contained, Marlow hadn't revealed the secret, even to his own men. The only thing they knew for sure was that it wasn't rapeseed oil; but then nor could it have been gold, or *Berolina* would have moved it on and converted it to cash. The fact that they hadn't meant the great Dr M. was equally puzzled.

Wolter had been surprised when Franz Krajewski got in touch yesterday. If it weren't for his gun having featured recently, he would have forgotten all about him. He hadn't been expecting much from him, perhaps a few tip-offs from the porn scene, but nothing major, and had driven to the meeting sceptically, convinced that the man was merely seeking attention. Perhaps he wanted his gun back or to cadge some money. But Krajewski was exceptionally well informed. The porn Kaiser actually had a friend in *Berolina*. A friend who had pinched his girlfriend, and now Krajewski wanted to land him in it.

After Wilczek's death, Wolter hadn't been able to get any more information out of Marlow's organisation, and that had made things increasingly difficult for him as the weeks wore on. Now, at last, he was back up to date. He had played the innocent yesterday when Krajewski told him that Johann Marlow was no ordinary businessman but the real leader of *Berolina*. Krajewski didn't know anything about the gold; he merely said that Marlow was expecting several goods wagons full of weapons at *Ost-bahnhof*. Had Dr M. uncovered the secret of the gold and got hold of the weapons for the *Red Fortress*? It sounded almost as if he had.

If he had already sold off the gold, then they'd just have to take the weapons. Marlow and the Reds weren't entitled to them anyway. Seegers was already waiting impatiently; the majority was earmarked for *his* people. They had also promised a piece to Röllecke's SA. The *Sturmhauptführer* paid good money, and his troops were cut from the same political cloth as Wolter's.

Be that as it may, Krajewski had talked about *their* weapons, and now they were going to collect them. There had to be a huge amount to justify an entire goods train.

He had informed Rudi Scheer yesterday, and with Seegers's help managed to round up enough reliable soldiers, all of them good marksmen. Led by DCI Bruno Wolter, a CID officer from the Prussian police, they would pose as police officers. If the real police couldn't sound Johann Marlow out, then it would have to be this team of fakes. Wolter knew that Marlow didn't have much respect for his badge, but he might be more amenable to a handful of armed men. Some of his *Stahlhelmers* were better shots than the police. No wonder, he had trained them himself.

At the station he had chosen around a dozen men for the operation, all in plain clothes and without so much as their *Stahlhelm* lapel pins. The vans were now waiting in Friedrichsfelder Strasse and, when the time came, they were to make for the loading ramp.

Bruno marched along the platform, followed by his men. A shunting locomotive chugged past with a few empty cars. A single train was being unloaded. Not much else was going on. A few crows, picking at something indefinable on the ground, fluttered up as the men approached. Marlow's sheds weren't far away, but a large goods train blocked their view. Wolter crouched and looked from underneath the wagons. It appeared the tank wagons were still standing on Marlow's platform. It was time. They began to divide themselves up, Rudi leading the larger group, Wolter the smaller group. Wolter explained the route for a final time and away they marched.

It would be just like a police operation. He had his ID in his pocket, Rudi Scheer likewise. No-one would notice the others were only carrying weapons.

They were coming! He could already see them from afar. Johann Marlow knew where the best vantage point was, up here under the roof, by the narrow skylights where he usually posted his guards. From here you had a view of the entire station, without being seen yourself.

The young police photographer next to him began snapping before the faces of the men could even be made out. He had the easiest job today. All he had to do was take photos and make sure he wasn't seen.

Everyone else was taking a big risk. Johann Marlow too. No-one could predict what was going to happen. The man with the second Sorokin map would come, Rath had said he would make sure of it and, true enough, there he was below. The inspector hadn't said he'd be showing up with five companions, however. Marlow still wasn't sure if he could trust the cop, even though he had given him the first part of the map. Bruno Wolter had been Rath's boss once upon a time, why should he betray him now? To convict a black sheep on the force? There were a lot of black sheep at Alex; no-one knew that better than Johann Marlow. He had the feeling the police had come to terms with it. So why were they going to such great lengths with Bruno Wolter? What did Rath really want?

If it was to put one over Johann Marlow, then he wouldn't succeed. The inspector was a coke-head; if push came to shove Marlow had him well in hand.

The men were clearly visible now. Slowly but surely making their way towards platform six, hands buried in their coat pockets. Even from up here you could see they were carrying weapons.

When the men finally reached the loading ramp, Fred emerged from the shadows below.

'Evening,' he said. 'You're entering private property. Might I ask what you're doing here?'

The leader showed his ID. 'CID,' he said. 'I'd like to speak with Herr Marlow.'

The man had to be Bruno Wolter.

'What's it about?'

'I'll discuss that with Herr Marlow in private. Please take me to him. We want to have a little look round.'

'Sorry. I'm afraid if you don't have a search warrant, then I must ask you to leave.'

Right on cue, the three other guards emerged from the shadow.

It looked as if the cop below had turned away in resignation, only for him to draw his weapon and hold it to Fred's forehead.

'I'm the police, and you'd better do as I say,' he said.

Marlow saw that his men could be relied upon. The other three had likewise drawn their weapons and aimed them at Wolter and his companions. It would only take one of the men to get nervous, and this would descend into a murderous shoot-out.

Fred remained calm. 'You're trespassing on private property, Inspector,' he said. 'If you shoot me, my men will be forced to act in self-defence.'

'That's Detective Chief Inspector! Tell your goons to put down their weapons. Then send one of them to Marlow.'

'I fear, Detective *Chief* Inspector, that my men don't give a damn if you blow me away. If you do they will kill you and your companions on the spot.'

'If they are still able to, of course!' said a calm, friendly voice from the other side of the ramp.

Marlow swung round, just as surprised as the police photographer. Nine men had taken up position with pistols drawn. In the middle stood the man who had spoken, smiling politely.

'Do what the DCI says,' he continued. 'Believe me, it's for the best.'

'That's the guy from the armoury!' said the police photographer beside him. 'I don't understand anything anymore.'

Marlow was growing nervous. What kind of stunt were they trying to pull? His men laid their weapons carefully on the floor of the loading ramp.

Marlow decided to put an end to this theatre and went down to join them. The train should be here in twenty minutes. He could count on Kuen-Yao. Until then the main thing was to avoid a bloodbath. He had to intervene to gain some time. When he stepped onto the ramp, all eyes turned towards him.

'Good evening,' he said to Wolter. 'You wanted to speak to me?'

'Johann Marlow?' Wolter asked.

Marlow nodded. 'Why are you invading my private property and threatening my men?'

'I heard that you are expecting a goods train this evening.'

'Looks like it. Do you think I hang around goods sheds at night for fun? What about my people? They're just trying to go about their work, and you are preventing them from doing so. Does the commissioner know what you're up to?'

'I don't think you're the type to complain to the commissioner.'

'Wait and see.'

'Let's wait for your train first! Then we'll see what you're having delivered.'

'Then what?'

'Perhaps it's something I ought to have confiscated.'

'Believe me, you won't be able to haul it off on your own.'

'We have enough people. More than you think.'

He could see his men were getting nervous. The wait was making him uneasy too, more than he cared to admit. Wolter's left hand was in his coat pocket, playing with his ID; in his right he was still holding the pistol. Darkness was falling and there was still no sign of the train.

In the meantime they had frisked all of Marlow's men and disarmed them. Rudi had dealt with Marlow himself—and found no weapon. That had surprised Wolter. Now Dr M. was standing alongside his men. The five of them didn't seem chastened in the slightest.

'Are there still people in the shed?' Wolter asked.

'If there were,' Marlow said, 'I wouldn't have come out just now, but ordered them to shoot you.'

'Got anything against me sending a few people in?'

'As long as they don't break anything.'

Wolter was getting annoyed. The whole time Marlow was talking to him as if his people had the upper hand, not the other way round.

He was just about to give his men a sign when he was interrupted. There were two brownshirts approaching from the direction of Rüdersdorfer Strasse. What the hell was going on? Who had sent for the SA? In full uniform at that? Stupid fools!

Wolter recognised Heinrich Röllecke, marching purposefully towards them. Alongside him was Hermann Schäffner, the caretaker from Luisenufer, with a black leather bag.

Wolter gazed at the uniformed soldiers. When they had reached the ramp, the *Sturmhauptführer* stretched a hand out towards him. At least he didn't give the Hitler salute!

'Everything ready as arranged,' Röllecke said.

Wolter had no idea what was going on. 'What's the big idea?' he asked. 'Did Seegers request you as back-up? Not necessary! I have enough people here!'

'What do you mean, Seegers? You sent your man to me yourself. We just want our share. The truck's waiting in Rüdersdorfer Strasse.'

'What man? What are you talking about?'

'I've got the money with me anyway. I hope you have the weapons.'

'They should be here any moment.'

'Are they Reds?' Röllecke gestured towards Marlow and his men, who were standing huddled in a corner.

'They belong to Red Hugo, but that's about the only red thing about them.'

Dusk was encroaching ever more on the evening. At a distance, three lights emerged from the semi-darkness and grew gradually brighter. Everyone stared at the triangle as if spellbound. A locomotive was shunting two sealed goods wagons onto the platform. They approached, squealing and rumbling, moving ever slower until the buffers of the front wagon almost bumped into a tank car, and came to a halt. The locomotive hissed, rooted to the spot like a phantom train. No-one on the loading ramp uttered a word.

Wolter ended the silence.

'That's the consignment,' he said to Röllecke. 'Where's the money?'

'You'll get it once I'm satisfied with the quality of the goods.'

'Then take a look!' Wolter remained by the tank car, where he had positioned himself to keep Marlow's men in check. He had a bad feeling about this. If it was a trap, then it should be Röllecke who fell into it.

The two SA men marched to the first wagon. Eagerly Schäffner removed the bolt and slid the heavy door open, staring inside as if he had seen a ghost.

Röllecke stepped forth impatiently. 'What is it, man? Stand aside.'

Then he looked on in surprise too. Furiously, he approached Wolter.

'Is this a joke?'

'What?'

'Hiding this man in the wagon. Where are the weapons?'

'What man?'

'The messenger you sent yesterday.'

Röllecke gestured towards the goods wagon. Out of the darkness stepped Gereon Rath, with pistol drawn.

He must have looked at least as surprised as Hermann Schäffner. Rath hadn't counted on it being his caretaker, of all people, who opened the wagon, but rather one of Marlow's people or even Bruno himself.

A successful entrance, nevertheless. He looked around, and saw that all eyes were on him. It was starting to get dark. Hopefully Gräf had what he needed in the can.

'I wouldn't shoot if I were you,' he barked at Wolter's companions, who had aimed their weapons nervously in his direction.

'Well, if it isn't Inspector Know-it-all,' said Wolter. 'And why,' he asked with a smile, 'shouldn't I tell my people to simply blow you away?'

'Because there are marksmen positioned under the roof of the goods shed who have each one of you in their sights and are just itching to pull their triggers. Besides, I haven't come alone.'

Rath raised his left hand. The men inside the goods wagon had been waiting for this sign and leapt out with weapons drawn. In no time there were two dozen armed plain-clothes officers standing on the platform. Behind them Liang climbed out of the locomotive.

'Quite a little army,' Wolter said. 'Scary stuff. I trust they're not actually going to do anything.'

A few of the younger *Stahlhelmers* grinned uncertainly. The two SA officers obviously found it less amusing that their weapons deal was off. Röllecke looked as though he was about to breath fire.

'This little army consists of upright police officers who will now arrest you and your men, DCI Wolter.'

'Why would they do that? Is it illegal to be in a train station?'

'Drop the act. We've heard enough, and we have enough in the can too.'

'I'm afraid I don't quite understand what you're saying.'

'Up there with the marksmen there's also someone who's good at taking pictures.'

'What's that supposed to mean?' If Wolter was surprised, his face wasn't giving anything away.

'It means that the Berlin police force now has enough evidence to prove that one of its officers, DCI Bruno Wolter, is in cahoots with the SA and engaging in illegal arms deals.'

Wolter laughed out loud. 'Where did you get that idea?'

He hadn't even finished his sentence when the shot rang out. Wolter had squeezed the trigger with a smile, and shot as casually from the hip as other people light cigarettes during a conversation. A single shot.

Heinrich Röllecke gazed more in surprise than horror at the little red stain that was growing ever larger on his brown shirt. He wheeled halfway round as his knees buckled, and toppled onto the concrete of the ramp.

Hermann Schäffner crouched by his side and felt for his pulse. Nothing there. The SA man gazed at his dead commander in disbelief. It took a moment for him to work out what had happened.

'You bastard,' he cried, before, still squatting, he pulled a heavy Colt-Browning and started firing wildly in Wolter's direction. He was able to squeeze the trigger five times before a shot from Wolter's Luger blew the gun out of his hand.

Wolter laughed, as Schäffner was overpowered by two police officers. He hadn't been hit by a single shot.

Nevertheless, several had gone into the tank wagons beside him; and one of them must have caught the drain valve of the middle chamber.

As if in slow motion, Rath saw a metallic bolt fall to the ground at an angle behind Wolter. There was a sound like the banging of a gong as the heavy part struck the floor.

In the same instant that Wolter turned to fire at his putative attackers, hydrochloric acid spurted out of the defective valve.

The acid sprayed out of the tank at high pressure, hitting Wolter in the face and transforming it within a fraction of a second into a confused grimace. He fired a desperate reflex shot, before covering his eyes with his arms. The pistol clattered to the floor.

Wolter was swaying, trying to support himself, but could find only the acid that was forming an ever greater puddle on the concrete floor. He recoiled, and his whole body crashed to the ground, only for him to leap back to his feet. Driven wild by pain, blind and disorientated, he moved in the wrong direction, hit his head against the still spitting metal tank, stopped screaming and plunged back into the steaming puddle of acid.

Schäffner, whom two officers had taken between them, looked on in horror and everyone else stood as if paralysed.

Marlow was the first to react, issuing his men instructions and disappearing inside the shed. When he emerged a moment later with a bucket of water, the pain had caused Wolter to regain consciousness, but his strength had left him completely. From a safe distance Marlow tipped the water over the twitching, writhing body. It was impossible to move him away from the wagon, as the acid shower still hadn't abated. Meanwhile, two of Marlow's men had climbed onto the wagon from the other side and were trying to close the valve using an iron bar. They managed to stem the flow just enough for Liang, who had donned a pair of heavy leather work gloves, to close it properly with a few nimble flicks of the wrist and refasten the bolt that had been blown off.

Marlow grabbed Wolter by the feet. His clothes had in large part dissolved, and scraps of material and flaps of skin were left behind as Marlow dragged the heavy body across the acid-soaked concrete. Finally Wolter lay at a safe distance from the tank wagon, unconscious once more, acid steaming from his entire body. It took some time for one of Marlow's men to emerge with a second bucket of water. Rudi Scheer and the *Stahlhelmers* were still gazing disbelievingly at the gruesome spectacle, while Hermann Schäffner continued to stare wide-eyed at Wolter's steaming, acid-ravaged frame, forgetting his own bloody hand in the process.

After a few showers of water the steam began to clear, though it only made the sight of Wolter's devastated body even more horrific. There were still shreds of clothing hanging to him. Blisters had formed on his skin, which was massively inflamed and coming loose in places to expose raw flesh. His eyeballs had melted and were leaking like undercooked soft-boiled eggs. It was impossible to say whether he was still alive. Marlow, too, had donned leather gloves, and was searching Wolter's jacket. He lifted a damp scrap of paper and flung it furiously onto the ground. The sorry, now worthless, remains of the second Sorokin map, Rath guessed. Now the one he had given Dr M. earlier was worthless too.

The valve was still spitting slightly and stank like hell, the pungent stench of acid mixing with the smell of raw flesh and blood. A repulsive mixture.

Rath held a handkerchief over his nose and went over to Wündisch's people.

'We need the paramedics now,' he said. 'If there's anything they can still do.'

On his signal, one of the officers opened the second goods wagon and a troop of uniformed officers sprang onto the platform, around fifty men in total.

'Put your hands in the air,' Rath called out to the *Stahlhelmers*. 'But put your weapons down first.'

The young men obeyed immediately and one by one the handcuffs clicked. Rath issued the operation commander with instructions. The men waiting outside in the vans were to be arrested too. Only Marlow's people were spared. There was no reason to take them to the station. None had previous convictions and they could provide firearms licences for their guns. Their boss, the owner of an imports business, had even helped police lay the trap by placing his property at their disposal.

Marlow went over to Rath.

'Bloody hell! Turned out just the way you pictured it, no?'

Rath shook his head in silence. He thought of Zörgiebel's words: *it'll be alright.*

How wrong he had been.

Rath still wasn't sure how he was going to tell the commissioner. They had wanted to punish Bruno Wolter and take him out of circulation. And they had done so, at least after a fashion.

'How are we supposed to get hold of the gold now?' Marlow asked. It sounded almost reproachful. 'Do you think the DCI made a copy of his map?'

Rath shrugged his shoulders.

'No idea, and to tell the truth I couldn't care less.'

He left Marlow where he was and went over to the goods shed, from which Reinhold Gräf emerged, legs still wobbly, camera on his shoulders.

'I hope you didn't photograph the finale,' he said to the pale man.

'Too busy being sick,' said Gräf. Rath offered him an Overstolz and this time the assistant detective helped himself.

The men smoked in silence, examining the faulty tank wagon. Liang, still wearing work gloves, took a closer look at Schäffner's bullet holes. He used a knife to pick a bullet out of the tank wall. His face gave nothing away. At all events he soon interrupted his work to whisper something in Marlow's ear. Dr M.'s expression brightened again. He went over to Rath and Gräf.

'Inspector, you assured me this operation would be carried out discreetly. I trust you'll be true to your word.'

'Don't worry. The press won't get wind of anything that happened here.'

'Your Buddha isn't about to move in and turn my place upside down?'

'There'll be no CID investigation. Officially, nothing happened here.'

'There were loads of witnesses.'

'The officers involved can be relied on.'

'My people too. Then I hope you have the *Stahlhelmers* under control. They saw quite a bit too.'

'They won't say anything.'

'Good. Then we should start tidying up. It's about time normal business was resumed.'

Rath nodded.

Marlow gave the Chinese man a sign. Liang connected the tank wagons, climbed back into the locomotive and the train moved off slowly, leaving as it had arrived: like a phantom.

35

The *Nasse Dreieck—Wet Triangle*—lived up to its name. The lounge was actually triangular, just like the whole building, squeezed as it was between two tenement houses, and it was so small that one was seldom dry for very long. The pub had its advantages: the prices were decent, and the modest dimensions meant there wasn't room for fights. If push came to shove it was close enough to Rath's flat for him to crawl home.

There were only four tables in the public bar. Rath didn't mind. He usually sat at the counter anyway. Just like now in fact.

'Schorsch, another glass of beer and a short for both of us!'

'So, two beers, and two shorts.'

'Yup.'

'Nothing for me?'

'Then make it three.'

Three or four weeks had gone by since the shoot-out at *Ostbahnhof*. It was mid-June, and the summer had the city firmly in its grip. In the *Nasse Dreieck*, it was pleasantly cool. The barman placed two beers and two schnapps on the counter.

Rath raised his schnapps glass. 'Cheers, Detective! To your promotion!'

'Fuck the promotion,' Reinhold Gräf said dismissively. The whole station was talking about it, a detective at twenty-three! During a moratorium on promotions at that! The subject was clearly making him uncomfortable. 'Let's drink to life,' he said.

They downed the strong schnapps. In a strange way the incident at *Ostbahnhof* had bound them together, even if they never spoke of it. To compensate they met up with one another and drank, mostly in the *Nasse Dreieck*.

'Have you heard? Buddha wants to finally assign the Selenskij/Fallin file to the wet fish,' Rath said.

Gräf drank his beer in silence. 'Charly was grilling me again today,' he said after a while.

'Does she still want to know why you're meeting up with me?'

Gräf nodded.

'What did you tell her?'

Gräf grinned. 'The same as always. That it's your irresistible eyes.'

Rath laughed, even if he didn't really feel like it when his thoughts turned to Charly. After the botched operation at *Ostbahnhof*, their relationship had grown noticeably cooler again. Too many things appeared strange to her. No wonder. She must have noticed the inconsistencies in the story the commissioner was pedalling about the operation. Meanwhile Gereon Rath was saying nothing, likewise Detective Gräf.

They often talked about Charly. It was their way of talking about what happened at *Ostbahnhof*, and about their silence. Zörgiebel knew how to buy silence. The newly appointed Detective Gräf felt uncomfortable in his own skin. Rath no less so—and he hadn't even been promoted.

But then how many police officers felt comfortable in their own skin?

It was late by the time the *Nasse Dreieck* closed, and the bricks and asphalt still reflected the heat of the day. Rath just needed to go across Wassertorplatz to be home. He didn't even feel that drunk, despite the bill in the *Nasse Dreieck* being rather sizeable again. When he stepped into the rear courtyard on Luisenufer, all the lights were already out. People went to bed early round here. There were no curtains on the windows of the caretaker's flat. The Schäffners had moved out. The caretaker Hermann Schäffner, unable to work due to the injuries sustained to his hand, had been awarded a generous disability pension by the Prussian state. Meanwhile Lennartz, the new caretaker, was still renovating.

The police seal on the attic flat in the rear building had long since been removed, but the place still hadn't been rented out, since Frau Steinrück alias Sorokina had paid half a year in advance. One evening Rath had seen Ilja Tretschkov hurrying across the yard. He dashed out of his flat and tried to catch up with the Russian, but by the time he made it outside Tretschkov had disappeared.

That was a week or two ago now. Rath couldn't help thinking back to it as he opened his front door and heard a noise upstairs. It couldn't be the

Liebigs. The communists went to bed early. Rath didn't think long before quietly ascending the steps.

He had heard right. There was someone in the attic flat.

There was light coming into the stairwell through the crack in the door. He heard quiet steps. Had Tretschkov come to clean again? It was already past midnight.

Rath decided to knock.

It took some time, but at last the door opened slightly and he found himself looking into the eyes of a beautiful woman.

Svetlana Sorokina. She had dyed her hair black.

'Good evening,' he said. 'I saw the lights were on and . . .'

'Well?'

'We haven't met.' He stretched a hand through the door. 'Lennartz, Peter Lennartz. I'm the new caretaker.'

'Ingeborg Steinrück.'

'I'd like to speak to you a moment, Fräulein Steinrück.'

'At this hour?'

'I urgently need a few signatures. You were never at home when . . .'

'I was away.'

She seemed suspicious, but opened the door. Rath went inside. The flat hadn't changed since his previous visit.

'So, Herr Lennartz, if you could show me the papers I need to sign, we can get this over with. I'm tired.'

In the electric light Rath could see how beautiful she was. It almost knocked him off his feet.

'I lied to you,' he said. 'My name isn't Lennartz, just as yours isn't Steinrück. I'm Gereon Rath and I work for the CID, Countess Sorokina.'

'I know your name,' she said harshly. 'You're the policeman who issued a warrant for me! What do you want? To arrest me?'

'To talk to you. I . . .'

Suddenly he was staring down the barrel of a gun.

'Don't worry. I'm not going to betray you,' he said. 'Now put that thing away.'

'Why should I believe you?'

'Because I've helped you many times already.'

'Not that I'm aware of. Put your hands in the air, and don't try anything. I'm a proficient markswoman.'

Rath obeyed. 'I found your hiding place in *Delphi* and kept quiet. I know it was your hairdryer that ended up in Selenskij's bathtub, and I also know you were in Yorckstrasse when Nikita Fallin fell from the fourth floor. Yet I haven't put you on the list of murder suspects.'

'Am I supposed to be grateful for that?'

'It would be enough if you stopped waving that pistol in front of my face.'

'I don't owe you anything,' she said. 'I didn't kill those two men. Even if they deserved it. I wanted to kill them, I admit, but you can't be punished for intent alone.'

'No,' Rath said. He tried hard not to show his surprise. Was she telling the truth? 'Then why were you at Yorckstrasse when Fallin died? It was you who lured him into the trap.'

'I was waiting for him a floor higher, that much is true. I wanted to shoot him, just like I wanted to shoot Selenskij. But when I arrived at the house here, the police were already outside the door. I didn't find out he was dead until a day later.'

'So how did your hairdryer end up in the bathtub?'

'I didn't throw it in, anyway.'

'And you didn't cause Fallin's fall either?'

'When I called him, he was leaning over the banister. I wanted to pull the trigger, but then he fell, and I ran downstairs after him. I swear I'd have shot him, if he had still been alive, but there was a man crouching beside him who said Fallin was dead.'

'My colleague.'

'At any rate, I got away. I had a pistol in my handbag after all.'

Rath considered for a moment. There was someone else who might be interested in seeing the two Russians dead: Bruno Wolter. The pair had become a security risk and he must have disposed of them, before attempting to lay the blame at the Countess's door.

He nodded. 'Sounds plausible to me. In the meantime the dust appears to have settled on the matter. Homicide have been looking into other cases for quite some time.'

'So why are you paying me a visit?'

'You haven't been here for a long time. I'm your neighbour.'

The astonishment suited her.

'Believe me, I'm not trying to trick you. The case is closed. Even the police know Fallin and Selenskij got what they deserved. Can I lower my hands? My arms are beginning to hurt.'

She nodded. Nevertheless, a tiny bit of suspicion remained in her eyes. She kept hold of the pistol.

'I've just made some tea,' she said. 'Would you like a cup?'

'Yes, but no rum please.'

A short time later they were sitting at her small kitchen table drinking tea. She had to get a second chair from the bedroom.

'You're the only person who knows what happened with the gold,' Rath said. 'Did it ever leave the Soviet Union? Or did the *Red Fortress* get it after all?'

'You're very inquisitive.'

'Occupational hazard, but the question is private in nature.'

'The *Red Fortress* doesn't exist anymore,' she said. 'The organisation still calling itself that doesn't merit the name.'

'What about the gold?'

'In its rightful place.'

'Marlow found the hiding place, didn't he? Even without the map. And he gave you your share?'

'The gold has long since been sold. Everyone got what they were entitled to.'

'Marlow most of all.' Rath nodded. 'So the deal has already taken place. Then can you tell me how you smuggled it?'

'Why do you want to know?'

'Because I don't understand. I assume it was in the tank wagons.'

'Correct. Only the outer wall of the tanks was steel. On the inside they consisted of a thick layer of gold.'

'How did it get there? The cars didn't come from Russia, they came from East Prussia.'

'They were built in Russia though.'

'Sorry?'

'My family didn't exploit serfs, but was involved in industry. That's where the Sorokins's fortune comes from. In St Petersburg we owned a rail wagon factory. By the time the war began, my father had already invested a large percentage of his assets in gold. When the Bolsheviks staged their coup, he had it melted. After that a whole series of tank wagons were built, whose actual worth only very few people knew about.'

'But they weren't built to the Russian track gauge.'

'No. That way the Bolsheviks wouldn't get it into their heads to confiscate them for their own purposes. Father wanted to get them out of the country, there had been orders placed for all of them from abroad, from family friends.'

'One of whom was from East Prussia.'

'Correct.'

'So the gold has been in Germany for years?'

'No. During the Civil War normal trade was impossible. Then the communists started making trouble, so it took almost ten years before the wagons were finally allowed to cross the border. Foreign capital makes even the Bolsheviks weak.'

'The buyers were *Vereinigte Ölmühle Insterburg?*'

'The company belongs to a good friend. He was in on it.'

'So why didn't he just send the wagons to you in Berlin?'

'Someone would have noticed. Too many people knew about the gold. Some people knew who I was and were waiting for me to make a move.'

'What about the rest of your family?'

'No longer alive.'

'So everyone was circling around you like vultures?'

'That's why Alexej and I arranged this spectacle. We thought if everyone was concentrating on the cargo, no-one would be paying any attention to the wagons.'

'Which is why Marlow had to order chemicals in Leningrad when he could have got them far cheaper along the Rhine . . .'

She smiled, and it looked as if she hadn't done so for a long time.

'The chemical company he ordered them from also used to be a Sorokin factory,' she said. 'It was all pretty obvious—but then it was supposed to be.'

A little later Rath was climbing the stairs back down to his flat. There were a thousand different thoughts milling around his head. But he knew what he had to do; he knew exactly what he had to do. He wanted to feel comfortable in his own skin again.

He fetched the keys to the caretaker's flat from the shed. Lennartz had started to repaper the flat, but left the poky grey corner where he did his paperwork. Everything looked the same as always. Schäffner's old typewriter was still there, it was part of the inventory. Rath sat down and took a few leaves of paper from the drawer. Then he wrote it all down, the whole story. From the perspective of the simple SA *Scharführer* Hermann Schäffner. With every letter that he typed he felt his heart grow lighter.

In the distance were the eight chimneys of Klingenberg power station and the great hall of Görlitzer station amidst the sea of houses that formed Kreuzberg. Finally Rath was able to savour the view. It was the same as before, only this time unaccompanied by feelings of dizziness, as a large balustrade prevented visitors to the rooftop restaurant from plunging onto Hermannplatz below.

The new Karstadt department store had opened today to an indescribable hullaballoo. Rath had requested a meeting with Weinert and the journalist had suggested the roof garden because he had business there anyway. The Karstadt building seemed suitable. Perhaps because the whole story had started here when this department store was still just a building site, a building site on whose scaffolding he had chased Franz Krajewski. Where Bruno Wolter had saved his life. DCI Bruno Wolter, whom the commissioner had posthumously decorated for his bravery a few days ago.

Hermannplatz had changed its appearance. The sand-coloured colossus dominated the square and seemed as out of place here as an Aztec pyramid. As two Aztec pyramids. This twin-towered example of modern gigantomania in Neukölln, of all places, where only weeks before the police and communists had been engaged in bloody street fighting! Rath doubted that the huge store would lend a touch of New York to the workers' district. Nevertheless, the residents of Berlin had been awaiting its opening with feverish anticipation for weeks and loved the store from day one. The rooftop restaurant in particular, it seemed.

Rath had trouble finding Weinert in the crush, but in amongst the pushing and shoving the journalist had actually managed to get them a seat, and one with a prime view at that. Was it due to his press card? Perhaps he had just had coffee with Herr Karstadt himself.

The journalist had reserved the seat opposite with his coat. Weinert stood up to greet Rath and as he did so a brash type almost snatched away his chair. A stern glance sent him on his way again. The men sat down.

'I've ordered you a coffee,' Weinert said. 'It takes forever for a waiter to come.'

Rath nodded. In the confusion of voices around them, it was hard to make oneself understood. It was scarcely believable that anyone was being served at all in the chaos. Still, the waiters were weaving their way through the crowds with trays raised like circus artists.

'Nice quiet spot, this,' Rath said.

Weinert laughed. 'We're less conspicuous here than we would be in an isolated clearing in the middle of a wood.'

'That could be. Every sensible person is somewhere other than here today.'

A waiter placed two pots of coffee on the table, settled up and disappeared straight back into the crush.

'You wanted to speak to me?' Weinert asked. 'Do you have something for me at last?'

Rath lit a cigarette before replying.

'I do.'

Weinert looked surprised. 'Really?'

'It's not what you think.'

'Of course not. Birds of a feather flock together.'

'You'll just have to deal with the fact that you're barking up the wrong tree. It's a part of everyday police life.'

'I'm not a policeman, I'm a journalist.'

'With a little too much imagination.'

'This weapons trafficking is real. Rifles and submachine guns with police and *Reichswehr* serial numbers are being used for *Stahlhelm* reserve duty training exercises. My informant isn't just some crazy, you know.'

'You've been getting on my nerves for weeks with this crap.'

'Yeah, because you're suddenly praising an officer to the skies who has more dirt on him than a Kashubian swineherd!'

'DCI Wolter died in hospital as a result of injuries sustained in the execution of his duty.'

'You sound like a prayer mill, do you know that? Wolter was a staunch

Stahlhelmer, even Zörgiebel didn't deny that. And he belonged to a network of old war comrades. I know that from Behnke.'

'The *Stahlhelm* is a league of front soldiers. Lots of police officers served in the war.'

'But not all of them train young people for a paramilitary organisation. So that one day the *Reichswehr*, when it's big and strong enough again, can call on enough trained soldiers. The *Reichswehr* itself comprises almost only officers. The ordinary soldiers are being cultivated by the right-wing para-military groups like the *Stahlhelm, Scharnhorstbund, Wiking* and the rest of them. They're all being fed by the *Reichswehr* and their financiers from the armament industry. The same goes for the Nazis with their SA.'

'That's a problem for the *Reichswehr* rather than the Prussian police.'

'There are links to the police, or at least there were. I know it, I just can't prove it. The police aren't as democratic as the social democrats would have it.'

'The police aren't political. It's their job to maintain law and order.'

Weinert shook his head. 'Don't tell me you still believe that.'

Rath blew a final cloud of smoke across the table and stubbed out his cigarette. During the last few weeks, he had told himself over and over again that Bruno Wolter had got the punishment he deserved. In truth, he had never believed it. The commissioner had made Wolter into a hero and the press had swallowed his story. A story that kept the *Stahlhelmers* who had been at the station that night in check. If they wanted to question the of-ficial police version of events, they'd have to damage the reputation of their own man, the hero Bruno Wolter. That it didn't happen was down to Rudi Scheer, who might no longer have access to weapons in the Department of Building Regulations at Charlottenburg, but remained an important fig-ure in the *Stahlhelm*. In the meantime Rath knew that, had Wolter sur-vived, his fate would have been similar, demoted but not punished. The commissioner had never intended anything else. It meant a man like Major General Seegers went completely unchallenged. A total farce. Only, Rath couldn't discuss it with Weinert.

Still, there were other ways.

Deal with official business first.

'Do you know the Deutsche Bank Branch Office on Reichskanzler-platz?'

Weinert nodded. 'Pretty flash isn't it?'

'Rich customers. Big cash deposits. The *Nordpiraten* are hoping to pull a job there, a big one—like the job on Wittenbergplatz . . .'

'Like the Brothers Sass?'

'Only not as successful. My colleagues from C Division are going to catch them red-handed. If you position yourself in good time tonight with a few photographers, you'll get some nice snaps.'

'Not exactly the revelation to end all revelations.' Weinert seemed only moderately enthusiastic.

'A whole *Ringverein* is being taken out of circulation. There ought to be some spectacular photos. It'll make your boss happy, believe me.'

'*Your* boss too.' Weinert's index finger drew a headline in the air. '*Berlin's police in fight against organised crime.*' He stood up and stretched out a hand. 'I have to go. Thanks for the tip-off Gereon.'

'Wait!'

Weinert stopped in his tracks. Rath passed him a black file with the typed confession of a simple SA *Scharführer*.

'What's that?'

'No idea. Someone must have forgotten it. Perhaps there's something interesting inside. About arms trafficking for instance.'

Weinert finally seemed to understand. His face lit up. 'Do you think?'

'Well, I wouldn't be handing it in to lost property if I were you.'

'If the information is correct.'

Rath shrugged his shoulders. 'That's for you to decide. You're the journalist. I'm a police officer.'

Weinert waved the file. 'If there's anything I can do for you—let me know.'

Rath didn't have to think long. 'Do you need your car tomorrow?'

'If you dare show your face again in Nürnberger Strasse, you can have it.' Weinert laughed and turned round.

Rath gazed after the journalist until he had disappeared into the crowd. He stayed at the table and lit another cigarette. Sometimes you had to lie to reveal the truth. Weinert was all fired up for this story; he would write it, that much was certain.

Rath's gaze wandered over the sea of houses. He still didn't know what to make of this city, but in summer Berlin definitely had its charm. It was completely different from the winter. Perhaps it wasn't so bad here after all.

Now he just had to persuade Charly to take a drive out to the country with him tomorrow. That was the trickiest part, but he would manage it somehow.

FROM THE INTERNATIONALLY BESTSELLING AUTHOR
VOLKER KUTSCHER
BOOK 2 OF THE GEREON RATH MYSTERY

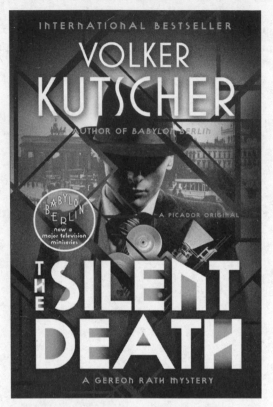

ISBN 978-1-250-18701-7 (TRADE PAPERBACK)
ISBN 978-1-250-18702-4 (EBOOK)

"EXCELLENT." —*Kirkus Reviews*

"JAMES ELLROY FANS WILL WELCOME KUTSCHER'S [GEREON RATH MYSTERY] SERIES,
A FAST-PACED BLEND OF MURDER AND CORRUPTION SENT IN 1929 BERLIN."
—*Publishers Weekly* (starred review)

"RIVETING AND ATMOSPHERIC." —*Library Journal*

"A GRIPPING, EVOCATIVE THRILLER." —*Mail on Sunday* (London)

PICADOR

PICADORUSA.COM • TWITTER.COM/PICADORUSA • FACEBOOK.COM/PICADORUSA • INSTAGRAM.COM/PICADOR
AVAILABLE WHEREVER BOOKS AND EBOOKS ARE SOLD.